THE MAN WHO GAVE IN

Joan W Probert

Books by the same Author
*Song for a Sparrow**
*Flight on a Broken Wing**
Sips of Water

**Title will also be available as an e-book soon!*

The Man Who Gave In
Copyright © 2016 by Joan W Probert

Published by Uplift Publishers
33 Jensen Drive
Urraween, Queensland, Australia

National Library of Australia
ISBN 978-0-9802864-3-4 (pbk)

Printed by IngramSpark

The Author wishes to advise that the characters in this book are fictitious. If in some way they reflect real people or their activities this is purely coincidental.

Cover: original artwork by the Authoress

Dedicated
To Him
With my love

And
To my spiritual daughter and son-in-law,
Sue and Marlon
Without whose generous help
This book would not have seen the light.

Table of contents

CHAPTER ONE

The Challenge

The tall countryman moved slowly around the deeply carpeted art gallery. He stared at some paintings for long intervals. Then he thumbed through the Catalogue for the number. Finding it he would either survey the work for another interval or show no further interest.

For want of something else to do Morris Anderson-Smith tried to follow the stranger's line of thought as he sat at his ease in the small office. It wasn't the exorbitant price of some of the paintings that turned the viewer off. Of two artworks of the same price the Westerner stared long at one while the other was immediately rejected.

Suddenly Morris tumbled to it. He was picking out the paintings of James Somerville II. Morris was sorry for him. Of the exhibition's total of a hundred and fifty paintings only nine were by Somerville and he had had a hard time even getting them. All had been sold on the Opening Day. The westerner was wasting his time and Morris decided not to waste his. No chance of a sale there even if the viewer turned out to be a wealthy cattleman down for the Show[1].

As he turned back to his papers a young woman entered the gallery, paused for a moment to take in the westerner who was standing like a statue in front of a Somerville, and then moved into the office. A laconic greeting passed between the two and Morris cocked an eyebrow at the lone occupant of the gallery.

"Another Somerville fan in the making."

The girl smiled slightly as she sat down. She was attractive without being an eye stopper: fairish brown hair worn in a short windswept style, humorous blue-grey eyes, a firm chin and a pretty mouth. Not tall but beautifully in proportion. Morris found her easy on the eyes

---

[1] *The Royal Queensland Agricultural Exhibition*

and her soft voice was pleasant to the ears. They fell into desultory conversation.

From where she sat the girl could see the solitary viewer and the more she looked him over the more she liked him. Tall and well built, dark hair with a faint curl, dark eyes, an excellent chin. He was dressed in a lightweight summer suit and carried a wide brimmed felt hat as he made his slow voyage of discovery. Then she got caught into real conversation with the stout fair haired owner of the gallery and forgot him.

"Excuse me. These little red spots. They mean?"

Morris rose to his feet to courteously assist the stranger.

"Yes, they signify a sale. Can I help you?"

The westerner looked disconsolate.

"All these James Somerville paintings are sold then?"

"I'm afraid so."

"What's this two after his name?"

Morris glanced involuntarily down at the girl who had turned away.

"Second generation. Jamie's father was the first artist."

"Better than this James?" The slight accent on the name showed what the speaker thought of such a milksop nickname for a man. The girl turned away a little further to hide a spontaneous grin.

"Well, that's a moot point," replied Morris blandly. "Both have their following."

Very neat, thought the girl.

"Does Mr Somerville take orders?"

Morris rubbed his nose and felt like boxing the girl's ears. She was being of no help whatsoever.

"You mean commissions?" doing his own bit of correcting. "Very rarely. Jamie likes to work from inspiration."

"Would Mr Somerville paint a certain scene if it were pointed out to him?"

Morris seemed to gaze vaguely around the room as if seeking information from the walls. The girl gave an infinitesimal nod.

"Yes, if the fee were attractive enough."

"That's no problem. The distance might be."

"The distance?" Morris repeated, buying time. By all the canons of good salesmanship he should now invite this richly prospective customer to sit down and then introduce himself. But what then would he do with this wretch of a girl?

"Yeah," drawled the westerner. "I'd like him to come out to my family property and paint a scene there. He can stay as long as he likes."

"A pastoral scene?" queried Morris pleasantly, giving Jamie a chance to think.

"More or less." The stranger turned his hat in his hands as he thought aloud. "It doesn't look much. Just a stand of trees and a creek but they'll be mining there shortly. The creek will be diverted and the trees will die so –"

He broke off as the girl turned sharply in her seat.

"That shouldn't be allowed," she snapped.

The man looked her over coolly and apparently saw nothing to impress him.

"I'll thank you to mind your own business, miss," he said bluntly.

Jamie blushed scarlet and got up and stalked out of the office. Morris was grateful to see she did not leave the gallery but contented herself with walking to the end.

In the meantime, he had no end of a prickle on his hands. The stranger was still watching the girl.

"I'd like to have the schooling of her for a couple of weeks," he remarked and turned back to his business. "I've got an aunt who is cutting up rough about it – like her – only Sarah's lived there all her life. She's got a fancy to have the scene painted and she likes James Somerville's way of doing it."

"Please sit down Mr – Mr –"

"Hugh Lawrence – of Fairlie Downs," supplied the westerner amiably as he took the proffered seat.

"Morris Anderson-Smith," said Morris offering his hand which was firmly shaken. 'Lawrence Bros. Fairlie Downs,' the director was thinking quickly. Something had got into the papers about Fairlie Downs…this odd business of not owning the mining rights of one's own land. There had been a bit of a dust-up that had to be sorted out legally with the Lawrence brothers ending up with a good deal and no mining rights. Obviously this brother had no regrets.

"Well, we must try and please your Aunt Sarah," he said cheerfully but with an anxious glance down the gallery. Goodness knew whether

Jamie would accept the commission now. She probably had a hate session going for this client but, with her known views on conservation, she was just as likely to dash out and paint the doomed trees.

"I'll have to get in touch with Jamie," he said. "Might take a couple of days."

"That's okay. We'll be down for the rest of the Show. I'll call in again and bring Aunt Sarah with me." He glanced out at the paintings. "I'd have liked to have bought her one of those. You don't suppose one of these buyers would sell?"

"Well now…sometimes…" Morris dithered knowing none of his clients would cough up a Somerville unless at a substantial profit.

"They could name their figure."

Heavens! He was not going to let this one out of his sight. "I have a couple at home, Mr Lawrence. You might care to look at them when you return."

Hugh Lawrence brightened. "I'll do that. Are there any other galleries that have Somerville paintings?"

"None." Morris was in this favoured position by reason of being Jamie's uncle but he was glad that she was not within earshot for there was no contract binding her.

Hugh Lawrence rose to go. "Just in case the two you've got don't take my fancy, you might give me the names of some of these buyers."

Morris was properly shocked.

"Mr Lawrence, all sales of these paintings are done exclusively through this gallery. I don't think.. "

"Oh, I mean to have one," said the westerner and there was that in the line of his jaw that gave the art-dealer pause.

"I have two particularly good ones, Mr Lawrence," he said firmly.

They were two of Jamie's best and he had been holding them back till her prices rose. This was the moment to let one go and gain a valuable client.

They shook hands and as Hugh Lawrence turned to go he caught sight of the girl making her slow way back to them.

"Nice little filly," he observed dispassionately. "A firm hand on the bridle and a bit of spur and she'd be right."

"A bit of spur in that young lady's flank and she'd be more likely to pigroot," Morris remarked acidly.

Hugh Lawrence grinned disbelievingly, waved a hand and went.

"WELL!" Jamie's sharp ears had caught the last exchange. "Mr High and Mighty is in for a shock."

"Are you going to go, Jamie?" Morris grinned.

"Oh…I don't know for sure." The girl sounded a little confused.

"You could name your figure."

"Could I now? Well if I go it will be a whopper."

"Now don't go scaring him off."

The young artist looked him over shrewdly. "Got a deal going already?"

"Could be. I'm pretty certain he'll take one of those I've been hanging on to. You know, Jamie, if you'd just settle down to painting full time you could make some real money."

"Don't want to. I like painting but it's not my life."

Morris sighed. Jamie earned her living as a freelance photographer with a news team and went all over the place. It was on these trips she saw the scenes that took her eye and returned later to paint them. The nine on show were the full result of two years' work and Morris saw no immediate hope of being able to stage a one-man Show with her.

He sighed again. Jamie's widowed father had cared for her since her childhood. A wanderer himself he had begrudged the years of school, taking her everywhere with him during the breaks. Jamie had dabbled in paints from her earliest years and displayed unusual talent from her teens. She actually had been christened James for he and his wife had longed for a son. He had dressed her as a boy until the school authorities had taken over. Jamie had turned out to be a very feminine little person and had taken most kindly to dresses and ribbons but had had little chance to wear them.

She had started exhibiting with her father at eighteen years and had kept the name of James. Only her friends and special clients knew the truth. The rest of the world took it that the second James was of masculine gender. She had brushed her hair well back for the catalogue photograph. This little ploy had afforded father and daughter some amusement. They had been very close and his death two years before from a virus caught overseas had devastated the girl. Now, Jamie, at twenty-six still carried on the harmless deceit for nostalgic reasons.

She flopped into a chair and proceeded to hold forth on the black sins of money hungry mongrels who ripped up and destroyed God's beautiful earth.

"He gave us all things to enjoy – not destroy," she declaimed.

"Now don't start on this religion business again," Morris warned. He did not know what had got into Jamie since she had been to some meeting or other at the invitation of a friend. "And don't go spouting that kind of talk if you go to Fairlie Downs. You'll set their backs up and –"

"God goes with me wherever I go," announced Jamie flatly. She sat frowning at the opposite wall and suddenly gave a funny little laugh.

"What's that for?" Morris asked curiously.

"He's a nice hunk of a man. Tall, dark *and* handsome. Could be interesting."

"Since when have you been interested in men?"

"Since I discovered I was a girl," said Jamie with a delightful grin.

Morris laughed with her. "It's on then?"

"Umm, but don't tell him I'm me."

"You won't be able to pull that off. He'll want to meet you."

"He'll have to forgo that pleasure till I get there. Just say I'm out of town and you had to ring me."

Morris sat back. "I'd like to be a fly on the wall when you two do meet. A couple of gladiators if you ask me."

Jamie stood up. "I've wasted enough time here, Uncle Morris. I've got to get to work." She kissed the top of his head before he could dodge and, on her way out the door, looked back.

"If I got into difficulties would you rescue me?"

"Sure would."

"Right. Tell him I'll arrive by whatever transport is available a week after he gets back to his property. He can meet me."

Morris shook his head. "For some reason you think this is all play, don't you, Jimmy?"

A shadow swept across the girl's countenance. "Yes, I haven't played for a long time," she said softly as she went.

Morris put his two hands together and rested his chin on the thumbs. Was Jamie at last getting over her father? The older Somerville had been all in all to his daughter and, after his death, Jamie still seemed to live as though a glass wall separated her from the rest of the world. Come to think of it she had been more with it since that meeting she had gone to. Which was the only good thing he had seen come out of that religious experience of hers, he reckoned, as he prepared to go to lunch.

CHAPTER TWO

Round One

It had been quite a business arranging both transport and meeting place. Evidently the Lawrence brothers were picking up a new truck and the coming artist had to be where the vehicle would arrive – not vice versa. This caused Jamie some amusement and she finally ended up on a small plane with only pilot, co-pilot and two other passengers.

One was a stockman who, true to his calling, had little to say. The other was a pretty fair-haired young woman who had been looking askance at Jamie ever since she had heard she was headed for Fairlie Downs. Jamie's name meant nothing to her and she took care to inform the artist that she was Stella Cousins, a great friend of Hugh Lawrence.

"Aren't you a great friend of the other brother as well?" asked Jamie, purposely innocent-eyed.

"Mark? Oh, well, yes, of course," Stella answered vaguely

Evidently our Mark isn't the tall, dark and handsome kind, thought Jamie shrewdly.

Stella could not draw her on the reason for her visit and her indifferent remark that she had not really met the Lawrences properly was received with patent disbelief.

Then Jamie began to have her own problems. Her idle question as to who lived at Fairlie Downs was received with a darkling look and the information that only the brothers lived there with their housekeeper.

"Aren't either of them married?" asked Jamie anxiously.

"Nooooo… but one of them is likely to be before long," announced Stella dampingly.

"Where does Aunt Sarah live then?"

"Who gave you the right to call her Aunt Sarah?" demanded Stella belligerently. "Even I don't."

"Oh, I wouldn't address her as such," Jamie assured her hastily. "Mr Lawrence referred to her a couple of times. I naturally thought when he said 'she lives at the old house' that that's where I'll be staying during my visit."

"How could you hear Hugh speak of his aunt if you haven't met him?"

"Oh, he was talking to someone else. I just happened to overhear," explained Jamie. She was beginning to think that the mystique in which she had wrapped her identity was not paying off.   "I think I'll probably have to stay with this aunt anyway. It's an awkward business. I never thought…" she trailed off vaguely

When Hugh Lawrence had spoken of his family property she had taken it for granted that it had a family ensconced. Aunt Sarah had added to the comfortable picture. Well, they would just have to work it all out.

From Uncle Morris's description of the aunt, who had been delighted with the painting that her nephew had bought her she seemed a sensible woman looking forward to the artist's visit. How much would this change when she discovered that Jamie was a girl? Jamie suddenly surmised –and correctly – that a bedroom would have been provided in the house the brothers occupied for the expected male artist.

She had to push down a bubbling giggle and began to try and draw Stella out a bit about herself. This overture was received with suspicion so she desisted and found herself looking forward to getting the shock of the introduction over. It was actually a good thing that Stella was here. Me fine Hughie could hardly kick up a dust in front of a special girlfriend.

As the plane circled and came down it appeared to Jamie that they were on the outskirts of a very small town which was nearly correct as it was just an outpost at a meeting of roads.

Drawn up beside the primitive airstrip were a number of cars and a shining new truck which had been overlanded on a trailer.

Jamie turned to see to the unloading of her luggage which included her special folding easel, a roll of canvas and a large paintbox. Stella had only one big suitcase beside her carryall. The pilot and co-pilot obligingly helped and the silent stockman and the girls finally landed intact with their belongings on the ground.

"There's Hugh!" cried Stella unable to suppress her excitement. "And Mark too," she added perfunctorily.

Jamie saw two men approaching them. There was no mistaking the striking figure of Hugh Lawrence. Beside him walked another man equally tall but fairer, slimmer and wearing dark wraparound glasses. Both wore khaki pants but where Hugh was all khaki, Mark had on a white shirt.

Then the stockman waved to the two approaching and walked off towards another car. Both men stopped short as recognition had come, stared after him for a moment and then back at the two girls.

Stella immediately claimed the field. She went straight to Hugh with hands held out and raised her face. Hugh kissed her full on the mouth but turned back to the stranger. His eyes were puzzled and now there was a faint hint of recognition. He was coping with two facts: one that the confounded artist hadn't come and two that he had seen this girl somewhere before.

Mark, as a matter of course, walked towards Jamie. He invariably acted as backup for his brother. He touched the brim of his hat.

"Were you expecting to be met, miss?" he asked kindly.

"Yes," said Jamie briskly. "I'm Jamie Somerville and you must be Mark Lawrence." She smiled up at the dark glasses and held out her hand.

The small group was locked in momentary silence. Mark held on to her hand as he gazed down at the mischievously smiling girl. Then with an exclamation Hugh strode forward. With Jamie's words had come recollection.

"So you're the mysterious artist," he said sharply. "Why all the secrecy – or do you habitually engage in unisex tricks, Miss Somerville?"

This slid right off Jamie's back. She had intended to surprise and confound. Round one was definitely hers.

"Lots of writers hide behind a nom-de-plume," she said gaily. "Why shouldn't artists?"

She went to extend her hand and discovered that Mark was still holding it. He released her hurriedly with a stammered apology. Hugh took it, gave it a brief shake and dropped it.

"Aunt Sarah's going to be very surprised," he said in a hard voice, thus intimating to Jamie that he felt no surprise himself, "and also disappointed."

"Why?"

"She met your father a long time ago and she thinks she's going to meet his image," explained Hugh dryly.

Jamie was hurt. The inference she drew that being a female she could never please Aunt Sarah gave those points to Hugh. He was an adversary to be reckoned with.

Mark had turned away to deal with the luggage. Before Jamie could move he had her easel under one arm and his hands grasped her suitcase and paintbox. She picked up her canvas roll and carryall and prepared to follow him. Hugh picked up Stella's case and walked beside the blond girl who was talking animatedly to him. A station wagon was drawn up beside the truck. All the luggage was stowed in the back of it. Now, apparently, all waited for Hugh to sort out the parties.

He did this in a way calculated to put Jamie further in her place. He gave her a charming smile that made her pulses quicken a little and then turned to Stella and opened the door into the wagon.

"We've got a lot of catching up to do," he remarked as he looked down at the palpitating girl and his smile for her was even more dazzling.

Poor Stella, thought Jamie cynically as she followed Mark over to the truck. Stella had been more clad for the truck in her neat white slacks. Jamie's green linen suit was smart but she was going to show an awful lot of leg as she got up into the truck. Before she could even try, two firm hands were under her armpits and she was up and in her seat before she could draw breath.

She settled herself comfortably as Mark went around and sprang up into the driver's seat. Then they were on their way following the station wagon. Jamie opened her large white bag and drew out her camera. As a news photographer, she had a habit of having her camera always at the ready. It was not her usual camcorder but a still one she used exclusively on painting trips. Mark glanced over at her activities but asked no questions. He was a man who took in all or most of the information he required through observation alone.

For thirty kilometres, they travelled in absolute silence, Jamie being much taken up with her own observations. She liked to spend considerable time in getting the feel of her surroundings. The fine nuances of her paintings owed much to her ability to capture the intransient atmosphere at any given time of day.

At last she felt it was only polite to engage in a little conversation with the silent man beside her.

"Have we very far to go?" she ventured.

"Over a hundred k's," was the laconic reply.

"Goodness!" exclaimed Jamie. "I wish I'd eaten more before I boarded the plane."

An attractive smile flickered around the man's firm lips.

"We'll be pulling up for a bit of lunch," he vouchsafed.

And that was that. After a moment Jamie went back to her ceaseless scanning of the land. There had recently been some good rains and the countryside was greening with the inevitable but poignantly brief flushing of wildflowers. Jamie watched a pretty grouping of trees for a while till she realised the road was turning away from it. She turned impulsively to her companion.

"Do you think there's a chance of getting closer to that group of trees, Mr Lawrence? I'd have liked a shot or two of them."

Mark bent his head and looked past her, following her pointing hand. Without more ado, he left the road and began making his winding way over the rough ground. Jamie was charmed by this. It was just how she would have acted herself had she been driving. There was no terrain she and her father had not tackled in their own four-wheeled drive.

The trees were further off than they appeared but were well worth the diversion. The reflected light on the water showed up soon and at last Jamie was able to pick up the shape of a billabong. As the truck pulled up she sat there entranced. This particular grouping of trees was a real find; the billabong was covered with waterlilies and other green bushes testified to a never-failing spring. A lot of birds had risen in the air at their approach and, in a flash, Jamie snapped them in flight.

Mark was around and had opened her door. He held out his arms. Jamie came down neatly and he released her at once.

Nice man, thought the girl and ran a finger around her skirt to adjust her blouse.

"If you want the birds back we'll just sit quietly for a little," Mark said as he moved over to the shade of a tree. Jamie followed him and as they seated themselves on a fallen log she delved into her capacious bag and produced a sketching pad and a box of oil crayons. She never wasted a moment on location although this was not a good time for sketching. The sun was almost overhead and the shadows packed densely under tree and shrub. Jamie used this fact to give the necessary drama and, under Mark's amazed eyes, a delightful picture grew in the most delicate tints. She caught the effect perfectly of the drained away colour and the somnolence of the midday bush. The birds coming shyly back were touched in here and there, just enough to give life to the scene. It took her about twenty minutes in all.

"That's mighty clever," Mark drawled as she looked up. "If Hugh's still got any doubts he won't after he sees that."

"I'd like to get some good photographs of the birds now," said Jamie hopefully, wondering if he would allow her any further time.

"Go ahead." Mark got up and walked over to the truck. In a moment, he returned with the esky which he proceeded to unpack.

"We'll have lunch here," he said as she looked around. "The others will pull in to the stop we arranged and begin on theirs while they wait for us. That way we'll save time."

"Great," said Jamie who saw nothing wrong with inconveniencing anyone else when she was on an artistic high. "This is a glorious place," she added enthusiastically as she put a zoom lens on her camera.

Mark built a fire and boiled the billy while she crept about to get her shots and was more or less satisfied when he called her. They ate the thick sandwiches and drank the scalding tea. At least Mark did. Jamie blew on hers till she could manage to get it down. As soon as they finished he began to pack up methodically and refused her offer to help.

"You get all you want. I can handle this,' he remarked.
Jamie watched him for a moment. He might have little to say but he was a marvellous companion in his quiet competent way. She stared around and above her looking for any specimen she might have missed. She caught the egrets, greater and lesser, the magpie geese and one or two pelicans which seemed quite out of place so far inland. Then she saw a strange bird high in a tree near them.

When Mark had put the stuff away and stamped out the fire she called softly to him and pointed.

"What is it?" she asked.

Mark strained upwards for a moment then jerked his head back with an exclamation and Jamie saw a grey and white blob on one of the lens of his dark glasses. Quick as thought she pulled the glasses off.

"You were lucky you had them on," she said gaily and with a smothered laugh pulled out her hanky and went down to the billabong to clean off the bird-dropping. As she returned to him polishing the glasses she remarked seriously. "It's pretty potent, isn't it?"

Mark nodded into her face of concern. "Yes, you were very quick."

"Oh, just habit. I always cleaned my father's glasses," and Jamie looked up into the nicest blue eyes she had ever seen. She smiled involuntarily. A small flame leapt in the back of those eyes and her heart gave an odd thump.

They both turned away on the instant.

Back in the truck Jamie noticed that Mark made no attempt to catch up with the others. Nor did he make any attempt at further conversation. Brooding over this she suddenly realised she had not taken a picture of the strange bird. A silent party finally arrived at the lunch spot and an exasperated Hugh.

"Surely you haven't had a breakdown already," he queried as he strode to Mark's side of the cabin.

"Nope. Miss Somerville wanted to take some photographs and do a drawing."

"The devil she did," drawled Hugh sarcastically, "and I suppose Stella and I were to patiently starve till she finished."

Mark merely grinned knowing that each vehicle always carried its own provisions but Jamie was pipped.

"Surely you've eaten," she said loftily. "We have."

Hugh looked at her across his brother. He did not like the tone of that remark. It sounded as though she were in cahoots with Mark already. This would never do. The thought that he had had in the art gallery returned. Time to begin the schooling of James Somerville the Second.

"Well you can drive with me now," he snapped. "That way we'll make sure we get home tonight."

"I don't want to," said Jamie quickly as Hugh moved around the bonnet to get to her side. She made her voice mischievous, "Please drive on Mr Lawrence. Let's have some fun."

Mark frowned and started the truck reluctantly. As they passed Hugh's amazed figure Jamie felt a small sense of triumph but it was short lived. Mark drove the vehicle slowly whereas Jamie wanted him to speed away. Within minutes the station-wagon was right behind them.

"Can't you go any faster?" urged the girl. Mark was watching his rear vision mirror and did not answer. Then he drew over as the wagon passed him with a flourish. It went on a little way and then was turned to straddle the road. As Hugh got out and went around to jerk open the door for Stella, Mark pulled up and spoke without turning his head.

"You'll find that it's just as well to give in to Hugh first as last," he said quietly.

Jamie turned to him in exasperation but her door was pulled opened before the hot words left her lips. Hugh stood there with one hand held up to her. There was a small silence. This Mark's not going to help me one little bit, she thought angrily, to pot with him.

She took the proffered hand, sprang lightly down and marched off to the wagon. Stella passed her with downcast eyes and an injured air. His point won, Hugh chatted amiably to his passenger, telling her more about her destination and his aunt's pleasure in the painting he had bought for her. Jamie tried to ignore him but responded in spite of herself. Both vehicles picked up speed now. There was a short break for afternoon smoko and then the long drive was resumed till finally they were going over the cattle grids.

A big old-fashioned house set among mango trees, its greenery draped around it like a shawl, rose on a slight incline.

An older couple came out on to the veranda and soon Mrs Templeton – Aunt Sarah – was exclaiming with amazement and, yes, obvious disappointment at Jamie's identity. Over the evening meal Jamie almost had to give her life history before Sarah Templeton was finally satisfied.

Her brother, Ashley Lawrence, said little and seemed a second Mark. In fact, the two men were very alike in colouring and build except that the older man's muscles were fined down to whipcord. Jamie found herself thinking that Hugh must take after his mother.

Stella, who had to take a back seat to all this, seemed satisfied merely to be seated beside Hugh who threw a tit bit of conversation her way now and then. He, his aunt and Jamie carried the talk apart from these occasional asides. We're the talkers and the others are the listeners, thought Jamie with an inward grin. Then Aunt Sarah broached the difficulty which had reared itself over the artist's changed sex.

"I suppose Miss Somerville had better stay here," she suggested to Hugh in a way that expected nothing but an affirmative in answer. Hugh frowned.

"I don't know. It's twenty minutes to our place and another twenty or so to Feldings Creek. I don't see why she can't stay with us. Mrs Howard will be there and after all Miss Somerville's here on business."

Jamie saw the jealousy flicker across Stella's face and her heart ached for the girl. She was so obviously the one in thrall. Jamie glanced at Mark. He had removed his sunglasses and put on his ordinary ones. They still seemed to act as an effective screen. He couldn't care less, she thought, and was annoyed with herself for minding. She decided to be completely unhelpful and shrugged her shoulders when asked what she would like.

There was no further argument. Stella and her goods were left at the homestead as originally planned and Hugh put Jamie and her luggage into the truck. He drove, Mark jumping in after Jamie. The station wagon was left for Stella to drive over in the morning.

Mrs Howard got her share of the surprise as they drove up to the Homestead in the dark. Jamie was tired and in no mood for another long explanation. However, the housekeeper did not require it. Hugh's brief statement had been sufficient. What she did was to precede the girl into her designated room and whip off the plain bedcover. Even as Jamie began to unpack, a flounced cover in autumn tones was placed on the bed, a charming set of doilies on the dressing table and a pretty gold-shaded lamp was brought in and placed on the bedside table. To Jamie's appreciative thanks Mrs Howard replied with a smile,

"It's just lovely to be able to use them again. There hasn't been a woman in residence here since Mrs Lawrence died four years ago. I'll put some flowers in tomorrow and a couple of nice ornaments. Do you like pretty things?"

"Oh, yes," responded Jamie with enthusiasm, "I had very little in that way when I was a child and I just lap it up now."

They smiled into each other's eyes and were friends at once. Mrs Howard withdrew with a little sigh. Would this charming young woman, turning up so unexpectedly, be the one to finally take with Hugh? She did not give much for Stella's chances. This was the third visit the girl had wangled and Hugh was still as nonchalantly casual as ever.

Over supper Hugh surveyed the artist speculatively.

"I suppose you'll be wanting to get started on the picture tomorrow. I can drive you over and – "

"Nothing of the kind," answered Jamie composedly, wishing she was game enough to dip her toast into her tea, "I may not be painting at all this first week."

Hugh jumped to a totally wrong conclusion. He thought she was after a free holiday into the bargain. As girls made all sorts of excuses to hang around him he could hardly be blamed.

"You're here to paint, not to grace the landscape, Miss Somerville," he drawled.

The two protagonists measured glances. Jamie dropped into a tired teacher's voice as she explained with infinite patience that she had to study a landscape at all hours of the day and do several sketches before she could decide on the mood she needed.

Hugh was nettled by the tone although it brought a quirk to his silent brother's lips.

"I can save you all that bother, Miss Somerville. It looks its best at sunset."

"Does it now," said Jamie with a sarcastic inflexion in her weary voice. "I never paint sunsets, Mr Lawrence. If that's the kind of chocolate box art you want, you'd better drive me back tomorrow."

Hugh suddenly remembered the art-dealer's remark as to Jamie's propensity for pigrooting if the spur was driven home and he involuntarily chuckled. There could be an interesting few weeks ahead.

"Right. We'll play it your way." He smiled charmingly and utterly disarmed her. "By the way its first names around here except for Howie. But I don't care for your nickname. What's your proper name?"

"My full name is James Elizabeth Somerville."

Mrs Howard gasped. "But surely the girl's equivalent is Jaimie, J-a-i-m-i-e, isn't it?"

"I wouldn't know, Mrs Howard. Dad christened me James because he had wanted a son." Jamie was bored. She had gone through this time and again ever since she had started school. What did it matter?

"Well, I never!" Mrs Howard glanced around at the others.

"I like it," said Mark with his slow smile. "It suits you…Jamie."

Jamie smiled gratefully back at him and that decided Hugh.

"Then Jamie it shall be," he said heartily and the party broke up for the night.

CHAPTER THREE

Surveying the Field

The next day Hugh only waited for Stella's arrival before driving both girls out to Feldings Creek. Jamie had been surprised to find that the much vaunted scene was nearly half an hour's drive from the homestead. Hugh explained that it was the place they had always gone for picnics when they had visitors and it was indeed a lovely spot. Much larger than the pretty billabong that had first caught her fancy, it had a backdrop of low blue-hazed hills that set it off and, amongst the bush growth, one magnificent old gum. Hugh averred that the water would not be lost just merely diverted but, because of this the great tree would die. Jamie grieved over the business but realised that there was no help for it.

The emotional traumas over the proposed Gordon below Franklin dam and the Daintree road blockades were still within living memory. This was such a small spot in comparison, and so far away, that it would be impossible to mount a defence. The thought formed in Jamie's mind then to do two paintings. The second one she would do when she returned home and would mount it with its story in a suitable exhibition. Then another thought flashed into her head: to paint other doomed spots and she saw a life's work ahead of her. This all made her very vague and non-committal as she wandered around and the other two finally left her to her own devices.

Jamie sat on the bank of the creek and gave herself up to contemplation of the brown sunlit waters, the softly swaying branches above her head, the magnificent dashes of colour on the trunk of the old gum. It was very old, had been split by lightning and, in its degenerative state, more picturesque than in its slim youth. "Never mind," said Jamie softly, "you'll live forever in my paintings."

When she returned to the others she found them sitting close together on a rock. Hugh was fondling Stella's hand and the girl's expression was one of absolute beatification. Oh, if only he meant it!

Why doesn't he get married, thought Jamie irritably. He must be close on thirty. That made her speculate on Mark's age. He looked younger than Hugh who was in the heyday of his rich manhood. Yet she had heard Mark spoken of as the older brother. He must be about thirty-two or three she guessed and had no irritable thoughts as to why Mark had not married.

She got out her sketch book and made the first of her sketches: one small overhung corner of the creek. The others eventually sought her out and gazed down at the drawing.

"I'd never have thought there was a picture there," marvelled Stella.

"Me neither," agreed Hugh, glancing from the scene to the clever sketch. "What makes it a picture?"

Jamie put her hand over the slender sapling leaning out gazing at its own reflection. Immediately the sketch lost point and emphasis. Both viewers could see it and looked respectfully at Jamie as she scrambled to her feet.

"I'd like to prowl around the whole property when we get home," she said as she dusted herself off. "I can see a lot of stuff I'd like to record."

"Then Stella can take you around. I'll be busy -"

"Playing with the new truck," finished Stella playfully.

"No cheek from you, young woman," said Hugh giving her a playful smack on her backside. He happened to glance at Jamie and found her glaring at him. What Stella had taken as a compliment Jamie would regard as an insult. Too bad!

On their return Stella faithfully showed Jamie over the immediate environs of the station. Jamie was a bit staggered at the obvious wealth and up to the mark of everything. There was a big machinery plant, garages for the cars and motorbikes, stables for the splendid riding horses, storehouses, a small piggery, fowl yards, holding paddocks, stockyards, quarters for the men, a special office for Mark attached to one storehouse. They paused outside his door where he was busy working and Jamie made it plain that she was interested in what he was doing. To her polite but firm questioning he admitted that he did the books for all their business ventures but described none of his work. It was Stella who told her that Mark did the buying and selling of cattle, all the ordering of goods and the hiring of the men. Mark stood where he had risen at their entrance and listened to the girl with an indulgent half-smile

"You run the place then," stated Jamie.

"Only from the inside. Hugh handles all the outside work. He's tops at that."

Jamie nodded and they soon moved on. She glanced back to see him bent once more over his books. She went on feeling a trifle flat.

After lunch SarahTempleton drove over and whisked Jamie back to Seven Trees. The young artist fascinated her and she still wanted to hear more about her father and her life with him. In fact, she was so interested that Jamie began to wonder if she had been fond of him. There had been those years in school when James Somerville had had to do his own thing and could have met up with the divorced Sarah Templeton then.

Jamie did not like this peering into her private life and countered with personal questions of her interlocutor. But Sarah liked talking about herself and the Lawrence family generally. In no time the photo albums were out and she was calling across to her brother when he came in for smoko to verify this or that fact, which he did with nods and grunts. After Ashley had gone back to his work, Sarah smiled at Jamie.

"The non-talking Lawrences – they're the ones that don't marry."

"How do you mean?" asked Jamie, feeling as though some unauthorised person had just squeezed her heart.

"We've got an odd tradition in this family. This is the fourth generation of Lawrences. In the second, third and the present fourth there have always been two sons regardless of how many daughters. One is fair and the other dark. One's a talker, one is not. One marries and the other doesn't."

"W-Who's the – the likely one to marry this time?" stammered Jamie.

Sarah smiled knowledgeably, "Oh, Hugh, of course. He's the marrying kind."

"Well, why doesn't he get on with it then?"

There was a careless shrugging of the shoulders. "Oh, he'll get there eventually. He's a bit of a flirt, our Hugh. Breaks all the girls' hearts around here."

And he's in the process of breaking another one, the creep," thought Jamie viciously. "But it's not quite the same tradition," she said hopefully. "There are no sisters this time so –"

"Yes, there are: two sisters. The girls came later, twins, and went off like hot cakes. Ed, their father who always spoilt them, took them with him once when visiting in the States. They were a hit and were grabbed by two ranchers. Ed was furious. Of course they are married and living in the States now. Ed never encouraged exchange visits."

Jamie took a moment to digest this. Typical behaviour of the dominant brother.

"Er…hasn't Mark ever shown an interest in girls?" Jamie tried to keep the forlorn note out of her voice.

"He did once about seven or eight years ago. Hugh was away at Uni when Mark got engaged. When he came home for the holidays Hugh gave Claudia the run around, just testing her out for Mark he said. Of course, she fell for him and that was that. Mark had a lucky escape, we all thought."

"How do you mean?" Jamie seemed very dumb that afternoon.

"Well, she was obviously fickle. That wouldn't do for Mark. He's the old faithful type."

Jamie could hardly keep her seat and her countenance. She turned page after page of the albums without seeing the contents or hearing Sarah's voice. What chance would Mark have with all Hugh's charm and address? But how stupid of Claudia! Hugh had obviously dropped her when he had proved his point. I'd like to choke him, she thought savagely.

"How do you rate Stella's chances with Hugh?" she asked anxiously.

Sarah frowned. 'Very good during her last visit. Not so good now."

"Why?"

"She's got to the cow-eyed stage. Follows him round with big adoring eyes and it's yes and amen to everything he says. All the salt's gone out of her. Hugh will be bored in no time, you'll see. He likes a challenge."

What a callous lot they were. As if there was anything wrong with a girl loving a man dearly. Not that anyone would catch her, Jamie Somerville, making cow-eyes at a man.

Ashley drove Jamie back for dinner but did not stay. Jamie took covert stock of them all at the meal. Yes, Hugh was definitely the talker. Yes, Stella was agreeing with everything he said and sounding a dead bore. Mark was saying nothing even though he was following the conversation with interest. It's not because he's dumb, Jamie thought. Hugh's probably held the floor from the moment he was born.

She made a subtle and carefully casual effort to get a second conversation going but she had no sooner got Mark answering when Hugh paused, caught the gist of it and took over. After that he initiated a rallying kind of conversation with Jamie, a teasing game of thrust and parry at which Jamie excelled but she worked hard to include the others. There were some spontaneous bursts of laughter at hers and Hugh's wit. When they rose from the table, he put a casual arm around her shoulders.

"You're in form tonight, Jamie," he complimented.

Jamie shrugged his arm off. "Oh, really?" she said in a way that suggested that he would not know whether she was in form or not. Hugh was sharp enough to catch the subtle nuance of meaning she intended and his brow darkened.

When it was time for Stella to go, Jamie expressed extreme surprise that the girl should be expected to drive back on her own. It certainly did not compare well with city manners.

"We country girls are used to looking after ourselves," Stella said with a lopsided smile.

"Sure," agreed Hugh, "she wants the car for tomorrow."

"I'll drive you home, Stell," Mark got up as he spoke. Hugh glanced complacently at Jamie and settled back to watch the news. Jamie waited till she heard the car being started, then jumped up and shot out of the room. As the car turned into the driveway she rapped at the window.

"Take me too," she pleaded. The car stopped and she ran around and got in the front beside Stella. Mark put his foot on the accelerator and they were away, Jamie grinning hugely to herself in the dark. She then proceeded to initiate a bright conversation that was mostly carried on by herself and Stella but enjoyed by all.

When they dropped Stella, Mark promised that one of them would drive over for her in the morning and with that she was content. As they drove off Jamie had time to assess her impulsive action. It was Hugh's complacent glance at her that had triggered it. He was obviously contemplating an uninterrupted evening with her and, being a predatory male, the thought had not been unpleasant. Mrs Howard had gone off to her own quarters and, short of going to bed herself, Jamie could not have avoided Hugh's company. She was already getting Hugh's measure.

The only thing was that she was now alone in the car with Mark and an unhappy thought struck her. Would he think that she had engineered this? She began a light and airy conversation, the words of which fell in the silent car like lumps of lead.

Finally, Jamie gathered her bright thoughts together and dismissed them. Let him think what he liked. She wound her window right down and leaned out to catch the breeze and the beauty of the night.

After a while a feeling of wellbeing stole over her and she thought dreamily of that moment by the billabong. In the course of her work she had met plenty of men, and had often been taken out on dates, but none had stirred her pulses for more than one outing.

Now she felt that, no matter how often she stood by that billabong, if Mark looked at her with that tiny flame in his eyes she would feel that same thump in her heart. Right to the end of time, she thought drearily.

Then she brightened. Mark must have felt something to have had such an expression. How did he get started with Claudia? Or had Claudia made the going? She glanced surreptitiously across at him. He was driving with one hand on the wheel and the other resting on the open window ledge, very relaxed. His profile showed cleanly against the moonlit earth. What a good profile he had; such a nice straight nose. Hugh's nose would probably have a hook in it by the time he was sixty.

But why, why, why should she, Jamie Somerville, who moved with ease in cosmopolitan circles, meeting the most attractive of men, feel a thump in her heart over a quiet, undemonstrative man whose true personality she could only guess at? Perhaps that was why, she thought dismally. She knew Hugh's type. He might stand out up here in the

outback but in the city he would not be the only stud in the other girls'
corral.

She laughed a little low laugh at the thought. Where on earth had
that come from? A real Americanism.

"Care to share it?" a laconic voice queried.

Jamie almost jumped. Oh, what a pity she couldn't. It could have
been the start to a decent conversation.

"Just laughing at myself," she said lamely.

"Why?"

Jamie sat up and tried to think.

"Don't you ever laugh at yourself?" she parried.

"Nope."

"It's good for you. Stops you from taking yourself too seriously."
Silence.

Well, that's that, thought Jamie.

But Mark's mind was turning over.

"Couldn't imagine myself laughing at anything you did."

"Not even if I meant to be funny?" pleaded Jamie with exaggerated
concern.

Mark gave a genuine chuckle. "I see what you mean," he said.

Jamie laughed too and settled back contentedly. No need for
conversation all the time. Just a remark now and then. And that was
how it went.

When they pulled in she deliberately waited for him to come
around and open her door. As she stood upright she was quite close to
him. The moon was shining and Jamie felt reckless.

"Thank you for a delightful drive," she said dulcetly, "most
enjoyable."
Silence.

She stepped away and prepared to throw in her hand for the night.

Mark shut the car door.

"Second nicest drive I've ever had," he remarked and got back into
the car in order to drive it into its narrow berth in the garage.

Jamie strolled up to the house wishing she had kept her mouth shut.
Mark could do his own work of thrust and parry quite well when he
put his mind to it. Would she ever know when that first nicest drive
took place and with whom? Shades of Claudia! She felt a pricking

behind her eyelids as she ran up the three steps onto the darkened veranda.

"Not dallying in the moonlight with my brother?" asked a deep voice.

"Not dallying in the moonlight with any brother." Jamie whisked past Hugh thankful she had not been tempted to overplay her hand that night.

The next few days saw Jamie well entrenched into the ways of the homestead. It was finally decided, despite Sarah's protests, that Stella should move over with Jamie who thoroughly approved. It was Stella who drove her out to the creek at various times of the day so that she could assess the light and do her sketches. Hugh always insisted that the two go even though Jamie asserted she could find the place herself.

"Safety measures," he said. But Jamie felt that he used it as an excuse to get Stella out of his hair. The men were busy about their own concerns but Stella was apparently welcome to share the outside work. She was superb on a horse and could take her place in any mustering with the men. Her tall slim-hipped body showed off the tailored jodhpurs and her long blond hair, tied back with a brown bow, made her a lovely sight.

While Stella rode with the men, Jamie pottered about with Mrs Howard, learning more of the personal history of the Lawrences. During this she was surprised to discover that Howie had a favourite spot in her heart for the older brother and it was easy to initiate a conversation about him. As Mrs Howard made the beds Jamie hopped on to the other side to do her bit or wielded a duster as she led the housekeeper on. Jamie learned that Mark walked in his younger brother's footsteps, backing him up in every venture, putting out a steadying hand if Hugh's ideas proved too rash, picking up the pieces when Hugh's temper blew things. Jamie wondered at this.

"Must be some temper," she remarked as she lifted the ornaments in the dining room for the housekeeper's duster.

"Haven't you noticed the way his eyebrows meet across his nose? Sure sign of a bad temper."

Jamie's mind brought up a picture of Hugh. He had finely marked brows which, together with the widow's peak of his black hair, gave his face a striking emphasis. Yes, there was a thin line of hairs across the bridge of his nose.

"Mark's eyebrows don't meet, do they?"

Mrs Howard laughed. "No, and they wouldn't need to. One temper around here is enough. All the lassies are mad about Hugh but the one who gets him will have plenty on her hands."

Jamie carefully lifted a heavy ornamental vase. "Do you think that Hugh will be the one to carry on the tradition and marry?" she asked tentatively.

Mrs Howard whisked the duster roughly across the polished wood. "I guess so,"

"But Mark is attractive too," the girl said, greatly daring.

"Yes, but he got his fingers burned once and, while Hugh is single, he hasn't got a chance."

"Oh, hasn't he?" thought Jamie grimly.

"Besides," added the housekeeper, "it would take a bomb to get him moving now. He's thirty-two and well settled in his ways. No, he'll be a second Uncle Ashley like his Uncle Harry before him. Only there's no sister in the offing to keep house for him." She sighed and swept the room with a glance that dared any malcontent speck of dust to show its face.

One night they all drove over to the other homestead for a game of cards. Another time Ashley and his sister drove over with some visitors who were anxious to meet the artist. Sarah had been showing off her own recently acquired Somerville. Jamie could see further commissions looming. She made it clear that she had just managed to squeeze in this particular assignment. If she was in danger of becoming too emotionally involved at this station it would be the last.

By the end of the week Jamie had concluded that the morning light was the best for the painting and this had nothing to do with Hugh's choice of the late afternoon. The creek had a pellucid quality in the morning and the soft light caressed the old gum highlighting the pearly trunk emerging from its rough red brown stocking.

She had marked out a very good frame around an old print up at Seven Trees and asked if it could be used for her painting. It was most cordially given, one and all thinking it a good idea to use a frame already available. Jamie then proceeded to cut the large stretcher frame to fit. She was discovered in this by Hugh who promptly took over, insisting on doing the cutting for her – to her extreme annoyance. She called it a day once the frame was ready and did not go back to work till the next day when she was sure he was out of the way.

Once satisfied, Jamie unrolled the expensive canvas and cut and tacked it to the stretcher frame, driving in the little wedges till it was firm and tight. She then gave it a light wash of Rose Madder Tint and turps and left the paint to dry.

Next day she and Stella drove off after a very early breakfast with her painting gear. They were back soon after ten finished for the day and the painting was put away in the empty end of a shed Mark had cleared for her. Jamie refused flatly to let anyone see the work in progress and Stella grinned smugly.

Things went smoothly for a few days then some heavy clouds blew up and called a halt to proceedings, Jamie refusing to paint without the exact light much to the others' mystification for the light was still good and it was much cooler.

The clouds did bring some rain to everyone's delight but Jamie was annoyed afterwards with the clear-washed aspect, which had destroyed the heat haze for the time being, and the disturbance of the creek waters. She was short-tempered during this period and everyone knowledgeably blamed the artistic temperament. That is, everyone except Mark who seemed not to notice.

Hugh set out to humour her into a good mood with much light hearted teasing and enjoyed her lightning ripostes. Jamie realised with dismay that, simply because they were communicating, something was building up between her and Hugh. It was nothing but camaraderie yet Hugh contrived to shut the others out with it, including Stella.

When other visitors were present he ragged her unmercifully and the visitors laughed and nodded to each other. Sure, this was Hugh's latest and very charming at that. Stella's moon was so far on the wane that Jamie wondered why she stayed with one breath and was very glad she did with the next.

She remembered reading once that women loved to suffer in love but did not think Stella was enjoying the experience. She finally broached the subject one day when they were back out at the creek and she had finished her daily stint.

"Bring the thermos over here," Jamie called as she folded the heavy easel. Once seated in the shade she cut the ground from under Stella. "You're madly in love with Hugh, aren't you?"

Stella flushed darkly. "Is it so obvious?" she asked bitterly.

"Very," said Jamie, intending to be kind in her cruelty. "That's what sticks in Hugh's throat. You want to stand back a bit, give him as good as he gives, tease him a bit. Be standoffish when he least expects it."

Stella turned from Jamie's earnest face and began to draw pictures in the sand with a small stick. "I used to be like that. I could do what you do but I can't now. I – I care too much. Do you find him attractive too?"

Stella was blunt in her turn.

"Me? Not jolly likely." Jamie tossed her head. "His type's a dollar a dozen where I come from." This was not strictly true but Jamie wanted to blast such a thought right out of Stella's mind. She brushed her fairish hair out of her eyes and knelt up beside the unhappy girl

"Isn't anything worth a try?" she asked gently.

Stella held her countenance for a moment and then broke, her head coming down on Jamie's shoulder. Jamie held her while she wept herself out. When Stella finally pulled herself together Jamie poured their tea and they sat companionably over it.

"I think I had better go home," said Stella at last. "Every day I keep hoping… but it's just the same."

"The trouble is there's no competition." Jamie frowned heavily.

"No," agreed Stella forlornly. "If Mark had a bit of go in him I could try playing him."

"I wonder if we could ask him to help us," suggested Jamie even though the very thought was like knives digging into her.

"Oh, no," Stella grasped her arm in alarm. "If he should refuse I'd die of humiliation."

"I suppose so. But what say we don't tell him."

"How do you mean?"

"Make your own little play for him." Jamie nobly disregarded the knives. "After all he did offer to drive you home the other night."

"That won't work since I've moved over."

"Well, let's see what we can do about it. Anything's better than doing nothing." Jamie had begun to wonder if she played up to Hugh more herself whether she could surprise a reaction in Mark. Anything was better than nothing.

Stella was withdrawn during the rest of the day. Jamie spent time in the shed ostensibly brooding over her painting. It was going to take a bit of careful thinking out.

The following day was Saturday and Hugh decided that they would all have a break and go riding. He hauled Mark into the party and Jamie winked at Stella. Step one had, of course, been to prise Mark from his office.

Jamie could just ride and that was all. Hugh brought out a plump little mare for her. He fixed the stirrups and put a hand on her blue-jeaned leg. "We should have been giving you riding lessons all along," he teased.

"That won't lower my fee," stated Jamie, letting his hand rest there in full view of Mark. Unfortunately, that was the moment Stella chose to engage Mark's attention with some remark about the ride. Instantly Jamie roughly shook off Hugh's hand as her mare moved forward.

Hugh reacted at once. He mounted and slapped Jamie's mare hard on the rump. The horse took off and Hugh galloped beside her while she sought wildly for balance.

Stella stared after them bleakly and turned to find Mark white with anger.

"Damn fool thing to do," he muttered and took off with a running mount after them. Stella was left to follow and decided that the first effort was a flop.

Jamie bouncing around, clung on for dear life, determined not to be thrown. Out of the corner of her eye she saw Mark's big red horse ranging alongside her. Before he could do anything, Hugh divined his intent and himself caught Jamie's rein and eased both horses to a steady canter. Mark kept beside the inexperienced girl and Stella came up on his other side. Nothing was said and the small party headed towards the closest spur of some foothills.

Stella knew the area. There was a very colourful gorge and the riders could not go more than two abreast. Here was a chance to put their roughed out plan into operation. She deliberately eased her horse back beside Mark allowing the other two to go ahead. She at once initiated a conversation and was pleased to find Mark answering readily, even though she suspected that it was out of courtesy. As they chatted their canny horses idled to a walk.

The others had entered the gorge by the time they got there so, having been there several times, they tacitly drew their horses off into some shade.

They had got into a discussion on horseflesh of which Mark was an expert judge for he bought most of the horses for Fairlie Downs. Stella seized the chance to pick up some tips and, when Hugh and Jamie returned, she did not so much as look around till her attention was claimed.

Jamie was aglow with the beauty of the earth colours and slid off her horse to pick up some samples. They all ended up helping as Jamie demanded their handkerchiefs as receptacles.

"Are you going to make one of those coloured sand bottles?" queried Stella with interest.

Jamie shook her head. "Much better than that. Wait and see."

When she had gathered what she could and the little cloth parcels were disposed in various pockets, they rode away from the gorge.

Stella stubbornly stuck to Mark's heels and he seemed nothing loath to have her. Jamie noticed this with little pleasure so she was sure it would not escape Hugh's sharp eyes. It hadn't. He moved adroitly between the two and turned a laughing face to the girl.

"It's a long time since we had a race, Stella," he shouted and was off.

Stella was riding a splendid brown gelding which she knew could match Hugh's big black. She dug her heels in and was off after him, confident that her lighter weight would carry the day. Jamie's little mare jumped forward after them and she struggled desperately to hold her. The mare would soon have got her head but for an iron hand gripping the bridle. Mark pressed the mare around with his own mount and eased her to a steady walk.

"Phew!" breathed Jamie. "Trixie's too fat for me to get a good grip on her. I think I need a few lessons before I go again."

"You need a more reliable horse," said Mark grimly, "not an excitable flirt like Trixie."

Jamie laughed. "Is she? Oh, how gorgeous. Is she always after the boys?"

Mark grinned and nodded. Now that their first little ploy had succeeded Jamie meant to use the time with Mark. She glanced around her.

"This is a lovely area, Mark. Are there any other gorges we can explore?"

"Not close but there is a cave. In fact, Hugh was going to include it but he must have forgotten."

Too busy with his dog in the manger tactics, thought Jamie.

"I'd love to see the cave."

To the cave they went forthwith, the horses picking their way delicately up the slight rise. The cave seemed nothing more than a shallow indent. Jamie waited for him to tie the horses securely and change his glasses, then followed him to find that, once inside, there was a sharp drop. She did not like the damp darkness and made no bones about getting a good fistful of the back of his shirt. They pussyfooted their way along, backs bent till Mark was able to straighten.

"Now just give me a minute." He pulled out a flat torch and shone0 it around.

Jamie gasped. They were in a small limestone cave and there glowed before her eyes some exquisite formations. Mark held the torch steadily on a delicate veil and told her to stand still and hang on to the wall while he went behind the veil. He shone the torch through it and the almost transparent crystals were breathtaking. Jamie's beauty loving soul was enthralled. How glad I am I saw this with Mark and only with Mark, she thought. He patiently shone the torch around till she had looked her fill. Then they turned and made their way back, for once in a silence that Jamie was reluctant to break.

Once on the surface again, Jamie turned to Mark with shining eyes. "Thank you so much. I wouldn't have missed that for anything. Do many come here to see it?"

He shook his head. "Only our guests. We haven't registered it and swear to secrecy the privileged few we bring."

She met his whimsical smile with one of reassurance. "It's safe with me."

It was a moment for a real exchange of glances but he had slipped on his dark glasses. I'll have to call on another bird's help if this state of affairs continues, she thought as she got up on Trixie before Mark could help her. Jamie was not going to play helpless to get his attentions.

They rode home slowly and Jamie hugged every moment. She was pretty sure now that what had happened to her was for real. I'm getting that way that I'm cherishing every moment with him like pearls, she thought ruefully. Maybe that's all I'll have. She tried to ride a little behind him that she might better study his broad back and straight shoulders but he kept dropping back too so that they were moving at the slowest of paces. Jamie half expected Hugh to come galloping back. It would be like him not even to leave this part of the field to another.

CHAPTER FOUR

Tactical Experiments

As soon as they were in sight of the homestead they saw the cars. They seemed to have been invaded. There were young people everywhere. Introductions were swiftly made and Jamie discovered it was a surprise party for her and was touched. Of course, everyone was in the know. Ashley and Sarah were there with Sarah directing the unloading of the foodstuffs. They had gathered from far and near; some having driven through the night. They were a high spirited but orderly group and all knew each other well. Jamie hurried away to change and was glad to see Stella the centre of a laughing crowd.

A picnic lunch was quickly served and then the fleet of cars took them all to Feldings Creek for a last sighting of the doomed trees. There was disappointment that Jamie's painting was not ready to be seen but Sarah assured them solemnly it would eventually be on view at a dollar a go.

Jamie looked at the bronzed young men, all familiar with a hard day's work. She looked at the girls, not so sharp in fashion as their city counterparts and the better for it. Hugh was in the thick of it, at ease with the younger ones while Mark seemed to be classed with the older guests. It's his manner that puts him apart, she thought. With his thick fair hair and clear faintly freckled skin he did not look his thirty-four years. His dark glasses gave him an unfair advantage as she realised when she saw his slow attractive smile grow and knew he was returning her look. She coloured faintly and turned her attention to those nearest her.

As they were returning, young Geoff Rossitor who was squeezed in beside her, asked for a dance that night.

"Dance? Where can they possibly dance?"

"On the surface of the moon if necessary. If we want to dance, we dance. In the meantime, Geoff is willing."

"Then Jamie is willing too," she laughed.

The dance floor turned out to be the cement surfaced tennis court. Swept clear of the encroaching debris, the high wired fences hung with coloured lights, it seemed twice as large.

But first there was the barbecue. Jamie saw for the first time the true outback barbecue chop with the long rib bone still attached. Bacon rashers were curled around and secured with toothpicks and eggs broken into the cups. Bananas, onions, potatoes and sweet corn were roasted on the coals. Huge thick steaks were flung on the scorching hot stones. Strips of damper dough were wound around green sticks, held to the fire till they puffed crisply and then dipped in honey or syrup. Soft drink there was in plenty but very little beer.

Hugh was everywhere: the perfect host. Jamie had to search for Mark to find him in the background keeping supplies up. He looked perfectly happy and she had to remind herself that some people are just not made for the limelight.

When everyone was replete the fires were allowed to die down and a temporary lull fell on the proceedings. Gradually the girls melted away and Jamie found an arm around her and a voice in her ear.

"Now we get ready for the dance."

"Oh, no,' Jamie wailed. "I'm stiffening up already from that ride this morning."

"Well, you'll have to unstiffen then," decreed Stella mercilessly and bore her off.

It was only by a fluke that Jamie had anything suitable to wear, not having given a thought to the social side of her commission. At the last minute, she had put in a soft white organza and the silver filigree belt studded with real turquoises that her father had once given her. Thankful that she had washed her hair that morning, she fluffed it out and slipped on her white sandals.

The girls gaily complimented each other and moved out in a solid group that no boy would have had the hardihood to penetrate. Sarah broke them up and moved them around. The boys had all changed and had a slick look about them. Jamie tried to keep in the background but Ashley sought her out and brought her to the fore.

"Now, Jamie," he said in his light pleasant voice, so like Mark's, "you're to open the dance and choose your own partner."

Hugh was standing in full sight. Mark was nowhere to be seen.

"I choose you," she said and held out her arms to Ashley.

There was a shout of derision and Ashley started to back away.

"Haven't been on the dance floor for years, young woman."

"Well, you can just start again," said Jamie, hanging on to him. She turned to the musicians. "Give us something simple."

They did with a waltz and in no time Ashley and Jamie were matching their steps for he was as light on his feet as the girl. Jamie smiled up at him.

"I wish I had been around twenty years ago," she said.

"I wish you had, too, my dear," he said with some wistfulness and Jamie's heart cried for him. The non-marrying Lawrences. Please God, don't let Mark end up like this. To Jamie's surprise they were allowed to finish the dance on their own. It seemed these young people did not know how to waltz. Now everyone wanted to try it and Jamie was kept busy till they tired of it and went back to their own style.

Jamie found that she was expected to go through these gyrations with Geoff but pleaded her encroaching stiffness.

"Anyone who wants to dance with me has to order something slow," she announced as she sank exhausted on a seat. Stella sat down beside her and something about her demeanour made Jamie ask: "Has Hugh -?"

Stella shook her head miserably. "He seems to be avoiding me."

Jamie was annoyed. Why couldn't Hugh at least observe the ordinary courtesies. After her efforts with Ashley she had little hope of Mark asking her but she would have liked to see Stella happy. Just then she saw Hugh approaching her with an intent look in his eye. He's going to ask me in front of Stella, she thought and braced herself. When he was almost upon them she slipped her hand to her belt and undid the clasp. The heavy belt slid down at once. She stood up with a little gasp as she caught at it. "I'll have to fix it properly," she said and was off calling her excuses over her shoulder.

Once inside the house she peered around one of the veranda posts. Hugh and Stella were dancing. Pleased with herself for having for once outsmarted him, she turned to go inside for a breather and collided with Mark.

"What are you doing in here?" she scolded.

"Just helping Aunt Sarah lay out the supper."

"Isn't Howie helping?"

"Sure. I just got the drinks ready."

Jamie stood before him, blocking his path. "Why aren't you dancing?"

"I don't dance much, Jamie. I —"

"You and Ashley are a pair. Well, you're going to dance now. Listen, they're back at the waltz again. Come on. You'll soon learn."

"Not here," he said hurriedly. They were standing in the full light from the dining room.

She dragged him along the shadowed veranda and ordered him to put his arm around her. 'Now just follow me. One two three…one two three…"

Either Mark had never danced before or he was in the grip of nerves. He held Jamie so hard against him that she could scarcely breathe. After a while he got the hang of the step and relaxed his clasp. They moved harmoniously together and Jamie was in the seventh heaven. Her whole body was thrilling to his nearness and that extraordinary sense of wellbeing swept over her again.

When the music stopped, she continued to hum the tune, willing the precious moments to last. Then they heard a step outside and Hugh ran up the steps.

"Don't move," she whispered and froze. Fortunately, their steps had taken them to the turn of the veranda where it was darkest. Hugh went inside and she heard his voice inquiring for her. Shamelessly she clung to Mark, determined not to be found by his brother. Eventually Hugh stamped out and back to the others. It had not occurred to him to glance along the veranda.

Jamie was just breathing a sigh of relief when Mark dropped her like a hot coal and turned away. There was almost a rebuff in the movement.

"Didn't you like it?" She tried to keep the hurt out of her voice.

"It was well enough," he replied in a thin dry tone. "I'm no dancer. Better get back to the others."

He went inside again and Jamie made her way slowly back to the tennis court where she was claimed at once by Geoff Rossitor. As soon as the dance finished Hugh was at her elbow to sweep her once more on to the floor. Jamie did not have to fake her aches and pains by now. She stumbled and pushed against him with a little moan.

"Please, Hugh, take it easy. I'm so stiff from that ride this morning."

"Exercise is the best thing for it. How's your belt?"

"What belt? Oh.. this…"

"You seemed to find something wrong with it as I was coming to ask you for a dance."

"Did I?" said Jamie dreamily. "I wonder why?"

Hugh gave her a little shake. 'Don't rouse me, Jamie girl, or you'll be sorry."

Safe in her love for Mark, Jamie smiled enchantingly up at him. "I think you would be the one to be sorry, Hugh."

He stared down at her. She was bewitching in the soft light and there was a teasing gleam in her eyes. A strong desire swept him to bring her into subjection. He drew her closer and she stiffened.

"Don't try any funny stuff, Buster,' she said sharply.

"Grow up, Jamie."

"Grow up, yourself. I'm here on business and I intend to leave on the same terms." She raised her voice a little and those near looked around. Hugh scowled and released his hold a little. The dance was finished in a cold silence.

By the end of the night Jamie could hardly stand. It was a relief after supper when everyone was bedded down for the night. There was an abundance of air mattresses and the girls were accommodated in the house and the boys on the veranda. Before she crept to her own bed, Jamie felt her way to Stella and pressed a kiss on the soft cheek. There was the taste of salt on her lips.

Everyone slept late. Those in the habit of waking early simply turned over. Jamie found herself unable to do this and reached for her Bible. She was a very new Christian and had not had any good follow-up. All she knew was that she should read her Bible every day, pray and go to church on Sunday, but she was sure that there was much more to it than that. There would be no chance of church at the station so she read carefully through the great high priestly prayer of the Lord Jesus in the Gospel of John. She was greatly taken with His request for His disciples: 'that they may be one even as we are one." Jamie murmured the words over and over. She found herself thinking of Mark and felt at peace at the idea of oneness with him. She offered her newborn petition shyly to the Lord and then turned her thoughts to her new friend. But when she thought of Stella and Hugh in the one breath, prayer would not come. A sense of unease replaced the harmony that had accompanied her prayer about Mark. Jamie lay and puzzled over this. Was God telling her that nothing would come of Stella's love for Hugh? That their efforts were wasted? She wished she had more experience in prayer. The sense of unease grew. She ended up offering a simple prayer for guidance and drifted off to sleep again.

By ten thirty the last of the revellers had staggered up and were immediately served a large brunch as they would be taking to their cars straight after the meal. Jamie moved among them, thanking them for coming on behalf of someone they did not know.

"Any excuse for a party," stated Geoff gracelessly and was howled down. At the end Hugh announced a toast to James Elizabeth Somerville.

"Not really," gasped someone.

"Yes, really. On your feet, everyone. James Elizabeth."

They all stood, solemnly drank and shouted: "James Elizabeth."

"Honestly I'll really have to change it." Jamie put her hands to her scarlet cheeks. She looked up straight into the smiling eyes of Mark.

"I like it," he mouthed and raised his mug high.

By noon they were all packed in, waiting to be waved off. Geoff Rossitor still stood at the open door of the last vehicle, grabbing a last word.

"Jamie! You got a steady?"

"No, but I'm a pretty busy girl," albeit smiling kindly upon him. He was such a nice young fellow.

"I was just thinking…I go down to the big smoke now and then."

"Well, look me up by all means." She gave him the address of Morris's Gallery. "They always know where I am…but I don't want to raise any false hopes."

He nodded. "I'd like to see you again all the same…since Stella won't look at me."

Then Jamie really looked at him. Tall, dark and good looking, a younger edition of Hugh.

"Keep trying," she said urgently. They were starting to yell at Geoff.

"It's no use," he said. "She's mad about Hugh."

Jamie grabbed the collar of his shirt. "It's not going to last," she said triumphantly and shoved him towards the car. He scrambled in somehow in a daze and soon they were gone.

Jamie stared after them, in a bit of a daze herself. What made her say that? Was it guidance? She did a little step dance and found the others watching her.

"Not too stiff today, I take it," drawled Hugh sarcastically.

"Not too stiff," agreed Jamie and pirouetted towards the steps. Hugh grabbed at her. She ducked, ran up the steps and disappeared into the house. Stella followed her soberly. It was noticeable that Hugh made no attempt to grab her.

Jamie was just about to stretch out on her bed again when Stella appeared in the doorway. The two girls sat companionably on the bed. Jamie put her head on one side and studied her friend.

"You look…you look stiff and sore in spirit," she decided.

Stella smiled faintly. "Good shot."

"What happened last night?"

"What didn't happen is more to the point."

"Were you expecting something special?"

Stella brought one knee up and hugged it. "Yes, I did, more fool me. You know that race we had back in the morning?"

"Umm."

"We were neck and neck. Then we saw the cars and Hugh gave Vulcan the spur. He just had to show off. Then, when we took the horses to the stables, he said the loser had to pay a forfeit. He grabbed me and really kissed me. I couldn't help but respond and we ended in a real clinch. So I thought – I thought – "

"He'd follow it up at the dance?" finished Jamie. She looked around restlessly. They needed to be somewhere where they would not be interrupted.

"Let's drive out to the Creek," she said. They told Mrs Howard their plan and went outside.

Outside everyone was cleaning up. Stella went off to beg a snack from Mrs Howard while Jamie told the men that they were going out to the Creek for a while. She would rather have not done so but it was a golden rule she had the good sense not to break. Hugh looked up from where he was cleaning down the barbecue.

"Wait half an hour and I'll come."

"*I'll* come," snorted Jamie to herself. "The great Mister I."

Mark had not even looked up. Jamie made sure no one was looking and poked a small pink tongue at him. Stella arrived back with a small esky and the car keys and they drifted casually down to the garage. The station wagon was a quiet car but Jamie held Stella's hand till the men had moved around the building. Then she nodded and Stella turned the key. They got away easily and Jamie did not care if they were seen then. Let Hugh come belting after them if he wanted to.

The drive was peaceful. The sun had passed its zenith and the shadows were beginning to lengthen. She studied Stella's profile.

Stella was a really lovely girl. With her slim figure and poise she could have been a model. As a wealthy station owner's daughter Stella neither toiled nor spun. The social life seemed to satisfy her. Apparently, she was just marking time till she should marry and set up her own establishment. Just an old fashioned girl, Jamie thought whimsically, and too good for me fine Hughie.

Stella glanced around, caught her eye and smiled. They were fast becoming close friends, and Jamie was determined to be a very good friend to Stella. Her own particular friend, Helen McArthur had hauled her off protesting to an evangelistic crusade and look at the result! A total ignoramus in religious matters like herself had been born again…and *knew* that she had. It had just come before Helen's marriage and she had not had the chance to nurture Jamie in her new faith but had assured her of her prayers.

Arrived at the Creek which lay dreaming in the afternoon heat, they found a shady spot and spread the rug. Jamie's head was almost bursting with all she had to say so, with a quick prayer, she began.

"What would you say if I told you that I'm pretty certain that God thinks it would be wrong for you to marry Hugh?"

Stella paused in the act of adjusting a cushion behind her head and stared at her friend.

"And what would you say," continued Jamie, "if I told you that a much nicer young man, Geoff Rossitor, thinks the world of you?"

This double attack made Stella vocal. "How would you possibly know about Geoff?" she asked in astonishment. Apparently knowing Geoff's thoughts was equal to knowing God's in Stella's eyes. "I can't imagine Geoff blurting out his feelings."

"And what would you say," added Jamie, well satisfied with her shock tactics, "if I told you that Geoff asked to be my steady?"

Stella sat up. "Did he now?"

"Only because you won't have him."

"Did you take him up?"

"No… I'm a busy girl. I'd have to be hit on the head with romance to allow it into my life." As I was, she thought ruefully.

Stella picked up a handful of leaves and threw them away.

"Actually I'm quite fond of Geoff," she said with some irritation.

"Where did you meet him?'

"He was a jackeroo on our property for a couple of years but he was very young… my age. His Dad owns *Silky Oaks* which is one of the real show places. Geoff's a marvellous rider … we used to have a lot of fun… but he's so young."

Jamie had let her ramble on but gave a sniff at this reiteration of Geoff's youth.

"How old is he?"

"Twenty-three."

"Good grief. I thought you were going to say eighteen or something."

"He seems younger."

"Because he's fresh and untouched. There aren't many like him these days. How long have you known Hugh?"

"Most of my life. I had a bit of a crush on him in my early teens. Then I didn't see him for some time while we were overseas visiting Dad's sister in the States. When we came back he seemed to see me with new eyes and straightway did a line for me."

"And you fell for it. I think all you've got is a hangover from your original crush on him."

Stella surveyed Jamie with some amusement. "Setting up as an advisory bureau?"

"Better than that," said Jamie and got out her small Bible. "Now you be quiet and listen to me."

She told Stella quite bluntly about her prayer to God that morning, the sense of unease she had had about her, the desire for guidance and Geoff's few snatched remarks which had been so revealing. Stella made no attempt to reject any of this.

"Could be," she said slowly. "I've got a couple of friends who reckon they get guidance like that. They believe that God has a real plan for their lives. I'm not doing so well with my own plans for my life." She stared disconsolately across the shadowed waters.

All inexperienced as she was, Jamie realised that this was the psychological moment. Stella's heart had known the rough ploughing of pain; the soil was turned; it was ready for sowing.

Jamie began by telling about her own conversion, so recent yet so satisfying. She followed it up with an explanation of the Way and what Christ meant to her now. When she had finished, she suggested gently that Stella could find the answer not only to her present problem but also to the problem of life itself if she would respond here and now.

There was silence as Stella thought it over. Pain-filled, unhappy, full of doubt in herself, she felt a strong understanding hand was being held out to her. This same hand had the promise of bearing her up on her thorn filled path till she was safely through. She turned and reached for Jamie.

"Show me how and I will," she said simply.

An hour later, during which the girls' tongues had not eased for a second, Stella looked knowledgeably at a puff of dust approaching them.

"We seem to have overstayed our time."

Jamie looked up and frowned. Just like Hugh to come and spoil it all. But it was Mark who unfolded his tall figure out of the 4-wheel drive. He was greeted cheerily by the girls who suddenly remembered their forgotten afternoon tea.

"Worried about us?" asked Jamie hopefully as she pulled forward the basket.

"Not really, but Sarah rang to ask us all over for tea. Thinks we will be feeling flat and dull after yesterday."

The girls looked at each other and burst out laughing.

"Do we look it?" asked Jamie merrily.

Mark studied them as they moved over to give him a spot on the rug.

"You look like you've found the rainbow's end now I come to think of it."

"We have – we have," crowed Stella. "At least I have today. Jamie had already found it."

By the turn of his head Jamie knew that he was looking at her, not Stella. Is he more interested in what I've found rather than Stella, she thought breathlessly. I'm going to buy myself a good pair of sunglasses when I get home. What a comfy hiding place they make!

"Let's have that tea first," said Mark unexpectedly.

The girls exchanged glances. Here was an open invitation to witness to him. Jamie mentally bowed out of the arena, telling herself that it was better for Stella to state her new stand at once. She did not admit to herself that she had hesitated to tell Mark of her own standing in Christ so early in their acquaintance. Now she was agog to know how he would take it from Stella but she said nothing while they enjoyed their brew and the passionfruit sponge left over from last night.

If it had not been such an important moment Jamie could have relaxed and enjoyed herself. It was fantastic to have Mark without Hugh. She could hardly keep her eyes off him: loving the ruddy flush under his fair skin, the little gold hairs that grew thickly on his bare forearms, the rise of the sandy hair from his broad forehead. She observed all this with quick glances sandwiched between contemplation of the countryside, Stella and her tea.

When he had finished, Mark brushed away the crumbs and sat more comfortably.

"Well, Jamie, what is your rainbow's end?"

If he would only ask that question another time in another way.

"Actually it's the same as Stella's but it is rather important for her that she should be the one to tell you."

As yet Stella hardly understood the principle of confessing with the tongue but she trustingly followed Jamie's lead. Leaving out all reference to Hugh, she said that she had hit a bit of trouble in her life and Jamie, in helping her, had explained what salvation really was and that once she had accepted Christ as her Saviour, God was free then to reveal His own plan for her life. As she finished she turned to Jamie who was watching Mark anxiously. What she could see of his face revealed absolutely nothing. She longed to reach forward and whip off those wretched wraparounds.

Mark picked up a twig and bit on it with his strong white teeth.

"I think I did something like that when I was eight," he remarked.

"Whe – when you were eight?" squeaked Jamie looking as though the heavens had opened for her.

"How was that?" asked Stella with interest. "I never thought that you and Hugh were particularly religious."

Jamie was glad that Stella had drawn his attention. She wanted to laugh. She wanted to cry. She wanted to stand on her head and shout Hallelujah. And she had to hold herself in and listen keenly to Mark's answer.

"We had a Governess who was very religious. She was the best Governess we ever had and I was pretty fond of her. She only stayed two years because she reckoned God wanted her on the mission field. During that time, she taught me how to read the Bible and pray daily and showed me how to be saved. So I did."

It was the longest speech Jamie had ever heard him make. She wished she could have recorded it in gold. She found that she was trembling.

"Do you – do you still…" Jamie paused in agony.

"More or less. I had good fellowship at Uni with other Christians but it's a bit tough going here."

"What about Hugh? Did he -?"

"He was only four and more interested in play than lessons." He resumed biting his twig.

Jamie was speechless. All those years on his own and he was still doing it – more or less. It was all she could do to stop herself falling on his neck with joy. That was why God had given her that extraordinary peace this morning. It *was* right to love him.

"You've stolen the march on both of us, Mark. Stella came through today and I – I came through just a few months ago."

Mark reached out a hand and grasped hers warmly and then did the same to Stella. But he took my hand first, thought Jamie.

"I don't know too much," he cautioned. "I've been marking time I guess. I've got a lot to learn."

"So have we all," encouraged Jamie, "but we have all –" she stumbled and began to busy herself packing the tea things. She had been about to say that they had all their lives to learn and the vision of herself and Mark being together had been too much for her.

She was not questioned, however, as they prepared to return to the homestead. It went to her heart to leave Mark to drive back alone but her place was with Stella. It was as well she was not driving for she was lost in a beautiful dream of a future that now could be prayed for in good earnest. Maybe God would put a bomb under him.

CHAPTER FIVE

More Revelations

The upshot of this glorious high was that Jamie could not concentrate
on the painting. She and Stella faithfully went out to the Creek and the
girl just stood in front of her easel dreaming, her thoughts full of Stella
and the wonder of fruitful witness. When she tired of that she thrilled
over Mark's confession and what it would mean for their lives.
Eventually she would throw down her brush and sit beside Stella and
encourage her in her study of the Bible

On Wednesday, she gave up altogether and explained to the others
at breakfast that she was not in a painting mood at the moment. On
Hugh's sceptical query she explained in her tired teacher's voice that
she had either to work under inspiration or not at all so she could come
back next year if he liked.

This silenced Hugh and brought an irrepressible smile to Howie's
lips. She thought Jamie handled Hugh very well, very well indeed but
she, like Jamie, did not think where it might lead.

By rights Stella should have gone home by now. Her visit was to
have lasted the month but certain unmistakable signs showed that she
should call it a day with Hugh. However, her conversion had changed
all that. Jamie did not want her to leave till she had learned all she
could.

The girls were obviously such good friends now that no one really
thought it odd that Stella should stay on till Jamie herself left. Such is
the hospitality of the outback that it was not begrudged even though it
was obvious that Hugh had gone stone cold on her.

His attention was becoming more and more fixed on Jamie and
Stella inadvertently gave him more opportunity by suggesting that
Jamie take a break and come out with them as they worked the cattle
while she worked on her riding. This took her right out of Mark's
realm but she thought the experience would help her to adjust to her

future station life. Mark supplied a much better horse which Hugh was pleased to approve. A sweet mouthed grey with a good tolerance of his inexpert rider, he won Jamie's heart even apart from the fact that he had been Mark's selection.

Inevitably Jamie had her camera and sketching pad with her. Once they reached the stockyards she chose to sit on the rails, making lightning records of the unceasing movement before her. She revelled in the dust, the sweating stockmen, the clever horses, the bawling steers and thought it would be perfect if only Mark were there.

She had given up asking anything about him since Mrs Howard had begun to answer her questions with a half-smile

One question she did ask however. Next morning Mark announced that the Maddisons were picking him up and he would be away for a couple of days. This was said to everyone but Hugh who naturally knew about it. When a light plane circled over them as they rode out, Stella glanced up.

"That'll be the Maddisons coming for Mark."

Jamie watched it land on what she had taken to be a deserted airstrip.

"I didn't think that airstrip was in use now."

"It isn't," said Stella briefly, "just for other people's planes."

Jamie turned around and stared at her friend.

"I don't like the way you said that. Was there an accident or something?"

Stella reined in a little to let the men get ahead of them. Jamie followed suit.

"I take it you haven't been told," she said.

"No. Mrs Templeton and Howie have talked me blind about the family but nobody's mentioned any accident."

"You'll find that all their stories stop short about four years ago. I think you should know even though it's not my place to tell you. Haven't you ever wondered about the boys' parents?"

"I thought they must have died, of course, but I wouldn't dream of prying."

"They had their own plane then. Mr Lawrence used to fly himself everywhere and both Mark and Hugh had pilot's licences. But if Mr Lawrence was in the plane he flew it."

Jamie thought of the marrying Lawrences, the dominating ones.

"Go on."

"This time they were flying home from a party. Mr. Lawrence had had too much to drink although the family won't admit it. Mark was with them. I forget where Hugh was. Before they boarded the plane people heard Mark pleading with his father to let him fly but Mr Lawrence was stubborn. Mark had to give in and – what did you say?"

"Nothing."

"To cut a long story short, Mr Lawrence badly misjudged the landing and hit a big tree. Mark was thrown out. He was badly concussed and had some broken ribs but it saved his life. The plane burst into flames. They never had a chance."

"Great heavens! That old burnt out stump?"

"Yep."

"What a tragedy!"

Stella had not finished. "Mark had bad headaches for over a year and his eyesight was affected. Hence the glasses. His doctor said he had to give up working continually in the open and he always has to wear very dark glasses when he's in the sun."

"Oh, no," Jamie gave a whimper. She had been thinking sub-consciously that those sunnies were a bit of an affectation. She had never seen in films stockmen or cowboys so equipped. It just shows you, she thought guiltily, you should never make rash judgements. Thank goodness I never tried to tease Mark into taking them off. Then a terrible thought struck her. He was getting into a plane right now. She turned wildly to Stella,

"He shouldn't be flying," she cried. "Not after –"

"Nonsense. Jim Maddison's a good pilot and flying itself does not affect Mark."

"But – but –" Jamie knew not how to put her nameless fears into words. "They don't have a plane themselves now, do they?"

"The doctor advised against it with Mark because of the strain on his eyes and Hugh's now got a thing against planes. He blamed the engine not his father."

He would, thought Jamie. She was thoroughly shaken by Stella's recital. Mark could have been killed four years before she had a chance to meet him. When the plane went over she watched it anxiously out of sight.

The day seemed to drag. Jamie determinedly busied herself making sketches and snapping the various actions of man and beast.

She became aware of a young aborigine stealthily watching her. He was perched on the rails a couple of metres from her and he craned his neck to see her work till she glanced up when he would shoot it back in like a tortoise and pretend to be interested in the horizon.

It was some time after they had lunched with the stockmen that Jamie saw the scene that fired her inspiration. It happened so suddenly that there was no time for the camera. A bullock broke free and charged one of the men who happened to be on the ground. Hugh shot after it and, launching himself from the saddle, brought the animal down by the sheer force of his weight. Jamie got a glimpse of the propping horse, the flying figure, the falling steer and the dodging stockman. The whole scene was partially shrouded in the red gold dust that the descending sun was striking.

Jamie turned away with her hand over her eyes as she secured the whole thing in her memory. She opened her larger sketch book and, grabbing a handful of dust, threw it over a clean page and rubbed it in. A brown pencil moved like lightning in her hands. Stuck for colour she looked wildly around and grabbed a handful of darker dust and some grey ash. These were spilled on the ground beside her and her flying fingers dabbed into them as she worked.

Only one person was aware of her frenzied activity. Two slender black hands deposited two small piles of earth near her book. Where he had found them in that short time she could not guess but one was a light yellow and one a dull orange.

Jamie looked up, smiled a brief thanks and spoke rapidly:

"Get me a couple of burnt sticks from the fire place and see if you can find a white stone – oh, and bring me a piece of bread without any butter on it."

The boy flew to do her bidding and by the time Stella noticed her and rode over, she was carefully lifting out the highlights with the bread while the aborigine breathed down her neck.

"There." Jamie sat back triumphantly as Stella dismounted. She stared at the work and then walked back to where Hugh was.

"Come and see yourself," she called.

Hugh looked around and Stella pointed to the two on the ground. He frowned and rode over. He too dismounted to have a better look.

"Wow," he said softly. "I'll buy that, Jamie. What are you doing here, Maxie?"

"I couldn't have done it without him. He found me the dirt,' said Jamie, raising a smudged face.

Others began to gather around and all were silent. Out of the clouds of shimmering golden dust could be seen glimpses of the writhing bodies, each caught in a symphony of movement that told the tale of the cattleman. Here and there a dark stroke outlined a hoof or a horn, the curve of Hugh's body and a white dash picked out the shine of sweat so that now you saw them, now you didn't.

"Do you mean that you did all that just with dirt, Miss," someone asked.

Jamie nodded and glanced at the boy. "That's all the aborigines use. Oh, and of course, they use bark instead of paper."

Maxie nodded, his eyes shining, and put a tentative finger on the picture. "I do you one, Miss."

It was plain that, in his simplicity, he was asking for the picture in exchange for one of his. Jamie knew how fragile it was. It would have to be fixed or she would lose it the moment it was rubbed.

"I'll do you one for yourself, Maxie, if you'll show me how to use your colours in your way."

Maxie grinned and the bargain was struck.

Jamie promptly asked to borrow Maxie for the day. The two rode back to the homestead and nothing more was seen of them till dusk when Jamie came in, weary but satisfied. She had brought out the colours she had found in the gorge which he had approved and then they had gone bark hunting for the rest of the afternoon. The sheet was well on the way in its preparation having been burned and scraped.

Indoors she found Hugh studying the picture where it had been hurriedly placed on the dining room table. He had just passed an experimental finger over a corner.

"It's going to come off," he said, displaying his finger.

"Oh, naughty, naughty," she scolded, pushing him away and inspecting the paper. "I've got to fix it."

She went off to her room and came back with her hairspray. To Stella's horror she proceeded to spray the drawing which immediately went dark.

"You've ruined it."

"No worries. Hairspray is a lacquer and has stood in for me before this. The picture will lighten again when it dries. This will hold it till I have a chance to do the painting."

"You're not going to use this just for a painting?" exclaimed Hugh.

"Oh, yes. That's just a rough sketch. I'll have to slap it under glass in order to protect it for the time being."

"I don't know. I'd rather have it as it is. You know. Local dirt and all that."

"You haven't got it yet. I haven't said I'd sell it."

"But you do paintings to sell them. Why would you want to keep this one?"

Jamie met his eyes and saw the dark challenge in them. She weakly yielded rather than have him think she wanted to keep even a sketch of him.

"Okay but there won't be any lifetime guarantee coming with it."

Next day she literally sat at Maxie's feet while he did his bark painting for her and marvelled at his sure touch. It was filled with transparent goannas and kangaroos that cheerfully showed their insides. A careful design of dots and strokes brought the whole thing together and Jamie acknowledged that it was a genuine work of art. The tedious design took Maxie all day so that it was not till the following day that Jamie did her sketch for him. She deliberately stylised the drawing more and Maxie grinned his appreciation.

During all this Jamie showed Maxie her painting of the Creek and he begged to be allowed to watch her. Mark was back by this time and, besides adding his admiration to that of the others, put in a word for Maxie with Hugh and the boy's father.

The next day saw the three troop off to Felding's Creek. Maxie did something Stella would never have dared to do. He took up his stance right beside the artist and constituted himself her brush-holder. Jamie, who ordinarily could not bear anyone watching her on a major work, felt quite unselfconscious with the boy and worked like a small fury. The inspiration had flowed over and she knew she was on a high.

She worked long past her usual deadline, still seeing the right lights in her mind's eye. Stella was staggered when she was at last permitted to look.

"I'll finish it tomorrow," announced Jamie with a satisfied sigh and smiled at Maxie. "You've been my Muse."

Maxie did not understand the term but he heard the warm tone and flashed a white-toothed grin.

Jamie was true to her word and the following day saw the painting finished. Just at the last she put a brush in Maxie's hand and got him to do a bit of dabbing in a corner.

"Oh, me too," cried Stella.

"Well, I'll guide your hand," smiled Jamie and did so to Stella's immense satisfaction.

"When this picture is counted with the Old Masters I'll point to that spot and say that I, Stella Cousins, helped."

As they were packing up Jamie cautioned the others not to say that the painting was finished.

"I like to look at it after a couple of days in case anything jumps out at me. Besides I want us to come back here tomorrow."

"Why?"

"You'll see."

Next day they set off again with a smaller canvas prepared overnight. Maxie set up the easel and Jamie placed the canvas on it.

"Set the colours out, Maxie," she commanded.

Maxie did so in the order she liked. Then she handed him the brushes.

"You've watched me for two days. Now you paint the scene...my way."

Maxie's mouth opened and shut without a sound. Stella also was silent with astonishment. She got off the rug where she had settled with a book and stood where she could see. Jamie constituted herself Maxie's brush-holder. The boy began with hesitant strokes because he had not seen Jamie begin the painting. She gave him some advice and a demo or two. Eventually he got going and his own artistic sense took over. For two hours, he worked with his tongue gripped between his teeth till Jamie called a halt.

"That's it. Anymore and you'll spoil it."

"I'd never have believed it if I hadn't seen it with my own eyes," marvelled Stella. "Why, I couldn't do that in a million years."

The oil sketch was rough but it had caught something of the joy of water in the outback. Jamie knew it was a good effort and praised him mildly. He had much to learn yet but his grasp of the new medium was extraordinary.

They showed Mark as soon as they got home and Jamie was pleased to see that he looked amazed. That evening Maxie's father was called up and he brought the head stockman with him.

"Well!" was the general remark of approval but said with much emphasis. Hugh looked quizzically at Jamie.

"Don't tell me that all this talent was lying around just waiting for you to find it?"

"Well, if Rex Batterbee could do it with Albert Namatjirra, why shouldn't I do it with Maxie?"

The general feeling was: Why not?

"There'll be no getting an ounce of work out of him now," grumbled Maxie's father.

"Let me teach him what I can while I'm here,' pleaded Jamie.

The man grinned reluctantly but he was really proud of his boy and the fuss they were making over a style of painting he did not think matched their own inimitable way of doing it.

The three disappeared into the improvised studio that night. While Stella guarded the door, Maxie was introduced into the art of preparing a canvas and they did a couple of small ones.

Next day they were gone after an early breakfast to the indulgent amusement of those left.

Looking to Stella for guidance they ended up at a dry creek bed beside a picturesque grouping of rocks and some straggly gums.

"You can imagine what the water would look like," said Jamie as she set Maxie up with her palette and easel. When he was right she squeezed some paint on to an old board and selected a few brushes. Armed with these she propped her canvas against a rock and found another for a seat. Then she opened her sketchbook at the first scene she had done. Stella stood watching her for a while.

"I've a feeling I've seen that place."

"Umm. I saw it from the truck the day we came. Mark and I had lunch there."

"Goodness. That seems a long time ago."

Jamie nodded absently. She wanted to make a good job of this because she intended to give it to Mark, come what may. Time was running out and as yet he had made no move. Not that he had much chance to, she admitted to herself.

She glanced at Stella who had drifted off to the rug and was opening a book. Her face had showed much less strain these last few days. The unusual activities had been of absorbing interest to her. Whether it was that, the coming of the Lord into her life, Jamie's friendship or all three combined, her fixation with Hugh had been broken. Her poise and self respect were returning and her release was imminent. Jamie sighed: as long as the cat that was Hugh did not capriciously lay a claw on the mouse that was Stella, she would be all right.

CHAPTER SIX

Religious Do's and Don'ts

Stella was perched on the veranda rail and Jamie was in a cane chair industriously mending a tear in her shirt. Mark had been out with Hugh on some inspection tour and they had just returned. Hugh went through to claim first shower and Mark dropped into a deckchair to await his turn. He lounged back with his hat still on his head, his dark glasses keeping his secrets as he listened to the girls.

Stella was trying to give Jamie a list of Christian do's and don'ts as she had seen them practised by her two Christian friends which she said Jamie must meet some time. Jamie was inclined to cavil at some of these edicts.

"You can't shut yourself away from the world altogether," she protested. "How would you ever get to witness to people?"

"You've got to be in the world but not of it," quoted Stella "For instance the present morals of society are non-existent so –"

"I know, I know. Christians must lead fully moral lives and not watch immoral films or read immoral books. I go all the way with that but I can't see anything wrong with good clean sport."

Nor I… but my friends will not play even a game of tennis on Sunday. It's not a case of its being wrong, just that Sunday is to be given to the Lord," explained Stella.

"And just what would you do with a pack of kids all day Sunday? Couldn't they even play a game of cricket in the backyard?" persisted Jamie.

"You've got me there," said Stella. "Maybe – it's just organised sport."

"What's the difference?"

Suddenly Mark spoke up. "My Governess would never go to any dances."

61

Jamie jumped and turned to him. "Not go to any dances," she repeated.

"Nope."

"There's nothing in the Bible against dancing, surely."

"My friends wouldn't either," chirped up Stella.

Jamie laid down her sewing. "I'm sure I read something the other day about praising God with musical instruments and dancing."

"Maybe that's a kind of sacred dancing," volunteered Mark.

"Well, my friends said –" but Jamie was getting tired of Stella's friends.

"You can't tell me there's anything wrong with Scottish dancing or – or bush dancing like we had the other night. It was all good clean fun."

"I don't think that kind of thing was meant. They wouldn't go to places where there was drink and all that –"

"Well I don't like that either. We didn't have –"

"… and they reckon it's wrong to let a strange man hold you closely."

Mark tipped his hat over his face and Jamie dropped her scissors which entailed much scrabbling on her knees around the chair legs.
I wonder whose face is the reddest, she thought crossly. I might have made him dance but he did the hugging. Jolly near squeezed the breath out of me.

Stella continued, serenely oblivious of the silent uproar near her.

"Actually liquor is something most Christians don't touch at all. They –"

"Not touch it at all!" exclaimed Jamie, upright once more and turning her flushed countenance to good account, "my father and my uncle and aunt wouldn't have an evening meal without a sherry or two before hand and I've *never* seen any of them drunk."

"I think it's a case of setting a good example," said Mark from under his hat, "the alcohol problem being what it is in Australia."

"That's right," replied Stella. "Marie told me that her father works for AA and they have to show that Christians can be bright and happy without drinking at all because, you know, a reformed alcoholic just has to have one small dri –"

"I know, I know," interrupted Jamie impatiently, "but the Bible says all things in moderation."

"Well, it doesn't work these days," persisted Stella, beginning to realise just how much she had been indoctrinated by her two friends.

"Well, just tell me," demanded Jamie, "who gave the grape the property to ferment: God or the devil?"

There was an upheaval in the deckchair. Stella leaned over and snatched the hat away. Mark was in a paroxysm of silent laughter. Once exposed he let go. The girls could not resist joining him and the resultant roars broke up the discussion for good. Finally, Mark took off his glasses and wiped his eyes.

"I'll have you on my side any day, Jamie," he said, their glances meeting for a fleeting second, and Jamie felt an unbearable sweetness in her breast. Surely...

"What's the joke?" queried a freshly showered Hugh. "I haven't had a good laugh for days."

Mark sprang up and went inside for his shower. Stella slipped off the rails and followed, feeling retreat was the order of the day. Hugh dropped into Mark's vacated chair as Jamie was gathering up her sewing.

"Now, don't you run off. What was the joke?"

"I really can't say," Jamie floundered

"Oh, come on. You were all laughing your heads off."

"All right. We were arguing about the drink problem in Australia," she said baldly.

Hugh's countenance darkened a little. "And so?"

"I made some silly remark about whose fault was it that grapes ferment."

"That's not very funny."

"It seemed so to the others at the time," said Jamie as she rose.

"There's nothing wrong with drinking provided a fellow knows when to stop," stated Hugh with the touch of belligerence the subject always aroused in him.

Jamie said nothing.

"Now don't tell me you're completely against alcohol, Jamie."

Now Jamie had not really thought the matter through but meeting Hugh's derisive glance she snapped to a decision.

"Yes," she said with relish. And that was how Jamie was converted to a dry stand.

During dinner that night a phone call came for Stella. She came back to the table to announce that her father was flying in for her in a couple of days' time. "He wanted to come tomorrow," she said as she slipped into her seat again, "but I told him about your Art Show so he's coming the next day so he can see it."

Stella did not seem at all perturbed about leaving Hugh. Jamie was glad about this but she felt the wrench for she had come to love Stella dearly, but they had already arranged to meet up again. She felt it now behoved her to make some definite statement about leaving herself. She was thankful that she need not leave abruptly by Mr Cousins' plane as he was returning directly to his home.

"Yes," she said briskly. "As soon as my Show's over and I've tidied my corner I'll be ready to leave too." She looked straight at Mark with a questioning lift to her eyebrows.

"I can take you early next week," he answered. "I've got to go through to –"

"I'm taking her, Mark," interposed Hugh. "I'll run her in on Saturday. She can catch the evening plane then."

Jamie, desperately watching Mark, saw that his knife and fork did not falter although he hesitated a fraction of a second before pronouncing a laconic, "Right."

He continued steadily with his meal while Jamie could hardly swallow a mouthful in her passion of disappointment.

She felt like shouting to him to stand up for himself and had to take serious control of herself for she knew that Howie was watching her closely.

That night in bed Jamie sternly asked herself did she really want to be involved with a doormat. What would life be like with a man who did not have the strength to do his own thing? But did he want to do his own thing as far as she was concerned? The girl tried to envisage life on the station with Hugh in such close proximity and dominating his milder brother. What happened when a brother married?

She knew, from working with Mrs Howard, that of the two beautiful main bedrooms, Hugh occupied one while the other was kept for guests. Mark was apparently satisfied with one of the many large single rooms. Already preparing for his single state, she thought bitterly. She recalled some of Aunt Sarah's chatter. The boys' father had built this home for his bride. The divorced Sarah had come back to resume housekeeping, this time for Ashley. Of course, when Hugh married as everyone expected him to, Mark would move over with Ashley and Sarah, leaving Hugh in full possession of the big house.

Jamie gave a little sob and sat up in bed. Now, you listen to me, she said fiercely to herself. Do you want to live on this station for the rest of your life? Do you want this kind of strain of living under Hugh's foot for ever and ever? Do you want… yes, yes, YES! Jamie almost shouted it aloud. It wasn't the station. It wasn't the strain. It wasn't her career even… or anyone else's opinion in the whole wide earth that mattered. It was Mark. Just Mark. Wherever he was, she wanted to be. Whatever situation he was in, she wanted to share it. Jamie looked grimly down the years, seeing herself involved in contest after contest with Hugh for she would NOT take his dominance lying down. NEVER. But you have, a small voice said.

Jamie collapsed back on to the pillows recalling that last time they had driven over to Seven Trees. Hugh had openly insisted that Jamie sit beside him in front and Stella had meekly got into the back seat with Mark. She had seethed all the way and could hardly bring herself to reply civilly to Hugh's remarks. When they were returning she had made a bid for independence, quickly slipping in beside Stella in the back seat leaving Mark to ride with Hugh in the front. They would have a good chat between themselves and blast the men.
Hugh had immediately gone around to her door and opened it.

"Come on, Jamie," he had said pleasantly but with a ring of steel in his voice. "You can't do that to us poor men."

She had sat there stubbornly till Aunt Sarah had called out to know what was wrong. Mark had made no attempt to get into the front seat. She remembered his words with the taste of gall in her mouth: *you may as well give into Hugh first as last.*

She had got out and taken her seat in the front while Mark had slipped in beside Stella. If he had only got into the front seat she could have laughed at Hugh for wanting to disrupt them all. As it was…

Jamie turned over on to her side and stared into the darkness. Now she was doomed to a long drive with Hugh, alone and at his mercy. She was finding it increasingly hard to keep him at a distance. Her resistance had unfortunately roused the hunter in him. Jamie began to panic.

If the worst came to the worst: she supposed that she could beg Mark to come with them, confiding that she was afraid of Hugh's advances, but that wouldn't get rid of Hugh. How was she to get alone with Mark, really alone, in order to give him a chance to say something… that is, *if he wanted to say something*. Had Hugh, in some psychological way, drained all initiative from his brother? Yet Mark did so much business for the station. He had been away a couple of times while she had been here. He was perfectly capable of making decisions when on his own.

Jamie's eyelids began to droop… yes, if the worst came to the worst…came a thought…pray about it.

Jamie rolled sleepily out and knelt wearily by the bed. Her petition was brief and to the point.

"Dear God, please foil Hugh's plans." She paused and then added tentatively, "If you could manage to reverse the situation… it would be just wonderful. Thank You. Amen."

The impromptu Art Show was a great success. If Hugh had been wondering if Jamie had been deliberately spinning out her time, he had his answer. The dining room was used as it opened on to the veranda and had an excellent light. The main painting had pride of place on an easel and Jamie had draped a light cloth over it. Then hers and Maxie's works were placed around the room on the sideboard, shelves and chairs. All her efforts bar the one for Mark were on display: several oil sketches, the one on bark done in the aboriginal style, dozens of crayon drawings of all aspects of life on the station and her dust picture of Hugh which had found a home behind glass in a frame from which a rather poor watercolour had been dismissed. Then there were three oils by Maxie plus his own bark painting.

Ashley and Sarah came at the head of a fleet of cars bringing visitors and everyone on the property who could get away. Hugh's men came and Maxie's father with a host of relatives who had appeared from nowhere. Mr Cousins flew in with his wife and a friend.

They all had to form a queue and file past the art works for a preliminary inspection. Jamie did this deliberately so that the viewers might get used to her style. Maxie was beside himself with pride and excitement. The visitors gazed and were impressed. Then when everyone was ready she unveiled the main work and stood back.

It was not what people had expected. If they had thought about it, most would have said that they expected to see a typical Australian landscape depicting the dry air, a high sprung blue sky, the usual haze, the soft grey-greens of the outback. But Jamie had painted it in a minor key with discordant colours. She had painted the tree from an angle showing a single haggard branch reaching desperately up to a sky of bitter yellow, as though the sunlight itself had been soured for it fell in a sickly way on the sparse leaves and bushes. The shadows, of a jarring purple, seemed trying to hide something which was partly revealed right at the base of the painting – the bright red casing of a chainsaw, the ugly continuous blade pointing straight at the trunk of the doomed tree.

There was silence for several minutes as everyone readjusted their thinking. Then Sarah, her eyes filled with tears, said softly,

"Thank you, Jamie. I shall treasure it till my dying day."

Hugh looked and turned away, bothered by a vague sense of guilt. Mark? Well, Jamie could not see what Mark thought. He had on his ordinary glasses but they seemed to be reflecting the light.

Some pressed forward to congratulate the artist and praise her while others hesitated, feeling uncomfortable without knowing why.

Maxie came in for his share of praise and encouragement. He was told that he was a very lucky fellow indeed. Stella had an amusing story to tell of one of Maxie's efforts

She had found for the artists some picturesque rocks and one or two old trees by a dried up creek bed. Jamie and her protégé had had a right royal row over it. Jamie had insisted that he paint in the water in order to give the scene some life. Maxie had stubbornly refused to do so, maintaining that there was never any water in the creek at that time of year. The battle had raged all day. There was no water in Maxie's picture. Jamie had finally bowed to his artistic integrity.

Everyone loved the story. It showed that the bush still had something to teach the city artist.

After that everyone broke into groups the better to consider and purchase the works, and commissions began to come in. Jamie accepted a couple on the proviso that there would be a year or two's wait. She was not tying herself down to anything at the moment.

There were buyers for Maxie's works too but Jamie took control of this. She announced that she would use half of the money to buy proper equipment for him and freight it up. There was much disappointment among his relatives but others nodded their approval.

A large morning tea was served and then it was time to say goodbye to Stella. The girl had herself well in hand. She might not be fully out of Hugh's thrall but she was on top, turning her cheek to receive his final salute. The girls clung to each other at the last moment for a close and deep bond had been formed. When they drew apart with tears there was no doubt in anyone's mind whose Stella's were for.

As they waved the plane off Jamie felt the loss keenly. Stella had been a good bulwark against Hugh. He walked beside her as they returned to the homestead while Mark walked with his aunt.

All her stuff had to be packed up now. Hugh collected the few remaining sketches while Mark took the big painting out to Ashley's station wagon to be carried in state to Seven Trees. Jamie gave Sarah some advice as they watched its safe bestowal.

"It will take six months at least to dry adequately for the paint is very thick. It's got a skin on it now but a hard knock could break that and the paint will be quite wet underneath. Hang it in a light airy room for a few months before you put it in the lounge."

Sarah nodded and once again thanked her. As the car moved off Mark came to stand beside her.

"You know, Jamie," he began in his light drawl, "I never cared one way or another when the deal was going through… but when I saw your painting today it stirred something in me. I felt angry –"

"Did you?" Jamie turned to him eagerly. "Why, that's the best compliment I've had all day. I *want* people to feel angry… so angry that they will hesitate to destroy needlessly."

Mark nodded. His forehead wrinkled and he appeared about to say something else. Jamie, waited, almost holding her breath.

"This painting of yours – I guess it's your whole life."

"It is not," said Jamie vehemently. "I'm a woman first and an artist afterward."

Then she flushed and turned away, afraid that he would see her feelings standing naked in her eyes. Others came up to take their leave and her acute embarrassment faded in the general talk. She was glad she had said what she did but wished she had not been so violent in expressing it.

CHAPTER SEVEN

Desperate Measures

Late that afternoon she began packing up all her gear, feeling an unaccustomed depression which she put down to Stella's departure. Maxie had gone off to celebrate his brief moment of fame and the rest of the money with his family and friends.

A shadow darkened the doorway. Jamie looked up hopefully but it was Hugh. He deliberately shut the door, smiling blandly at Jamie's frown.

"I've an apology to make," he announced, coming to stand beside her.

"Oh? Well, it can't be so private that you need to shut the door."

Hugh grinned. "It's been mighty hard to get a moment private with you what with Stella and Maxie both living in your pockets."

And not Mark, thought Jamie.

"Well, what have you got to apologise about?"

"No hurry." Hugh surveyed her lazily. She glanced up, met his handsome eyes and looked away swiftly. There was a devil in those eyes.

"You could fold up that easel if you like."

Hugh did so and Jamie used his distraction to get on to the other side of the rough table that had served her as a painting bench.

"Well, first the apology, although I think you owe me one too."

"Oh, really?"

"You know, Jamie, you have a way of saying 'oh, really', that can be maddening to a man."

"Too bad."

It was not the best way to deal with Hugh but Jamie's temper was mounting. That Saturday trip still loomed before her.

Hugh frowned but decided to get the apology out of the way.

"Remember that day I first came into the gallery and you were sitting by the desk?

"Yes?"

"And you fired up when I spoke of mining at Feldings Creek. I can't remember just what you said but I told you to mind your own business. Well, I can see it was very much your business and you can be a formidable opponent with your brush. I apologise sincerely."

"Thank you, Hugh." Jamie was surprised and disarmed. She did not think there would be much apologising in his arrogant life.

"As for you," he said, absently fiddling with a paint brush and moving around a little, "you could apologise for your little deception."

Jamie looked blank.

"Letting us think you were a man right till you got here."

"Oh that," Jamie laughed. "I've been practising that particular deception almost since I was a toddler. I shan't be apologising."

"Then you can pay a forfeit," and Hugh moved swiftly around the table to grab her.

What he ended up with was a torrent of falling tubes and brushes as Jamie emptied her paintbox on him. She raced around the table and opened the door. Once there she lounged in the doorway. It was not her intention to make an enemy of Hugh. The wooden box had sharp edges and he was rubbing his barked shins ruefully.

"So you weren't born yesterday."

"No, Hugh. Remember I came here on business terms. I told you once before."

"You're unnatural."

"Sexual harassment is a real problem these days and I won't put up with it."

"If I make up my mind I'm going to kiss you then you'll be kissed. It's nonsense to call a mild flirtation sexual harassment."

"It is when it's only on one side. Look, Hugh, ever since the Sex Discrimination Act came in it is possible to make a complaint and have the offender hauled up before the Committee of Human Rights."

"Good heavens! You wouldn't go to all that trouble."

"Oh, yes I would."

"You wouldn't be getting me down to appear before any Committee. Why, they'd laugh at you."

"If you don't appear you will be fined a thousand dollars each time."

Hugh stared at her. "Well, I've heard of some methods of defence but this is the best yet. And you'd submit to all that unsavoury publicity just to get your revenge for a simple kiss?"

"Publicity can only do an artist good," said Jamie firmly. "Gets her name known far and wide. That's all that matters."

"Rot."

"It's not rot. My father told me of the time William Dobell won the Archibald Prize for Portraiture. He wasn't all that well known then. Some people took objection to his portrait of Joshua Smith. They reckoned it was a caricature so they took him to court. By the end of the case every man in the street knew there was an artist called William Dobell."

"Did the people win their case?"

"No. All they did was give him fame."

Hugh passed a hand across his mouth. "Well, James Elizabeth Somerville, if you're not a handful."

"I'm going up to the house."

"What about all your precious paints and brushes?"

"I'll pick them up later."

"Oh, come off it. I'll help you now. I promise not to touch you...today."

They measured glances and then Jamie came back and they soon had the stuff all neatly packed away again. Hugh walked back with her chatting easily. He never had any trouble with his tongue and her resistance had not done her any damage in his eyes. Nevertheless, Jamie renewed her prayers that God would intervene in some way.

Relief did come the next day and to Jamie it was a minor miracle. The phone rang and Mrs Howard went to answer it.

"That's interesting," she said to Jamie as the girl came through towelling her hair. There's an author and his wife calling in tomorrow: Craig and Eileen Nickerson. They've been out at Banksia Springs for a couple of months. We saw them on their way through. He's getting material for a book."

"Is he coming here for material too?"

"No, just calling in. He and his wife are making a leisurely journey back to the coast."

Jamie put the towel down. "Has he got a big car?"

"Four-wheel drive."

"And he just has his wife with him?"

"Yes. What's on your mind, honey?"

"They could take me," said Jamie slowly, the conviction growing in her that this could be her chance. The girl and woman contemplated each other, an unspoken thought in their minds. "Do you think we could ring back and see if it's possible?"

"By all means… if that is what you want to do, Jamie?"

"I don't want to drive back alone with Hugh."

Mrs Howard rang through and the author and his wife declared that it would be a privilege to take Jamie. The bush telegraph had been working and they knew all about the artist staying at Fairlie Downs. Jamie flew off to complete her packing.

Mark was over at Seven Trees all day doing their books so it was not till both men were at the meal table that Jamie told them in a bright voice that her transport was all arranged. Hugh took umbrage at once.

"I'm quite capable of looking after my own guests," he said in a hard voice. "We'll stick to our own plans."

Then Jamie called on her position as a guest. "It is my desire to go to the coast this way."

Mark looked up from his meal and for once put his oar in. "If that's what you would like, Jamie?"

"It is," said Jamie briskly. "I'm looking forward to meeting a real live author. It should be a most interesting drive after all."

This was a direct slam at Hugh and Jamie delivered it with a bland air of satisfaction that stung. Hugh's lips tightened angrily. Just then the phone rang. He got up and strode off to it. When he came back his mood had changed entirely. Ignoring Jamie, he spoke to his brother.

"Sylvia Morrison and her Dad have just arrived at Seven Trees. I'm going across. Coming?"

Mark buttered a slice of bread. "Don't think so. I've been over there all day. Might have an early night."

No invitation was offered to Jamie to her secret exultation. An evening alone with Mark. God was certainly working overtime for her. She could barely resist meeting Howie's knowing eye.

When he had finished his meal Hugh fingered his chin and muttered, "Think I'll have another shave."

A few minutes after he had gone they heard the shower. Jamie opened her eyes at this. The phone went again, this time for Mark.

While he was engaged, Jamie carried some plates in and placed them on the bench. She struck an attitude and softly trilled,

"Who is Sylvia? What is she, that all our swains commend her?"

Mrs Howard laughed.

"They've known her for years. Closer to Hugh than – "

"He'd take care of that. Cow eyed?"

"No way. Sylvia is very much her own person."

"Pretty, of course."

"Umm, but not eye catching. Got a cloud of lovely black hair."

"Shot with glancing starry beams," trilled Jamie dancing about the kitchen.

"Such a face that drifts through dreams,
This is Sylvia to the sight."

"Stop it, Jamie, you wretch." Mrs Howard was doubled up over the sink. "How come you know those old classics?"

Jamie's expression softened. "It's my mother's name. Dad had quite a voice and he used to sing all these ballads to her," she explained wistfully.

Mrs Howard no longer laughed but threw a tea towel at her.

"You're a minx. I'm going to miss you terribly."

"Oh, come. I'm sure you'll have a gaggle of lovely girls passing before Hugh's eyes once more."

"Yes, but not one who -" she stopped, thinking better of what she meant to say. Jamie had gone for the rest of the dishes.

When they had finished Mrs Howard, who often sat with them on the veranda of an evening, announced that she was fair fagged and would make it an early night. Jamie embraced her and said lightly,

"I think I will too."

"Jamie!"

The girl laughed and strolled out on to the veranda. After Hugh had left she asked Mark if he would help carry her stuff up from the shed. When they had it all up she stretched out in one of the deck chairs and breathed a sigh.

"I'd just like to take in the night for a while. I can't believe I'm leaving tomorrow. It seems only yesterday that I came."

Mark dropped into a chair beside her. "Not to me."

"Oh?" said Jamie invitingly.

Silence.

It continued for a solid half hour. Jamie, who had envisaged some light conversation that would gradually get more meaningful, stared resentfully out at the night sky. What should she do? Sit in stolid silence till he broke it? But would he? A mischievous thought came to her. She could shock the life out of him by proposing. Utterly impossible. That was the trouble with these Women's Libbers. They were all for equality of the sexes but they hadn't yet figured out how to get a girl over the psychological barrier of a proposal of marriage. Suppose he told her kindly that he loved her as a sister. Jamie's mental writhing put that idea dead in the water.

Eventually she asked about the author who would be taking her. Mark did not know much about him but he had read some of his books which he said were very authentic stories of the outback.

"Do you like reading, Mark?"

"Very much. Find it a bit of a strain though now I do all the bookwork."

Silence.

"Have you always worn glasses?"

"No. Do they worry you?"

"Not at all." Except when I can't see your eyes.

Silence.

After half an hour Jamie tried again.

"The Morrisons. What are they like? A nice family?"

"Yep."

By now it was getting on for ten o'clock. Jamie looked across at him. Totally relaxed, one arm behind his head, long legs stretched out. The exact opposite of her, sitting in hopeful tension. It dawned on her then that he had absolutely no intention of making any sort of move that night. Or ever?

She got up quietly and went through to the kitchen. The supper things were all set out for them: Mark's favourite cake, her favourite doughnuts. Howie had done her best. Jamie wanted none of it. A hot temper was mounting in her. Could one actually boil with disappointment? She jerked open the fridge and got herself a glass of cold milk hoping to ease the growing pressure. Then she went out silently through the back door and out into the star filled night to make her own pilgrimage of farewell.

Jamie lifted her hot face to the coldness of the remote star fire. She could love this place if she let herself go. On the night breeze the inimitable sounds of the country came to her: the far howl of a dingo, the leaves rustling against each other: the comfortable nicker of a horse nearby, the heart-catching loneliness of a curlew's cry. Jamie leaned her face against the slim bole of a young gum tree for several minutes. Passing the herb garden, she plucked a handful of mint and pressed it against her cheek, finding comfort in the homely fragrance. Her aimless wanderings brought her without intent to the garden near the front veranda, her pale blue dress making her visible.

"Is that you, Jamie?"

"Yes," she said wearily.

Mark was standing near the steps.

"I wondered where you'd got to. I looked in the kitchen but –"

"I went for a stroll just to say goodbye."

"Why didn't you tell me? I was thinking myself a stroll would be nice."

Jamie had reached the bottom of the steps. Her disappointment coupled with frustration reached flashpoint.

"Were you now?" she spat. "And just when were you going to suggest it? Ten thirty? Eleven thirty? Twelve thirty? Well, let me tell you, Mr Mark Lawrence, I'd as soon go for a stroll with an iceberg. Sooner. Icebergs do melt."

With that she shot up the steps past him and into the dining room. His voice stopped her.

"Jamie."

She turned and presented her profile: "Yes?" and as nothing was forthcoming she repeated the word impatiently.

"Don't you want any supper?"

"I've had it."

Silence.

Jamie went on to her room. She shut the door and removed the bedcover and folded it with meticulous care. Then she lay face down on the bed, pulled the pillow over her head and let the tears in her heart well up and spill through her aching eyelids as she lay in the dark.

Much later she heard Hugh's car come in. Probably had had a very successful night according to his lights. Jamie waited till she was sure he had gone to bed and then got up and switched on her light, busy now in the throes of regret and self doubt. She could at least have suggested he join her in the stroll. It might have made all the difference. Why not the supper? Much could be said in sharing a meal. To and fro in the room she went, battling with her thoughts. Supposing it was just a monumental shyness. Why hadn't she said how much she loved being here? It could have been a lead in. She was as bad as he was.

She was fast becoming distraught and looked around for some form of relief. Diving into her suitcase Jamie brought out her small writing case. She would write down what was in her heart whether or not she would have the courage to give it to him. In her firm rounded hand she wrote:

Dear Mark

My heart insists that I tell you something before I go. And my pride insists that I make sure I've gone before you get this.

I just want you to know, for what it's worth, that all the time you stood aside for Hugh to have a free go with me it was you and you only that I cared about. Right from the beginning.

If this means nothing to you, please forget it. I shall get over it eventually and hope to meet someone almost as nice as you some day.

Please do not try to contact me out of any feeling of 'kindness'. I could not bear it.

God bless you. Keep reading your Bible. Yours Jamie.

She folded the letter, put it in an envelope and placed it in her Bible. A further idea had come to her but she needed to sleep on it.

Jamie slept late and woke heavy-eyed She was glad she had missed the traditional early breakfast. The Nickersons would not be there till after ten. As she picked up her Bible the letter fell out. Jamie replaced it and as she did so her eye fell on a verse:

To him who knows to do good and does it not, to him it is sin.

Is it now? thought Jamie. Maybe it's not as strong as that but it's as good a leading as anything else I've had.

When she did make her appearance, the men had long gone to their work. Mark had left no message but Hugh had left his assurance that he would be back to say goodbye.

"How sweet," muttered Jamie, giving the top of her boiled egg a wallop to the bitten-back amusement of Howie. Nothing from Mark. That would be par for the course.

Guessing that everyone would be gathering to say farewell when the Nickersons came, she slipped out looking for Maxie and spied him hanging shyly around. She motioned him closer.

"You know that painting I want you to give Mark?" she whispered.

Maxie nodded vehemently.

"Well, I want you to wait one full hour after I've gone and then give the painting to him with this letter."

Maxie looked up at the sun but Jamie said, "There's a clock in the dining room. You can see it from the veranda."

The boy again looked up at the sun and again at her. "One full hour. This Mark. You like him, Miss."

"How do you know?" Jamie was astonished.

"I seen it in your eyes, Miss."

"Is that so? Well – well what about Mark's eyes?"

"No see 'em, Miss. Him got glasses."

Jamie sighed. "Well, Goodbye, Maxie. I'll send your stuff up. Keep painting."

As she went back up the steps the Nickersons' big four-wheel drive approached.

Now all was bustle. The couple had decided to make another station that same day where they had been invited to stay the night.

"You will be most welcome too, Miss Somerville. We explained that you would be with us when they rang and invited us."

There was only time for a quick cuppa as they still had to call in at Seven Trees. Hugh arrived while they were still having it but there was no sign of Mark.

Then it was time to go. Everyone gathered around. As her gear was packed in Hugh strode over to Mark's office and drew a blank. "Can't think where he could be."

"Well, we can't dally around." Craig Nickerson had his mileage to make.

"There he is," Mrs Howard pointed, "coming up from the stables."

However, Mark was not making for the group. He was heading for the end of the drive. Jamie avoided Hugh's final attempt to capture her lips and gave him her cheek. Then she gave Mrs Howard a mighty hug and got into the backseat of the vehicle. Hugh shut the door and Jamie locked it. There was a wave all round and they were off.

Mark was obviously waiting for them so Craig Nickerson pulled up. Jamie had wound the window up and now waved to him through it. She was giving no quarter, already regretting having left the letter. Mark reached his hand through the open front window, unlocked her door and pulled it open. He leaned right in over her.

"'Bye, Jamie."

"'Bye, Mark." She would not look up.

"See you in Brisbane?"

"If you wish," she replied coldly.

He bent close and swiftly pressed her lips with his. Then he was standing back, shutting the door and waving them on.

It had all been too quick for Jamie. She lay back, tasting and retasting that precious fleeting moment. If that isn't like him, she fumed. He does and says nothing for ever and then makes one statement, one gesture… and the whole world changes. She dashed a hand across her eyes and glanced at her watch. Ten thirty. At eleven thirty he would have her letter.

Jamie straightened her green skirt and leaned forward to answer Eileen Nickerson's question.

Soon they were stopping at Seven Trees.

Having been warned that the Nickersons were pressed for time Ashley and Sarah came out to the car. They were joined by Sylvia and her father. While everyone chatted, Jamie took quiet stock of the girl. A slender poised creature. Pale classic features framed by a glorious cloud of black hair. Humorous dark grey eyes. Jamie recalled Howie's remark about Sylvia being very much her own person. There would be no cow-eyed running after any man here. Jamie warmed to her.

"We'll be seeing you at Showtime, Jamie?"

"Oh, yes. Goodbye."

Then they were really on their way. Craig Nickerson wanted to get a couple of hours under his belt before they stopped for their picnic lunch. Jamie tried not to watch the time but eventually her watch showed her eleven thirty. Right now, Maxie is standing before him with the letter and parcel, she thought with a quickening heartbeat. I wonder which he will open first.

She was a bit out. At that precise moment, a man was leaping up the steps and calling to Mrs Howard to pack him a sandwich. By the time he came out of his bedroom, changed and with his case packed, Howie had the esky ready and Maxie had hurriedly checked the oil and water of the station wagon.

"What is it, Mark?" asked the housekeeper anxiously. "did you get a phone message?"

"That reminds me." Mark strode back inside and made a swift phone call. "Yes, Howie, I did get a message. I'll be away a while."

"What shall I tell Hugh?"

"Tell him…tell him…oh, tell him I'll ring him."

In five minutes the car was speeding away.

Mrs Howard looked at the grinning Maxie. "Do you know what that was all about?"

Maxie shrugged his shoulders. "Mark in one big hurry, Missus."

Maxie had decided to anticipate the hour by a good ten minutes. Mark was not much more than an hour behind the Nickersons' car.

CHAPTER EIGHT

Unexpected Roses

Craig Nickerson drove his car hard. He only allowed them a brief half hour to stretch their legs and have lunch for he wanted to make the distance in daylight. The sun was low in the sky as the big car made its way over the last of the cattle grids.

Lindsay and Belle Anderson and their three sons were awaiting them, quite thrilled to have both a bona fide author and artist in one scoop. The travellers were tired and stiff and grateful for the cool drinks eventually served to them on the wide veranda. The youngest lad, Clyde, who had a penchant for drawing, had persuaded Jamie to fetch her sketchbook and sat down beside her full of pleasurable anticipation.

"Now, don't you bother Miss Somerville till she's enjoyed her drink," Belle said complacently and turned to her other guests. "There's no hurry. I've set dinner back a bit as we'll wait for Mark."

"Mark who?" queried Eileen Nickerson as she settled back in her chair.

"Mark Lawrence. He's coming behind you. He rang to say that some urgent business had cropped up and also he had a message for Jamie."

All eyes naturally turned to Jamie to find her paling before their eyes.

"Oh, I do hope it's not bad news!" exclaimed Eileen sympathetically.

"I don't think so. Not from the way Mark spoke. I'm sure it will be all right," Belle assured them.

Jamie nodded mechanically. After a few minutes, she told Clyde to keep looking at her book and slipped away quietly to the bedroom allotted to her. Standing fair and square in front of the mirror, Jamie asked of her reflection,

"Shall I die of happiness? Or shall I die of fright?"

She pressed her hands to her still pale cheeks and moved to and fro in her agitation.

"It's all very well for him. He knows what is in my mind and he knows what is in his," she whispered, "but I only know me. If he dares to come to me out of kindness I'll – I'll kill him."

After which bloodthirsty threat she stood for a while at the window in a little dream till she had steadied down.

When Jamie arrived back on the veranda they were all admiring a very good drawing of Mark without his glasses which she had done from memory in her room at night.

"What a good profile he has," remarked Belle. "I didn't realise that Mark was so good looking. Pity he has to wear those sunnies all the time."

"Oh, well, Hugh's always been considered the big handsome hero," remarked her husband somewhat acidly. "Where's one of him, Miss Somerville?"

"I didn't get around to doing it," said Jamie, blushing at being caught out for she had never bothered. "Hugh was never still for a moment."

The Andersons smiled knowingly at each other, having known the family for years. The girl probably had one hidden away. Belle had seen young women blush before at the very mention of Hugh's name.

Jamie was grateful for Clyde's demands on her attention. On her return, she had contrived to move her seat more towards the back of the group. The two were in a world of their own when, later on, one of Clyde's brothers announced,

"There's Mark now. He's made good time."

Jamie could see nothing at first and then a tiny puff of dust. The eyes these westerners had! As the puff grew bigger she found herself growing hot and cold by turns. What I *will* die of, she told herself fretfully, is nervous apprehension.

The others went placidly on with their conversation. Craig Nickerson was a good talker and he was among those who admired his writings. Everyone but the tense girl was well entertained during the wait till the station wagon came over the last grid and drew in beside the Nickersons' car.

There was a natural pause and everyone watched as Mark got out, took hold of his case and came towards them with easy deliberation. He was wearing a lightweight safari suit with short sleeves and, in Jamie's eyes, looked his best. He came up the steps, greeted his host and hostess and their family pleasantly and acknowledged the Nickersons with a touch of his hat. Last of all he murmured, "Jamie," and placed his case on the veranda.

"Well, Mark, dinner is about ready but we'll wait while you have a drink if you like."

"A wash will do, Belle. If I could just have a word with Jamie?"

"Of course."

Everyone rose and politely began to make their way indoors. Seized by a sudden shyness Jamie was following when a firm hand grasped her right elbow. Mark took off his wide-brimmed hat and dropped it on a chair. Jamie began to tremble.

As soon as the last heel had disappeared, Jamie's arm was pulled around him. Her body was gripped in a crushing vice and a hard mouth proceeded to bruise her tender lips in a decidedly painful kiss. What with the pain and the ecstasy and her nerves Jamie was mentally and physically awash. At last a convulsive gasp made Mark release her mouth.

"Mark, you'll break me into a hundred pieces."

"I just want to make sure you don't think there is any of that 'kindness' in the way I feel about you."

Jamie lifted her free hand to push up his dark glasses. "Let me see your eyes."

There they were: blue and bright; the tiny flame she had seen beside the billabong now a blaze.

"I'm crazy about you, Jamie. I have been right from the very first," he said with an odd restrained violence not characteristic of him at all.

"Then why didn't you do something… say something?"

She saw the shadow darken his eyes.

"I couldn't. I dare not. Hugh would have stymied every move I made once he guessed."

"The beast! But, Mark, last night. Surely you could have said something."

"Too short a time slot. I wasn't sure how you would react. I needed room to move so I was planning a trip to Brisbane."

"Oh, Mark, last night…while we were sitting there?"

"Yep. I—"

"Well! Is this the urgent business?"

They moved hurriedly apart under the indulgent but amazed gaze of Belle Anderson. Mark changed his glasses.

"It would be nice if it were," he smiled noncommittally at his hostess.

"Well, you had better have that wash. You know where the bathroom is."

Belle made one of her sons move and by the time Mark came back there was a chair for him beside Jamie. She made no teasing reference to what she had seen nor, during the table conversation, did she speak of the two collectively. Inwardly she was dumbfounded. Was the quiet reserved Mark going to steal a march on his brother after all? Good luck to him! It would do the arrogant Hugh a pile of good.

Under cover of the general chatter, Mark whispered, "We must get alone for a while as soon as we can. We've got a lot to talk about."

Jamie caught his eye. "It's not the talking I'm anxious about."

Then the clear glasses could not disguise the flash in his eyes. He caught her hand and held it hard against his thigh.

But they reckoned without Clyde and his brothers. It was not often that the three boys got a pretty girl all to themselves and they closed in on her. Jamie finally broke the strangling attention by announcing she would do a sketch of Clyde in his own book. The others had to sit back while her pencil flew. The host and writer had their heads together and Belle and Eileen engaged in women's talk. Mark could have seemed the odd man out but he lazed back in his chair, lending an ear to the different conversations as he watched the progress of the drawing, content as always to be in the background.

Finally, Jamie signed her name and stood up. While everyone was admiring her work she moved nearer to Mark.

"I need to move around after all that sitting."

"Come with me to the car while I get my case," said Mark, rising.

"You've already got it," chirped Clyde. "I saw you —"

"Shut up," said Mark with a wink and piloted Jamie through the door.

Outside, on the dark veranda, they stood wordlessly in a close embrace, savouring the exquisite moment of mutually acknowledged love. Then his kisses took her to joyous heights. Goodness, thought the girl breathlessly. There might not be any scintillating conversation at the breakfast table but in other areas he positively shone. Cuddled against him, Jamie asked:

"How far are you coming, Mark?'

"All the way. From the conversation back there, the Nickersons are being invited to stay for several days which leaves us free to go on."

And so it proved. Next morning, after an early breakfast, Jamie's gear was packed into the station wagon and goodbyes were said with mutual goodwill on everyone's part but that of the young men.

As they went over the first cattle grid, Mark glanced across to where Jamie sat decorously belted by the window. "At last!"

They drove in a heavenly silence full of anticipation for about twenty minutes. Mark wanted to get clear of the Anderson property. Eventually he saw a group of trees and pulled up in their shade. The two seatbelts clicked in unison.

Jamie turned eagerly to him but Mark put his arms on the steering wheel and leaned his head on them. He prayed a most beautiful prayer of thanksgiving. Only then did he take the humbled girl in his arms. They seemed so completely at one that Jamie hesitated to ask the thousand questions in her mind. Just to hold each other was enough for the moment. When they did drive on Mark put her hand under his on the wheel. Jamie leaned back in blissful peace. Mark actually broke that silence.

"We must be married as soon as possible, Jamie."

"Actually I don't think I've had a proposal yet."

Mark glanced across at her. "I think I proposed to you in my heart the first day I met you, sweetheart."

"That'll do," said Jamie, quite charmed. "I think I gave my actual consent a few days later."

They smiled at each other. Mark looked back at the road and just swung the car straight in time. "Love and driving don't mix," he said ruefully.

"Mark, when was it with you? At the waterhole… when I was cleaning your glasses?"

"Goodness, no. Hours before. When you stepped off the plane and stood there, your face brimming with mischief. I was that bucked when

I found you were the artist we were expecting. Best surprise I've ever had in my life."

"You can talk when you get going," observed Jamie with satisfaction. And so it proved.

As the station wagon devoured the kilometres it was a time of self-revelation for, really, they knew little about each other. Over a brief stop for their packed lunch, Jamie told of her motherless childhood, with her father being all-in-all to her, of her half-boy, half-girl life, the early following in her father's footsteps artistically. Mark was surprised to learn that she actually earned her living as a free-lance photographer.

"I just thought you painted all the time. Can't you earn enough?"

"I couldn't in the beginning. Now I like the variation. I don't want to stand in front of an easel all day. I've better dreams than that. Up till he died, Dad was everything. When I got over his death I found I wanted a home of my own, a husband and a family."

"Put wife instead of husband and you've got my dreams too."

"But I thought –"

"That I was one of the non-marrying Lawrences. Well, I'm not really."

Jamie was silent, thinking about Claudia, as they repacked the lunch things and returned to the car.

At last she succumbed to the irresistible temptation to draw him out.

"Well, why haven't you then?"

Mark was silent for so long that Jamie thought that she had trespassed on a situation still sensitive but at last he said,

"The only time I attempted to get married was such a disaster that I was pretty browned off."

"What happened, darling… if I may ask?"

"Someone's bound to tell you some time. I fell in love really for the first time when I was about twenty-four. We were engaged. Then Hugh came home from Uni and my fiancée fell for him. That's all."

"Was that Claudia?" she asked, wanting to let him know that she had been told.

"Who told you?"

"Mrs Templeton. She said you had a lucky escape."

"I don't know so much. Claudia was a nice girl. She was just dazzled by Hugh. Can't blame her."

"I do blame her. Tell me, Mark. Did it happen naturally or did Hugh set out to make it happen?"

Mark did not answer. Now Jamie knew that she had trespassed onto sensitive territory. He doesn't want to betray his brother, she thought, but it's true.

At last he said reflectively, "It takes two to tango. Had Claudia really cared… I did feel a bit bitter up till now. After Hugh threw her over, she married a pastoralist. Got two bonny kids. They could have been mine."

"We'll have much more beautiful children."

Mark smiled. "I don't care what they look like as long as they're yours and mine."

"Do I really compensate for Claudia?" Jamie asked wistfully.

"Compensate? Good heavens, girl, I'm not carrying a torch for Claudia. Just telling you how things used to be before you came along."

"Well, what made the bitterness go?"

"For over a month you've been exposed to Hugh. Claudia had never met him till we were engaged. Hugh had every chance with you."

"You saw to much of that," Jamie interposed quickly.

"I had to be sure. When you told me in your letter that you had cared for me from the first, and obviously had never changed, I was over the moon. That drive, while I followed the Nickersons' car was one of the happiest of my life."

"That reminds me. What was the nicest drive you've ever had?"

"The nicest? That would be the first one we had together before we caught up with Hugh and Stella. I was right in the midst of falling in love with you."

"And yet you meekly let me go with him."

"Can't you see why? Mark spoke very seriously.

"Yes, I can," Jamie answered honestly, "but what were you going to do about us?"

"Well, I obviously couldn't court you in front of Hugh. I haven't taken much of a holiday for years. I was going to take a month off, nip down to Brisbane and start from there."

"I'm thankful to hear it," said Jamie and she *was* thankful but something still niggled at her.

"Mark, seeing you felt like that about me how could you let Hugh take over and say he alone was going to drive me to the plane?"

"I wasn't going to."

"So… you were going to stand up to him."

Mark shook his head. "I never argue with Hugh."

Jamie stared across at him in some exasperation. "Well, what were you going to do?"

Mark gave her a teasing glance. "There are other ways besides confrontation, my dear."

"Well, what?" demanded Jamie impatiently.

"I was going to come with you."

'Ohh!" Jamie sat back with a gasp. She was just beginning to get a dim idea of how Mark had handled Hugh over the years.

"Well, you might have given me at least a hint of how you felt."

"You might have given me a hint too."

"Couldn't you see I wasn't attracted to Hugh? I was always sparring with him."

"All the girls start by sparring with Hugh. Then end up falling madly for him."

"Well, my sparring was for real. If he tries any of his tricks with me he'll get short shrift."

"We've got to get married as soon as possible, sweetheart."

Jamie looked anxiously across at him. Was there a troubled note in the even voice?

"You don't seriously think Hugh will make any trouble now? For one thing, I won't be at the station."

"I don't know," Mark moved uneasily in his seat. "I'd like to get all the preliminaries over quick smart and settle down to married life."

Jamie frowned. She could see Mark was in earnest. But there was nothing to worry about. She couldn't stand Hugh anyway. She made an attempt to lighten the situation.

"But I want to enjoy our engagement. My uncle and aunt will want to throw a party and I want to take you around and show you off."

"I'm staying down for a week. We can get all that over then. How soon can you marry me?"

Jamie gave up. "Well, whether we like it or not we have to give a month's notice to a marriage celebrant – in this case it will be my nice Minister."

"A whole month!" Mark groaned softly.

"Yes, it's the law. You obviously haven't been associated with anyone getting married lately."

Mark grinned. "Well, we'll have to get to that Minister of yours as soon as possible."

Jamie glanced out of the window where the sun was casting long shadows through the bush.

"We'll have to start thinking about where we'll pull in for the night. There's a town not –"

"We'll just be stopping for a meal."

"Mark, we don't want to leave it too late to find a Motel."

"I'm driving through to Brisbane."

"Driving through? But there's no need to do that. We've plenty of time and –"

"No, we haven't. I'd like to get everything settled as soon as possible."

Jamie thought this attitude was silly and put forth some sensible arguments as to why they could and should take their time. Mark listened courteously but did not reply. When she finally insisted on an answer he turned his head a little and remarked,

"We should get into Brisbane in time for an early breakfast, a quick shower at your unit and make an appointment to see your Minister. I hope he doesn't mind being disturbed so early."

Jamie sat back thinking and decided that there must be some paranoia here. Mark was definitely feeling insecure despite her confident assurances. Well then, the best cure was to get married as soon as they could.

CHAPTER NINE

Fast Work

Morris was seated at his desk working on his latest catalogue just before going for lunch when Jamie burst in.

"I'm engaged! I'm engaged! I'm engaged!" she chanted doing a whirling pirouette before him.

Morris put down his papers and whistled. "Whew! I've heard there was a shortage of women out west but I did not think it was as bad as that. So he snapped you up."

"Not so. Not so. I snapped his brother up."

"Wow! He must be something then. Stand still, you're making me dizzy."

Jamie subsided breathlessly into a chair and flung her hands across the desk. "Oh, Uncle Morris, I'm so utterly *utterly* happy."

Morris took both small hands in his warm clasp. "I can see you are, my dear. I'm very happy for you even if it does seem a bit sudden. Where is he?"

"Paying for the ring. He'll be here in a minute. I just had to see you first. You've no idea how busy we have been. We got in early this morning, grabbed a McDonald's breakfast, dashed off to my flat, had a shower and a shave - at least Mark did – and changed, then out to my dear old Minister to book our wedding…"

"Burning your boats that fast. I'd like to see him before I give my blessing."

"You shall, you shall. Oh, Uncle, did we get into a dither over our names. You'd have loved it. When Mr Hartley grasped our names properly he got all upset and announced that no way was he going to marry a James to a Mark. It would not look right on his books, he said. We finally settled it by emphasising our second names. So you and Aunt will be witnesses to James *Elizabeth* taking Mark *William* as her husband, emphasis loudly accented."

Morris laughed. "Good for him. One of the old school."

Jamie agreed. "So is Mark. Oh, Uncle, I've a favour to ask. Mark won't stay with me in my flat and I don't want to put him in a Motel or something –"

"Then you'll both stay with us. Alison and I would love to have you."

"You're a real pet. That's what I wanted."

"Is he coming to fetch you here?"

"No, I'm going to pick him up right now so –"

"Well I'm taking you both to lunch right now."

As Jamie hesitated Morris said whimsically, "No 'buts,' please." You can spare a jaded middle-aged man some of your stardust."

Jamie laughed and, arranging to meet him at his favourite restaurant which was nearby, flitted off.

Mark was waiting for her outside the jeweller's and she hurriedly explained that they would have to postpone the special moment of the ring giving till after lunch. Mark was disappointed but as they walked to the restaurant he remarked amiably that a telephone box would do or any booth for that matter. Jamie was convulsed and started to point out all the various corners or nooks where their betrothal could be sealed as they went along.

"Of course, I could put on dark glasses too," she giggled, "and then we could pretend we were in a dark corner."

As they entered the vestibule of the classy restaurant Mark saw a convenient nook behind some potted palms. He whisked Jamie over there and put the ring on her finger without more ado, saying that she had to be properly engaged to present him to her uncle. He then changed his glasses so that the first impression Morris had of him was of a tall fair bespectacled man who let Jamie do most of the talking. Remembering the dynamic Hugh, Morris sincerely hoped that Jamie was not throwing herself away and wondered what she saw in him.

The lunchtime conversation was taken up with a recital of Jamie's artistic exploits. Morris was very interested in Maxie and complimented his niece on her find.

"Did you bring any of his work back?"

"Only the bark painting he did for me. The rest were sold and half his relatives turned up for a share but I kept some of the money to pay for some art equipment for him."

"Now there's a business head for you," remarked Morris glancing across at her silent fiancé.

"She's pretty smart all round," said Mark with his attractive smile.

I like him, thought Morris, he grows on one. But he seems a bit slow for a firecracker like Jamie. It was obvious to him, and later to his wife, that Jamie had regained all her old zest for life. It might not be obvious to others but Mark certainly had the key that turned on the ignition in Jamie.

The afternoon was taken up with collecting their gear and having haircuts – and Jamie found that no way in the world would she be able to get Mark into a unisex salon.

When they drove into Morris's driveway Mark was impressed. Coming from the spaciousness of station life he immediately took to the wide lawns embracing a tennis court and a half-Olympic size pool. On entering the house, he found that the spacious note was everywhere. The carpets were pale and deep, the rich curtains were a neutral shade, the furniture kept to a minimum, that Morris's impressive collection of artworks should be fitly displayed.

As Morris went off to fetch his wife, Mark glanced around and observed that art-dealing was more profitable than he had thought. Jamie grinned.

"Uncle Morris has more irons in the fire than just paintings. He's something of an entrepreneur."

"What's that?"

"Oh… someone who more or less takes risks staging things and pulling them off, I think," said Jamie, vague about the exact meaning of a term she used without hesitation in its right place.

Alison, forewarned by her husband, was exuberant in her welcome and embraced them both. The aura of their happiness had a good effect on their host and hostess and, by the end of the evening, Morris and Alison were in a fair way to loving Mark for his own sake. They both looked on Jamie as the child they had never had and were jealous of her well-being and future. When they went to bed that night, they were convinced that Jamie would provide the excitement and Mark the stability in their barque of life.

Fully bent on a programme of visitation in order to show him off, Jamie found that she could not drag Mark hither and yon. To be in her presence was the ultimate with him and that with not too many distractions.

"I believe you're a real stay-at-home," she said teasingly as they drove off one afternoon to see her Aunt Miriam, an elderly relative on her mother's side. This was one visit she had insisted upon.

"Could be," replied Mark. "Living on a station makes you that way, I guess. We make our own fun."

Jamie grew thoughtful. After a while she said,

"You know, Mark, I don't think I'd be satisfied with station life twelve months of the year."

"I wouldn't expect it. You are an artist. We should be able to work it so that our different lifestyles dove-tail together."

Much heartened Jamie continued.

"I was born with the wanderlust. All my life, apart from the school years, I trod in Dad's shadow. It's not the social life I crave but I would want to go on painting trips. For instance, I want to paint in Carnarvon Gorge – some lovely stuff there. Would you be happy for me to go off and spend a couple of weeks there and –"

"On your own? No."

Jamie jumped at his tone.

"If you want to paint Carnarvon or any Gorge for that matter, I'll take you. There's a lot of difference between trips like that and making time pass with endless cups of tea and cakes."

Jamie smiled at this pithy summing up of the social round while wryly acknowledging to herself that the marriage state was a new ballgame.

"Mark, the girls want to give me a shower and –"

"A what?"

Jamie giggled. "A kind of engagement party with gifts. I've hardly any time to get a trousseau ready even."

"What the dickens is a trousseau?"

"Really, Mark. Where were you when your sisters got married? It's a special set of clothes to get married in and wear afterwards."

"I like all you've got now."

"Yes, but I want some new things, some pretty – pretty night dresses and things."

"Oh, yes, have plenty of those. You'll be needing 'em."

Mark, glancing across, caught the blush.

"Do we really have to visit this aunt of yours?"

"Yes, we have to. Keep your mind on it, boy."

Mark sighed, "I wish it was all over."

Jamie glanced uncertainly at him. Morris liked to do things on a grand scale and had been talking about a big wedding. Mark had said nothing but there had been a closed expression on his face.

"Darling, about the wedding. I could see you weren't keen on a big do but I have lots of friends and then there are your friends and relatives. You'll want –"

"I want the ceremony itself to be very private. We can have a big do afterwards."

"But you'll want Hugh and Ashley and Sarah –"

"I don't even want them to know the date."

"Don't even want –" repeated Jamie, bewildered.

"I don't want to give Hugh a deadline. Just let him know we'll be married some time when we tell him."

Here was paranoia indeed.

"What am I to say to Morris and Alison?"

"Just tell 'em that that is what we want."

"What *we* want?"

Mark caught the emphasis and pulled the car over to the kerb and stopped it. He turned around to face her.

"Jamie, I've had twenty-eight years with Hugh and I know what I'm doing. Will you trust me on this?"

For the first time Jamie felt the tension in him.

"Yes, Mark, I will," she said stoutly.

She was not quite so stout when it came to combating her uncle's protests. She tackled it while Mark was having his shower next morning. Morris took instant exception. Jamie made it sound as though it were more her idea than Mark's in order to shield him.

"I don't like it, Jamie," Morris fussed. "It's too hole-in-the-corner. Makes it look as though you have to get married."

"I'll use the pill for six months," said Jamie, getting over that hurdle. "That'll prove that we didn't."

"Don't you even want to be a bride?" Alison asked wistfully. She so longed to have the joy of preparing a daughter for marriage.

Jamie looked at her with softened eyes. "I will be in the truest sense, my dear Aunt, but if you want to make me a white bride you can."

Alison's eyes lit up. "May I make your dress?"

"Of course, and you'll be Matron of Honour so you will have to wear something glamorous, too."

Alison was off in a world of styles. Morris grunted,

"And what have you got for me in this very private wedding, minx?"

Jamie considered with her fingertip to her chin.

"Well, you'll have to give the bride away. Then you'll have to nip over to Mark's side to be Best Man which means you will be in charge of the rings. Then the two of you will have to be witnesses to our signatures. After that you'll have to cough up the dibs for a smashing wedding break –"

"Enough, enough," Morris cried, laughing. "Next thing you'll have me arranging your honeymoon. Well, you're not having it all your own way. If I can't give you a big wedding what I will give you is a big engagement party and it will be this Saturday."

"Fair enough," the girl assented; glad to have cleared the hurdle in Mark's absence.

Morris decided to throw one of his pool parties which were really something. They were all day affairs. The guests could swim, play tennis, mini golf or just lounge about. A delectable lunch was served by the pool with a barbecue for the evening meal. Professional catering freed Alison to do nothing but prepare the guest list which, considering their situation in the world of art, included some well-known names as well as their social circle. She was all day on the phone as the reason for the party had to be explained and exclaimed over.

Mark had no idea what he was in for but, seeing the size of the surprise party he and his brother had thrown for her, Jamie felt he would take it in his stride.

As he did not have any tennis things or swimmers with him, Jamie went with him to purchase them. He would not have her anywhere near him as he dealt with his shorts but Jamie made good the time searching for a fashionable pair of swim trunks.

When she showed him the flimsy white things with a black dart at one side, she had trouble even getting him to consider them.

"They'll slide off," he protested.

"No, they won't," assured the salesman. "They'll cling like a second skin." But this was quite the wrong tack.

"I don't want a second skin. I want a decent pair of trunks," asseverated Mark.

"I want you to have them because they match my swimsuit," Jamie said persuasively. Mark was horrified.

"If it's like a second skin on you."

"No, no," Jamie dared not laugh. "Wait a minute." She went over to the women's section and soon came back with swimsuit similar to her own. It was a simple white one piece with a black dart down one side.

Mark eyed it dubiously. "As long as it doesn't go transparent in the water."

'It won't," chorused Jamie and the salesman in unison. Mark was eventually persuaded but insisted on taking a plain pair of black trunks as well just to be on the safe side.

The next hurdle they had to get over was the engagement notice in the paper. Morris undertook to do this as a matter of course and was dumbfounded to find Mark demurring over it.

"It's the official announcement," Morris explained with a touch of impatience. "It must go in Saturday's paper to coincide with the party."

Later Morris cornered Jamie. "He's not a recluse, is he?" he asked anxiously. "You're not going to live on a desert island?"

"No, it's not that, Uncle." Jamie was at a loss to explain Mark's dread of a public announcement. She decided to tell part of the truth. "He was engaged once before. It was publicly announced and everything and then the girl jilted him. It has stung him for years."

Morris's brow cleared at once. "What rotten luck! She must have been a nark. Well, he's got nothing to worry about this time the way you sit in his pocket. I doubt if you know that any other men exist."

"They don't."

"*Thank you.*"

CHAPTER TEN

Celebrating the Coup

The pool party was successful as all Morris's parties were. Jamie,
hoping that Mark would appear at this best, need not have worried.
Quite unexpectedly, a cloak of glamour fell on him. Among the guests
were a couple who knew him from his University days and informed
one and all of his prowess in the sport of swimming and diving. He
was a good tennis player, too, and, when his game was over, Jamie got
him into the pool, white swimmers and all. Mark was quite reconciled
on finding that every other man wore the same style. Although he was
out of practice his dives had the touch of the expert
Jamie lay back and listened with pleasure to admiring remarks about
his slim graceful physique and abilities.

It was another guest who put the cap on Mark's attractions
however. This young woman had a cousin who moved in horsey
circles, and, after inquiring if Mark was one of the Lawrence brothers
who owned Fairlie Downs, volunteered the information that he owned
the Reserve Champion stockhorse of that year.

"Went around with Derek to see the gee-gees and I saw the horse.
I've never seen anything like him. A great big red-gold horse with a
neck like the curve of a strung bow and –"

"Why, that's Red – Redmaster to give him his full name," cried
Jamie, sitting up on her towel. "They've got a wall of ribbons up there
but Mark never told me he had won one with Red."

Mark got hauled over the coals for this when he got out of the
water. Standing there, his slim body gleaming with the drops of water,
rubbing his fair hair with a towel and without his glasses, he was
enough to turn any girl's head. As he smiled his engaging smile and
informed Jamie that Red was a shy horse and didn't like it mentioned,
he charmed them all. Someone asked sotto voce just what Fairlie

Downs was and, on hearing that it was one of the larger cattle stations out west, looked at Jamie with a healthy respect.

After that Mark was in danger of being lionised and Jamie kept a possessive eye on him. He spread out his towel and stretched out beside her as she fished out his dark glasses from her holdall for him. She knew, of course, that had the more magnetic Hugh been there Mark's star would not have shone so brightly but he was *not* there and Mark had his chance for once.

Later that night when she stood in his embrace to say goodnight, she asked him if he had enjoyed himself. He seemed more concerned with nibbling her ear than chatting but he gave a satisfied grunt.

"Isn't it wonderful, Mark? Being in love I mean."

"Umm. It always is," murmured Mark, his lips wandering up her hairline.

That word 'always'. Was there a hint of reminiscence in the tone? Jamie felt a little prick which she wished with all her heart she had not. Was there still warmth in that old memory? She turned her head so that her lips met his and she put everything into the kiss in an endeavour to erase all recollection of Claudia. She was in danger of succeeding too well. After a long moment Mark raised his head a little and muttered against her lips, "Don't start something you're not prepared to finish tonight."

"Sorry, darling," Jamie pulled back but he would not let her go. She stood there quietly, her body raging within her, sensing his own urgent need. "Sorry," she repeated and firmly pushed him away.

"I won't do it again till our wedding night," she whispered and flitted away down the hall to her own room.

"I won't give him a chance to think of Claudia," she told herself as she undressed. "And I won't be using any pill. The sooner I put our child in his arms the better."

Mark had decreed that he must start for home early on Monday morning as he wanted to keep all the time he could for his honeymoon. He had not as yet made any move towards informing his brother and uncle and aunt. Jamie knew that Saturday's papers would be there by Monday and asked about it on the way home from Church on Sunday.

"I suppose I'll have to let them know," he said reluctantly. "If we hadn't put that notice -"

But this would not do for Jamie. "He can't touch you, Mark. They've got to know sometime. Ring them from here. I'll be at your side. I think Sarah and Ashley – and Howie – would be hurt if they only read of it in the paper. You're making too big a bogey out of it,"

They put the call through after lunch and Hugh's sleepy voice came over the wires.

"Well, you old son-of-a-gun, I thought you must be at the South Pole by now. What gives?"

"Well, I have got off the beaten track a bit." Mark paused and Jamie, standing close so that she would hear Hugh's voice, smiled encouragingly. "I've got myself engaged."

There was total silence at the other end for a few minutes and then Hugh's voice with something of a grate in it. "The devil you have... and who is the enterprising lady?"

Jamie's hackles rose. Enterprising indeed!

"Jamie Somerville."

"*Jamie Somerville?* What damned nonsense is this? She never looked your way and –"

"Yes, I did." Jamie grabbed the phone. "I more than glanced his way. Aren't you going to wish us well, Hugh? We're wildly happy."

Then she was hanging on to the phone herself, enduring an agonizing wait till Hugh answered. At last his voice came, light and mocking, "Clever girl."

Jamie flushed with anger. She turned to Mark who was reddening. Why didn't he grab the phone from her and give his brother what for? Her face was hot but her voice could have frozen the wires.

"Don't you think your brother is capable of getting a woman?"

Again that long pause which was in itself insulting. Then:

"I've no intention of discussing my brother's abilities with you."

Jamie fairly gasped.

"Is Mrs Howard there?" she asked sharply. "I'd like to speak to her, please."

"Well in the saddle, aren't you? She's not here."

"Not there? Where –"

"That's her business. Put Mark on."

Jamie felt like throwing the phone through the ether as she handed it to Mark.

Hugh immediately asked in a businesslike tone when his brother was coming home and launched into some matter concerning the property. Mark's replies were brief and to the point whereupon Hugh uttered a laconic "See you," and hung up.

Jamie turned to Mark. She was trembling from head to foot.

"The pig!" she stormed. "The absolute pig! Why, he treated us like criminals."

Mark put his arms around her. He had gone a little pale.

"I knew what it would be like,' he said sombrely.

"But it's ridiculous," Jamie cried. "You're a grown man with heavy responsibilities on the station. You can marry when and where you like."

"He's got it into his head that he's the marrying Lawrence and I'm not."

"That's just a stupid coincidence. You're all behaving as though it's some unbreakable tradition. The laws of the Medes and Persians or something. Let's ring the others at once."

It took them twenty minutes to get through. Jamie suspected Hugh of being the cause of the engaged line and she was right. Ashley answered and before Mark could give him the news he broke into congratulations.

"Best thing I've heard for years, boy. Good on Jamie."

Jamie choked and nearly swallowed her tongue. Didn't they think that Mark had any initiative at all? She would have liked to box Ashley's ears. Then Sarah came on and asked for Jamie. Congratulations did not trip off her tongue.

"I can't understand it, Jamie," she said plaintively, "it was always Hugh and you."

"No, it wasn't, Sarah. It was Mark all the time. Aren't you going to wish us happy?"

But Sarah would not come off the threshold of wonder. She kept on harping about the rapport between them and the way she and Hugh were always teasing each other. Jamie found herself involved in explanations and assurances till she was sick of it. Mark just stood silently by, his arm comfortingly around her waist. Before she hung up Jamie asked where Mrs Howard was.

This was a new puzzle for Sarah.

"Howie? She's with Hugh."

"Are you sure?"

"Of course, Jamie. I was speaking to her just before lunch. I rang to see if there was any news of Mark. Why?"

There was no request to speak to Mark. Jamie rang off and stood there, running her tongue around her dry mouth.

"Now I know what it means when they say 'mad enough to spit chips'. Let's go outside."

They left the house by the side door and wandered around, their arms entwined about each other. Jamie had to get her feelings off her chest and did so. Mark said nothing but the shadow on his countenance conveyed more than any words. At the end of a solid hour when Jamie had figuratively thrashed his present family and all his forebears, all he said was,

"I wish we had just kept quiet and cleared off and got married."

Now Jamie agreed with him. "If I'd any idea we'd get such a reception I wouldn't have had that wretched notice published and – and – oh, darling." She pressed her head into his chest. "It's all so silly and selfish."

Suddenly a thought struck her.

"Mark, how is the property left? Is there any advantage to Hugh in being the only one to marry?"

Mark frowned. "Not on the books. It's just so happened that the non-marrying brother's share is willed back to the one with the family. That's why after three generations it's still intact."

"So if Hugh's the one with the family Ashley's share would go to him?"

"Actually Ashley's willed his share to both of us. Sarah has a share and hers is willed to Hugh."

"So Hugh would be sitting back expecting that the whole property will go on through his line when – or if -," she added savagely, "he decides to marry. Well, it's more than time that the whole stupid setup was blown apart."

They walked on in silence while Jamie gathered her thoughts. She wondered what Mark was thinking. Hugh could not force them apart. A small fear sprang up in her. Mark had been under the domination of his forceful brother for most of his life. She remembered with a cold chill that Mark had said that it was easiest to give in first as last. But surely he would not let Hugh spoil his second chance for happiness.

The situation was totally different. She was a wake-up to his tactics, not like Claudia. Also, she had the advantage of detesting Hugh. He would not be able to sweep her off her feet in order to 'test her out for Mark.'

It suddenly hit Jamie that there was no getting away from Hugh when they were married. She wondered why the thought had not occurred to her before.

"Mark, had you – had you thought about our living quarters?"

"Sort of," he glanced down at her unhappily, "but I haven't come up with anything yet."

"What if Hugh had already married?"

"I was going to move over with Ashley and Sarah and give Hugh a free start to married life."

"And now that you are the first to marry, Hugh should move over and give you a free start, shouldn't he?"

There was a trenchant pause. Then Mark said slowly,

"He already considers the place as his."

Jamie thought of the big master bedroom that Hugh already occupied. There was one identical room across the hall from his but it seemed to be kept for married guests. Mark had a good sized room behind his and Howie the one opposite. She and Stella had been accommodated in the guest wing.

Jamie could not see herself and Mark occupying the one opposite Hugh and meeting him at every turn. Her wrath drained away leaving her puzzled and a little afraid.

"Mark, have you made a will?

He smiled down at her. "Yes, darling but I will be changing it on our wedding day."

"I'm not looking for –"

"It's right and proper that a man should provide for his wife in case of death."

At least he could still see himself marrying her. They heard a call and looked across at the house.

"It's teatime," said Jamie, "we'll have to hurry. I don't want to miss Church tonight."

During the Service, which was not particularly well attended, Jamie endeavoured to regain her spiritual poise. She wondered how one went about praying for a situation like this. It was during the Bible reading that she came across a verse for the first time:

Roll your burden on the Lord and He will sustain you.

She put her finger under the line and drew Mark's attention to it.

He nodded and said unexpectedly, "Been following that all my life."

The girl was quite stricken and did not pay much attention to the sermon. Had Mark's life been such a burden with his overbearing brother that he had needed the Lord's sustaining hand? Or had he just meant it as a general philosophy?

On the way home, she brought up the subject and put the point to him. Mark waited for the lights and, as he changed gears, remarked thoughtfully,

"It had a lot to do with managing Hugh and then I guess it finally became a habit."

Jamie began to feel her way. She was looking for a clue to the fact that Mark never fought back, never asserted his rights.

"What was it like while you were growing up? Did your parents give Hugh more attention?"

"He always claimed more attention. He was younger, livelier, better looking –"

"That's a matter of opinion. I for one don't care for very dark men."

"The Lord be praised," said Mark fervently but with a twinkle in his eye.

Jamie knuckled him in the ribs. "Did you ever have an out and out clash?"

"When we were very young – but I always had to give in because he was the younger and used to throw such tantrums. They were really something. When I got to my early teens I made up my mind that, rather than suffer continual defeats, I'd avoid open contests. Where it didn't matter much I let Hugh have his way before he realised he was getting it."

He fell silent. Jamie forbore to press him for a while. A whole life's programme and philosophy set out before he was even out of school. Yet questions kept sprouting in her mind.

"What about in sport, Mark? Alan spoke of the trophies you'd won."

"Hugh and I never competed. I was four years older and had a different set of interests and friends. He chose field sports and I got into the aquatic. I had a thing about water… it's so dry at home."

"What about the station? Does Hugh make all those decisions too?"

"Dad used to make them all. We were just the workers. After he died we seemed to gravitate to our own spheres. Hugh manages most of the outside stuff. I do the books and a lot of the buying. There's no need to quarrel with a decision just because he makes it."

"Mark, Stella told me about your parents' deaths. If you don't want to talk about it –"

"I don't mind. It's never discussed at home because it always leads to argument."

"Then you do stand up for your opinion sometimes."

Mark glanced across at her. "You've sure got me in the witness box tonight."

"Sorry, I just want to get the picture. I'd like to hear you present all of your arguments."

"Then you'd be disappointed. Hugh knows my opinion. I've never altered since the accident. He's the one who has tried to change me."

"Why? Does he want to win every argument?"

"No, it's just that we won't have a lot of drink on the place particularly at parties."

"So! And who's 'we?"

"Ashley, Sarah and myself."

"This is interesting. How come?"

"Hang on. I'm worn out with all this questioning. Need some refreshment."

They had turned into the driveway and Mark brought the car quietly into the garage. Jamie, her head full of what she had been hearing, remarked that her aunt had some delicious new mango and orange drink and prepared to get out. A hand reached across and held the door shut.

"It beats me," said Mark with a soft laugh. "You've been engaged to me for a whole week and you still don't know what I mean by refreshment."

Jamie giggled and surrendered. Mark gripped her hard and she felt his hunger as his lips set her on fire. Dear God, how was she ever going to let him go back to Hugh? Thank heaven there were now only three weeks to their wedding.

When they eventually made themselves go in for supper they found that Alison and Morris had been putting their heads together.

"How about moving in here till you're married, Jamie," suggested Alison. You're going to have to give up the flat anyway. You could be here for the fittings and I'd love to have you, seeing you're going to live so far away from us."

It seemed to be a good idea all round.

"We should have thought of it earlier," said Mark. 'I could have moved Jamie's things and –"

"You would never have it done in time with all your canoodling," announced Morris. "I'll move Jamie before she knows it."

"Will you also pay the month's rent in lieu of notice, Uncle dear?"

"I'll pay that," said Mark. "I'll give you a cheque now."

"No need to –" began Morris but Mark had gone.

In a few minutes, he was back with his cheque book. Ignoring Morris's protests, he inquired the amount from Jamie and completed the cheque.

Morris, who felt he stood in loco parentis to his niece, took umbrage at this highhandedness and scolded him soundly.

Mark said nothing.

Later, when he walked upstairs with her, Jamie got hold of the lapels of his jacket.

"You're not going to bed till I hear how you and Ashley and Sarah managed to put the screws on Hugh."

Mark sighed. "I could think of better things to do."

"No." Jamie held him off. "Not till you've told me."

Mark rubbed his ear and marshalled his thoughts in the dim hall.

"Ashley and Sarah knew how under the weather Dad was at the time. They had failed to persuade him to wait till the next day. I couldn't get him to give me the controls. It galvanised us into action. We just decided next time not to turn up if Hugh ordered a large amount of drinks for a party."

"No arguments?"

Mark grinned. "You try holding a big do out west with no one to manage the food like Sarah, no one to play the fiddle like Ash and no one to do the organising like yours truly. Hugh never thought we would do it but we all cleared off to Brisbane, taking Howie with us. We've had no trouble ever since except that periodically Hugh tries to change my mind."

"And what do you say?"

"Nothing. I never argue with Hugh."

"So it can be done," mused Jamie. "You've just got to find the right ball play."

"Well, that's all the questions I'm answering tonight. I've never talked so much in all my life."

Jamie slid her hands up from his jacket to his face and said softly, "You're getting better at it every day."

"I'm getting better at everything all round," said Mark and proved it.

CHAPTER ELEVEN

A Surprise Manoeuvre

Next day Jamie was in tears as she saw him drive off. He was such a darling and so vulnerable in his new love. He was also a conundrum. There was nothing wishy-washy about his character; just a hang-up where Hugh was concerned.

Jamie did not want to admit it but she had begun to be apprehensive about Hugh. She threw herself into her move with Morris's help and then Alison swept her off for some trousseau shopping. Mark rang her twice on the long trip home and finally from his office on Wednesday.

"How's everything, Mark darling?"

"Fair weather," he answered in his light pleasant drawl. "Here's someone who is dying to speak to you."

Mrs Howard came on the line and, although she spoke in low hurried tones, her genuine pleasure made up for some of the distress caused by the others. She innocently asked when the wedding would be but Jamie was noncommittal, "Goodness I've hardly got used to being engaged yet. Got to get a trousseau together first."

Eventually she handed back the phone and must have gone back to the homestead for Mark spoke much more freely. It appeared that Ashley and Sarah had come over for the day specially to see Mark.

Sarah had been pleasantly congratulatory but there was a dry note in Mark's voice which showed that he had not been particularly impressed. Ashley had been his usual easy-going self but still a little amazed. Jamie did not ask about Hugh and Mark did not volunteer anything. The call ended with Mark promising to ring her every day.

By Friday Jamie had plucked up courage to ask Mark directly how Hugh was behaving.

"He's not here. He's gone over to Cannington. They picked him up by plane this morning."

"What's at Cannington?"

"Cattle."

"No beautiful girls?"

There was a chuckle on the line. "No, seems he's all wrapped up in cattle at the moment."

On Monday morning Jamie was coming down the stairs dressed for some personal shopping. Morris had already gone into the city and Alison was in her sewing room, crooning over some delicate embroidered voile.

The doorbell rang and Jamie called. "I'll answer it."

She opened the door and was flabbergasted to find Hugh Lawrence on the doorstep. He stepped in quickly, grasped her shoulder and kissed her warmly on the cheek.

"What are you doing here?" demanded the girl, jerking back.

"For goodness' sake, Jamie, you look as though you've seen a ghost. It's your future brother-in-law." He let her go and stood smiling down at her.

"You didn't appear to be all that thrilled with the prospect a few days ago."

Hugh frowned and turned his wide-brimmed hat in his hands.

"I'm ashamed of that, Jamie. I needed kicking around the stockyards for that. I just somehow had the picture of old Mark —"

"Not so much of the 'old Mark'. He's only four years older than you. What do you want?"

"Nothing, honey. I had to come to town on business and thought I'd look you up... and apologise for my behaviour." Seeing her stony face, he added, "Look here, Mark and I are the best of pals. I can't quarrel with his wife-to-be."

He had her there. Mark had said nothing of any trouble since he had got home. It behoved her to be on good terms with his relatives. She peeped out the door and saw a big sleek rental car while Hugh eyed her clothes.

"If you're on your way out, may I take you. Actually I'd like to take you to lunch and celebrate."

Jamie wanted to get rid of him off the doorstep before Alison came through. She knew Hugh's charm.

"Okay but it'll have to be a quick meal. I've got a lot of shopping to do."

"And not much time to do it in?" queried Hugh sympathetically as he escorted her to the car. Jamie was not to be caught by such tactics. Suddenly she stopped short and exclaimed, "My goodness, I've forgotten the sample. I won't be a minute."

She shot back inside and up to her room where she picked up a small speech recorder. Grabbing a piece of ribbon out of her handbag she flourished it as she rejoined Hugh. She often used the recorder when interviewing people and it occurred to her that Hugh might let slip something that would be useful. Once in the car she picked up the conversation where it had been left off.

"Actually I've haven't got much time," she paused and saw Hugh give a quick glance in her direction. "I'm going to the ballet tonight and want to wear my new dress but I haven't got the right evening bag for it. It takes me ages to choose one."

This was perfectly true but not what Hugh had hoped to hear by his expression.

He obviously knew his way about town for he took her to one of the best restaurants. She let him order while she glanced around.

"It's a bit early but we must have champagne."

"Provided it's non-alcoholic," she said tranquilly.

"Oh, come off it, Jamie. I'm ordering the real stuff."

"You can order it but I won't drink it." Jamie smiled sweetly at the approaching waiter. "I'll have fresh orange juice, please."

Hugh grinned appreciatively for there was nothing he liked better than to spar with a pretty woman.

Under cover of settling down Jamie set the recorder going and left her bag slightly open on the edge of the table. However, it seemed all for nothing for Hugh kept up easy small talk throughout the meal which was very good. Then, as they relaxed over coffee, he remarked out of the blue:

"What puzzles me is how you got so far in one week."

"Actually," said Jamie, quite unable to resist, "We fell in love at first sight."

Hugh gave a derisive snort. "So I noticed. I've never seen two people look less in love. In fact," he continued with a quick frown, "I wish I could be sure Mark was really in love now."

"What do you mean?"

"He's not himself. Seems in the doldrums."

Jamie could think of very good reasons why Mark was not himself but she was not giving anything away. "Just missing me, I guess," she said airily.

"I'd like to think it. You know you didn't give him enough time."

Jamie frowned and merely looked a query.

"After all it was all your doing, wasn't it?"

"I don't know what you mean."

"If you hadn't written that letter, you wouldn't be engaged today, would you?"

If anyone needed split second divine guidance just then it was Jamie. The cogs whirling in her brain, she pulled her handbag toward her and drew out her compact.

"Letter?" she said vaguely, conscious that Hugh's eyes were boring into her like gimlets.

"The letter you wrote Mark when you left."

How could Hugh know about her letter? Mark would never have shown it to him. Had he stolen it out of his brother's pocket? As she casually repaired her makeup Jamie remembered a piece of advice given to interviewees on television: Answer an awkward question with another question. She shut her compact with a snap.

"Why did you lie to me and make out Howie was away when I asked to speak to her?" she demanded belligerently.

Caught out Hugh struggled for a moment and then took refuge in another lie. "I thought she had gone over to Seven Trees," he said hastily.

"Particularly as she had just been talking to Sarah on the phone herself," purred Jamie and finished the last of her coffee. She was definitely holding her own in this verbal duel.

Hugh looked like a thundercloud for a moment and then grinned with reluctant appreciation.

"Up to all the tricks, aren't you?" he said softly.

"Aren't you?" countered Jamie.

Hugh laughed and picked up his coffee. He sat back to enjoy it, gazing out the window.

Reviewing his arsenal, thought Jamie and was content to wait for his next attack. It came with a thoughtful concerned air:

"I'd let the dust settle for a while before you make any marriage plans," he said quietly. "You don't really know Mark and it is a very big step for him to take. I for one would like to be sure that he's completely over Claudia."

This was a mistake. Jamie fired up at once.

"If it hadn't been for your interference he would be happily married now," she flashed.

Hugh stared and then recovered quickly. "Which means you would not now be in the picture at all," he observed blandly.

Jamie was confused. She hated the nagging little doubt as to whether Mark was really over Claudia but it was still there.

"Let's just suppose Mark had married his Claudia and you had come out to do that painting. Would it still have been love at first sight, Jamie?"

Jamie turned her troubled gaze away. What was Hugh doing to her? She could not think straight where Claudia was concerned. "Of course not," she said hurriedly, "he would have been a married man and –"

"Did you know that Mark was not married when you fell for him 'at first sight'?"

"Yes," crowed Jamie triumphantly. "Stella told me on the plane."

"Saved by the bell," said Hugh good humouredly and added as the thought occurred to him, "so you were checking up on us on the plane."

Jamie had had enough. She picked up her handbag but Hugh forestalled her by signalling the waiter and ordering more coffee. He was not going to let her go yet. As she hesitated he said,

"You're a very attractive young woman, my dear. If you'd given me half a chance it would not be my brother's ring you would be wearing."

This was coming out into the open with a vengeance. Glad she had her recorder running Jamie showed Hugh the face of astonishment.

"But, Hugh. There was Stella. She and you…"

"Jamie, dear. You must have seen that was only a flirtation. I –"

"Not to Stella. You hurt her badly."

Hugh put on the face of contrition. "I was sorry about that."

Jamie could not help it. "You're a chronic flirt, Hugh. It would take some fancy girl to pull you down."

"Not if it's the right girl. You didn't give me a chance. You assured me that it was all business and here I find you engaged to Mark. When did the business end and the pleasure begin?"

Jamie flushed. There had been nothing between her and Mark till she actually left. If he could tie her into knots what could he do to Mark? She stood up.

"Thank you for the lunch," she said stiffly and turned to go. Hugh was immediately at her side, a hand under her elbow.

"Sorry, Jamie, but you hit first. This thing has knocked me for six, you know."

"I don't know and I don't care. Let me go."

"Hush. People will be looking at us."

Nobody was but Jamie paused. She let Hugh pay the bill and escort her out of the building while she did some quick thinking. Once on the footpath she turned smiling to her adversary.

"I really have to go now." She then added on a doubtful note while looking at the ground, "I really thought it was Stella so - I didn't –"

"Silly girl." Was there an eager note in the smooth voice? "If you'd given me half a chance."

"But I can't – I mean - the way things are –" she floundered artistically.

"Listen, honey. Just take things quietly. No rush. I'll be down again soon."

"Please, Hugh," she put a hand to her forehead and then held it out with an air of brave resolution, "I must say goodbye now."

Hugh took her hand and held it in both of his. "Not goodbye, dear. Just au revoir."

Jamie turned and hurried away. Once in a shop she took out the recorder. It was still going. She clicked it off with a sigh of satisfaction. But she was not satisfied when she thought of her letter. She cringed at the thought of his cool gaze taking in her avowal of love. Surely Mark would not leave it lying around. Jamie did her shopping rather abstractedly. Hugh's poison was beginning to work.

With a group of friends Jamie had a season ticket to the ballet and was glad to be going out that night. She had told Mark she would be out at the theatre and impatiently awaited the call he would be putting through earlier. When it came, she took it in Morris's study.

The preliminaries over she asked him where Hugh was. Mark sounded surprised.

"At Cannington… on some cattle business. I thought I told you."

"Well, he's not. He's here in Brisbane. Called on me this morning."

Mark was dumbfounded.

"He reckoned he was here on some cattle business. Is that possible?"

"Could be. Cannington is part of a big concern; they have an office in Brisbane. What happened?"

"He insisted on taking me to lunch." Immediately she felt the drop in temperature. Mark's 'Did he?' had the emptiness of an echo. To him it was a score for his wily brother.

"Now don't drop your bundle, Mark. He did not charm me into it. I had to get rid of him quickly and I had a purpose in going."

"Did you?" Again the empty echo.

"Yes, I did," she said patiently. "I wanted to see what he would be up to. I took a small speech recorder I use for interviews and got our whole conversation."

She was relieved to hear Mark laugh naturally. "There's no doubt about you. Was it worth it?"

"Very much so. Hugh can twist your words and mine and hint at all sorts of things but he can't erase his own recorded words."

"What sort of things did he hint?"

"Actually he more than hinted." Jamie took a deep breath and plunged. "He inferred that he had read the letter I wrote to you."

The amazed ejaculation that came over the wires was sweet music in Jamie's ears.

"Read your letter? Why, I'd cut my right hand off rather than let him see it. How did he know there was a letter?"

"I don't know. Did you leave it lying around?"

"I should think not. I –" He paused, thinking back. "Wait a minute. Maxie brought your letter and parcel to me in my office. I'm ashamed to say I didn't open the parcel till I got back. It's a delightful picture and I'll treasure -"

"Never mind that. Keep thinking."

"I slit open the envelope, read the letter and dashed off to the house and –"

"What did you do with the envelope?"

"I don't know. I guess I just dropped it on my desk."

"And it had your name on it in my writing," said Jamie. "I'll bet Hugh found it and later, when he heard about our engagement, did some pretty shrewd guessing."

"I suppose that's what happened." Mark said wearily.

"Listen, darling. Whatever Hugh tells you about me and whatever he tells me about you we must make a pact never to believe it."

No answer.

"Mark?"

"I heard you, darling. I was just wishing it didn't have to be like this."

"We'll weather it, Mark." Jamie's fighting dander was up but she felt she could not say the same for him. Why wouldn't he stand up to his brother? They talked of other things and Jamie was as loving as she could possibly be. He seemed to be in better spirits by the time they hung up.

Tony and Aileen Campbell were calling for her and chatted brightly in the car. Jamie made an effort to respond.

"Brooke's back," said Aileen over her shoulder.

"None the worse for wear, apparently," Tony laughed.

"Don't be awful." Aileen turned towards Jamie in the back. "I think she's had a rotten deal."

"Yes, two marriages and two divorces before she's twenty-eight," replied Jamie who had known Brooke Tarrington for years. "We all thought she was headed for a totally glamorous and successful life."

"Well, she's successful in every department but love," interposed Tony. "Isn't she one of the top models? I saw a smashing photograph of her in – er –ah – damn these lights."

"In *what?*" came Aileen's arctic tones and Jamie burst out laughing. "He'll never tell you now." And he didn't.

They were a congenial group and as they moved into the theatre, Jamie saw that Brooke was unpartnered like herself and moved to her side. Heads were turned as they took their seats as people caught sight of Brooke's remarkable beauty.

This always happened and Jamie was long used to it. Her features were classic, her auburn colouring vibrant but there was something more which photographers were always trying to capture. Hers was the profile that seafarers wanted on the prow of their ships, hers was the face desired by artists who wanted to depict the legendary Helen whose looks could cause wars. Her figure would have been sought by sculptors of old to model for their goddesses.

And Jamie, glancing at her during the performance, thought that the hardness of her expression made her look as though the exquisite features were actually carved in marble. Her heart ached for her friend.

During the interval, Brooke who had heard of her engagement, congratulated Jamie sincerely.

"I hear we are losing you to the outback."

"Oh, we'll be down every year for the Show."

"I believe he's really something."

"Umm… umm."

"I hope you won't be disillusioned, honey," Brooke said sombrely.

"I won't. His kind's the salt of the earth."

"Glad to know there's any of that kind left." Brooke could not keep the bitterness out of her tone. "All I seem to come up with are womanisers and wimps."

The lights dimmed and, in the darkness, Jamie sought Brooke's hand and gave it a good hard squeeze. "After I'm married you must come up for a good long visit."

Brooke turned to her. "Don't say anything you don't mean. You won't want anyone around during your honeymoon months."

"Oh, we won't be alone and, anyway, I do mean it. Station life would do you good. Get the fog out of your soul."

"Yes," said Brooke slowly. "I've never been on a cattle station. I'd like to do something really different. Thank you, Jamie, you're a real friend."

After a moment, Jamie began to wonder whether she really was a friend. She had completely forgotten about Hugh. What would this beautiful disillusioned woman and the handsome habitual flirt make of each other? Perhaps nothing. They might both have the other's measure.

They all went to supper afterwards and stayed late. Jamie enjoyed the outing. Her little talk with Brooke had lifted her thoughts off her own problems. When she got home the house was in darkness so she got out her key and let herself in.

CHAPTER TWELVE

Another Surprise Manoeuvre

She slept in and came out to breakfast in her brunch coat. The first thing she saw was Hugh, dressed in casual slacks and reading the paper while Alison bustled about preparing breakfast. He was the only one facing her and glanced up smiling,

"'Morning, Jamie."

Jamie whirled about and fled to her room. She stood in the middle of it, all her senses in a perfect pandemonium of shock and fury. The rotten scheming beast! He must have come back last night knowing she would be out. Of course he knew Morris, having had dealings with him over the purchase of the painting for Sarah. He had not quibbled over the price and Morris would be eating out of his hand. She had not thought it necessary to acquaint her uncle and aunt with the peculiar problem at Fairlie Downs.

Marching into the shower Jamie turned on the cold tap in an effort to cool her raging temper. When she eventually arrived at the breakfast table she was wearing a pale turquoise tracksuit, giving at least the appearance of cool poise. Hugh rose and pulled out her chair.

"This was a surprise, eh, Jamie?" Morris was smiling at her. 'You should have told us you'd seen Hugh."

Hugh!

"I am surprised," said Jamie, picking up her glass of orange juice. "I can't imagine how he comes to be actually in this house."

Alison came forward with a fresh plate of toast and gave Hugh a big smile. "We couldn't leave your future brother-in-law out in the cold. When he told us that he was going to a Hotel we insisted he come here."

Well did Jamie see how he had wangled the invitation.

"Clever boy," she said, looking coolly at him over her glass.

119

Hugh had the grace to drop his gaze to his plate. He soon recovered and Jamie had ample opportunity to watch him at work. All his considerable charm was in full working order as he chatted easily bringing them all into the conversation. When Morris rose to leave he dropped a hand on to Hugh's shoulder,

"Jamie will see to your entertainment when you're through with your business. Feel free to do what you like."

He kissed his wife and Jamie and was off, having effectually hogtied his fuming niece.

"I hope you do have some business, Hugh. I shall be very busy this morning."

"So shall I, dear. I've got to go into town straight away but I hope you will be showing me that lovely pool later."

"Of course she will. We always go for a swim when Morris gets back about four… and don't worry about swimmers. We have extras laid on."

Did she have to drool over him? When Hugh rose, he insisted on helping with the breakfast things. Jamie could have choked. He never lifted a plate at Fairlie Downs. She was forced to stay for she dared not leave him alone with her aunt. Who knew what poisonous seeds he would sow in Alison's open mind?

While Hugh wiped and she put away, Jamie's brain was in overdrive. Should she grab her aunt and uncle at the first opportunity and put them wise? But what could she say? Hugh had not done anything objectionable yet and the tale of an old broken engagement would not ring a warning in the ears of those who had been the first witnesses to the happiness of the present one.

The phone broke into the turmoil of her thoughts and she went to answer it. The caller was Brooke with an invitation to lunch in town.

"Hang on a tick," Jamie was thinking fast. A scheme – a rather devilish one – was beginning to take shape. "I'd love to have lunch with you but I want it to be here. Will you come and spend the day with me?"

Brooke, who was at rather a loose end, agreed at once and Jamie danced off to her room, not deigning to leave it till she heard Hugh drive off.

Brooke drove in about ten looking smashing in a black and white turnout, her magnificent auburn hair loose in rich curls and waves down to her shoulders. That she was a trifle pale did not detract from her loveliness.

After a few pleasantries with her aunt who was preparing to get back to her sewing, Jamie swept the girl off to her room.

"I've got a job for you," she announced, gesturing her friend to the window seat and dropping down on to a floor cushion, "a rather ticklish one in public relationships."

"Sounds interesting," remarked Brooke disposing herself with habitual grace. "I feel like a bit of a lark."

Jamie laughed. "That's just what it could prove to be."

She thereupon set to and told the whole story from when Hugh had first walked into the gallery. The only bits she left out were the intimate details relating to Mark and herself. She ended with the climax that Hugh had actually inveigled himself into her home.

Brooke listened with keen interest, smiled a couple of times and, at the end, delivered her verdict on Hugh.

"I know the type well. A real womaniser. Not fit to wipe your Mark's shoes. Fancy deliberately setting out to break his brother's engagement. He needs taking down a peg or two, that one."

"How would you like the job?" asked Jamie.

Brooke looked at her for a moment and then threw back her head and laughed. "You schemer, you."

"It's dangerous, Brooke. He's terrifically handsome and has oodles of charm."

"That type always has. I've cut my teeth on 'em. What do you want me to do? Break his heart? It'll be a pleasure."

"If he's got a heart to break," said Jamie sceptically. "I'll be honest with you, my dear. I thought afterwards that it was not fair to invite you to Fairlie Downs until you had met Hugh and knew what you were in for."

"I appreciate that. You're suggesting a preliminary skirmish?"

Jamie giggled. "What I really want you to do at the moment is to draw Hugh's fire. I'm fairly sure that he's out to get me like he got Claudia but he can't resist a pretty woman. I had a grandstand seat of the way he shed Stella when he decided to try for me – not that I'd hold a candle to you," she added hastily.

"Don't be so modest. You can be enchanting when you smile that mischievous smile of yours and that windswept hairstyle makes you look as fresh as a breeze."

"That's as maybe," said Jamie practically, "but it doesn't add up to cover girl stuff. I'm looking to you to put me completely in the shade."

The girls had a good morning together, got lunch for themselves and Alison and then decided to sun themselves by the pool while they waited for the others. Jamie knew that it would take time for her model friend to prepare herself and waited with anticipation. Brooke had never been seen emerging from a swim with wet straggly locks. She braided her glorious hair and coiled the short braids in a crown on top of her head secured so that the wildest romp would not disturb the style. Jamie had thought her own white swimsuit was smart till she saw Brooke's white one-piece high cut to show her superb thighs and with a glittering border of jet jewel embroidery.

All Jamie said was 'Yummy!" and promptly changed into an old black suit.

"You'll look even better with me as a foil," she declared to Brooke's rueful protests.

They lounged by the pool chatting till they heard Hugh's car arrive. It was some time before he came strolling out in his borrowed swimmers with a towel around his neck.

"I'll bet he's been buttering up Aunt," said Jamie scornfully. "Now we'll see what he's made of."

She made Brooke move her chair till it had its back to the house and waved nonchalantly to Hugh as he approached them. Hugh returned her greeting and as he came closer Jamie rose. Brooke rose too and turned.

Jamie had an excellent view of Hugh pulling up short. He actually blinked before resuming his progress.

"Oh, Brooke, this is my future brother-in-law, Hugh Lawrence. Hugh, this is Brooke Tarrington. Well, I see we're all ready. Let's try the water."

She dived in. Brooke gave Hugh a lazy devastating smile and followed suit. The girls were halfway up the pool before Hugh recovered himself and joined them.

As she broke water, Brooke murmured in Jamie's ear, "I'm glad you warned me. He's a humdinger."

Jamie frisked around the pool and awaited events. It was not long before the other two were laughing and teasing each other. Brooke was like a sea sprite as she ducked and dived around him but Hugh was a match for her, pulling her under with him till she rose gasping to flee away from him .

Satisfied, Jamie left them to it. She had had her shower and was busy blow drying her hair when she saw the two of them coming back to the house, having some kind of tug of war over a towel.

Soon Brooke peeped into her room. She was showing a lovely colour and her honey brown eyes were snapping. Jamie waved her off to the shower as she worked for the windswept look. She would invite Brooke to stay for the remainder of Hugh's visit.

Eventually Brooke was back. She had brushed her hair out into its natural curl and now borrowed Jamie's dryer to finish it off. Her own eyes were full of mischief when Jamie stated her plans and she giggled her acceptance. When the girls were ready Jamie rose but Brooke pushed her back.

"Let him stew," she said and glanced out of the window. "Well, bless my soul."

"What?" Jamie went to the window.

Hugh was not stewing. He was back at the pool with Morris who had just come home. In a moment Alison joined them.

"Huh!" said Jamie.

"He'll keep," said Brooke.

Dinner was a gay affair that night. Brooke always sparkled in company and when the company admired her very much she was dazzling. Jamie's eyes almost ached with the splendour of her and she could see Hugh reacting despite himself. But he had not lost his wits by any means.

When the phone went later and Jamie jumped up he watched her covertly. She took the call in the hall out of earshot of the others. She let Mark talk for a few minutes wondering desperately how she could tell him that Hugh had had the hide to move in. Then an arm went around her waist and Hugh leaned close and said, "Hi, brother!"

Jamie pushed him roughly away. "Get out!" she hissed. Before Mark could say anything, she spoke, "Yes, it's that wretched brother of yours. Gate crashing as usual."

"Break it up, kid," Hugh spoke loud enough to be heard on the phone. "You know you've all made me very welcome. Quite a setup they've got here, haven't they, Mark?"

It was unbelievably cruel. The tears sprang to Jamie's eyes. She could not think how to reassure Mark and damn Hugh's eyes in one breath. Then a slender arm reached over and took the receiver from her.

"I'll hold it till you can pick it up upstairs," Brooke said and held Hugh's eyes with her own limpid gaze. "Let's give the lovers a chance."

Jamie flew upstairs and grabbed the receiver, "Right." There was an immediate click. "Thank heaven for Brooke," she cried as she threw herself into a chair.

"What the dickens was all that about?" came an uneven voice over the wires.

Jamie promptly poured her heart out, telling him of Hugh's clever ruse to get into the house and his ingratiating attitude to Morris and Alison. She was upset but it was not the wisest thing to do. Mark was already worried. Then she told him of her scheme to use her glamorous friend, Brooke, and the effect it was already having on Hugh.

"I suppose it will amuse him for a while," Mark said doubtfully.

"Darling, you haven't seen Brooke."

"He might hurt her."

"Brooke's grown a pretty thick skin where men are concerned and she's going into it with her eyes open. Oh, I wish you were here."

"I don't."

"You *don't?*"

"I never shine in the arena with Hugh. You know that."

"But – but it doesn't matter whether you shine or not. My eyes wouldn't be on Hugh. Mark, darling, didn't I live in the same house with him? He never turned my head once."

"He didn't have any cause to then."

Jamie could have wept with vexation. "Look, darling, I'm madly in love with you. I think of you all the time. The more Hugh tries to wreck our happiness, the more I despise him. Believe it, Mark."

"I will, sweetheart," but his voice lacked the ring Jamie wanted to hear. Why oh why was he so enervated where dealings with his brother were concerned? He went on to say that he wouldn't be ringing her the following night.

"Oh, why not?"

"I've got to go over to Seven Trees tomorrow and will take my turn with the cattle."

"But you mustn't stay out in the sun all day."

"I'll do the night shift. I've done it before."

"I see. You've got to fill Hugh's place, haven't you, while he fools around down here."

Mark just grunted. A yearning for him swept Jamie. Oh, to have his strong arms around her. "I don't know how I'm going to stand it till our wedding day,' she said forlornly.

"What? He's not staying down there till then, surely?" Mark's voice was ragged with anxiety.

Jamie's laugh had a touch of hysteria. "I mean stand being apart from you."

"That makes two of us."

When he rang off Jamie went along to her room and lay on the bed for a while. Already there was a faint shadow on their happiness. She felt a faint sense of pique and immediately shook it off. He was alone up there. If he'd just trust her. Then she remembered the pricking doubt about Claudia that had plagued her. She was as bad as Mark with her doubts and fears. One thing she was sure of: her aunt and uncle must be made aware of the true situation if only to stop them succumbing any further to Hugh's laid on charm. There was a tap on her door and Brooke came in.

"I'll have to be going, honey. I shan't stay for supper."

"You're not going at all." Jamie jumped up and grabbed her arm.

"Listen, Brooke. I want you to stay here till Hugh goes. Will you do that for me. I've got to avoid being alone with Hugh at any cost. Mark's upset as it is."

"Yes, of course I will if you think it will help. I'll have to get some clothes though."

"I'll lend you what you need for tonight – no – get Hugh to drive you back for them."

"He's pretty wary since the phone call."

"He'd need to be. Much more and I'll be gouging his eyes out."

"My, you have got it bad."

"You bet."

The girls went downstairs and found the others watching the television in the lounge. Hugh glanced up, took in Jamie's black looks and returned to the screen.

"Jamie's asked me to stay a few days," Brooke said to Alison, "so I'll just slip home for some clothes."

"I'll go with you for company," offered Jamie.

"I'll take you, Brooke," Hugh announced, rising to the occasion as they had hoped he would.

When they had driven off in Hugh's car, Jamie turned off the TV.

"Hey, what are you doing, girl? I was interested in that programme." Morris was peeved.

"Are you more interested in that then in my future happiness?"

"Your future happiness?" they echoed in unison.

"Yes." Jamie launched into the whole sorry tale. They were quite incredulous at first but Jamie went over the salient facts. On second hearing the breaking up of Mark's first engagement did seem pretty shabby and Jamie brought out her recorder and played it for them. Alison, still under Hugh's charm, took longer to grasp what he was doing but, at the end, Morris was fully convinced albeit he gave Jamie a shrewd glance.

"You led him on quite shamelessly, my dear."

"I wouldn't have needed to if he had been loyal to his brother," riposted Jamie. She then told them what he had done while she was on the phone, impressing on Mark how well he was ensconced in the family stronghold.

"That's a bit of cheek when you come of think of it," said Morris, frowning, "we really only welcomed him in for Mark's sake."

"Do you really think he would go so far as to prevent the wedding?" asked Alison anxiously, thinking of the half-made wedding dress.

"He's already stopped one," said Jamie grimly. "He knows now he can't charm me like he did Claudia but who knows what other spanner he might toss in the works?" She did not mention the faint shadow that was already evident between her and her fiancé.

"It's a pity you've got to use a nice girl like Brooke as a red herring," remarked Morris.

"Oh, she's a wake up to him. Thinks it's a bit of a lark."

"Well, all I hope is that she doesn't get her fingers burnt. He is such an attractive man," said Alison a trifle wistfully. She had been still wondering how Jamie had taken to Mark with Hugh around and now she had received this rude shock.

"They say snakes are attractive to their victims when they hypnotise them," said Jamie meaningly.

Alison laughed and shook herself as though shaking something off.

"Right," said Morris briskly. "We want your and Mark's happiness above all things. What do you want us to do?"

"Just be on your guard and don't under any circumstances let him think the wedding is so close."

"We don't even know ourselves how close it is,"

"Better you don't," said Jamie darkly. "then he can't surprise it out of you."

They waited supper till Hugh and Brooke got back. Evidently she had used the time well. They were engaged in a merry badinage even as they came into the lounge room. Everything seemed just the same but by the time they went to bed Hugh was conscious of a subtle change in the atmosphere that he could not quite put his finger on.

There followed an interesting two days as Hugh endeavoured to do a delicate balancing act. The Anderson-Smiths kept a very open house, always encouraging their guests to treat the place as their own.

There was plenty to do as other callers came and went, with Jamie putting on the charming hostess act to leave Alison free for her dress-making. During all the activity Hugh never lost sight of his original quarry.

His colossal conceit would not admit of his brother being anything other than a consolation prize somehow achieved by Jamie in a fit of pique; all of it aimed at him. Her present hostility meant nothing. He had encountered it before when engaged in defeating a rival and knew how to charm and dazzle till his victim had eyes for no one but himself.

He had always been stimulated by his passages with Jamie so the thought of conquering her was sweet and, in other circumstances, would have fully engrossed him. However, placed gracefully across his path by Jamie, was the most beautiful woman he had ever seen. While covertly booking her for the future, he had to deal with her in the present. He wanted to place her in a niche while concentrating on Jamie but Brooke was having none of it. She stuck to her friend's side, drawing his attention in a friendly merry way that was hamstringing him at every turn. Brooke did not use the age old feminine allurements. She was no flirt; her beauty was too dangerous for that. She just used her presence and Hugh found it hard to turn his eyes away.

He had to go into town a couple of times on the pretence of business in order to satisfy Alison's innocent query as to whether cattle business brought him down to the city very much. Using the time to think, he played with the thought that, rather than trying to charm Jamie away from his brother, it might be better to see if he could sow some seeds of distrust and misunderstanding and break up the relationship that way since Jamie showed no sign of warming to him. Driving back the second day with this thought still tentative in his mind, he was provoked into decision when he saw the girls sporting in the water. Yes, he would give his full attention to Brooke; it might even stir up some jealousy in his true quarry.

Morris was home and strolled down with him to the pool. Alison had stayed back to finish a ticklish bit of sewing and they heard her call to Jamie. The girl walked back to the house and Brooke caught up, seizing the chance of a council of war. Jamie looked at her friend curiously,

"How's it going?"

Brooke smiled. "I never thought I'd be thankful for my experiences but I am now. Downright grateful in fact. I can see through Hugh, right to the bottom of his mean little nature. He may look good but inside he's a small man."

Jamie gave vent to her frustration. "Well, I'm fed up with him. It's time we gave him the boot."

"Give him enough rope, honey. I'd like to see him hang himself."

When they got to the side terrace, Alison called from her room, "Visitor, Jamie."

"I wonder if it's Stella," remarked Jamie. "Come with me, Brooke, and meet her. She promised to look me up in a couple of weeks."

CHAPTER THIRTEEN

Enter Another Player

The girls walked into the front lounge still in their swimmers.

Standing near the window with one foot on the seat was a tall man in a brown safari suit in the act of changing his glasses. Jamie let out a shriek and threw herself across the room into the arms hastily held out to catch her.

The surprised Brooke watched them indulgently for a moment and was in the act of leaving when Jamie turned and called her back.

Brooke came forward and was introduced to the man who had no eyes for anyone but the girl in the circle of his arms. She was soon at her ease for Jamie promptly acquainted Mark with all their ploys up to date. He said little but his appreciative smile gave Brooke a little ache around her heart. Oh, that such a man had come her way.

"How did you manage to get here so soon?" Jamie was asking.

"A friend of ours flew in on business so I took the bull by the horns, flew out with him and caught a plane down here."

"What made you change your –" began Jamie and hesitated.

Brooke recognised her cue and excused herself. Back at the pool she took a leaf out of Alison's book.

"Where's Jamie?" Hugh asked suspiciously.

"Some visitor," she said nonchalantly and went to the diving board. Hugh, watching her graceful performance, forgot about Jamie temporarily.

In the meantime, Mark and Jamie were making up for lost time. In answer to her question he had replied that he couldn't stand being away from her, Hugh or no Hugh, and caught her in a fierce embrace. At the end of it Jamie pulled back and laughingly pointed to the wet patches on his suit. "I'd better change."

She took him upstairs and parked him in her bedroom while she grabbed some clothes and dashed for her shower. She returned fully dressed to find Mark studying the books in her bookcase.

"So you like adventure stories," he remarked as she got out her blow dryer.

"Oh, yes, you'll find I've got a masculine taste in books. I read everything Dad read."

"I wish I'd met him," observed Mark, watching her machinations with the dryer in some mystification. "Why don't you just let it dry?"

"Because I look just awful with it dead straight," she replied, thrilling to the delightful intimacy of having him watch her purely feminine activities. He moved closer to her as she sat on the bed. Jamie turned the dryer on his hair and, in the resulting scuffle, he took the dryer from her;

"Now you'll have to pay a forfeit to get it back."

"With pleasure," said Jamie. "How many thousand do you want?"

"How long can you stay down?" she asked when they had come to their senses again.

"I'm not quite sure," he said slowly, "but it will be at least till Hugh goes. He's needed at home more than I am at present. The books can wait. One thing about my charges. They can't run off into the bush."

When Mark recollected his suitcase, and went downstairs to fetch it, Jamie flew along to the bedroom Alison had given to Hugh. As Morris often entertained international visitors, his spacious home had all mod cons. Besides the rooms he, his wife and Jamie had, the two main guest rooms had ensuites. The other guest rooms had to share a communal bathroom. Jamie grabbed all Hugh's things and took them along to one of these, barely managing it before Mark returned. He showed no disposition to unpack his case while she was there. Jamie respected his shy reserve and did not press him. She suggested that they join the others.

Hugh was sporting with Brooke, lifting her clear of the water and then plunging under with her. Brooke was shrieking and laughing and, to all appearances, having a whale of a time.

When Hugh did happen to glance away, there was Mark standing at the edge, his arms enclosing Jamie in front of him. They both caught his look of chagrin before Morris hailed Mark.

Getting out of the pool, Jamie's uncle greeted her fiancé with a hearty handshake.

"Knew you two couldn't bear to be parted for long," he said jovially. "Great to see you again, Mark." He remained chatting with them for a while and then went off for his shower. Hugh dragged Brooke out of the pool and was following Morris when Jamie called cheerily after him,

"I've changed your room, Hugh, to one further along. You were using Mark's."

This brought Hugh up short in mind as well as body. He went on without looking back and eventually contemplated his stuff bundled on to the bed in an inferior room.

This was a greater slap than Jamie realised. Spoilt from childhood, accustomed to the first and the best in everything, this denigration was felt as a wound not only to his self esteem but to his whole person. He saw it as a prince would on being dealt with as a commoner. Yet there was an unconscious acknowledgement that the meanness in him had met its match by a meanness in Jamie as he searched for and found the bathroom.

As he showered, Hugh began, for the first time, to feel some apprehension regarding Jamie.

That night, at the meal table, they had an excellent view of Hugh at work. It was a duplicate of his behaviour at Fairlie Downs. On his mettle, he gained control of the conversation early and never lost it. He did not bore on about himself but drew everyone in including his brother to whom he appealed occasionally for corroboration on some fact he was giving. They all found themselves answering and participating in the lively give and take. That is, all except Mark who sat silently as usual except for the required assent now and then. Jamie made a solemn vow to herself that, if she had to live in a tent, she would not share a meal table with Hugh. Something just had to be done.

As they moved to the lounge for coffee, Mark whispered in her ear, suggesting a drive. Jamie blithely announced this as they finished their drinks. Hugh, although still smarting over the removal of his clothes, made a determined attempt to keep Mark in the shadows.

"Great. What about it, Brooke? We'll make up a party and go up to Mt Cootha."

"Let Jamie and Mark go off on their own, Hugh," Morris said sharply. "He's just got down here."

Seeing the darkening of Hugh's countenance, Brooke sprang up.

"I'd like to go to Mt. Cootha," she said brightly, catching Hugh's hand and pulling him up.

Hugh had perforce to respond with what grace he could muster while Mark and Jamie slipped off in her car. During this precious evening she conceived a furtherance of her plan. She was not going to sit by and watch Mark being tortured.

Accordingly, when Hugh came to breakfast next morning neither Jamie's nor Mark's place had been set. He queried this rather petulantly.

"Oh, they've gone," said Alison carelessly. "Jamie wants Mark to meet some of her relatives and they will be staying over."

Brooke, arriving late and luscious, for breakfast, also seemed to be in the know.

"I'll be getting along too, Alison. It's been a delightful visit, just the break I needed. Quite delightful," she repeated in her pretty way, smiling at Hugh. "Jamie has suggested that I come up to Fairlie Downs later on for a visit when she is married."

"There's no need to wait for that; goodness knows when it will happen," Hugh said deliberately. "I issue my own invitations. Come whenever you like. In fact, you can come back with me."

This was going too fast for Brooke who was committed to throwing her weight when and where Jamie wanted it.

"I'd love to do just that," she said slowly, "but I have some modelling assignments coming up. Perhaps the next time Jamie visits you I'll come with her."

Having cleverly given Hugh the impression that the engagement would be of some duration, she addressed herself to her dry toast and coffee, one of the less happy side effects of her career.

"So the party's breaking up," said Morris, slapping plenty of Alison's home made orange marmalade on to his second slice of toast. He looked deliberately and expectantly at his remaining guest.

There was no help for it. As gracefully as he could Hugh declared that he must be getting home too. He added frowningly that he had better be the one to pick up his responsibilities.

"There was no need for Mark to drop his bundle like this. We generally work our trips away separately."

This final subtle attempt to discredit Mark fell on totally barren soil. Nobody even bothered to answer him.

He and Brooke were both gone by ten and Alison gleefully rang Aunt Miriam who informed her with all the imperiousness of an old lady that, now she had the two of them, they could actually stay for one night at least. It was just lovely having young things about her again. Mark and Jamie did their penance.

When they were leaving on the following day, she told them rather tartly that she hoped they would be a bit over each other next time she saw them. A more lovesick pair she had never seen. Anyone would think they were Siamese twins.

"Aren't Siamese twins always of the same sex?" asked Mark in all good faith and received a rap over the knuckles with a knitting needle.

"That's enough of your cheek, young man, and don't go giving me that smile of yours. My heart's quite happy where it is."

When the unrepentant pair drove off, Mark looked across at Jamie, "I really love Aunt Miriam."

"Umm. She never really forgave Dad for not letting her bring me up. She was my mother's favourite aunt."

"Well, your Dad made a pretty good job of you. I can see he brought you up to be a fighter."

Jamie thought over these words.

"Mark," she said presently. "Wouldn't you put up a real fight for anything, especially anything you really valued?"

"There are different ways of fighting. I take it that you are thinking of Hugh. The way to fight him is not by direct confrontation."

"How do you know if you've never really tried it?"

"I did. When I first saw what Hugh was doing to Claudia. I swallowed my pride and asked him to lay off her. He just said that if he could take any girl off me she wasn't worth bothering about."

Jamie all but ground her teeth. That would not have been the way she would have tackled Hugh. The thing to do was to sweep Claudia out of his reach just like she had done with Mark yesterday. They had not gone many kilometres before she had mapped out a plan whereby Mark could have outwitted his brother. At that point she suddenly came to herself and smartly washed her hands of past history.

Jamie had persuaded Mark to stay over Sunday although his conscience was troubling him. There was a visiting preacher and she wanted Mark to hear him although she was soon to regret this.

The preacher was Dr Edmund Tracey, a Minister of some renown who had been a qualified psychiatrist before he had decided to move on to illnesses of the spirit. He took his address from the Sermon on the Mount, entitling it 'Winning by Losing'.

He shocked his hearers upright by saying that Christians were a lousy lot of fighters and deserved to lose most times. It was of God's mercy that some of them actually fell over the finishing line ahead of their enemies.

Then he went into an in depth analysis of the great Sermon and Jamie seriously considered feigning illness and getting Mark to take her home.

"How many of you," he asked the now keenly interested congregation, "really turn the other cheek when one is struck? Oh, you may not actually strike back but the content of your prayers is that God should do so on your behalf.

"How many of you give your cloak when your coat is taken? Even if you have released the coat the tug of war is still going on. Why did Jesus not put it in reverse and say that if your cloak is taken then give your coat also? This would have made sense to his hearers. The cloak was often the only covering a man had to keep himself warm at night and, once it was taken, then the coat may as well go too for the owner would be without protection anyway. But Jesus actually said that if the lesser was taken then give the greater also, if you want to fight your battles according to correct Christian ethics."

Jamie glanced apprehensively at Mark. His eyes were steadily fixed on the speaker whose magnetism was enough to hold the attention of his listeners without the content of his words.

If Mark had not been there Jamie could have taken an unbiased interest in his proposition.

It appeared that if you retaliated you fought under the rules of the world and spiritual help would not be available. If you appeared to behave like a mad man and used rules directly opposite from those in use in everyday life, then spiritual help did become available. Even then victory did not always appear to be won. The Christian might even be commiserated with as a loser yet, according to the speaker, the very heavens would be ringing with the trumpet calls of victory.

In that hidden deep spiritual world there were forces undreamed of by the rest of humanity, massive forces working towards the final triumph that brought the forces of evil under subjection. The apparent losses of the Christian were often the catalyst of final victory.

Dr Tracey then gave a demonstration from Watchman Nee's writings. One day some of the converted Chinese who worked in a communal rice field, came to him complaining about their neighbour one step down on the crowded terrace. This neighbour had quietly opened the gates and allowed their precious allocation of water to seep down into his patch. What was the Christian answer?

"Let him do it and then water your own again."

They did so and came back, complaining that they still had no joy and no victory.

"Then water his first and then water your own."

They went away profoundly puzzled but faithfully followed the instructions. They returned next day jubilant. Yes, this was victory for they had the joy of the Lord.

Jamie gave an audible sniff. Dr Tracey glanced her way. He could not pinpoint the sniffer to Jamie's embarrassed relief but he said with a chuckle,

"I've had my sniffing days, too, but that's not the end of the story. The neighbour was so amazed by this totally unprecedented act of generosity that he came enquiring as to what could cause anyone to do such a crazy thing. His enquiries eventually led to his being converted to Christ."

"The reward of losing? One soul. To the world the Christians often appear as weak doormats. To the heavenly Father they were about His work. Try it next time."

When they rose for the final hymn, Jamie thought bitterly: He's just about negated my entire campaign. Does he mean that Mark should let Hugh walk off with me? *Well, I wouldn't go anyway.*

When they reached the door, Jamie was all for slipping past the Minister in the crowd, not wishing to shake hands with such a radical but Mark held her back and shook hands warmly.

"I've been trying to follow that principle most of my life but I'm not sure that I've really got the hang of it."

"Keep trying. If you really want to succeed you will."

Dr Tracey then turned to take Jamie's flaccid hand and received a cool non-committal nod. His bright brown eyes summed her up with a twinkle.

"I fancy we have a sniffer here. Don't you trust Jesus?"

"Of course," Jamie mumbled, going red.

"Well, just remember they are His rules, my dear, and He is Captain of the Lord's hosts. Rather a formidable General."

These words rang in Jamie's ears as they went to her car. A formidable General. Oh, if only He would fight on their behalf and bring down the Jericho wall of Hugh's arrogance and jealousy. She just could not go along with the Minister's precepts. She wanted to see Hugh outsmarted, beaten at his own game; not to lie down and let him walk all over them.

In the car she watched Mark, trying to think of a line of approach with him. At last she asked,

"If you go along with that, Mark, does it mean that we will be under Hugh's thumb for the rest of our lives?"

Mark smiled. "If it meant winning Hugh to Christ, would you be willing?"

Jamie sat up straight. "Dr Tracey spoke of winning battles – not a lifetime of hell," she said flatly. She tried another approach. "If Hugh makes a real play for me, are you willing to give me up?"

His lips tightened. "Only if you were willing to go."

"Mark!" It was a cry of pain.

"Can't you see, Jamie? I wouldn't want you if Hugh could take you."

"But you still wanted Claudia."

"No, I didn't."

"Yes, you did. You said she was a nice girl. I think you still love her a bit."

"Nonsense."

"You said you looked at her children thinking they could have been yours." Jamie was weeping now.

Mark turned into a quiet side street and stopped the car. He unclipped their seatbelts and took her protesting form in his arms but she would not listen to his assurances.

"If Claudia had come back to you then you would have taken her back," she cried into his shoulder.

"She did come back."

Jamie raised her head and stared at him through tear-spiked lashes.

"Hugh threw her over as soon as she broke our engagement and she came running back to me."

"How cheap! What did you say?"

"Nothing."

"Nothing? Didn't you tell her off."

"That's not my way. But nothing would make me take Hugh's leavings. The magic had gone."

"Oh, Mark," Jamie threw her arms around his neck, Claudia's ghost slain for good.

"Now supposing we stop crossing our bridges before we come to them. Darling, what you and I have going for each other is beyond price. We have each other and Christ too. I hate all this pettiness. I'd like – well – to stand above it somehow. I believe this principle works. When I lost Claudia, I read a verse in the Bible about trusting in the Lord and He would give me the desires of my heart. I tried desperately to believe it despite what had happened. Faith in that verse enabled me to go on living with Hugh in amity when I longed to get out… sell my share and make my own way. If I had I would not have met you and you, Jamie, are my heart's desire in a way Claudia never was."

"Oh," said Jamie. "If only I'd had my recorder with me. I could listen to that speech a hundred times."

Mark laughed and held her chin up with one hand. "Okay?"

"Let me see your eyes?"

He removed his dark glasses and Jamie looked into the serene depths.

"Okay," she said.

CHAPTER FOURTEEN

Fun and Games

When they entered the house, Morris informed them that Hugh had rung twice for Mark. Even as he spoke the phone rang again and Morris told Mark to pick it up.

Jamie looked sceptical. "I'll bet it's some grand excuse to get Mark home again and away from me." She dropped her bag and Bible on a chair and went through to help her aunt with lunch.

Mark was some time on the phone and when he came through to the dining room, Jamie called out:

"How soon do you have to leave? In twenty minutes? You'll just have time for a snack. No roast chooky for you."

Mark came into the kitchen and filled a glass of water at the sink. Then, like lightening, he turned on Jamie and held her with one hand against the fridge. Holding the glass high he proceeded to drip the water on to her head. It ended in a free for all and Alison scuttled out of the kitchen and plumped down in a chair near Morris.

"What it is to have a pair of lovers in the house!" she exclaimed.

By the time Jamie had promised him chicken for breakfast, lunch and dinner and thrown in supper for good measure, Alison judged it safe to return and was amazed at the way a glass of water had spread itself. After they had cleaned up, the meal was served to the accompaniment of much high spirits. Alison decided once and for all that Mark was a darling with hitherto unsuspected depths of fun in him. Yes, he was well worthy of their beloved Jamie.

During the dessert, which was a delectable mango trifle, Mark finally admitted that Jamie was right. Hugh did want him home as soon as possible. "It's quite genuine. There's a problem with some cattle we're sending to auction. That's my department." He smiled into Jamie's downcast eyes. "I would have to go home in any case just once more before our wedding for I want to take time for our honeymoon."

Jamie nodded bravely. "Only a few days now."

"Only a few days!" cried Alison. "Jamie, you wretch, and here I am taking my time and enjoying my sewing."

"Just what is the date?" demanded Morris in his turn.

The lovers looked sheepishly at each other.

"Tomorrow week," Mark said and they could hear the exultant note in his voice.

They got him on the plane on Monday morning. He had rung through for a charter flight to take him out to Fairlie Downs. After they had seen him off, Alison grasped her niece by the shoulders.

"Now, young woman, hop to it."

And hop to it, Jamie did. Her girlfriends gave her a hasty shower mainly for her trousseau for they did not know what to buy for her station life. She stood nobly still while Alison fitted her, offered to do all the housework and spent the rest of her time out in the big garage giving her father's caravan a thorough cleaning.

They had had many ideas about their honeymoon, not being able to decide till Jamie thought of the caravan. She had not used it herself since her father had died but Morris and Alison had taken it a couple of times on their own holidays. Mark had rather fancied the idea of being their own boss so now it was being all shined up and outfitted once again. When she had made her final check, she passed a hand that trembled slightly over the teak woodwork. "Only with Mark, Daddy," she whispered. "Only with Mark."

Mark rang her when he could, often very late at night, and they spent ages on the phone. Morris remarked teasingly that he was glad Mark was paying the bill. Alison reminded him that when he had had a trip to the States during their courtship, he had burned the wires ringing her.

"Oh, well, lovers will be lovers," he excused himself, retiring behind his listings for his next Art Show.

On Thursday Jamie had a visit from her friend Helen who had taken her to the evangelistic meeting where she had given her heart to the Lord. Helen had been feeling guilty over neglecting Jamie while in the throes of the first rapturous months of her marriage and had been unable to come to the shower. Helen came prepared to spend time with her friend. She had read of the engagement and had a burden about it which vanished when Jamie told her that Mark had been a Christian for many years, even if a hidden one.

"Oh, that will change now," she said delightedly. "Jamie, how glad I am. You know, Christians should only marry Christians."

No, Jamie did not know and read the relevant verses pointed out to her with interest. "Of course, I didn't know he was a Christian when I fell in love with him but, when I was praying about it and wondering if the Lord would give Mark to me as a husband, I had a real peace in my heart."

Helen nodded vigorously. "That's as it should be. I'm so looking forward to meeting him. When will he be down again?"

"Just in time for the wedding."

"The wedding? Jamie, *when is the wedding?*"

"Monday," said Jamie guiltily.

Helen looked amazed and hurt. There was no help for it.

"Now, look, Helen, what I am going to tell you is in the strictest confidence."

"Of course." Helen settled herself comfortably.

Jamie launched into the tale once again, feeling this time that she was telling someone who could help her with the spiritual values involved. When she had finished, Helen sat for some time in silence and then she looked sympathetically across at her protégé.

"Rather a deep pool to be flung into so early in your Christian walk," she said. "The Sermon on the Mount isn't for kindergartners."

"Helen, do you go along with this principle of turning the other cheek?"

"Yes, but it is a costly road. It takes great strength to live that kind of life."

"Strength? I think it's – it's –" she floundered, not wanting to voice the unwelcome thought that it displayed weakness in Mark.

"Jamie, don't confuse meekness with weakness. Our Lord referred to Himself as meek and lowly in heart. Do you think He was a weakling?"

"Oh, no, but – but that minister spoke of Jesus as Captain of the Lord's host, a formidable General."

"Then can't you see that if He chose to be meek that it must have been a mighty meekness? I wish I'd heard that sermon. You must have a wise Pastor."

"It wasn't our regular one. A Dr Tracey – it said in the bulletin."

"Not Edmund Tracey? You were indeed fortunate."

Jamie was silent for a moment. Then she asked abruptly,

"Do you think Mark is paranoid about wanting to keep our wedding day a secret?"

"No, from what you've told me he is trying to look after his personal interests and yours. It's his brother who is paranoid. He is making a normal situation abnormal. I'd say this Hugh is a selfish and immature man. Your Mark simply towers above him in character."

This pleased Jamie so much that she issued an invitation to Helen and her husband. All this had to be explained to Mark together with a petition for Brooke. Mark laughed and assented, "provided you don't think more about wedding doings than about me."

Saturday brought another couple to her doorstep. Jamie took one look at Stella and grabbed her in a huge embrace. Stella had heard of the engagement and wanted to know ALL ABOUT IT. Jamie was a dark horse if ever there was one. She had in tow young Geoff Rossitor but pulled Jamie aside and whispered,

"Don't go getting ideas. He just won't leave me alone. Reckoned he had business in Brisbane."

"Did he now," said Jamie and winked roguishly at Geoff who returned the salute.

"And are you going to have a big country wedding, Jamie? They are really something."

Once more Jamie was on thin ice.

"Well, no," she said casually. "Mark said we can have a big do afterwards up there but we – we'll be married here from my uncle's house."

"Well, let's know in plenty of time," said Stella comfortably. "That's one wedding I'm not going to miss."

"Me neither," agreed Geoff who felt he owed Jamie a lot.

Alison glanced knowingly at Jamie who rather helplessly returned the look.

Stella sat up. "What gives?" she demanded.

"You'll have to promise me in blood that you won't tell a soul," demanded Jamie, knowing they both had open lines to the west.

"Right. We'll cut our fingers," promised Geoff pulling out a pocket knife.

"Do you promise?"

"Stop fooling, Geoff. Yes, Jamie dear, we promise," assured Stella realising that Jamie was deadly serious.

"In blood anytime you like," vowed the irrepressible Geoff.

"Shut up. Well, when is the wedding?"

"Day after tomorrow."

Stella squealed and they would have made mincemeat of her only that Alison interposed.

"Leave the poor girl alone or there will be nothing left for Mark to marry. I guess they've got their reasons."

"Jamie, do you mean that no one – *no one* – out west knows?" asked Stella awed.

"No," said Jamie flatly. "Time for me fine Hughie to find out when he can't do anything about it."

Of course, Stella had heard various versions of Mark's broken engagement so she wisely did not pursue the matter. She only wished she could be a fly on the wall when Hugh did find out. Getting his comeuppance for once. She and Geoff went away secure in their invitation.

That night Mark listened with some resignation to her explanation and agreed that there was no help for it and they were very welcome but his dream of slipping away on their own was beginning to fade. Still it was wonderful to have such friends.

That night Jamie prayed very hard that nothing would prevent Mark getting away. He had had to take Mrs Howard into his confidence. They were all supposed to go over to Seven Trees on Sunday for some old friends were calling. The housekeeper simply said that Mark would drive her over later as she had things to do: the things being a complete packing for Mark's honeymoon which she did with mischievous enjoyment, thrilled to death with it all, and keeping an eye out for the plane Mark had chartered. She had it all planned that she would drive over when Mark had gone and give only the vaguest answers when queries were made as to his whereabouts.

Mark had always been her favourite and she would play out this little drama to the hilt.

On Sunday Jamie was neither to hold nor to bind. She barely managed to sit through church, then rushed home to drive Alison mad going over and over the arrangements for the next day.

The connection was late but by nine that night Jamie had Mark safe in her arms at the airport.

"Oh, darling," she whispered, "I've been praying and praying that nothing would prevent you."

"I needed your prayers," he said a little grimly. "Heaven and hell seemed to be combining to stop me."

"Oh, not Heaven, Mark," cried Jamie shocked.

He grinned and kissed her again. "I stand corrected. The skies and hell. We had bad weather getting out of Fairlie and then we had engine trouble on the Brisbane flight and nearly had to turn back."

"Oh, darling." Jamie clutched him to her. 'I wish you didn't have to fly."

"Now, don't let old fears worry you. I was safe in your prayers, wasn't I?"

As they drove home Jamie had one more confession. "Oh, Mark, darling, I felt I just had to invite –"

"Oh, no," Mark groaned aloud. "We'll be having a full scale reception at this rate. Who is it this time?"

"Aunt Miriam," said Jamie and went off into a gale of giggles.

"Aunt Miriam? But she was invited wasn't she?"

"That's the funny part," said Jamie when she could. "She was so close we really didn't see her. She rang up to invite me over on Monday to see some things she has for me, and Alison and I nearly fell apart. We had a simply terrible time trying to tell her that the wedding was on Monday and that we had not forgotten her. She really told us off."

"She's coming though, isn't she?"

"Umm. Says she's only coming because she wants to see her boy again. That smile of yours knocked her for six, she reckons."

"As long as it knocks you for six I'm happy, sweetheart."

"It did and it does and it will," yawned Jamie. "We've strict instructions not to linger over supper tonight. This early wedding you want means an early night tonight."

"Enjoy it," said Mark as they turned into the driveway. "It's the last one you'll be getting for a while."

Mark found that they were organised within an inch of their lives by Alison who was, if anything, more excited than they were. After a quick supper they were separated and sent off to bed.

Sleep did not come quickly to Jamie. Their wedding day was about to dawn and nothing had happened to mar it. Yet she was troubled a little by the secrecy. Some people were bound to think they were callous in their cavalier treatment of Mark's nearest and dearest. There could be hurt feelings and some unpleasant reaction on Hugh's part. Jamie finally pushed these awkward thoughts aside. Like so many young people in love, she decided that the important thing was to get married. They would deal with all the other problems afterwards. She finally fell asleep in the midst of her prayers and her sleep was sweet with her maiden dreams.

CHAPTER FIFTEEN

Victory

Morris was the prosaic herald of her wedding day holding the door open while Alison brought in her breakfast tray. While she ate, he informed her that he had to get back to his charge who was champing at the bit and she had to stay out of sight till he got Mark off the premises. Observing her picking at her bacon and scrambled eggs, a favourite meal, he announced that Mark had hoed into his and then vanished.

"Mark never shows any nerves," commented Jamie. She ate what she could and then headed for the shower. Alison held her armful of delicate embroidered voile while Jamie put on the satin slip and voiced a wistful thought.

"Would you have preferred a real bridesmaid, darling? One of your girlfriends?"

"No and no and no," said Jamie, managing to kiss her amidst the froth of material. "Apart from Mark, you two are the closest people in the world to me."

Alison gave a satisfied nod and put the dress over her head.

Mindful of the fact that Jamie would be spending much of her life out west, they had chosen a simple ballerina style with shoestring straps and a tiny bolero to cover her shoulders.

Jamie had refused a veil, announcing that Mark had a right to know what he was getting... not like poor Jacob, whose story she had read recently. Her hair brushed out and caught at the side with a cluster of roses and stephanotis, a small white Bible that Mark had given her in her hand and she was ready.

"You look... you look like a summer breeze – if one could see it," announced Alison. "Now I must rush and get ready or Mark won't be getting his early wedding."

They used Jamie's little car and Alison drove it while Jamie sat in the back in state. They did not want a chauffeur much to Morris's horror who said he had never heard of the shenanigans that went on for this wedding.

"Mark looks splendid," Alison remarked as she drove. 'I've never seen him in a full suit before."

"A full suit?" echoed Jamie in disappointment. She wanted her westerner in his safari suit.

"You wait and see, Miss," advised her Matron of Honour.

Morris was waiting at the church door in a dark metal blue suit and a light blue tie, his usual business attire, so Jamie knew just how Mark would look.

Oh, I do hope I like it, she thought as Alison fussed about her. She peeped in to see the entire congregation occupying the second front row with Mark sitting in dignified solitude in the first one.

When she was ready the organist was given his cue and Jamie began walking slowly up the aisle on Morris's arm to the traditional strains of Lohengrin. The congregation rose and a tall distinguished looking man stepped into the aisle and held out his arms.

Jamie took one look, Oh, he can hold his own anywhere, she thought and would have taken off but for Morris's tightening grip on her elbow. Even then it was the fastest bridal walk anyone had ever seen. They battled it out till Jamie reached Mark. Morris thankfully released her, said his piece and then skipped around to support the bridegroom for the rest of the service, all in a cold sweat.

They had chosen the full wedding service and the listeners were intrigued to hear the quiet voiced Minister suddenly loudly ask Mark WILLIAM to take James ELIZABETH to be his lawful wedded wife and James ELIZABETH to take Mark WILLIAM to be her lawful wedded husband.

Mark never took his eyes off Jamie's face throughout, the Minister having to push Jamie's ring into his hand during the exchange of rings. During the prayer, some people peeped to see if he would shut his eyes but they never told what they saw because they had no business looking anyway.

The kiss was the piéce de resistance. Not for Mark any dutiful salute with promise of more later. It was his own longed for wedding and he was untrammelled by any traditions. He took Jamie by the shoulders, gazed deeply into her eyes for a moment and then enfolded her in a long hard embrace. Aunt Miriam sighed gustily, Brooke sighed softly and the rest of the congregation prepared to wait it out.

"Now where," queried Geoff Rossitor in some astonishment, "did stay-at-home Mark learn his technique?"

"Obviously from a master," said Stella soulfully.

"You'll keep," Geoff said taking her hand in a grip she would not get out of in a hurry.

They waited patiently while the bridal party went into the vestry to sign the register and on its emergence were struck by two things: the triumphant smile on Jamie's face and the blinding happiness on Mark's.

Morris had chosen well for the wedding breakfast. It was a restaurant on the river's edge and the spread was served on the balcony. They just about had the whole place to themselves and made enough noise to account for a crowd.

Mark made the shortest speech on record by saying that on behalf of his wife and himself (loud cheers) he thanked everyone, and then sat down, colouring up even with this brief effort. He was hauled up again to propose the traditional toast to her attendant and forgot her name. They all supplied it as they rose and drank to Alison who was dissolving into laughter. "Never was there such a wedding," she declared.

To Alison's amazement Jamie had not wanted the traditional cake but the restaurant chef came up with an icecream one, which was much appreciated as the day was growing hot.

"First time I've had icecream for breakfast," remarked Helen to her husband as she beamed fondly on the newlyweds.

"Well, don't go giving Junior any ideas," he said, smiling, as he patted her swelling tummy.

The company was so congenial that the guests were inclined to linger and Mark was well content. He had Jamie now and was at peace.

When they did finally go they were showered, not with rice or confetti (the restaurant mindful of the clean-up afterwards) but with thousands of tiny bubbles supplied in miniature bottles. Jamie laughed in delight as they got into Morris's big car which they would be using to pull the caravan.

They drove straight back home and in an hour were away, Mark driving cautiously for a while as he had never pulled a big caravan before. As Jamie relaxed beside him, he remarked,

"I think I'll have to put this drive at the top of the list. That first drive I didn't own you. This one I do."

"Do you now?" challenged Jamie.

"Yep. You'll find me a real old-fashioned husband."

"What if I'm not a real old-fashioned wife?"

"Then I'll teach you to be… according to the Bible."

"Aren't you the clever one?"

"Yep."

"Did you know that according to the Bible a real old-fashioned husband is to love his wife as Christ loves the church?"

"No, but I'll do my very best."

"Then you won't have any trouble making me a real old-fashioned wife."

They dawdled along the way, picnicking for lunch, all the time heading inland to a small caravan park beside a pretty creek that Jamie knew of, finally arriving when the evening shadows were closing in. The perfect cloudless day had yielded to a perfect moonlit night. After they had eaten, the lovers were beguiled into a stroll along the creek. As they wandered along the bank hand in hand Mark gazed around him. From where they stood they could see no sign of human life as they were hidden from the park; nothing but the soft sounds of the bush about them, the moonlight silvering everything.

"It must have been like this in Eden," he said breathing deeply. "Just the two of them on the unsullied earth, nothing to do but tend a beautiful garden."

"Oh, yes," said Jamie entering into his mood. "All the food supplied, the animals harmless as pets, the same moon, *the very same moon,* looking down on them as on us. What a pity they had to mess it up!"

Mark nodded. "One act of disobedience and Adam found himself digging weeds - and they have been multiplying ever since."

Jamie laughed. "Well, everything was told to be fruitful and multiply, wasn't it?' she asked mischievously.

"Well, that command was never rescinded," said Mark thoughtfully. "It still stands today – or rather tonight."

With one accord the two turned and, arms around each other, directed their steps purposefully towards the van.

When Adam tentatively took his lovely virgin bride into his arms to experience for the first time with her one of the great joys of mankind, it was no more precious to them than was Mark and Jamie's hour.

And that same shining moon witnessed both.

CHAPTER SIXTEEN

Honeymoon Bliss and Brickbats

Meanwhile Alison stood near the phone table studying a sheet of paper in her hand. There had been a lot of discussion as to how to let Mark's family know. Telegrams were now out, a letter would take too long, and Mark felt it was wrong to put the burden of explanation on to others.

They had finally decided to put the great news in the form of a telegram and have it read over the phone. Alison had undertaken to do this as she had a sneaking ambition to see how Hugh took the fact that this quiet brother had beaten him to the post.

By way of practice she rang Seven Trees first and fortunately got Ashley. Announcing in an impersonal voice that she had a telegram for him she read it out slowly:

MARRIED TODAY stop OVER THE MOON stop BE BACK IN A FORTNIGHT stop LOVE TO ALL stop MARK AND JAMIE LAWRENCE.

There was a gasp and then a delighted chuckle. "The old son-of-a-gun. So he's done it. Well done, Mark. Would you read it again, please so I can write it down? This'll knock Sarah for six."

Much encouraged, Alison did so, and then gave Ashley a few more details. During the whole conversation it was borne in on her that Ashley was not so much wishing them happy as getting a huge kick out of the situation. Apparently he was one who was glad to see the old tradition smashed at last. Alison had not yet grasped the fact that Ashley had lived most of his life in the shadow of a more dominant sibling

Fortified by this reaction Alison then rang Fairlie Downs. Hugh happened to pick up the phone. Alison went through the same procedure with this difference. There was silence and then a sarcastic laugh.

"I don't know who is perpetrating this joke but they've forgotten that you have to give a month's notice to marry."

Alison felt her hackles rise.

"It's Alison, Hugh. and it's no joke. Mark and Jamie put the notice in the first time he came down, exactly a month ago."

There was that aggravating silence and then a voice, thick with molten anger:

"We can thank that husband-hungry niece of yours for this."

"*Hugh.* It takes two to tango and –"

"Rot. My brother would never do this to me on his own. That Jamie is one smart cookie but if she thinks she's going to lord it up here she's got another think coming. Good bye.'

He put the phone down but before the cradle shut it off, Alison heard the muttered words: "That damned bitch!"

She stood there trembling. The beast! The rotten beast! With shaking fingers she dialled Morris at the Gallery.

Mr and Mrs Lawrence drifted steadily south, avoiding all the famous spots and finding nooks in less popular places.

They crossed the border and eventually reached the Hawkesbury River where Jamie introduced her husband to the houseboats. Mark promptly hired one and they deserted their travelling home for a delightful few days on the river. He was rather amazed that they had been so easily entrusted with the vessel after a minimum of instruction but he found he had no trouble. They were in a blissful world of their own. Jamie cooked the few fish he caught and bossed the boat while he steered it. They were blessed with glorious weather and lay under the stars at night, dragging out their mattress on to the open deck.

Halfway through one night Jamie remarked that it was wonderful to be able to make love all over the place.

"It was wonderful in our caravan under the whispering trees and it's wonderful here under the great night skies. Just think… on top of a high mountain –"

"Not in the Snowies. We'd freeze to death in the open," said Mark sleepily.

"Stupid. We'd be in a log cabin with a glorious fire going and a lovely big doona to cuddle under."

"For Pete's sake what's a doona?"

"That's a modern word for eiderdown. Or –" added Jamie, zestfully pursuing her romantic thought, "in a tropical rainforest –"

"We'd be eaten alive by mossies."

"No, we'd just use repellent."

"*All* over us?"

"More or less."

"I can imagine it," remarked Mark dreamily. "I'm about to make passionate love to you and – 'just a sec, dear, there's a mosquito' ..."

Jamie's hearty laugh rang out across the quiet waters and scared the life out of a lone fisherman around the bend.

"We could also make love in the desert with the balmy breezes blowing through the tent and –"

"Any breeze that blows off the Simpson is bitterly cold at night."

"How would you know?"

"Spent a couple of nights there in my wild salad days."

Jamie smiled up at the blazing stars. Anyone less likely to have wild salad days she couldn't imagine.

"I trust not with a woman," she said naughtily.

"Most certainly not," rebuked Mark. "You shock me, young woman."

"I'm glad," said his unrepentant wife. "One of the nicest things on God's earth today must be a shockable man."

After having had their fill of life on the river, they did not journey much further south as they wanted a leisurely trip back.

The return drive inevitably invoked thoughts of the future. These began happily enough with plans for their future family. Jamie first opted for a pigeon pair, then three boys and three girls, then four boys and two girls – announcing that extra boys would be needed on the station. Mark said nothing.

They were sitting on the bank of a stream or rather Jamie was sitting with Mark lying behind her, curled around her body as she sketched the farm buildings on the other side. Her pencil poised as she became aware of his silence, Jamie turned anxiously to him,

"Surely you want children, Mark."

"Surely."

"Well, why don't you say something?"

"You haven't come up with my idea yet."

"My goodness, don't tell me you want an even dozen."

Mark shook his head, smiling.

Jamie put down her pencil and leaned over him.

"Okay, shock me."

"I don't care how many we have or what sex as long as –"

He paused and, wondering, Jamie held her breath.

"I'd like a little daughter named William."

Jamie let out her breath slowly. "But, darling, you know the trouble I've had with my name… always having to explain, even spelling it sometimes."

Mark said nothing.

"It was only because Dad never had a son. I've always found it awkward."

Mark said nothing.

Jamie sat up properly and shook him.

"Now you just state your reasons, Mister Lawrence."

"I haven't any. I just like it. You've had a lot of fun with your name. I haven't had any with mine."

"Well, I'll think about it. It's too early to promise. We've got to start our family first."

"Well, haven't I been doing my best? I must have unloaded thousands of potential –"

Jamie threw back her head and guffawed. "You have, you have," she said delightedly. 'You've been magnificent. You're a copybook lover."

"Seeing I know what I know about your body, how would you know?"

'Now that's a tricky sentence. You pulled it off very well. I got hold of a book and boned up about it all."

"You might have told me. I could have done with some –"

"No, no. Don't you read a single word. You're a natural. It would only make you self-conscious. I love you exactly as you are."

This naturally called for a few minutes' refreshment but when she would have returned to her sketching, Mark held her.

"A little daughter called William?"

Jamie pulled his dark glasses away and looked into his eager blue eyes, soft with the love light.

"A little daughter called William," she agreed gently and solemnly sealed the pact.

That same evening Morris was watching television when Alison came in and dropped into a chair beside him.

"This business of their living in the same house as Hugh when he's such a nark, worries me. You should have heard the venom in his voice when he muttered that last. Mark's the older brother but you can bet Hugh will make him feel like the prodigal son."

Morris touched the remote control and switched the screen off.

"I'm a bit worried about it too," he admitted. "I did question Jamie about other living quarters and she said the head stockman has a cottage and –"

"But that's not good enough for Mark and Jamie. They should be on equal footing with Hugh. It must be a big house judging from what she told us about the guest rooms. Could it be divided?"

"Well, they'd know if the house is suitable. I have thought of their building their own home but that would take time."

"Two full dwellings on the one estate?"

"Honey, the size of those stations is measured in square kilometres. Didn't Jamie say it was a twenty-minute drive to Seven Trees? Of course the decent thing would be for Hugh to move over there for a while."

"I'll bet he won't... and oh, Morris, what if he develops a real animosity to Jamie and makes it hard for her?"

"I don't think it will come to that. He'll have cooled off by now and Ashley and the housekeeper will make a good buffer."

"And what if they don't?"

"Then we'll just have to move up there," remarked Morris to his wife's amazement. As he switched the television back on, he concluded, "We don't want to make premature plans. Let's see what the two lovebirds come up with. Mark said they'd work on it."

The two lovebirds did work on it during the final few days of their honeymoon. They had left the van in a park for a while, and were taking time to explore the coastland as they journeyed north. They talked it over as they went. It was not so easily solved as the future family. Jamie tentatively asked Mark if the estate could stand another house being built.

"Of course it can. If Hugh's determined to keep the present house, we'll build our own. It'll take a bit of time but with these prefabricated jobs –"

"But I wouldn't want a makeshift one. That house is beautiful."

"You could have one just as nice."

"It'll be better. I –"

"No one-upmanship, darling."

"What do you mean?"

Mark eased the car on to a headland they were crossing and stopped the car. He sat gazing out at the sparkling blue waters for a minute. Then he spoke in that quiet drawl that sometimes had an inflexible quality in it.

"Just what I said. I won't have any competitiveness. Hugh is bound to marry some day and I'm not having you two wives vying with each other as to who has the best house."

"But there are all sorts of new conveniences that house hasn't got."

"Put in all the mod cons you like and, if Hugh hasn't got them, we'll put them in his too."

Jamie stared at him. "He'd never do that for you."

"It's not what Hugh does to me but what I do to him that gives me a good sleep at night."

Jamie undid her seatbelt and leaned over and kissed him on the lips. "You're just too nice for words," she said soberly.

Mark undid his belt and pulled her close. "It's not a case of being nice. It's plain common sense. Two families living closely together must have harmony to make the whole thing workable. If Hugh brings home a nice little bride one day you wouldn't want to be trying to get the better of her all the time, would you?"

"Of course not. I wouldn't even think of it ordinarily but –"

Mark held her hard. "I want at all times to be proud of my wife."

Jamie dropped her head on his breast. "I want to be proud of you too."

"Meaning?"

"I don't like the way Hugh walks all over you. I think there are times when you should stand up and fight."

"There are different ways of fighting, Jamie. Christ's method of fighting satan was to go to the cross."

"But we're not like Him."

"He said the servant is not greater than his master. He also said that a grain of wheat has to fall into the ground and die before it will bear fruit. My dying to certain things may one day seed new life in Hugh."

Jamie raised her head in amazement. "Hugh? I couldn't imagine Hugh ever becoming a Christian."

"All things are possible with God. Now, how about a little refreshment."

When they were next near a shop Jamie bought an armful of magazines featuring beautiful homes and thereafter fancied a different house every day. But this did not solve the immediate problem as to what they would do when they got back to Fairlie Downs.

Jamie was more or less resigned to the fact that they would have to use the big bedroom opposite Hugh's and share the same table at mealtimes till their house was built but she did not like it. It was so wonderful to be alone. Jamie had many dark thoughts of Hugh which she did not share with her husband.

The obvious and simple solution came to them as they entered the outskirts of Brisbane. Jamie said dreamily, "I wish we could just keep driving and never stop."

Mark slapped his thigh. "That's just what we'll do. We'll pull the caravan to Fairlie and use it till our house is ready."

"Oh my, oh my, oh my," sang Jamie. "It's you who have the head, Mark Lawrence. I must have cotton wool in mine."

The slight depression that had hung over them because the halcyon days were concluding vanished. New plans burst like fireworks in their heads and they could not cover the final kilometres fast enough.

CHAPTER SEVENTEEN

Grand Plans

Morris and Alison, expecting to receive a couple of star struck honeymooners, found themselves greeting a brisk team brimful of plans and ideas. Mark, who had been greatly impressed with his new in-laws' taste, swept Morris off to look at prefabricated houses and whatever else was going.

Jamie likewise tore into town with a most willing aunt and began looking at furniture and curtain materials. Brooke, ringing up to see if the honeymooners were back yet, got caught up into this.

As the three women had lunch in town they got a news report on how Hugh was taking it all.

"Mad as fire at first," described Brooke gleefully. "The great Hugh Lawrence was not in control of events. I tell you he's dying hard. Next time, after I had shown him I wasn't taking kindly to some of his remarks, he was the wounded brother betrayed. The time after he was…" she paused, her hearers were staring at her.

Alison found her voice. "What is this 'the time after…the next time'? Has he been ringing you every day?"

Brooke coloured a little. "It means nothing to me but he's been ringing about every second day."

"Well… Well… WELL!" exclaimed Jamie on a rising crescendo. "I'm surprised he hasn't dashed down again."

"Oh, he'd like to," laughed Brooke. "It's all the fault of that inconsiderate brother of his that he can't with all this business about the mining lease. As a matter of fact…"

"Well, go on," cried Alison and Jamie in unison.

"He's determined that I come back with you but that's entirely up to you, Jamie. You may not want —"

Jamie was all smiles. "By all means come back with us. Then he can sob on your shoulder and leave us alone."

"I can see some fun and games up there," commented Alison enviously. "I'd like to be a fly on the wall. More coffee?"

"Thanks," said Jamie, handing over her cup. "Why don't you?"

"Be a fly on the wall?"

"Umm. You and Uncle Morris come back with us too. The more the merrier. The way I see it," she added, warming to her theme, "Hugh's just about got everyone under his thumb. Sarah dotes on him and Ashley doesn't know any other life. If there are more on our side we can crowd him, make it harder for him to throw his weight about."

"I see what you mean," said Alison thoughtfully. She and her husband had agonised over whether they should warn Jamie of Hugh's personal hostility to her. "Maybe we could educate him a little."

"That's it," agreed Jamie, a wicked light in her grey eyes. "A firm hand on the bridle and a bit of spur and he'll be right."

She and Alison burst out laughing and Brooke begged to be let in on the joke so Jamie told her of Hugh's estimate of how she could be brought into line.

"Did he now?" said Brooke, her lovely brown eyes gleaming. "How little he knew you. This promises to be fun. I haven't been so entertained for years."

"But don't tell Mark," warned Jamie.

Alison's gaze sought the ceiling. "The rot's setting in already."

"It is *not*," flashed Mark's wife hotly.

Her aunt laughed and put her arm around Jamie as they rose. "Just teasing, pet. All we loving wives have little secrets from our husbands for their own good." They passed smiling out of the restaurant and did not notice the rather drawn look on Brooke's beautiful face.

The grand achievement of all this rushing about was to find out what they did not want. Mark summed it up by saying that they needed to decide on the actual site before choosing the design especially as Jamie was favouring a split level one.

All plans were shelved for the time being as the company turned its collective face towards Fairlie Downs. The decision to take the caravan had taken the heat off the situation. Secure in the fact that they would have their own nest, they looked forward to returning with their house party. Morris found he could take a few weeks away from the Gallery, leaving his assistant in charge. Brooke, who could pick up work any time, gave herself a further holiday and they prepared to enjoy the long trip out west.

Mark wanted to buy a car suitable to pull the caravan and replace Jamie's little one. Morris went with him and they chose a Falcon eight cylinder as a suitable estate one but he said that towing a
big caravan was no way to break in a new vehicle so they used Morris's car which he drove while Mark and Jamie tried out their new baby. Brooke alternated between the two vehicles.

The young Lawrences realised ruefully that the honeymoon was over when sleeping arrangements were made. The women occupied the caravan while the men used the annex which they put up every night.

However, there was much camaraderie over meals which Jamie cooked with the expertise gained from years of caravanning. During their conversations and discussions true friendship built up between those who had not known each other all that well. Various confidences about the situation were shared and Morris and Alison and Brooke were jelled into a solid phalanx of support behind Jamie rather than behind the young couple. Mark was still a bit of an enigma to them.

Before they left Mark had tried twice to ring Hugh but had apparently missed him and Hugh had not returned his calls. A call to Ashley prepared the homestead for the date of their return but not the manner of it. On her own initiative Jamie rang Mrs Howard when she was sure Hugh would be outside so she could get ahead with the inevitable preparations. Howie accepted the news of the three extra guests without a qualm but confided to Jamie that she had taken special pains to prepare the big bedroom opposite Hugh's for the bridal couple. That will do nicely for my Uncle and Aunt, she thought as she rang off.

As they ate their meals with laughter and jest, ignoring the faint overhanging shadow, Jamie was sure that Brooke was getting back into the human race again. Her laughter was more spontaneous and her repartee quicker. Watching her one evening as she took on Morris in matters of artistic taste, listening to his greater wisdom with attention and then offering her own view firmly but respectfully, Jamie thought what a gracious and considerate person she was. Brooke should have her own settled home by now and queening it properly instead of warming herself at other people's fires, sighed Jamie. She did not realise that what she was seeing was a surface healing. Brooke's wounds were very deep. Nevertheless, she prayed that God would not let Hugh hurt her friend.

A phone call from the closest town put everyone on the alert and a royal welcome was waiting as they drove over the first of the cattle grids. The stockmen, meaning to gallop alongside the bridal car, were transfixed by the sight of the caravan creeping slowly towards them followed at a comfortable distance by a second car in order to avoid the inevitable dust.

Everyone had to do a kind of double take and here Hugh made a tactical error. Ascertaining that the bridal couple were now in the first car, Hugh deliberately strode past them to welcome the second party containing his latest flirt.

This left Ashley to do the honours which he did with enthusiasm backed up by the whole station. As the second car drew to stop, Brooke jumped out, waved to him and ran to join the crowd about her friends. Hugh was caught welcoming Morris and Alison and had to walk beside them in their leisurely stroll towards the group. He found himself on the edge of the excited crowd and for once a nonentity, for those who were not looking at the two stars were eyeing off the most beautiful woman any of them had ever seen.

Hugh was caught off balance and it was Mark who performed the introductions to his in-laws and friend. Good wishes and congratulations were showered on him and Jamie, and the caravan had to be exclaimed over and inspected

"What are you going to do with it, Boss?"

"Live in it," said Mark and struck the company dumb.

There had been various cogitations as to how the brothers would deal with the unprecedented situation. This solution had not even been dreamed of. There were some knowing looks and before the day was out the caravan had been christened 'the *Lovenest*' and its fame went far and wide.

Mark's party of five outnumbered the home party by two and set the tone for the evening as they gathered around the table. Hugh might still resume his seat at the head and Mark his old one at the side with Jamie by him but there is an old Scottish saying: 'Where the McGregor sits is the head of the table' and so it proved. Mark's happiness sat on him like a mantle, Jamie had the bridal flush on her cheeks and their glow attracted the spotlight of attention.

Morris and Alison set themselves to be model guests and charmed Ashley (when he wasn't looking at Brooke) and Sarah into relaxation and participation. Hugh's intention to freeze his brother and Jamie with the frost of his disapproval only resulted in freezing himself almost out of the picture. Brooke paid him little notice, giving her attention to the table at large and holding her own in the gay conversation. He shrewdly realised he had to play the genial host or lose his place.

Ashley valiantly did his part in keeping the focus on Mark and Jamie but he could not get over Brooke. Hugh had jocularly announced that he was bringing the loveliest woman in the world to the station and it had gone the way of his other descriptions of his previous flames. But Brooke, alight with the success of their manoeuvre, her rich brown eyes sparkling, her glorious mass of auburn waves and curls setting off beauty of feature and body, seemed the absolute incandescence of womanly perfection to the dazzled man. She seemed like some goddess who had stepped down from Olympus and taken his nebulous dreams and unrealised hopes and moulded them into her own shape.

Ashley Lawrence was then fifty-two, being eight years younger than his deceased brother. Jamie's remark that she wished she had met him twenty years ago and her subsequent surprise marriage to Mark, whom he had felt sure was on the same barren path he was travelling, had blown a draft over the banked fires of his warm but reserved nature. Once over the shock he was sure Jamie would be a great asset to the family and wistfully looked forward to many a cosy time with the newlyweds.

Now, into this gentle fanning of the coals had stepped Brooke and the flames unexpectedly flared. He worshiped her from that moment. Poor Ashley. He knew he had no chance but his dreams were his own and that night they were enriched with a quality of womanhood that had never come his way before.

Hugh had soon seen that if he did not exert himself he would be losing his position as the psychological head of the family. He made gestures of insisting that his brother and Jamie (he would not use the word 'wife') sleep under the home roof but everyone of Jamie's party soon put him right.

"You leave the honeymooners alone, Hugh," advised Morris with a wink. "They're still star struck, you know."

As Jamie hopped up to help Howie with the plates, quite unconsciously taking the bemused Sarah's place, she saw a thin sceptical smile on Hugh's face. He hasn't really accepted it yet, she thought, but there is nothing he can do now.

When the party broke up to repair to their allotted quarters then Jamie deliberately assumed the role of hostess as she escorted her Aunt and Uncle to the big bedroom. Hugh immediately seized the chance and showed Brooke to the bedroom that Jamie had used. He hoped for a few minutes alone with her but she merely waited till he had placed her cases on the floor and went out again.

Mark wanted to manoeuvre the caravan into a good position behind the house and everyone ended up outside giving advice. Jamie could have done the job herself but she let them struggle with it. The company then grasped that the new car was Mark's and the men had to give it the once over.

Sarah, who had not ceased to cast her doubts on the success of Mark's marriage because she had felt that Jamie was the one for Hugh, did a complete about face. There had never been a woman like Brooke Tarrington on the property before and, by the time the evening was over, she had marked her down for her favourite and abandoned the whingeing that had so got on Ashley's nerves. When they finally drove home she subjected him to a new kind of torture by singing Brooke's praises and he soon saw where her thoughts were tending. He heard her with the resignation that had characterised his life and his fine profile gave nothing away.

Brooke managed with considerable adroitness to evade Hugh and slip away to her room but she knew that she would not be able to keep it up. She had come up with the intention of cramping his style but there was something in Hugh's gaze that gave her pause and she needed time to think.

As she lay in bed that night Brooke's thoughts were sombre. She had never been a flirt and the offer to break Hugh's heart, made laughingly, had not been her intent. To keep him occupied and have a little fun had been the sum total of her ambition as a justification for the holiday she intended to enjoy. But this was Hugh's own territory and, if he decided to get serious, it would make things very difficult all round. After two disastrous marriages, Brooke shied from the very word. If she did marry again it would not be for a long long time. Men! Brooke was sick of them. She turned restlessly on her pillow. How fortunate Jamie had been! First time up and she had hit the jackpot. You could see Mark's innate goodness in his eyes. He might not be as dashing as his younger brother but Brooke had had enough of dashing men. Before she went to sleep she had decided to simply exude friendliness and take each day as it came – which was extremely sensible of her.

The station gradually quietened down and the moon silvered the tranquil scene, poking delicate fingers here and there.

One finger slanted across the bed where Morris and Alison were talking things over quietly. On the whole the return had gone well but it was obvious that their help was needed. It had taken most of the evening for Hugh's scowl to lighten completely. Without their presence he would have made the lovers' homecoming difficult – if not downright uncomfortable. They felt fiercely protective of Mark and Jamie.

The lovers themselves could not have cared less. Snug in each other's arms they were long beyond the stage of needing the romantic touch of moonlight.

CHAPTER EIGHTEEN

Settling In

The riding party was almost ready.

Hugh and Mark were long familiar with the viewpoint held by most first time visitors: that life on a great cattle station was mainly conducted from horseback. This view held till stiff and aching muscles finally rebelled. Then the guests were ready to settle for less strenuous forms of entertainment and the station staff could get back to the ordinary business of the day.

The policy at Fairlie Downs was 'ride 'em early and ride 'em hard'. At the moment all was enthusiastic anticipation.

The horses provided were excellently graded and the inexperienced Morris and Alison found themselves on well-mannered beasts with easy gaits. Hugh had already found out that Brooke could ride so had provided a pretty palomino mare that was kept for guests.

Mark put Jamie up on Greystock, saying with a smile as he tightened the girth: "One day, when you can really ride I'll be getting you a present. Something you'll really like."

"Shh!" cautioned Jamie. "Don't hurt Greystock's feelings. I think I'll be needing his help and guidance for a while yet."

Mark laughed and turned to swing himself up on to Redmaster. As he turned the horse he found that he and his mount were the centre of attention.

"We heard in Brisbane that you have the Reserve Champion of the Show there," remarked Morris. "I'm no judge of horseflesh but anyone can see that sure is some horse."

"What a glorious colour he is," admired Alison. "Red gold – wasn't that the description? Marvellous!"

Jamie, who had not taken that much notice of the horses on her previous visit, being much more concerned with the business of staying on her mount, found herself in full agreement.

"As a matter of fact," she said, glancing across at Brooke, "with the sunlight on them both, Brooke and Red have the same colour hair. I'd like to get a shot of Brooke on Red, Mark."

"I'll wait till I've seen Brooke ride," said Mark teasingly. "Red's a gentleman but —"

"He doesn't abide fools," said Brooke laughingly. "You've put me on my mettle, Mark."

She turned and rode up beside Hugh who had been listening jealously to this exchange. He quickly took the lead with her and had soon put some distance between them and the rest of the party.

Redmaster's taking out the Reserve Championship had been a sore point with him. They had both purchased their horses on the same day at the same stud. In fact the horses were half-brothers. Hugh had plumped for the black which was a year older and in his eyes the better colt but Mark's eye had been the finer in judgment as was proved later on in the Show Ring. Hugh was so accustomed to preferential treatment in all things as a veritable crown prince that he declared that the judges were at fault not the horse.

Mark was kind to his guests and kept them at a leisurely pace till they got used to their saddles. Alison had to recount her only two experiences on a horse, one ending on her back feeling the end of the world had come. Morris said nothing for he had nothing to recount. He was finding that he liked the feel of a living animal beneath him and made up his mind that he would really learn to ride. No doubt there would be plenty of chances in the future to foster this ambition.

Hugh urged Brooke's horse to a gallop and as they flew he expertly worked the mare, wheeling her in a great circle around the slower party. When they finally pulled up to a cantor Brooke turned to him with reproachful eyes.

"You didn't have to treat me as though I was some wayward steer."

"I wanted Mark to get a good look at you. He'll find nothing to complain about."

Her lovely smile flashed. "Thank you."

Hugh's glance deepened. "He's not the only one with nothing to complain about."

That was the moment to give her cavalier a saucy smile but Brooke in her uncertainty coloured a little and looked away. The effect was devastating.

They rode companionably back to the others, Hugh taking care to be his charming best. He had done a lot of thinking during the previous night. Although strongly attracted to Brooke his main aim in insisting she accompany the honeymooners back was to have her as an effective counterfoil to the excitement of the first bride at Fairlie for many years. Although his animosity towards Jamie had not abated a jot he put it aside as he assumed the role of the main host once more.

As they joined the other group he moved easily in to conversation with Morris and Alison, enquiring as to their progress. Brooke edged her horse to Jamie's side.

"Do you think I'll pass with Mark?"

"Oh, he thinks you're splendid but even if he didn't I'd have insisted you ride Red. You're glorious on a horse, honey."

"Nice to be good at something." Brooke smiled – and then straightway lost it. The shadow in her life had a way of flicking across it like that. Someone else had called her glorious on skis on her first honeymoon in the Snowies. The honeymoon that had promised so much.

As they rode into the yards the men were ready to take the horses but Jamie was insistent that she take her photos there and then.

"The sun's just right and I've got the feel for it just now."

Mark was familiar by now with Jamie's 'feel' and he dismounted and brought Red up to Brooke while Jamie flew indoors for her camera. He adjusted the stirrups as everyone else gave over their mounts except Hugh who allowed no one to handle Vulcan but himself. He watched sceptically while Jamie got Brooke to move her mount against various backgrounds. Redmaster obeyed her light and sure touch but showed no interest in the proceedings. This was not work and he was bored. Jamie wanted him to prance a bit and act up. At last she turned to her husband.

"I'd like to get more response out of Red."

Mark nodded to Brooke. "Take your hat off, slap his side and hang on," he called.

Brooke laughed, gripped with her knees and did so. Immediately Red rose on his hind legs, pawing the air and backing. Brooke leaned forward in sheer joy, her lovely hair mingling with the flaring mane. The picture was flawless: the perfect girl on the perfect horse. The watchers caught their breaths while Jamie jumped around, clicking furiously.

Hugh shouted, "You beauty!" and dashed his own hat to the ground in an ecstasy of reaction.

If an emotive experience could be wired for sound, then the crash when Hugh Lawrence fell utterly in love with Brooke Tarrington would have reverberated far beyond the station. In that moment, Hugh, who had held many a girl's heart in his hand and not valued it, gave his own to Brooke without reserve.

Jamie was triumphant. "I'll get a painting out of that."

"And I'll buy it," said Hugh going to Brooke as she brought the horse down.

"Don't let him, Jimmy," interposed Morris quickly. "I'd like you to do a Show on the Outback. Keep it for that."

"I can put it in as N F S."

"Clients don't like that."

"Have pity on him, Jamie," pleaded Alison. "Didn't Hugh snap up that marvellous dirt picture of yours?" They had seen it last night and Morris had been furious at missing it.

They broke off as the other two approached.

"By the way, Mark," called Morris. "Who took out the actual Championship?"

"Their sire," Hugh answered for him. "Greymaster of Yandowie for the third time. He's something of a legend."

"Well, he can't last forever," replied Morris. "Red's obviously his heir apparent."

"You never know. Different judges have different opinions," said Hugh firmly. "Vulcan's got as good a chance as any. He's got plenty of his dad in him." He paraded the horse before them showing the black's fine points.

"So they're brothers," commented Jamie.

"Half-brothers. Different dams."

"What was Red's mother like?" asked Brooke as she dismounted.

"Chestnut. Ginger Miss."

"Oh, I like that," approved Jamie, "but it should be Ginger Missus now."

There was a stifled guffaw. Every male eye fixed itself on Jamie charmed by her gaucherie. She looked at Vulcan sidling around his master.

"Vulcan's a splendid horse too," she said, determined to match Hugh in good will. "What about his mother?"

There was absolute silence as the men strained to hear.

"Tall black mare," said Hugh, desperately sober. "Night on the Mountain."

Jamie surveyed the horse thoughtfully. "Some night."

The men howled. She had not disappointed them. Jamie whirled around to find Hugh and Mark doubled up in silent laughter. Young Mrs Lawrence would have stalked off in high dudgeon but Mark collared her and made her come with him to the stables while he rubbed down his horse and showed her how to do the same with Greystock.

"You're not a guest now. Got to learn how to care for the Fairlie property."

Jamie watched him moving around the big chestnut, slapping his rump to make him move over and talking to him. Red answered with an occasional nicker, revelling in the touch of his master.

"He's a real pet, isn't he?" she commented.

"No, sweetheart, a friend if you like but never a pet. The same with a cattle dog. He is never a pet. He, like the horses, has his job and his dignity and well the man who recognises that."

"But you love him, don't you?"

Mark smiled to himself at her naiveté. "It isn't wise to love them too much," was all he said. Jamie was to remember those remarks.

As they were being groomed Mark had dealt the horses some extra rations and now turned them into the home paddock. As they were returning Hugh came up to them. He was back on Vulcan after escorting the others up to the house.

"Looks as though I'll have to go out with them," he nodded towards the other stockmen who were moving off. "We've got that job to finish we had to leave yesterday. Times like these I envy you your office job."

"It has its compensations," allowed Mark, slipping his arm around Jamie and moving off with her. Jamie wondered if he had yet noticed the way Hugh deliberately ignored her but decided to say nothing about it. He was putting a good face on it in other ways.

Hugh watched them for a moment, an odd smile playing about his lips. Then he turned to follow the men. He did not need to join in the job of bringing in the cattle for shipment but he wanted some space. He was coming down from the high to which his sudden revelation had swept him but he was still in a glow and needed to do some hard thinking. It would be a whole new ball game now.

Here was the chance to get his revenge on Jamie and feather his own nest in more ways than one. Right from their meeting in Morris's Gallery he had sensed the challenge in Jamie. He had been amused at first but she had been too smart all round. Working only from the facts that there had been no sign of interest from Mark and the discarded envelope, he put the whole hasty marriage down to Jamie's machinations. Somehow she had bewitched his easy going brother and would now be set to confront him all along the line. Knowing that the couple had Ashley's and Howie's approval he had been uncertain how to play his hand.

Now everything was falling into place. First Brooke had to be wooed and won and he did not doubt himself there. Once engaged he would set about rearranging the home property. Jamie and Mark could stay in their caravan till it was done. The house was L-shaped: the short wide arm comprising the main living quarters, the long narrow arm held all the guest rooms and extra storage space. That wing could be turned into self-contained living quarters for his brother. A bit narrow perhaps but it would do them. Separate accommodation would have to be built for the many visitors but the main entertaining would still be done in the spacious main area with his lovely wife presiding over all. Thus the main life of the station would centre around them. That would place Mark in his customary secondary position along with his smart little madam.

Hugh was of a very practical turn of mind. He worked out many details as he rode the mob. As far as he could see it was foolproof. There remained only the winning back of his former favour with Morris and Alison in order to get everyone on his side. Sarah was already there and Ashley... here Hugh dismissed his uncle as a nonentity who like Mark, had never pushed his point of view.

In the meantime, the guests had spent a good day being shown over the property and had helped with the stabilising of the caravan.

Jamie had the happy idea of rolling back the canvas walls of the annex and bringing across some of the pot plants off the side verandas. The caravan was well situated near some trees that gave it some shade during the day. Not that it needed it for the van had its own air-conditioning. The whole effect was quite charming. Mrs Howard came to summon them to a late lunch and remained to admire and to suggest that some little used cane chairs on the back veranda be added.

After the meal the guests, who were beginning to feel their muscles voted for a siesta. Mr and Mrs Lawrence did not look displeased. They went meekly off to their caravan as they still considered that there was part of their honeymoon still left.

"Getting into bad habits,' said Mark as he stretched out on the bed and watched Jamie as she fiddled about among her things. She had not yet had time to sort out their own stuff and was dying to get on with it.

"How do you mean?" she asked absently.

"Come here and I'll show you."

Jamie glanced at him under her lashes. "Some other time," she said nonchalantly and made as if to go out the door. The scuffle was short and sweet and she lay contentedly at his side.

"I think we'll have to have all our meals at the house while the others are here, don't you?"

Mark grunted his acquiescence.

"When do you think we should tell Hugh about building our own home?"

"Not just yet. Let things settle down a bit. We have to give the others a good time and there's the party coming up."

"What party? Oh, you mean –"

"The big at-home we'll be having. We can't get out of that."

"I don't want to."

"The whole countryside will want to see the new bride."

"You make me feel nervous. What will I have to do?"

"Nothing. Ashley, Sarah and Howie have it well in hand."

"I didn't think Sarah was all that keen."

"Ash got her moving. He said if she didn't want to run it he'd hire staff. She hates that. Likes to run it her way."

Jamie giggled. "I like Ashley a lot. I think it's a terrible shame that he hasn't married. As a matter of fact... I think I'll do something about it."

"How?"

"There must be some charming single ladies or widows around who would be just the right age for him."

"You might produce them but you still have to get him moving."

"Actually I've rather a talent for getting people moving."

Mark shook with silent laughter. Jamie pummelled him and nothing was said for a while.

Late that night, when they were having their evening devotions Jamie did think of something else she could do. She discussed it with Mark who said that they would have to move pretty smartly but he thought it was quite possible.

When Hugh, who had spent all day with the stock, finally came in for his shower his complete change of front was obvious to everyone. A benign and charming host presided over the dinner table, everyone was included in the cordial conversation and he even engaged in some of the old repartee with Jamie. Morris and Alison began to revert to their earlier estimate of him. He could not keep his eyes off Brooke but took care not to single her out in any way. His wooing would not be for public edification.

Everyone went to bed considerably cheered, feeling the awkward tension had been relaxed. Not a soul dreamed that they were on totally insecure territory.

The planners for the At-home had decided on the Saturday of the second week when the moon was full and the weather promised to be perfect.

Mark's remark that Jamie would have nothing to do was facetious to say the least. They were all in it up to their necks. An At-home outback meant simply open house for everyone who cared to come. The phones had run hot while food was ordered and flown in, tents and flies appeared, trestle tables set out, barbecues prepared, the tennis court hung with fairy lights and a big marquee erected.

The keenest interest was felt in Mark's bride. Without delving too deeply into the family traditions it was generally accepted that the older brother was the confirmed bachelor. Girls who had hardly noticed him while they competed for Hugh's favours, felt they had been caught napping and wondered where their wits had been.

Those of Jamie's friends who had given her the shower had told other friends with the result that quite a contingent was flying in, assured that they need only bring a sleeping bag and a towel each.

However, it was to be a function with a difference. These affairs generally followed the style of the surprise party for Jamie, people arriving early on Saturday, having fun all day and sleeping it off on Sunday. Now the word went out. Saturday evening would see the commencement of the celebrations; then on Sunday there was to be a special Service of Worship during which Jamie and Mark would confirm their wedding vows. This was Jamie's great idea and the novelty of it went down well even with those who had not been next or nigh a religious service for years.

Alison and Brooke threw themselves into the thick of it, helping wherever they could on the domestic side. Morris's delight in station life, his willingness to ride till his limbs were sore and learn all he could, endeared him to the men and he was always to be found with them.

They had a problem with Mark on the Saturday morning before any of the guests had arrived. He wanted to tow the caravan off to a spot a mile away.

"Why?" Everyone asked in mystification.

"Oh, I dunno," was all he would say but he was over-ruled.

"No one's going to run off with it, surely?" asked his wife, "and we'll lock it securely when we're not around."

Mark said dubiously that perhaps that would fix it and they left it at that.

Then the guests began to arrive. They came by plane and car and seemed never ending. Moving among them beside Mark, Jamie heard name after name till she felt dizzy but things seemed to go with a bang right from the start. All Mark's guests knew each other and all Jamie's guests knew each other and it was a case of mixing them. The family moved amongst them seeing to this.

The city slickers were charmed to have a chance to share station life and the country, glad to get together at any time, revelled in the romance of the two stars. For stars they were. Mark's joy radiated from him as the bridegroom coming forth from his chamber and Jamie was famous in her own right. The story of her protest painting had spread far and wide. As they moved among the crowd they seemed to leave a little murmuring wake of admiration and approval.

For the first time in his life Hugh was completely upstaged by his quiet brother. His dominant personality had to give way to the successful love story. Had it not been for the striking beauty of his latest girlfriend not much attention would have been vouchsafed him. As it was envious male eyes followed him as he took Brooke around and introduced her.

The evening meal was once again in the form of a barbecue and half a dozen fires were lit to accommodate the crowd. Mark and Jamie melted into the work party: Mark helping to supervise the cooking of the huge steaks and the long ribbed chops while Jamie got in with the ladies preparing tons of salads and other delectables. Here she made an excellent choice. So many young lovers saw nothing but each other and those country wives who had expected her to stick like glue to her husband's side were much gratified when she borrowed an apron and joined them. Immediately she found herself deferred to by women twice her age as the new Missus of Fairlie heading a team to whom hospitality was a sacred rite. Without intending it she put Sarah's nose out of joint but that rather negative lady accepted it with reasonable grace.

So Jamie shredded lettuce and arranged salad bowls industriously and with a secret amusement. Fond of domesticity she was not, but queening it at a huge function was a novel delight. She soon saw that sharing with Mark in his quiet service gave her a surer ground for popularity than a dazzling personality. Every now and then she caught Mark's eye as he glanced anxiously across and her radiant smile assured him that all was well.

Dancing was once again to be the chief entertainment for the young and, after the meal, the girls melted away to shed their jeans and dress for it. The older people, of whom there were many, were content to sit about sipping cold drinks and catching up on all the latest gossip. It was here that the serpent raised its head.

A friend of one of the girls who had given Jamie her shower heard of the excited planning and begged to be included with her husband. Alas we cannot vouch for the friend of a friend. She knew Brooke and was already jealous of her as having attracted the wandering eye of her husband. With no sense and less tact, she related Brooke's history to a group curious as to where Hugh had found her. Told at any time it was not pleasant: a divorcee twice over but to the old fashioned of the outback it came as something of a shock. Speculative gazes from various couples came Brooke's way. Why couldn't she hold her man? Some of the less gallant of the men began to consider her fair game. Some of this came Jamie's way and vexed her sorely. Why couldn't they leave Brooke alone?

She stewed helplessly over this in the caravan as she put on a pretty yellow frock. Someone had brought white frangipani with deep golden hearts. Mark came into the caravan as she was securing some in her hair. She looked at him a bit dubiously for she had not really sorted out this dancing business.

"Mark, they're expecting us to open the dancing with the bridal waltz."

He came close to her and put his hands on her tiny waist. "Well, I can still remember that lesson you gave me so I guess we'll get by."

Jamie grinned. "Never have I had a more reluctant pupil. Ashley would put you to shame."

Mark grinned in his turn. "Couldn't concentrate."

Jamie sniffed. "Then why did you drop me as though I'd stung you after Hugh went?"

"Because if I hadn't I'd have eaten you."

"Well, for pity's sake why didn't you?"

"You know why," he said seriously, holding her closer.

"Umm. But don't ruin my hairdo. I've had to stiffen it with spray."

"Come, let's get this dance over."

"Get it over? Well! Don't you want to hold me in your arms?"

"I'm doing that now."

"Yes, but it can be so romantic – dancing in the moonlight."

"What's romantic about simply putting one arm around your waist and hanging on to your hand when here I can –"

"All right, all right I get the point. I can see I won't be getting you on a dance floor too often."

"Nope and neither will anyone else. That goes for you too."

Jamie pressed away from him. "What's this?"

"I don't want any other man holding you the way I held you on the veranda."

"I don't either."

He looked down at her earnest face and kissed her gently. "We'll get it all sorted out one day, darling."

They went along to the tennis court in full accord to find they were being waited for. Ashley was watching for them and began a Strauss waltz. With a funny little grimace Mark took Jamie in his arms and after a false start or two they were away. They had only to do a couple of rounds before others could join in and Hugh swung Brooke into the dance. Others began to queue up for the privilege but they had little chance. It was the first opportunity Hugh had had of getting Brooke in his arms and he meant to make the most of it. He held her close possessively and Brooke stiffened and strained away from him. He glanced down at her, almost unable to bear the impact of her beauty so near him.

"Bit of an ice princess, eh?"

"I'd just like to be able to breathe," she said coldly. She was annoyed that her story was being bandied about and she did not relish being a rather notorious scalp to his belt. Hugh saw that it behoved him to move carefully with her, a procedure that had never been necessary for him before. However, his goal was the altar this time and he trembled slightly with a pinprick of self-doubt. He relaxed his grip and Brooke relaxed too. Their dancing became much smoother.

"Like to dance off on to Cloud Nine with me?" he said in her ear.

"There aren't any clouds tonight," Brooke replied teasingly.

"We'll make our own then."

"What can you make clouds of on a perfect night?"

"Dreams I guess. Glorious dreams of a glorious girl." For the life of him Hugh could not resist drawing her close again, letting his chin rest on her temple. If she thought she was going to see this night out without being kissed she was never more wrong. Brooke decided there was a better way of keeping him at arms' length.

"Dreams are all right as long as they stay dreams," she said.

Hugh drew back and looked down at her in surprise. "Hey, that sounds like you've been disillusioned somewhere along the line."

Perhaps her story would prove an effective armour here.

"Haven't you heard?" she asked airily.

"Heard what?"

"When you've been twice married and twice divorced you've not much faith in dreams."

There was an emphatic silence from Hugh. A man of his time he did not peer into the sexual history of his girl friends. Nevertheless, he had been placing this woman on a pedestal, seeing her as an elusive and chaste Diana that it would take some hunter to bring down. In wanting her to be his wife it was a bitter shock to find that two men had been before him. Brooke waited for the withdrawal but it did not come. As the music faded, Hugh kept his arm around her and steered her over to a clear space.

"What happened?" he asked bluntly.

Brooke stared at him. "What's my sordid past got to do with you?"

"I want to know why any man, having won you, was willing to let you go."

"I got rid of them. One was a womaniser. I was not married two months before he began looking over the fence. I found I was just another trophy to put on his shelf. He was a well-known racing driver, very popular. I thought him the ultimate in glamour. So did every other girl and he enjoyed picking the fruit."

Hugh said nothing. The description cut too close to the bone.

"The other one was an odd ball."

"What's that in your book?"

"He was not only interested in women. I fell for his 'sympathetic' nature on the rebound. I could not scrape him off fast enough." The girl shuddered. She was every inch a woman, and an exceedingly beautiful one at that, yet she had not been able to attract a normal decent man – one of character.

Hugh heard her with mixed feelings. She had presented him with two unlovely pictures of manhood, one a near reflection of himself. A sense of unease crept over him. He had no shy innocent maiden on his hands but a woman who, through bitter experience, was equipped to judge him and, if need be, find him wanting.

"Shall we go back?" She spoke in a light casual tone.

He turned without speaking and took her back to the dance floor where he was content to relinquish her for the time being. A sudden sadness swept over Brooke. Suppose Hugh had been the man she could love if she ever loved again. Could she have stood that thoughtful silence from him, the weighing of the pros and cons of her miserable confession?

The dancing was in full swing by now with modern steps and every male wanting a turn with the Bride and the Beauty. Jamie got them going in a Paul Jones number, her flying feet giving them no more than few seconds to partner her. It was otherwise with Brooke, all the men queuing for at least a turn around the tennis court. She was obliging but firmly pleasant with them and earned an ungrudging respect. With all but one man, that is. He was the husband of the woman whose jealousy had led her to 'spill the beans' on Brooke. He had never had much chance to get near the girl before but not for the want of trying. Here he seized his opportunity, piloting her off the cement ostensibly in search of a drink.

Brooke downed hers in a hurry but he had steered her against the wire netting of the court and kept her there as he dawdled over his drink, his breath in her face, his lewd gaze running over her body. At home Brooke could have easily got rid of him but dreaded making a scene where she was a guest.

Jamie, glancing over as she left the dance floor, grasped the situation and looked around for help. Hugh was not in sight. Mark was indulgently listening to an elderly station owner's reminiscences. Ashley had put his fiddle down and was enjoying a drink. Making up her mind never to invite this particular couple again Jamie crossed over to him.

"Ashley, I don't want a fuss made but that man is annoying Brooke."

Ashley turned and surveyed the scene. The man was grinning fatuously down at her closed face as he talked in an undertone. Ashley moved swiftly. Jamie saw what happened but even then she could scarcely believe it. He put his hand under the one holding the glass and knocked it up. The contents splashed in the man's face and he stepped back sharply with an angry expletive. It died on his lips as he was confronted with a menacing gaze of grey steel.

"Keep clear of this *lady* from now on. Understand?" The low chilling tone had its effect.

Without apology, the man nevertheless withdrew, quickly pulling out his handkerchief. Ashley put this hand on Brooke's back and gently compelled her towards the dance floor.

"Hey there, Ash," said a cheery voice. "No jumping the queue. This is my —"

A hand arrived on Bradley's chest and gave a quick shove. Caught off balance the young jackaroo missed his step and landed on the ground, staring up at his assailant in comical amazement.

"I'm no dancer," said Ashley briskly, "but we should be able to do a few turns till you settle down a bit."

As the dumbfounded Brooke went into his arms she peeped up at him, noting the high burn on his cheek. We both need settling down, she thought, peering around at Bradley. She was not laughing. She never felt less like laughing.

As Jamie turned away, hugging herself, Brooke adjusted her steps gracefully to Ashley's. One saw so little of knight errantry these days. Not only that. She was conscious of the light impersonal yet protective embrace. When had any man ever held her just like this? They got around the floor after a fashion, Brooke perhaps doing more of the guiding. Deeply appreciative of his quiet yet effective intervention, she wanted to show Ashley how grateful she was and was at her warm and charming best to him.

At the end of the dance, Ashley escorted his partner over to the young man he had shoved down.

"Here you are," he said cheerfully. "Got to get back to my fiddling."

Brooke and Bradley stood watching the lithe retreating figure.

"That," said Bradley, "had to be seen to be believed."

"You mean felt, don't you?" asked Brooke merrily, her poise and good humour quite restored.

Brad grinned. "Who'd have thought an old codger like —"

"Not so much of the 'old codger'," Brooke interrupted crisply. "I'd imagine he'd give as good as he got."

"You're telling me," said the boy with a new respect.

The incident had not gone entirely unnoticed; fortunately, the first part had happened too swiftly and Bradley's share became the subject of much ribbing which he took in good part.

A big supper was laid on and soon everyone was gathered around the food, Mark and Jamie in the thick of it. Afterwards, when the crowd began to drift off to their improvised beds, they found themselves isolated, being studiously ignored by their guests. Mark had expected quite a bit of ribbing regarding the 'Lovenest' but nobody had said a thing. They knew why when they reached the caravan.

"I knew they would be up to something," he said in despair. He had taken the precaution of locking the van securely and hiding the power cords. The high moon exposed the mischief. All over the walls graffiti had been scribbled – some in good taste, some not so good. Paper bows had been stuck all over it and right around its middle a huge chain had been placed securing the door. If they could not get into the caravan, then the merrymakers made sure the honeymooners would not either. Jamie was inclined to laugh.

"Now I know why we were so popular during supper," she said merrily. "I can see why you wanted to hide it."

Looking ruefully down at Jamie, Mark said,

"Looks like the bush for us, hon."

Jamie shook her head and led him around to the back end of the caravan. She pointed up to a long narrow horizontal window: the emergency exit. Between them they prised it open and Jamie clambered inside easily. Mark had a struggle but finally fell inside losing his glasses as he did so.

"I don't know how anyone could contrive to escape through this thing. It must be for women and children only."

They surveyed each other in triumph, Jamie remarking with a giggle that they would have to repeat the business in the morning in order to get out.

"Well, just shout 'Fire' and I shouldn't have any trouble," grinned Mark, immensely pleased that they had managed to outwit their tormentors. They undressed quickly in the semi-darkness. Jamie cleaned her teeth and turning back, saw a narrow shaft of moonlight from the half-opened skylight falling athwart the bed. She turned and fished in her drawer and brought out a delectable slip of a nightdress of smoke blue chiffon shot with silver threads. She changed again while Mark was cleaning his teeth.

When he approached the bed she was draped across it, the moonlight picking up the delicate shimmer and the paleness of her flesh.

"My," he said. "You look as though you've just come down on a moonbeam."

Mark lay on his side cupping a palm around the young breast.

"Don't you reckon this is more romantic than cavorting around a dance floor?" he pleaded.

"Yes, I do," said Jamie honestly, loving his touch. "It's just that it's associated with romance."

"Yeah but it's only the mating dance – a preliminary to better things."

Jamie chuckled. "I like that. The mating dance. I remember seeing an old nature film on TV once. It showed two scorpions gripping each other in their mating dance. Some square dance music was used which matched their jerky movements perfectly and the commentator came out with instructions like: 'Take your gal for the stingaree but just take care you don't sting me'."

Mark's deep laughter mingled with her lighter tones. Then they were silent. A lovely mood had fallen on them. The moonlight that etched her so exquisitely formed a silver nimbus behind his head as he leaned over her. His face was in shadow but she could see his expression dimly. Physical desire was naturally at a high between them but they were experiencing something deeper than mere physical union. They were far more than one flesh – they were one spirit – one in Christ.

Mark leaned back and switched on the LED lamp and picked up his small Bible. A family tradition was being birthed in their joined lives. They had discovered that Jamie liked to read her Bible in the morning and Mark liked to read his at night so they took turns in reading aloud. As he found the passage he wanted Jamie cuddled in beside him. Glancing across she was rather relieved to find it was not the Sermon on the Mount which seemed to have a peculiar fascination with him. He was reading from the twelfth chapter of the Gospel of John.

I tell you the truth, unless a kernel of wheat falls to the ground and dies, it remains only a single seed. But if it dies, it produces many seeds. The man who loves his life will lose it, while the man who hates his life in this world will keep it for eternal life.

Mark fell silent and after a while, Jamie stirred restlessly and looked up at him. He had his eyes closed.

"What does it mean?" she asked, a hint of impatience in her voice. "I certainly don't hate my life…our lives."

"I think it means the general attitude of the Christian to the very material world he lives in. It's the first part that gets me. We know that Jesus died and His death is producing a great harvest of souls but how could an ordinary man's death produce – perhaps it means death to self. It could be related to giving one's cloak."

"Oh, no – not again." Jamie sat up. "First you've got to give up necessary clothing … now you have to die. When do you start to live?"

"We will inherit eternal life and –"

"I mean live *now*. Isn't there more to the Christian life than giving everything up and dying? Aren't we looking forward to a happy future together here on earth?"

Mark said nothing.

Jamie leaned over and shook his shoulders. "Oh, no you don't. I'm not going to batter myself against these silences of yours. Answer me."

"I don't know the answer, darling. I think at some point in a Christian's life he could face a crisis when he has to place all on the line and die to himself."

"How?"

Mark shrugged helplessly. "I just don't know but –"

"But?"

Mark closed the Bible and put it back on the shelf. Then he put out the light and, turning, enclosed his wife in a firm embrace.

"Let's leave it to the Lord," he whispered nuzzling into her neck.

With a sigh Jamie acquiesced.

Morning found the young Lawrences early astir. The Pastor would be flying in for breakfast with the service to be held straight afterwards while it was still in the cool part of the day. They made use of their own shower, put on casual clothes and packed up their wedding gear – with Jamie insisting that Mark take his safari suit. They pushed their stuff out of the exit and then scrambled out after it. As they landed on the ground a long drawn out whistle was heard and a voice said,

"Well, blow me down!" Bradley Hartford was standing by with his arms folded.

"You old fox," he yelled. "To think how I sweated over those chains and padlocks."

"There's one of them," cried Mark and headed for the jackaroo with fell intent. Bradley took to his heels yelling for help. Round and round he dodged with Mark gaining on him. Everyone who was up rushed to see the fun but no one offered any succour to the hapless perpetrator. Mark's slim litheness stood him in better stead than Bradley's stockiness and the jackaroo was cornered, dragged to a water trough and summarily dumped in it.

"And if those chains aren't off by the time breakfast is finished you'll be dumped every hour on the hour," said Mark, stepping back in triumph, "and that goes for the graffiti too."

A streaming Bradley promptly fell on his knees. "You wouldn't do it when I've got me good duds on, now would you?" he wheedled. "Yes, you would, you old –"

"Ladies present."

"Well, save some breakfast for me." Bradley squelched off to find the keys swearing that everyone else of the mischief makers had to help or he would give their names to Mark.

Apparently his threat held for a small work party arrived very late for breakfast which was served on the veranda. The Pastor's plane had come in on time and Mark and Jamie were sitting with him as they worked on the programme.

The Rev Lee Savage belied his name. A man of indomitable spirit and frail health he had been forced to retire recently from the mission field through the repeated occurrence of Ross River fever in a body already affected by the rigours of malaria. None of this showed in his serene scarcely lined face although he was approaching sixty. He had not long been offered the wide flung pastorate that embraced Fairlie Downs and other stations as well as some small outback towns. A legacy had enabled him to use his own plane in the highlands of Papua New Guinea and he had brought it home with him, finding it so useful that he and his wife were prepared to go without in order to keep it in the air.

He had visited Fairlie Downs once before and was known to the brothers and had not yet realised that gold awaited his discovery. So the information that Jamie had given him over the phone had amazed and thrilled him. To think that there had been a secret disciple in Mark all the time!

Jamie and Mark did not want to repeat their wedding vows as they had already put their hearts into the actual Service but Mr Savage had come up with some words for them to say that they took to at once and carefully rehearsed with him. Jamie's were the immortal words of Ruth and Mark's were something the Pastor had adapted from Matthew Henry's description of the making of woman.

Every chair on the estate was gathered and arranged in semi-circular rows in the big tent. A simple table and chair provided the pulpit. All those who had had to go back to Seven Trees to sleep now arrived in full force including Ashley and his violin. He would lead the singing; the young guitarists would be content to strum the accompaniment as they scarcely knew a hymn between them.

Right on time the company assembled, full of anticipation at a novel experience. At the last moment Mark and Jamie came up the centre aisle, he in his safari suit and Jamie in her white dress with a circlet of small white flowers from Howie's garden in her hair.

The choice left to him, Ashley played *I'll walk beside you* as they took their seats in the front row with Morris and Alison, Stella and Geoff. Hugh had deliberately steered Brooke to a couple of rows back and Sarah followed them. To choose not to stand by his brother was a mean act but the congregation could not have cared less.

It has been said in Scripture that the one who has the bride is the bridegroom, naturally. All eyes were on the happy pair, some thinking that Mark seemed to have grown taller in his new happiness and many envying him the radiant girl by his side.

The Service opened with a hymn well known to the oldies. Then the Pastor read the Love Chapter from Corinthians. He went straight on to the wedding address he had prepared on *The Maturing of Love*. Using the form of engagement then marriage and family, he showed similar steps in the Christian's path with its first radiant acceptance of Christ, the maturing walk and finally the bearing of fruit in service. His message was ostensibly for the bride and groom but the teaching was for everyone present.

At the conclusion, he asked Mark and Jamie to come forward and required everyone to stand. Facing them he said,

"This young couple was married in Brisbane but they want to share with you the solemnity of their commitment to each other. He turned to Mark and simply invited him to speak.

His colour high Mark took just a brief glance at the small card in his hand and then took Jamie's hand and turned to the congregation.

"I call upon you all present here today to witness that I am committed to Jamie for all our lives. I have taken her as my true and loving wife, not to be at my head to rule over me, nor to be at my feet that I may tread on her but to be at my side, under my arm to be protected and near my heart to be cherished."

The Pastor nodded to Jamie who turned directly to Mark and said, "Where you go, I will go, where you stay, I will stay. Your people shall be my people and your God my God. Where you die, I will die and there will I be buried. May the Lord deal with me, be it ever so severely, if anything but death separates you and me."

Mark then took Jamie into his arms and once more sank into a deep embrace while the crowd remained standing and hushed. Hugh moved restlessly, impressed despite himself. He'd like something special in his marriage to Brooke, too. He half turned to her and was amazed. The tears were pouring down Brooke's cheeks. He pulled out his handkerchief, offering it to her as he tried to put a comforting arm around her. The girl pushed him away, heedless of everything but her own revelation.

"That's what was wrong with my marriages," she whispered under her breath. "There was nothing of God in them… nothing."

She looked past the people in front of her, past the embracing couple on towards the minister, unconsciously seeking help but his benevolent eye was on the two before him. Then her seeking glance encountered the kind eyes of Ashley standing near. He smiled encouragingly at her and lifted his violin bow. As his eyes held hers, the soft strains of an old wedding song filled the air:

> *Oh, promise me that some day you and I*
> *Will take our love together to some sky*
> *Where we can be alone and faith renew*
> *And find the hollows where the flowers grew…*

Brooke knew the words, the song had been sung at her own first wedding, a most elaborate affair where in an aura of tulle and lace she had light-heartedly made her vows to the debonair man at her side.

Instead of the bitterness of memory she felt an extraordinary sense of comfort.

There was a stirring around her as Mark finished his kiss. Geoff had timed him with the second hand of his watch. Brooke looked quickly down, not wanting to engage anyone else's attention for the moment. That music had seemed to hold a promise. Were the flowers of true love still waiting for her somewhere? Hand in hand with the right someone? A tiny ashamed hope was born.

"All right?" Hugh was bending solicitously over her.

"Yes, sorry." Brooke took the proffered handkerchief this time and used it. She felt cheered as they sang the final hymn and received the benediction.

Afterwards everyone said that it was as good as the wedding itself and old Mark was a dark horse if ever there was one.

It was close on eleven o'clock so, instead of morning tea, an early lunch was set out to fuel the travellers, many of whom had a long journey ahead of them. Mark and Jamie were in constant attendance on the occupants of the many cars and small planes as farewells were made. A few were remaining including the Pastor at Jamie's special request.

As soon as she was free Jamie sought out Ashley. All through the first part of the Service she had been intrigued by the Bible beside Ashley from which he had read when the Pastor had quoted from the Love Chapter. It was obviously an old well used Book. Taking hold of his hard calloused hand, she said tentatively,

"May I see your Bible, Ashley?"

"Of course." He fetched it for her and stood smiling while she thumbed the well-worn pages.

"This looks as though it has been well used." She looked up.

He nodded. "Read a chapter every night. Have done ever since it was given to me."

"Given to you? Who –"

"A Governess the boys had at one time. Actually, it was her own Bible. She said she could get another one."

Jamie was trembling. Surely… could it be the same one? She turned to the flyleaf and there was the name Mary Allingham and added underneath: Ashley Arthur Lawrence.

"Ashley, what happened? I mean how did she come to give it to you?"

Ashley looked a little embarrassed. "Well… she used to talk about God a lot and she wanted me to do something about it. What she called taking Christ as my Saviour. I kind of wanted to but I didn't. She was going away 'cause she said that God wanted her on the mission field."

"So – what happened?"

"Well, the very day she was going something came over me – a kind of panic. So I drove over from Seven Trees and bailed her up outside her room. She had one of those opening on to the veranda. I kind of stammered out that I wanted to do what she said." Ashley paused with a reminiscent smile that seemed to have something of tenderness in it. Jamie caught his hand again.

"Ashley, did you like her? I mean was there anything…"

'No – nothing like what you're thinking. I hardly knew her. She worked over here with Ed, my brother's kids. Her cases were just about packed but she dropped everything and got her Bible, this one, out of one of them and took me through the plan of salvation. She was praying with me when they started calling her, for the plane was ready. She pushed the Bible into my hands, told me to read it daily, locked her cases and I helped her carry them out. That's all."

Jamie drew a deep breath. "She must have been some woman – to give away her own Bible like that."

"She was. As I think about it now she was a very strong forthright lady. She was sadly missed when she went. We never seemed to get another as good."

"Why did you keep it a secret? Were you afraid of being persecuted or something?"

"Of course not. Why - back in my grandfather's day he had Sunday Services where everyone on the station that could be spared had to attend. The practice was kept up less and less after he went."

"A pity… but didn't you tell anyone?"

"There was no one to tell. People didn't talk about religion in those days."

"I think there was someone. How old would Mark have been then?"

"Oh, he was just a little chap – about eight or nine."

"I think it was this Governess who led Mark to the Lord right back then."

Ashley stared. Jamie became thoughtful. There they were: the two of them, quietly reading their Bibles and saying nothing to anyone, not knowing that fellowship was an arm's length away.

"Ashley, did –"

"Now listen, young woman, I've talked more to you than I have to anyone for six months. Just let's -"

"I was just going to ask if you knew that Mr Savage is staying for a while longer so we can have a chat about spiritual things. Mark and Stella will be there. Would you like to come along?"

"Sure would. He'd be the one to talk to if anyone was unhappy, wouldn't he?"

"Oh, yes. Why?"

"Maybe Brooke would like to come too. She was crying when you and Mark were speaking."

"Was she? I'll go and ask her."

Brooke declared herself most willing to come to the annex, to Hugh's chagrin for he had been looking forward to a long afternoon alone with her.

The group that finally gathered around the Pastor also included Geoff Rossitor who was determined to be in anything that interested Stella.

Jamie looked forward to a happy time but first she had to be sure.

"Mark, what was the name of the Governess who led you to the Lord?"

"Miss Allingham."

"There you are, Ashley." Jamie went quite pink with pleasure. She explained to the others all that had happened while Ashley and Mark looked at each other with new eyes. A most peculiar expression appeared on the Pastor's face. After they had all done exclaiming he asked to see Ashley's Bible. Mark showed his too: a small thick one such as is given to inquirers at a Crusade.

"Miss Allingham gave me this one," he explained. "I guess that's why she had to give hers to Ash."

Mr Savage picked up his own Bible, opened it at the flyleaf and turned it around for them all to read. They all leaned forward and read:

To Lee on the occasion of our wedding. May you be saturated in its teaching. All my love, Mary.

The writing was the same as that on the flyleaf of Ashley's Bible. They were all transfixed with astonishment and then joy flowed.

"Where did you meet?" asked Jamie, beside herself with excitement.

"On the mission field in Papua New Guinea. Wait till I see her tonight. Mary had told me that she had worked at Fairlie Downs many years ago but she had not liked to put herself forward."

"You must bring her next time," Mark said warmly. "It would be great to see her again."

Ashley assented heartily. This was all a bit above the heads of Brooke and Geoff but great joy and excitement are catching and they were intrigued despite themselves.

Knowing the status of most of them Mr Savage just chatted generally about the things of God, leading them on till their tongues loosened and encouraging them to ask questions. Geoff, it turned out, had dozens of unsolved problems about the universe and asked some pertinent questions. Brooke asked none. Having made up her mind that she was going to have whatever it was that Mark and Jamie had, she listened and drank in every word that fell from the Pastor's lips. Before he left that day, Mr Savage was firmly committed to a return visit in the near future, this time with his wife.

CHAPTER NINETEEN

Fruit Bearing

A certain lassitude lay over the company after the big weekend but the usual morning ride was now the rule with the three amateurs showing increasing proficiency. Jamie, like Morris, was learning to love the exercise and Mark saw, rather ruefully, that she was falling in love with the sturdy mount he had provided. Greystock was not up to the quality of the horse he eventually wanted her to have. Hugh, on the other hand, was giving Brooke the chance to try out others of the excellent stock horses and quarter horses that the station carried.

After the ride, Mark went to his office, Jamie to the caravan, Morris to the stockyards and Alison drove over to see Sarah, with whom she was getting on very well.

This left Brooke open to Hugh's attentions but she was proving elusive. Very friendly, interested, great company, but when he tried anything further she drew a veil. He had not even kissed her yet. Had he felt less he would soon have remedied this state of affairs. However, he was fast coming to adore the ground Brooke walked on and was unaccountably shy in this new love. In his need to make a good impression on her he showed her consideration in everything not realising that his feelings were an open book to the rest as his gaze followed her all the time. Jamie had a word for it: cow-eyed.

However, this all made for a good atmosphere and the visitors relaxed, finding that they were really enjoying station life.

Under all this congeniality and bonhomie two matters festered: on Jamie's side, she had not as yet broached the matter of a separate dwelling for the new family and on Hugh's side the opportunity for vengeance on Jamie.

Hugh's venom was well hidden but still flourished, for his objection to his brother's marriage had not abated. In his busy little mind Jamie had worked deceitfully from the very first, evidently

195

encouraging Mark behind his back, then inveigling his brother to Brisbane and springing the trap. Along with it went his refusal to acknowledge the fact that Mark had somehow upstaged him in attracting Jamie. When Claudia had fallen for Mark, he had not been around but he had soon sorted that one out. With Jamie, he had always been around and her lack of response to his attractions carried a smart that would not go away. All his life Hugh had been first in everything and, at this stage in his career, was not prepared to abdicate his throne.

Jamie had not lowered her battle colours either. She was determined that Mark should have status as the elder brother and had her own little schemes for bringing this about with the unblushing cooperation of Mrs Howard. By the simple expedient of having cold drinks available in the annex in the afternoon and inviting Althea, the overseer's wife, over (a gesture much appreciated) she made an attractive oasis which acted as a magnet for tired bodies. The overseer naturally followed his wife, Mark dropped into his rightful seat, Brooke and the others came without question and Hugh had either to sit alone on his veranda or join them which he did, marking up another score against Mark's impertinent wife.

These scores were mounting. Mrs Howard consulted Jamie on every domestic issue. Together they planned the meals, organised the help, consulted with Mark on the entertainment of their guests. All this of course was the legitimate female field where Hugh's interference would have been ludicrous. Jamie also stimulated Brooke and Morris to shine at the meal table, which both had a flair for anyway. Hugh found himself simply becoming one of the group instead of the genial dominating figure he was used to being. His one all-powerful trump card should have been Brooke and their new status as an engaged couple but he was as yet unable to play it.

Mark waited, troubled, for the waters to grow calmer. Not that their ruffled state appeared on the surface. Outwardly all was sweetness and light. Hospitality at Fairlie Downs appeared at its best.

The following Sunday, the Minister and his wife flew in and received a great welcome. Jamie looked curiously at Mary Savage, black haired and grey eyed, and decided that she was a force to be reckoned with. The ex-missionary was a fully dedicated woman, sold out to the Lord in every way. What she could no longer do on the outflung frontiers of the tropics she did in the outback, supporting her husband in his huge parish. She had an instinctive way of homing in on the neediest soul. While Jamie and Mark drove over to Seven Trees with Mr Savage to greet and bring back Ashley and Sarah, Mary took Brooke off for a long walk to Hugh's dismay.

Hitherto religion had been just a vague thing in his mind. He knew that, in the old days, regular services had been held at Seven Trees, his great grandfather actually taking some of them to which the entire station, black and white, had been summarily bidden. Was that pest of a Jamie going to resurrect all that with its benign influence over all and sundry, thereby adding more accolades to herself?

He sat with Morris and Alison who, while not in sympathy with him, went along with his views on this matter. They sincerely hoped that Jamie was not going to end up a religious fanatic.

The advent of Mary Savage into Brooke's life was equivalent to an ocean liner coming alongside a small distressed rudderless boat, tossing helplessly in the waves, and taking it aboard. Brooke was at the crossroads, dangerous crossroads. Brought up with her remarkable beauty recognised very early she had been idolised by her father and spoilt and exploited by her mother. The winning of a major beauty contest at fifteen had been the springboard to launch her as a professional model and photographer's dream. She was also launched into a shallow social set, over which she queened, knowing that any desirable male would fall into her lap, a ripe plum, without even having to shake the tree. This had not made for popularity among her own sex, only one or two, like Jamie, discovering the warm and endearing nature buried under the light artificiality she and others of her set wore.

Brooke's first marriage had occasioned a rude awakening. She might attract the moths but she had not the wit nor the experience to choose the best. She fell heavily for a glamour boy in the racing world and found he cared nothing for the personality inside that lovely body. Even then her body was only one of many to him. Disillusioned and humiliated, Brooke had finally faced the truth. She was nothing more than another trophy to be put among his cups. For some time her pride would not let her seek the divorce courts, thereby admitting defeat. When she finally did so, Brooke set about freshening herself and getting on with life. She had been wounded but did not think there would be lasting scars.

However, Brooke found herself unable to break free of the social set that was her milieu even though she could see it for the shallow thing it was. Her friendship with Jamie grew stronger at this time for Jamie's father had been still alive and they had taken her with them on a caravan trip to the red heart on a painting tour. On her return Brooke met a budding film producer and there was much talk of her going into films. He talked her blind on her star qualities and on the glamorous life she would lead. When she could no longer see straight he told her about himself and his troubles, leaving out one important factor. Rather on the rebound, Brooke fell for him. They married and he took her on location with him ostensibly to learn the ropes of screen acting. In no time her romance crashed at her feet. A totally heterogeneous woman, already feeling soiled from her first husband's adulterous behaviour, she could not handle this new problem. Bewildered and inexperienced Brooke sought advice and was told that these persons were sick and needed help. She finally came to the conclusion that the reason he had pressed marriage was so as to secure what he thought was going to be a highly successful product. Brooke got out only to find herself pursued remorselessly with promises of future success coupled with exemplary behaviour. Neither the changed behaviour nor the promised success materialised and the thoroughly disillusioned woman once again achieved her freedom through the divorce courts.

In the meantime Jamie's father had died and Brooke did not feel she could burden her grieving friend with her troubles. Coincidentally her own father passed away at this time so she went with her mother on a world trip ostensibly to ease their combined grief but, in Brooke's case, to take stock of her life which, like a whirling dervish, was defying every attempt to guide it into a safe and secure harbour.

Depression was setting in. Her always successful modelling career offered no challenges. There was no sure goal she could point to, no clearly marked path in life. In a cynical state of mind Brooke had returned to Brisbane and gone along to a certain ballet performance and caught up with Jamie again. Unknown to herself, Brooke had started down a new path that was to lead unerringly to this walk with Mary Savage.

Brooke unburdened herself completely to Mary who soon saw that here was a true-hearted woman who had tried and failed twice and was now shaken to the core. In a strange way, these trials had done the girl good for the spoilt artificial veneer had been stripped off. Brooke was seeking realities now, sure foundations and straightforward values.

Mary did not preach religion at the troubled woman. She simply treated the walk as a confessional, drawing Brooke out and listening, in a non-judgmental way, that encouraged her not only to confess the intimate details of her double humiliation but to find relief in so doing, much as a patient does with a doctor. Finally, Brooke told her about Mr Savage's conduct of Mark and Jamie's ceremony.

"Oh, I knew then that I had no idea what marriage was all about. Every word he said was like knives going through me."

They were sitting on some rocks under a tree. At least Mary was sitting thus. Brooke was crouching hunched on a slab at her knee while her new friend caressed the bright head and eventually drew it to rest.

"Let the knives do their surgical work, my dear, we must let all this poison out first. Once the cleansing has been done then healing can commence.'

"It's so wonderful to talk like this," Brooke murmured. "I did not want to burden Jamie with all this but – but you're different."

Mary smiled, letting the comment pass. She was wondering how much further she dared take the conversation when Brooke stirred restlessly.

"Oh, I can see it would be wonderful to feel cleansed but I want more than that. I'd like actually to *be* cleansed… to be as though it had never happened. You see I felt - feel so soiled."

Mary could not ignore this opening.

"It's others' sin that has soiled you in this case, Brooke, but we all have to deal with our own sins. There is a cleansing I can offer you, however, that will not only cleanse you completely but heal all your wounds."

Brooke pulled back and looked at her incredulously. "Isn't that a bit farfetched?' she asked sceptically.

Mary smiled. "There was a woman once who came out for counselling during a big evangelistic campaign some years back. I suppose I should explain it to you as a big church rally. The preacher had explained that Jesus could take the most sinful person who repented and make him as clean as a newborn babe and she had come out on this hope. But when it came to the crunch she could not accept it for herself. The woman who was trying to help her sought for a convincing example of the forgiving power of the Lord. At last she said, 'Jesus would not care if you were the most notorious prostitute in the city.' The woman gave a little gasp and said, 'that's exactly who I am.' God had guided the counsellor to give the one illustration that would reach the woman's heart."

Mary sat back and looked for the effect of this story on Brooke.

"I suppose you are going to tell me that this woman turned over a new leaf," the girl said doubtfully.

"I am, my dear. She had a wonderful renewal, a true rebirth. I met her once. She became a tireless worker for the Lord among the very women who had been her sisters in prostitution."

"I like that word 'rebirth'," said Brooke and then hid her face in her hands and began to sob, "Oh, to be clean… to be truly clean," she wept and Mary knew that her time had come.

Not long afterwards the greatest miracle in the world took place and Brooke was born again.

They were so late getting back that Ashley came in the car to fetch them. Brooke shyly stood back while the two greeted each other and renewed a friendship after a span of twenty-four years. The drive back was enlivened with much talk and reminiscence while Brooke sat quietly in the back with her new and beautiful thought patterns. She blessed and blessed again the day when Jamie had been used of God to set her on this path. So, much good had come out of Hugh's little tricks after all, she mused with a touch of mischief in her involuntary grin.

Mary and her husband were invited to stay overnight, something they frequently anticipated in their huge parish. Sarah and Ashley stayed for dinner and during a pleasant evening Hugh's and Jamie's hidden feud seemed quite buried.

Over three weeks had passed and, as yet, Mark had made no move about their house. Jamie was getting restless but Morris advised caution for he felt that Jamie herself was not in the right mood to handle the matter and, unfortunately, he was right.

CHAPTER TWENTY

Dangerous Corner

Jamie had been much pestered by Morris to do another dirt picture, this time for him. Remembering the lovely colours in the gorge near the caves she decided to work off some of her frustration by doing one there and taking Maxie along for a further lesson. Told of the caves the others naturally wanted to come too.

At the last minute Ashley arrived with a visitor, the nature of whose business was vital to the brothers.

"No help for it," said Hugh, preparing to lead Vulcan back to the stables. "I guess Maxie will have to guide them."

"Where are they all going?" asked Ashley trying not to fix his eyes on Brooke.

"Out to the caves – oh and some want to do a bit of drawing there," this with a nod in Maxie's direction only.

"Why don't you go, Ash?" asked Mark as he dismounted. "They need proper guidance to go down into the caves, more than Maxie can give them. Here." He threw Red's reins to his uncle.

"Sure you don't need me?" Ashley looked questioningly at the men. Alec Cartwright, the visitor answered for them.

"Nope. Just about pumped you dry."

They all laughed and, with a pleased grin, Ashley mounted Red with the incomparable ease of the stockman and the party moved off.

He had consistently fought every temptation to come to Fairlie Downs without a cut and dried pretext and one had unexpectedly fallen his way. May as well take what the gods offered. Nevertheless, he moved to Morris's side and queried his riding progress. Morris was feeling much more at home in the saddle now and they chatted amiably. Jamie, burning over Hugh's treatment of her as non-existent, held her tongue and rode with Maxie, leaving the other two women to their pleasant chitchat.

Arriving at the gorge, they all wanted to ride up it and were loud in their praise of the extraordinary and beautiful colours. Jamie and Maxie then unloaded their stuff and set off to collect their coloured dirt. Morris lingered but Jamie told him to go off and see the cave first.

Arriving at the shallow depression Ashley explained about the narrow drop.

"Best to have just two of us at a time," he advised.

Morris gallantly hung back for the women and Brooke politely stood back for Allison so they went in that order. The other two sat under a spindly bush while Ashley took Allison down. Morris surveyed Brooke narrowly.

"You seem a good deal happier these days."

Brooke smiled a secret smile. Both she and Jamie knew it was useless to explain the source of her happiness yet.

"Yes, I am. Much happier. This visit has been a watershed in my life."

"You haven't fallen for Hugh after all have you?" Morris queried anxiously. He had no time at all for Hugh.

"Good heavens, no…"

"Probably the only woman who hasn't."

'You're forgetting Jamie," Brooke reminded him with a mischievous grin.

"Yeah, so I was. Well, he's sure getting his comeuppance from you two… and one after the other. Must feel his technique is slipping badly."

"As far as Jamie was concerned she never saw him and as for me, his technique is old hat."

"And that's for me fine Hughie as Jamie would say." said Morris with a satisfied air and they both laughed. "You know," he went on with a serious note in his voice, "this whole business is a kind of watershed in Hugh's life too. How he eventually handles it will show what kind of character he really has."

Brooke nodded. "I think there's some good there but it's been warped by being allowed to have his own way all the time plus this stupid tradition. He should never have been permitted to feel that he is the heir-apparent. Mark was always the older brother just as their father was the older one."

"Yes, but Mark is so damned self-effacing that sometimes you'd hardly know he was there. Keeps his light under a bushel, that one."

"Umm… but he's an absolute gem," remarked Brooke dreamily. "those kind don't often grow two on a tree."

"Well, I reckon Ashley's one of the same breed. Pity there wasn't a Jamie in his life long ago."

Brooke got up. "How long are those two going to be?" she said as she moved restlessly to where the horses were tied. "We'll be all day at this rate."

Eventually they heard a rattle of stones as the other two came scrambling down.

"Fascinating," announced Allison enthusiastically as she landed at their feet. "Just you wait and see. There's a —"

"Well that's just what we've been waiting to do, honey," interrupted Morris. "Don't spoil it for us."

Brooke laughed and began to climb the rocky rise towards Ashley who had waited half way down for her. He did not offer to help which was perhaps why Brooke felt rather breathless when they finally arrived at the cave's opening.

"Goodness, don't tell me we've got to get down there," she said, peering dubiously into the darkness.

"Yep. I'll go first. Just hang on if you're scared."

"Of course I'm scared. I hate narrow dark places. Hope I don't touch anything slimy."

"Well, you'd better grab me then as the walls are damp in places."

Like Jamie, Brooke grabbed a handful of her guide's shirt and came down safely. She stood there amazed as Ashley shone the torch around. He did a more thorough job than Mark, pointing out each unique formation, lighting it up as he spoke. He left the shawl till last and, after showing it to her, left her stranded in the dark as he felt his way around in order to backlight it. Brooke caught her breath,

"What a purely perfect thing," she whispered.

"Like you," said a voice. It seemed to be disembodied, coming out of the walls themselves. Even Ashley wondered for a moment as to its source. "It's very fragile," he went on hurriedly, his face burning in the dark above the torch. "Wouldn't take much to shatter it."

"Like me," said Brooke involuntarily and again the words seem to speak themselves.

"No, not like you," stated Ashley firmly.

"I was like that once – complete, I mean, or I thought I was. But I was shattered and –"

"No you weren't," with that extraordinary note of firmness again. "You're not frail, Brooke, underneath you're very strong or you wouldn't have come through all that so well."

"So you know all about 'all that'."

"Just what was said at the party."

Brooke felt she might as well know the worst. "What did you think of me, Ashley?"

"Just what I thought before I heard. You're gold, Brooke. You can't damage a gold ingot. Oh, you can chip bits off it… or melt it down… or drop it overboard and let it sink into the depths of the ocean and leave it there for centuries. Then you can fish it up and it's just the same: a gold ingot, one hundred percent."

"That," said Brooke shakily, "is one of the most healing things that has ever been said to me."

"But – Mary said you've received healing from Christ."

"That's true, gloriously true," said Brooke, "but that was from God. This – what you've just given me – is from man."

There was a soft expectant silence. Ashley did not know how to reply either to her words or the tone of her voice. At last, with his own tones roughened by emotion, he managed to say prosaically, "Well, I'd better get you up so I can bring Morris down."

He came back and brushed past Brooke in order to take the lead. She followed him till they came to the opening above them.

"I hope you're at least going to give me a hand up," she said petulantly.

"Sure," his hard hand gripped hers unmercifully and Brooke found herself hoisted swiftly to his side. They went back to the others in silence and Brooke did not start raving about the cave as Allison had. She just sat quietly down beside Allison who thought she understood.

"Awe inspiring, isn't it?" she remarked.

Brooke nodded absently. "I wonder how Jamie's getting on."

"She should be finished by now, surely. Morry's a bit disappointed. He likes to watch her work."

"Well he should have gone first," snapped Brooke irritably. "Then he could have ridden back to them."

Allison glanced across at her in surprise. She wondered if Brooke was contemplating drawing her visit to a close. If she did not fancy Hugh, then his continual attentions must be getting on her nerves. Still, she need not take it out on them.

Eventually the two men returned and Morris was warm in his praise. It had been well worth waiting for.

They all mounted and rode back to the others. As Allison had predicted Jamie was finished. Her effort lay at one side in the shadow of a rock while she discussed Maxie's picture with him. The two paintings were of exactly the same scene yet were totally different. Morris leant over Jamie's for some time. It was a most delicately mysterious impression of the narrow part of the gorge where a minimum of sky could be seen, where the shadows were almost purple on one side and palest rose on the other.

Morris sighed his satisfaction and then turned to Maxie's. Here every twist and turn and moulding of the cliff face was clearly etched, the shadows sharp, the whole thing having a three-dimensional effect. There was no doubt the boy had talent. Morris nodded and smiled and patted Maxie on the back. He said nothing at all to Jamie but charged himself with the task of carrying the fragile work back. Jamie had brought the proper fixative this time and had already given the pictures their first light spray. After a few more sprays, she pronounced the works ready to travel, so they packed their goods and set off for home.

Brooke rode beside Maxie and asked him about his art before Jamie came along. It seemed that he had not been considered anything special by his peers. Most everyone could paint, according to Maxie, and mostly in their own style which was now selling well.

When they got back it was to find there were more visitors. Mr Morrison had arrived with his daughter, Sylvia. They were all well ensconced on Hugh's veranda with Hugh, Alec Cartwright and Mark. Hugh waved to Brooke and called out. "Don't wait to change. Drinks are here."

Jamie was happy to accede and a pleasant half hour was spent in chat till the riding party began to peel away and go for their showers. Jamie lingered as she was curious to watch Hugh with Sylvia and Brooke. It was very interesting. Hugh included both girls in his conversation, attending impartially to what each had to say. When he was addressing Brooke, Sylvia listened with a tolerant little smile flickering about her lips. I wonder if she really, really likes him… more than she lets on, wondered Jamie.

Brooke, herself, was giving nothing away either. She neither rebuffed Hugh nor encouraged him. Nobody would be able to reproach her with having flirted with him as he deserved and then left him high and dry. Yet she was careful to leave the gate open so that Hugh did not actually feel rejected.

Jamie knew that Brooke was doing this for her and she was troubled. Things would have to come to a head soon. She could not play around like this with other lives. They had to get on with the business of living too. Brooke could now get off to a flying start on her new life once free of the present situation.

In the end the whole matter came out in a way nobody could have predicted and all through a mischievous mischance.

Next day when the mail was delivered there was an oblong parcel for Mark and Jamie. Various wedding presents had been coming their way and Jamie casually opened this one in the presence of the others. Everyone was interested so they watched as Jamie took out a long white box, opened it and began to undo the Styrofoam packing. Eventually there was exposed what looked like three slender organ pipes, some long wires and a bell push.

"Door chimes!" exclaimed Allison. 'Oh, Jamie, how delightful! You know, for your new house."

Wrapped in the delight of the gift, Jamie caught up the card and read out a cheeky note from Stella and Geoff to the effect that no one would be able to sneak up to their front door and surprise them.

"As if anyone could," laughed Jamie. "Any visitors will be seen long before they cross the first cattle grid."

She turned to Mark and found him standing as though stuffed. She turned to Allison who now had her hand to her mouth. Morris was looking grim and Brooke wretched. It had been her easy confidential remark at the party that had let the cat out of the bag to Stella. In the suddenly frozen atmosphere Jamie found Hugh's hostile eye upon her.

"And just where will this new house be, if I may ask?" Everyone felt the menace in his voice.

"Somewhere on this property. We haven't quite decided yet," answered Jamie boldly before Mark could speak.

Hugh moved across to confront his brother directly thereby rudely cutting Jamie out.

"You're not thinking of wasting money building another house on the property, surely Mark?" His tone made it sound as though there was a superabundance of houses already.

Mark nodded. "Thought you'd like to keep this present one for when you marry."

"Nonsense. Plenty of room for us both here. Forget it." He nodded at the guilty chimes. "Just a silly joke. However, I'll have them put up here for you today."

He then strolled nonchalantly away, leaving the company like so many netted fish gasping on a bleak shore.

Allison who had stood up the better to see what was in the box now sat down suddenly as one who felt her legs could no longer hold her. Jamie caught up the chimes protectively, the tears springing to her eyes. "Oh Mark, don't let him put them up here, please."

Mark shook his head vaguely, a frown appearing on his clear forehead. No one else knew what to say. They had spent a lot of time marshalling their arguments for this occasion but none seemed to fit the total veto.

At last Morris bestirred himself and took control. "It doesn't matter what Hugh says or doesn't say," he stated. "He can't stop you choosing a site. He can't stop you ordering the building material or employing the men. Just go ahead, Mark, regardless of what he says."

They all looked at Mark to see how he would take this most sensible advice.

"And make an enemy of my brother?" he asked quietly.

"Haven't you forgotten something?" asked Morris testily. "You have someone else to think of now. Someone I hope is at least as dear to you as your brother. In fact, she should be more dear."

"Jamie wouldn't be happy either," replied Mark.

"I'll take my chance on that," said his wife sharply. "If I have to choose between the heaven of living in our own house with you and the hell of sharing the same house with Hugh I won't be hesitating."

Mark said nothing.

"It's utter nonsense," averred Allison, vexed to find that they were using their arguments on Mark and not on his brother. "How could your living in another house affect Hugh's happiness? He could have been married years ago and have a couple of kids himself by now. Where would be the room for you and Jamie then and the family you hope to have? You'd be building that extra house sooner or later so why not now and be done with it?"

Mark said nothing.

Brooke moved forward. "I can't tell you how sorry I am about this. I was the one who let the secret out to Stella and –"

"It's better out," said Jamie. "Seeing we're into this situation already I'm sorry we didn't go into battle sooner. I – I need your support." She looked appealingly at her aunt and uncle and Brooke. They all noticed that she did not once look at her husband.

"We'll stick with you till the end, Jimmy," Morris declared. "Even if I have to go, Allison will stay."

"I'm free too," added Brooke. "I know it's really a family affair but we are all your family in a way, Jamie."

Jamie's eyes misted again. "Thank you," she whispered voicelessly.

Mark said nothing.

Morris gazed levelly at Jamie's husband. "You know," he began in a cool tight voice, "since primitive days man has carved out a home for his wife and family. Pioneers here faced desperate circumstances when they went to the outback but they managed and survived. It was a mark of manhood. Now it's all done so easily these days…" he let his voice trail off but his meaning was clear.

Mark took off his glasses and felt for his handkerchief. Jamie automatically began to reach for them and then sharply withdrew her hand. Mark polished the lens slowly staring down at his hands. Then he put them back on and, for a fleeting moment, before they went into place, the others saw his eyes. There was a strained silence and then Morris spoke briskly:

"Well, let's leave it for the moment. Got to get our bearings again. What's for dinner Jamie?"

"Duck with orange sauce," muttered Jamie forlornly as though she was offering them their last meal on earth.

"One of my favourites," said Morris heartily.

"Will you excuse me? I have to go out to the office." Mark was gone on the words.

Allison walked over and put her arms around Jamie. "I think he's pretty upset, dear."

"Well, what do you think I am?" cried the girl. "It's all so stupid."

"It seemed to me," said Brooke slowly, "that Mark was thinking of greater issues than a new house would involve. That's just my impression."

"Well, there are greater issues involved,' asserted Allison. "the happiness of a new little family just starting out in life. Can't Hugh just for once put himself in Mark's place. I bet he would have been on Mark's heels to get him to move out if he brought you here as a bride."

A shadow slid across Brooke's face. "There's no hope of that," she said quietly and moved out on to the veranda as though she did not want anyone looking at her just then. After a few minutes she called to the others:

"Come and see. Quickly."

They all went out on to the veranda from where they could see Mark's office. Hugh was standing in the doorway and talking hard. With a little wounded cry Jamie turned into Allison's arms and they moved back inside.

"I know this," stated Morris grimly, "if we have to fight to the death, we'll get you your house, Jimmy, even if we have to stick a rod up the back of that jellyfish of a husband of yours. There... it's out now and I'm not sorry for it. He's absolutely spineless to let Hugh dominate him like that."

"Oh, Uncle, *don't*," Jamie wept. "I can't bear it. It's all got to do with some principle he lives by."

"Principle? I know of no craven principles that –"

"No, no, it's all to do with giving and –"

"Giving? Ay, you mean *giving in*. He's past master of that principle though what it's going to get him, I wouldn't know."

"No, Uncle. It means - it means dying to self somehow."

"Dying to self?" repeated Morris scandalised. "How can you possibly die to yourself? The whole instinct of life is towards survival and in the wilds, only the fittest make it. How long would your fine Mark last in the jungle? What's more to the point... how long would you last under his protection: a man who has not even the guts to provide a decent home for his wife *in this day and age*." Morris's final words were scorching in their burning contempt.

The only effect of this tirade was to increase Jamie's weeping and bring tears to his wife's eyes in silent agreement.

Brooke began to think that she had handled Hugh badly. She should have made it her business to so enthral him that her slightest wish was his law. And wouldn't she do some wishing, she thought vindictively. Perhaps it was not too late yet. Perhaps she could play him along till he gave in over the house. A small shudder shook her. No, she could not practice such tactics knowing what was in her own heart.

Dinner that night was a most difficult meal and the waste of a fine young duck. Hugh behaved as though nothing had happened and tried in the beginning to initiate the usual sprightly table talk. Receiving nothing but monosyllabic replies from his guests, and those only as a sop to good manners, he was finally reduced to dragging his silent brother in. Mark, who had not exchanged a word with Jamie when they showered and changed in the caravan, tried to meet him halfway but initiated no topic himself.

By dessert Hugh was angry and, when coffee was served in the lounge, he subsided into a sulky silence. Brooke moved to the piano and began to play softly something calculated to soothe the savage breast, of which there were quite a few in the room. Allison smiled, recognising the theme of Debussy's *The Engulfed Cathedral*. Pity they couldn't drop Hugh down there too.

Morris, feeling a trifle guilty over his criticism of Jamie's husband began to talk to Mark, recalling the days when she had travelled everywhere with her father in their caravan. Mark listened gratefully, smiling with genuine amusement at some of their exploits. Allison, covertly studying him, suddenly thought that he seemed the most serene of the lot of them.

Jamie went out to the laundry and brought in a kitten, one of the two spared from the latest effort of Howie's cat. She sat there cuddling the tawny ball and saying nothing to anyone. Both Morris and Allison knew what this meant. Whenever Jamie was deeply upset, she always looked for something to mother and had been known, in the absence of one of her own, to take even the family pets of neighbours up to bed with her. Allison had not forgotten the awful night when her beloved budgerigar had disappeared from his cage. Certain that he must still be in the house they had turned it upside down, not looking in Jamie's room for the door was shut.

It had been close to midnight when Allison had disconsolately gone into Jamie's room to check on the child, belatedly remembering that she had come home pretty upset about something at school. In the glow of the nightlight the sleeping girl lay, one arm out across the cover. With his feet tightly curled about one finger was the sleeping budgie puffed into a gold and green ball. She had beckoned to Morris and they had finally decided to quietly remove the bird lest she lie on it in her sleep.

Now she looked pityingly at the girl. Jamie must be in a bad way. Hugh recovered sufficiently from his sulks to go over to the piano and leaf through the sheet music. Soon he had Brooke playing some of his favourites. Allison moved over to Jamie and chatted quietly to her till Mrs Howard brought in supper.

As soon as supper was over, Jamie rose, said goodnight and went out without waiting for her husband. Allison saw Hugh note this with a sardonic smile. A point to him, she thought, you made a mistake there, my girl. Mark covered it as best he could by rising at once and following his wife.

When he entered the caravan he was amazed to find that she still had the kitten.

"Here, you can't keep it here all night. It'll be wanting its mother and keeping us awake. I'll take it back for you," he offered, taking the kitten out of Jamie's resistless grasp and departing with it.

Jamie sat on the end of the bed in slowly gathering wrath. Not only could she not have a house, she could not even have a cat.

Mark returning with a reassuring smile, meaning to comfort her himself, encountered a look calculated to freeze him where he stood He attended to his own preparations for bed and, once settled, picked up his Bible. After a few minutes, he realised that Jamie had not joined him. He glanced around and could not see his wife anywhere. He got up in a hurry and was just about to go outside when he saw her.

Jamie had quietly lowered one of the bunks at the other end of the van. With just a sheet over her she had settled nicely for a grand sulk when the sheet was jerked back and two arms came under to pluck her off her solitary couch. Mark carried her back and placed her in her usual position on their bed.

"We'll do our love-making and our quarrelling in the one bed," he said briefly, got back into bed and resumed his reading.

Jamie lay there in shock. *Quarrelling!* Were they actually quarrelling? They had not exchanged one angry word. It had been a war of silences. If this was to be what their quarrels were to be like, then she would have none of it. Better to get him talking. At least she could have her say. She turned and wriggled over till she was close to him. He immediately put his arm out and drew her close, never lifting his eyes from the printed page. Jamie cuddled in and rested a hand on his broad chest.

"What are you reading?" she asked tentatively.

"The Sermon on the Mount."

"But you've read that often before."

"I've been reading it all my life."

Jamie closed her eyes in despair. How could you fight the Bible?

Mark read on for a while. Then he closed the book and put it aside and lay for some time thinking. At last he stirred himself and glanced down at his wife. Something told him she was not asleep. She lay warm and delicious to his hand. He wondered if she was too tired and overwrought. Probably. This was one time when a new husband had to exercise tact and restraint, he thought wryly.

He took off his glasses and snapped off the light. Turning a little he lifted her chin in order to place a gentle kiss on her lips. But Jamie was not satisfied with a goodnight caress. She clung to him wanting the fullest possible comfort.

Her husband obliged her. He was better than the kitten after all.

CHAPTER TWENTY-ONE

More Tactics

The following morning saw several members of the party fighting fit and ready for the fray. The shock of the first encounter was over. They had remarshalled their arguments and were all ready for the opening fusillades. The trouble was that they could not pin down either quarry.

Hugh did not wait for the morning ride but went straight out with his men, taking his lunch. Mark announced that he had to go over to Seven Trees and tentatively invited Jamie to go with him. This put Jamie in a predicament. She would have liked to accompany her husband and grab the chance to get Ashley on side. Then the desire not to desert her loyal guests was strengthened by the thought of the ubiquitous Sarah always wanting to join in any conversation. So she made these same guests her excuses and waved Mark off. They did not urge her to go with him. It would be good to have the opportunity for another counsel of war.

After their ride, they all repaired to the annex where they told each other all over again how they felt which made them feel temporarily a bit better but did no lasting good.

"It's like boxing shadows," said Morris at last. "If the method around here is to have one conversation a week on the matter we won't be any further advanced by Christmas."

Jamie was feeling out of sorts. She stared disconsolately down at the beautiful home spread out at their feet. "You know Mark won't even take me over the ground so that we could at least have a site in mind. When I think of all the time we spent looking at curtain material…"

"And all the time Mark and I spent looking at plans," added Morris. "Damned waste of time."

"No, it's not," said Allison briskly and stood up. "Why don't we go and do a bit of surveying ourselves. Maybe we could pick out a couple of sites."

They looked inquiringly at Jamie. Ordinarily she would have wanted to keep this darling exercise for Mark and herself but now she got up wearily. "Let's. At least it's something constructive."

Mark had gone off in his new car so they took the station wagon and Morris drove it. They set off on a tour of the property considerably cheered by the activity. They roamed all over the place and Jamie welcomed every opinion or piece of advice. It was not long before they realised that the present house had the pick of positions in the near vicinity. Jamie agreed with Brooke, who said seriously,

"All things considered you really don't want to be in each other's backyard."

"Now I come to think of it, look how far Mark's father built from the old home."

Accordingly, they drew a wider circumference and eventually came upon a pretty rise with a dry creek bed at one side and a background of distant hills. The creek would only run in the rains but Morris, who had a flair for landscaping showed her how it would enhance the surrounding grounds. The more they looked at it the more they liked it and afterwards took only a perfunctory interest in other sites. It was necessary to be able to describe it to Mark so they took careful bearings and Morris noted the mileage as they drove back.

Mrs Howard met them with the message that they were all invited over to Seven Trees for dinner. Morris turned to Jamie.

"Do you reckon you could count on Ashley, Jimmy?"

"Yes, I do," said Jamie stoutly. "I'd count on Ashley anywhere and at any time."

Brooke looked at her with a veiled gaze as Morris began to outline his plan.

"You can bet your bottom dollar that neither Mark nor Hugh will mention it of their own accord. Why don't we spring it at the meal table? Announce to Ashley and Sarah the plan of a new house and follow it up at once with some suggestions for building sites. We can mention a couple of other sites that are not really suitable and toss in the real one. If I'm any judge of people they'll want to express their own views."

"If Sarah can stand the shock," murmured Jamie.

"What if Hugh ups and says 'nothing doing' like the other day?" asked Brooke dubiously.

"Well, surely there are enough of us to shout him down. Just laugh at him and say 'nonsense' like he did."

Jamie giggled. "Let's do it. We may as well have some fun and, if Hugh wants a thundering row, he can have it."

Oddly enough, not one of them, not even Jamie, let themselves think and wonder what Mark would like.

After lunch Sarah rang across to ask Brooke to bring some of her music over as Mark had said that she played beautifully. Brooke smiled at this. She was quite an accomplished pianist but sadly out of practice. She accordingly sat at the piano for the rest of the afternoon.

Allison took herself off for a nap as she was beginning to feel the heat. Morris wandered around the house looking for a suitable picture to dice so that he could claim the frame for Jamie's dirt picture. Jamie insisted he find one for Maxie's effort. Then she went off to lie on her bed but she was too tense to doze off. She reached for her Bible and, as though drawn by a magnet, began to read, very carefully, the Sermon on the Mount.

They were all showered and dressed by the time Hugh came in, work stained and weary. He brightened up at the news of the family gathering and was heard raising his deep baritone in the shower. Hugh was putting on a mask. He wished with all his heart that this present contretemps had not risen in Brooke's presence. He did not wish to appear in a bad light to his lady fair. People might just think he was being a bit mean whereas he was really out to stop Jamie wearing the pants around the property. His idea of a renovated wing would keep her in her place. Brooke was to be the acknowledged chatelaine of Fairlie Downs. He would not, of course, discuss it in front of Jamie. He and Mark would work it all out and she would have no choice but to accept it.

He was in a merry mood as he drove them over in his car. He complimented the ladies on their choice of dress and they, full of their own plans, answered pleasantly enough to lull him into a false security. Morris, the only one not thus complimented, did not bother to do any lulling but occupied himself with his own deep thoughts and plans.

The ladies were a pretty sight as they trooped up the stairs on to the front veranda where drinks were set out with Sarah presiding. Ashley stood with courtly grace to receive the party and charmed them all by saying that he had never seen such a bouquet of flowers in all his life. Jamie was in the soft blue that seemed to make her grey eyes bluer and her hair fairer. Allison was in the deep rose which set off her dark beautifully groomed hair. Brooke was wearing a filmy cream chiffon over a butter coloured silk sheath. Delicate panels of chiffon floated at the back from the shoulders. Her thick auburn tresses were dressed closely to her head and only allowed to fall to their full length at the back of her neck. With the slight pallor on a skin so fair that four weeks on the station had failed to affect it, the somewhat dreamy expression gave her an other-worldliness that was hard to pin down.

Two of the men present thought she simply dazzled the eyes. A third did not think about her at all. He had eyes only for his bride, a parting from whom for a whole day was still something of a penance. Mark always kept a supply of clothes at Seven Trees so he was also at his immaculate best. Sarah, in a familiar floral, had a moment of wishing she had taken more trouble but forgot about it in the business of preparing everyone's favourite drink.

The dinner started well with the men holding the forte as they discussed the day's doings. Jamie toyed with her food and Allison wondered anxiously if she were too nervous to eat. They must not leave her to do the fighting, poor pet. She had decided to fire the opening shot herself when a beautiful opening came. Sarah, not happy with the men hogging the conversation, asked:

"And what have you ladies been doing with yourselves today?"

"I'm glad you asked," Allison replied engagingly. "We've been looking for the right site for Mark and Jamie's new home. There are some choice positions. You have a wonderful property."

"Yes," agreed Morris. "Just wish I was building again. I'll be glad to come and take a hand when everything is under way."

"Of course, it's for you and Jamie to decide," said Brooke seriously, addressing Mark, "but Jamie, the artist, must have trees and water."

At this point Jamie laughed aloud. It was too funny. Ashley and Sarah were staring at the speakers. Hugh, taken completely off guard, had nevertheless rallied to the point of opening his mouth but was foiled by the quick comments of each speaker. Mark bit his lip but Allison could have sworn that there was a twinkle behind those glasses as he looked down at his plate.

But Jamie's laugh had given Hugh the break he wanted. He looked across at his aunt and uncle and said in a hard voice, "Just moonshine, my dears, just moonshine. Mark and I are going to renovate the wing and make it larger. We've been deciding just how to go about it."

This last was a mistake. Mark's surprised glance at his brother gave the lie immediately.

"Nonsense," said Morris loudly and with relish. "That's a whole bag of moonshine, my lad." Then he declared open war. "Jamie and Mark want a house of their own and they are going to have it if I have to camp on the property till it's finished."

Hugh went red with anger; Sarah white with shock. The colossal impertinence of it! Ashley, who by now had gathered his wits, looked across at Hugh and said quietly,

"I think another house would turn out the best in the end. Don't want to spoil the look of the main property with additions added higgledy piggledy."

With these few words, he announced where his allegiance would lie and also offered Hugh food for thought. Brooke glanced at him with approval. Behind that quiet demeanour lay a quick brain. Jamie did not like the inference that her house would be the inferior one but she saw the tact of such a thought at this stage. She too registered her approval to Ashley. He would make a good ally.

"But we can't go putting up houses every time someone gets married," objected Sarah with that air of disbelief that had so plagued Jamie.

"Why not?" asked Ashley coolly. "I'd have wanted a new house if I'd got married."

"*Well!*" That 'well' spoke volumes for the shattered Sarah. Panic leapt to her eyes as though Ashley were about to take off for matrimony there and then. He patted her hand.

"Not to worry, old girl. You look after me too well."

"The conversation's getting off the track," interposed Hugh. "No point in discussing the might have been. What matters now is the present situation. May I repeat myself? There will not be another house built on Fairlie Downs. An enlarged wing will supply all Mark's needs."

There was a concerted gasp. The selfish arrogance of it!

"What right have you, the younger brother, to lay down the law?" demanded Jamie, goaded to the limit.

Hugh's lip curled. "As I told you once before, it's none of your business, miss."

Everyone looked to Mark to see him defend his wife. He said nothing.

Jamie, her eyes filling with tears, began to rise from her seat but Mark placed a steadying hand on her arm.

"No need to get worked up," he suggested kindly.

Morris exploded. "She's every right to get worked up," he snapped, "seeing her darling dream of a new home shattered by this – this..." words failed him and he grabbed his drink wondering how far a guest could legitimately go in such a situation. There was not one sympathetic eye turned in Mark's direction. What kind of a doormat was he?

"W-would anyone care for d-dessert?" quavered Sarah.

It brought them to earth again. Everyone had stopped eating and now made haste to finish what was on their plates and turn their attention to the choice placed before them. The men took the steamed pudding and custard, and the ladies turned to the freshly made fruit salad accompanied by ice-cream or cream. Brooke chose neither so Sarah helped her to a double portion of the fruit. At all costs Hugh's latest and best must be kept sweet.

Dessert was eaten to the last mouthful in a heavy silence. No one knew quite where to go from here. Of course, they were all looking to Mark for a lead. One word from him and they would simply back him up to the hilt, over-riding Hugh and Sarah. By giving no leadership whatsoever, Mark was leaving Hugh in a position of strength. Even Morris realised that they could do nothing without the older brother's authority.

The minute that the last person had finished, Sarah, frightened that this terrible conversation would start up again, rose quickly to her feet and said, "Shall we have coffee on the veranda?"

As they rose, Morris, determined to make Mark speak and come down on one side or the other, spoke directly to him across the table.

"You've been very quiet, Mark. What is your preference? A house of your own or an appendage on your brother's?"

Then Mark spoke. "That's not the only alternative," he said and threw the entire company into doubting confusion.

What did he mean? What other alternative could there possibly be? Those who had been ready to continue the battle on the veranda now hesitated. If Mark had some other great idea, Jamie's supporters felt they could be wasting their breath arguing for the original plan. Sarah's worry frown increased. Hugh, for the first time, felt the ground give a little under his feet. Brooke thought and said nothing. She had lost interest in the conversation some time back.

When their coffee was finished, Sarah, making a brave effort to save her evening, timidly suggested to Brooke that she might like to give them a little music. Brooke, followed by Hugh, rose and slowly made her way to the living room where the much neglected piano stood. The rest of the company trouped after her with something of the air of lost sheep badly in need of a shepherd.

Hugh went to fetch the music that they had left in the car. While she waited, Brooke played a few arpeggios and was thankful that the instrument was not too out of tune. Sarah fussed over her, setting a lamp closer and remarking,

"I never had the gift. It was the children's mother and grandmother who could play."

Brooke nodded smiling. Then she took the first piece of music Hugh handed her and began to play. It was Beethoven's Fur Elise and she played the delicate thing mechanically. Steadily she worked through some of the music and her hearers sat back, thankful for the respite.

Then, as she started on *Traumerei*, the mellifluous tones of a violin began to mingle with the notes. She hesitated, lost the time and, with a murmured excuse, started again. By the time they finished she and Ashley were as one. Brooke now seemed to play with more assurance and feeling. Hugh, leaning over the piano, listened with a benign expression on his face. What splendid evenings they would have in the future! He could not remember one of his girlfriends having Brooke's talent. There was no doubt that she was the right one.

During the whole of the impromptu performance Brooke could not see Ashley for he had taken a seat directly behind her so that he could see the music. When she finally called it a day – or rather night - she swung around on the stool as Ashley lowered his instrument.

"Thank you," she said softly.

"Thank *you*," said Ashley and that was the total sum of their personal conversation although the piano and the violin had been talking to each other all night.

Sarah had gone out a little earlier to prepare supper and, once it was eaten the Fairlie Downs party got ready to depart. There were two cars for the return trip. Jamie would naturally go with Mark. Hugh would naturally take Brooke. While Morris and Allison were deciding which couple they should pay gooseberry to, Brooke gave them a wink which they grasped. She had a little ploy of her own to bring off and they wished her well.

Hugh thought it a heaven-sent opportunity. When he pulled up at a spot well short of the homestead Brooke had her defences ready. As he went to take her in his arms, she leaned back into her seatbelt and addressed him in Sarah's plaintive tones.

"Why can't Jamie and Mark have their own home?"

"We won't go into that just now, darling. I want –"

"But it seems so mean. I can't stand mean men."

"I'm not being mean, Brooke. I have my reasons."

"Well, what are they?"

"Not just now, Brooke. It's a glorious night and –"

"But it seems so mean. My first husband was mean. He –"

"Look, darling, I'm not being mean. It's just – well – I'll explain it another time but –"

"I wanted a house at the beach once so we could be alone but he wanted a unit in the city close to a race track. It's just the same thing. It had to be what he wanted all the time. Selfish."

"No it's not. I –"

"I wanted to be really alone with him but he –"

"Well, he was a fool if he didn't want to be alone with you like we are now. Brooke –"

"It was so mean. Just because the unit was cheaper. Are you so mean that you begrudge Mark the money?"

"Of course not. The alterations to the wing will probably cost just as much."

"Well, why can't they have their house then?"

"Oh, to hell with them. I –"

"Jamie is my special friend. I'm not going to sit here and listen to you saying to hell with my dearest friend," flashed Brooke.

Hugh drew back aghast at the flare of temper. Brooke was not red headed for nothing.

"I'm sorry, darling, but –"

"And what did you mean by calling her 'Miss' tonight just as though she wasn't married?"

"Did I? I didn't notice. She –"

"You made her cry."

"Oh, for Pete's sake let's forget about them. Look at the night. It's made for romance."

"With everyone upset? The last thing I feel like is romance. I want to go home."

For a moment Hugh toyed with the idea of getting his kiss regardless but the arctic profile turned to him decided the issue. With a sigh frustrating enough to rend the heart of the fair he turned on the ignition.

When they arrived at the homestead Brooke pranced out of the car as soon as it pulled up and was well on her way inside desperately trying to stifle her giggles. Poor Hugh. He'd be neither to hold nor to bind. She had her laugh out in her bedroom. Then, as she reviewed the evening, all desire to laugh left her abruptly.

Morris and Allison talked long in bed but could not come up with a fitting alternative such as Mark might have in mind. They had not questioned him in the car thinking he might prefer to discuss it with Jamie first. Still there was room for hope. If Jamie liked it, well and good.

"I still like that site we found," murmured Allison sleepily before they gave the subject away till further information was available.

Mark and Jamie had very little to say once they were alone in their caravan. Jamie naturally waited to be told the alternative but Mark was yawning and saying that he would be glad to hit the sack. Frustrated in one direction Jamie turned her attention to another grievance. She brooded till she boiled over while cleaning her teeth. She rinsed them hastily, gave a loud spit and turned on Mark.

"Why didn't you stick up for me when Hugh told me to mind my own business?" she demanded of his back. Mark turned around and surveyed her thoughtfully. Then he sat on the end of the bed and pulled her close to him.

"Jamie let's get this straight. It's far too early to be quarrelling over the issue in the first place. If Hugh had done you any damage I would be the first to defend you. But what I think you want at the moment to be able to do, is poke your tongue at Hugh and then run to me for protection."

Jamie stared down into his loving eyes and hung her head. "I don't know how it is but you say nothing for hours and then suddenly come out with something that knocks everyone flat."

He buried his head in her breast. She could feel him shake against her and pulled back. Yes, it was his silent laughter again.

"I've never known anyone like you for laughing silently."

"Hugh does it too."

Jamie sniffed. "I've never heard him."

At that Mark laughed aloud and, after a moment, Jamie got it and joined in. "Why do you do it?"

"It dates back to when we were kids and used to go over to Ashley and Sarah's for the night. Sarah put us in a big double bed and for some reason everything we talked about seemed excruciatingly funny. We were so often told off for keeping everyone awake and threatened with separation that we developed the art of silent laughter."

Mark's eyes were warm with reminiscence. Jamie leaned against him.

"You love him a lot, don't you?"

Mark looked up at her. "Jamie, I guided his first steps when he started to walk. He used to hang on to my belt. I steadied him on his first pony and helped him up the first tree he climbed. He did a lot of things earlier than others because I showed him the way."

Yes, and he seemed all the cuter for it, thought Jamie. No wonder he always had the limelight. Aloud, she said softly,

"I think you've so got into the habit of supporting his doings that you just about forgot to live your own life."

"But I've got you to make it worth living now," he countered and held her in a hard embrace to which Jamie responded heartily. The road he was choosing to walk was far harder than his wife or her friends had any conception of and he desperately needed her support and trust.

They went to bed in perfect amity. It was only through the night that Jamie awoke and realised that she still did not know what that third choice could be.

Hugh lay long awake. He too was troubled by that third choice and searched his mind for what it could be. Oh, to have the old days back when they had worked perfectly as a team. Jamie had a lot to answer for and in no way was she going to lord it over Brooke. This turned his mind to his frustrating love affair. He could not understand how he had made so little headway. It was not as though Brooke had actually repulsed him in any way. At first he had thought it was rather generous of him to accept that he was to be her third husband. Now he didn't care if he was the fourth or fifth as long as he got her.

He did not want to make a declaration before they had had a time of romancing but he might just have to dispense with it. This suspense was killing him. All these other guests and visitors milling around never let a fellow get a decent chance to do a bit of wooing. Well, he had got her alone and look at what had come of it. Brooke could be hot at hand but that only added to the spice. He wished that she and Jamie were not such buddies, conveniently forgetting that he had only met the love of his life through her. Depressed and uneasy he finally slept.

Back at Seven Trees Ashley lay awake, dreaming pleasant dreams, and lived the evening over again.

When Brooke eventually slept, her pillow was suspiciously damp.

CHAPTER TWENTY-TWO

Reinforcements

The next day brought Jamie's troops a new ally, Lilliputian but powerful.

While Mark showered and dressed, Jamie lay stretched out in bed. When she eventually looked up to find him hanging over her, she smiled sleepily.

"Think I'll lie in for a while."

"I'll bring your breakfast up."

"Horrors. I'll never be able to look Howie in the face."

"A cup of tea?"

"Thanks but NO," she said sharply.

Mark pretended to jump and cower away and Jamie threw a pillow at him.

After he had gone she lay there, glad of the respite. Hugh usually went soon after breakfast. She couldn't stand the sight of him at the moment. Her conscience pricked, she guiltily recalled what she had read in the Sermon on the Mount about a brother having aught against one. Despite trying to give her thoughts another direction some words about walking in the light came up. It was as clear as daylight. If she hated Hugh she walked in darkness. Jamie lay and mulled over it. If she called herself a Christian she had to love Hugh somehow. "But I can't, I can't," she wailed aloud and covered her head with the sheet.

After a while she poked a rebellious head out and decided to get up if only to escape these convicting accusations going on in her mind. She sat on the edge of the bed, strangely reluctant. She was certainly not hungry. Maybe if she asked Howie for something special like scram –"

Jamie shot off the bed and just reached the tiny sink in time. She hung over it for a while and then turned the tap on hard. Leaning against the wall she happily wiped her clammy forehead with a hand towel. It must be. She could never remember being sick just like that in the morning. Already she was nurturing his seed deep within her. Patting her tummy, she whispered, "Welcome, darlin', and God bless you."

Lying back on the bed Jamie heard a tentative knock followed by Mrs Howard's entrance with a bottle of something in her hand. She surveyed Jamie with wise eyes. "I've brought you some raspberry cordial. Best thing for an upset stomach."

Jamie sat up. "Wh – what makes you think I've an upset stomach?"

"A little bird told me."

Mrs Howard sat on the side of the bed and asked a couple of pertinent questions. Jamie must have given the right answers for Mrs Howard held out her arms and she flew into them like a homing bird. This was one time when a girl needed a mother figure.

"I've never heard that raspberry cordial could relieve morning sickness."

"Oh, yes. Scientists have at last stopped regarding it as an old wives' tale. They're treating pigs with certain stomach ailments with essence of raspberries."

Jamie thought this was wonderful. "I hope this doesn't mean I'll have a litter or something," she giggled.

Mark came in then to find them holding their sides. "Glad you've recovered," he remarked with a grin.

"Oh, she hasn't recovered at all," replied Mrs Howard airily. "She's going to have this problem for a long time." She departed with a flirt of her skirt leaving Mark staring anxiously at his wife.

"You haven't got some virus, have you?"

'What I've got is going to need a lot of T L C," said Jamie soulfully as she adjusted her pillows.

"For Pete's sake what's T L C?" demanded Mark sitting down beside her.

Jamie put her arms behind her head, cherishing the moment of revelation.

"Tender loving care. Both of us will."

Mark leaned over and put his arms around her. "You know I thought it might be that."

"Thought what might be what?" demanded Jamie, disappointed that her great announcement had fallen flat.

"Well… you've been so jumpy lately and –"

"Have I now?" cried Jamie, justly incensed and trying to push him away. "And, of course, I've no other reason to be jumpy, have I? Now, you listen to me, Mark Lawrence…"

But Mark held her tight and tucked his head against her neck and she could feel him laughing right through her skin.

"You miserable wretch! You must be the first man on earth to greet the news of a coming child with downright laughter."

"No, I'm not," protested Mark, trying to control himself. "I'm the second."

"Why – what?"

"Who. Abraham greeted the news of his promised son with laughter and the boy was named Isaac which means laughter."

"Really?" Jamie was enchanted. "Oh, I love it, I love it. We'll throw out the William and –"

"Over my dead body. I've got William booked. Besides that's for a girl. You can change James."

"Well, I won't. Maybe we could make Isaac the second name."

Then they stopped their funning and looked deeply into each other's eyes.

"Oh, my darling," whispered Mark and they were silent and still in each other's arms for a long time.

Jamie had too ebullient a nature to hold back their wonderful news even though Mark cautioned her that perhaps they should consult a doctor first.

"Howie's a good enough doctor for me," she said as she emerged from the neckline of a pretty frock. It was frilly and soft and suited her mood. She wished she had something remotely resembling a smock and for the first time regretted that she had never bothered with an artist's overall.

They arrived down at the house when the others were preparing for their daily ride. Jamie answered their concerned questions with a smug smile and the mysterious remark that she had to think of others now and would not be riding that morning. Allison, who had had her suspicions, guessed at once and they all went inside while Jamie was petted and Mark congratulated. For some reason, everyone felt marvellous.

"This gives us a deadline," said Morris, unblushingly smug at this turn of events. 'You've got to have a nursery now so the sooner you get started the better. Nothing but the best for the expectant mother."

Mark agreed heartily to everyone's relief.

"Let's forgo the ride," suggested Allison, "and drive out and show Mark you-know-what."

"Let's," agreed Brooke enthusiastically, seeking relief from her own unhappiness in her little friend's bubbling joy.

They sent the horses back, Morris not begrudging it for a moment, and piled into the station wagon with Mark at the wheel. They did not dither with him but led him straight to the rise. He did not seem at all surprised and, in answer to Jamie's pressing, admitted that he had had the spot in mind. They walked all over it and Jamie told Mark about Morris's landscaping ideas. The two men went back over the area while the women rested beneath a gossipy group of young gums under the determined concept that Jamie must take it easy. They recalled the strange alternative of Mark's and agreed that they would not press him for the explanation just then.

"It may be a trump card," remarked Allison wisely.

When the men came back, with Mark greatly impressed with Morris's ideas, they all returned to the house. Jamie was sent off to rest till lunch time and, feeling like a princess, did so. Mark invaded the kitchen and while Mrs Howard prepared the meal, had a long consultation with her. Taking her advice, he rang through to the doctor who had cared for him since the plane crash and got the name of a good obstetrician. Trying for an early appointment he picked up one for the following afternoon due to a cancellation. His third phone call booked the charter plane for the next day.

"Make sure it's not too early," warned Howie at his side. "Jamie won't care for an early morning ride." He made the reservation for eleven o'clock. They could have lunch in town. Maybe the others would like the break too.

When Jamie joined the rest for lunch he told her. She stared at him dumbfounded, torn between taking umbrage at his highhandedness and appreciation of his care.

"Howie strongly advised it," explained Mark hastily "You must have a doctor in attendance throughout your pregnancy."

"Dear me," said Jamie with a twinkle. "You evidently don't think I'm pioneer stuff."

"No," stated Mark baldly and got a box on the ears.

The others all fell in with the idea of a trip to town. When Hugh arrived back early in the afternoon, had a shower and joined them at the annex he found them all in animated discussion. He dropped into the vacant chair left for him, gave everyone a courteous nod and Brooke a special smile. He was pleased that everyone was in good spirits. It did not seem as though they intended to hold out on him.

"Drink a toast with us Hugh?" asked Mark as he poured his brother's lime and pineapple.

"Sure." He glanced around as he received his glass. Was there a subtle air of triumph in the gazes fixed upon him? "That is, if I approve."

They rocked with laughter. In fact, Morris nearly choked on his drink and it took some backslapping to set him to rights. Hugh took comfort from the genuine amusement and said good-humouredly, "Well, obviously I've put my foot in it. Put me out of my misery."

Mark raised his glass and the others followed.

"To the next generation of Lawrences of Fairlie Downs."

It took a moment for the penny to drop and then they all saw Hugh's features contort into a hideous grimace of jealousy. It was gone in an instant and the face smooth as Hugh's voice remarked expressionlessly, "Dear me. So soon. Cheers!"

In the ensuing silence, he took time to down his drink. Then he directed a question to Brooke who perforce had to answer it, albeit mechanically. Mark sat frowning at his feet and Jamie looked out into the distance, wondering how a child could evoke such a reaction. Morris and Allison were so shocked that the thing took on an unreality to them. It just couldn't have been!

Then, for Jamie and Mark's sake, they hurried into conversation trying to banish it from their minds.

Hugh stood up and asked Brooke if she would like to go down to the house with him. She rose at once and allowed him to draw her arm through his as they strolled off. Brooke had an inquiring mind and she felt that she just had to know what lay behind Hugh's extraordinary reaction.

She waited for a natural pause in their conversation, and, as they reached the house and she walked ahead of him up the steps, said,

"You looked anything but pleased at Mark's news. Why?"

Hugh said nothing for a while and, as he drew level she saw that his face had darkened. His good looks don't help him, she reflected. He looks positively diabolic. She shrank a little from him. Hugh felt this and made an effort to smile.

"I guess," he said with an air of wistfulness that was disarming, "that I always expected that the next generation would come from my loins."

"Well, it could have couldn't it? You've had plenty of chances from what I hear… girls ready to fall into your lap any time you like to name."

As she was the one girl who was not ready Hugh took umbrage at this. "That's not true. I'm sure some of them were just out for a good time."

"I've heard some very nice girls have looked your way. Stella and Sylvia."

"Leave Sylvia out of this. She's been a friend of the family for years."

"What about Stella?"

"You've been listening to Jamie's gossiping tongue. I couldn't help it if Stella got too serious."

"Well, there must have been one you could have married and have had your own toddlers around you right now."

"Well, yourself. It just so happened that the right one did not come along till now." He snapped and, gripping her arm, steered her into the living room. He caught her in his arms and was about to take his kiss when an elbow struck him smartly on the chin. He recoiled a little in surprise and Brooke pushed at him with all her might.

"If you think you are going to make love to me while you're in this filthy mood you can think again," she stormed.

Taken aback by her fierce resistance Hugh let her go. "Good heavens, what's a simple kiss?" he asked with an irritable laugh.

"Just a cent's worth in your book, I should imagine." Brooke seated herself in a single chair. Hugh looked down at her, his blood beginning to sing in his ears.

"Not where you're concerned. You've been here almost a month and I haven't pulled it off yet, I can't believe it," He said ruefully. He sat down in a chair near her, pulled out his handkerchief and wiped his forehead and hands. "You know you can bring me out in a sweat in nothing flat. We may as well get matters straight. I'm mad about you, my girl. Have been for weeks."

"Other men have been mad about me," said Brooke coolly. "It needs more than that to interest me."

"More? What the dickens do you mean? What more is there?"

Actually, Brooke was not sure herself. All she knew was that she had had a sickening of physical love in itself. It had something to do with Mr Savage's wedding sermon and the wonderful words that Mark and Jamie had uttered. It was the spiritual root of marriage she was feeling for. All she could think of to say was that she believed that there was more.

Hugh was mystified but made a guess. "Do you mean faithfulness and all that?"

"Well that would unquestionably be part of it," admitted Brooke. She looked thoughtfully at Hugh, wondering whether it would be fair to him to tell him then and there that he had no chance. She hesitated, feeling that, with matters still up in the air about the proposed house, she had better keep him at her side for a while longer. She stood up and Hugh rose with her.

"I couldn't imagine looking at another woman when I had you,' he said warmly.

"Other men have said the very same thing to me,' Brooke said flatly, "and it will be a jolly long time before I take another at his word."

That should give him something to think about without actually shutting the door, she thought.

"I hope you're not anticipating a five-year engagement or anything like that, are you?" asked Hugh in alarm.

"Nooo…" drawled Brooke, "but I'll have to be very *very* sure."

"You can be," asserted Hugh with all his old cocksureness. "In which case —"

He made another attempt to take her in his arms but the wily Brooke sidestepped smartly. At the same time Mrs Howard rang the dinner bell.

"You're as slippery as an eel," he growled as they went through the hall.

"Bitter experience," returned Brooke but she laughed at him over her shoulder.

Dinner was a strained meal with short babbles of conversation followed by awkward silences as everyone sought for another safe topic.

Afterwards Hugh begged Brooke for some music as a means of getting her to himself. Mark brought out some old board games and, in the ensuing easy competitiveness, everyone relaxed. During supper Morris remarked that the simple pleasures had a charm of their own. As he had won most of the games the others were not at all inclined to agree with him.

It was not till breakfast the next day that Mark mentioned their trip to town to Hugh. As Jamie, despite the raspberry cordial, was still not present the mention of a doctor's appointment had point. Hugh just grunted and then asked Brooke if she would like to spend the day in the saddle as they were working close to home.

Brooke shook her head. "Sorry, but I'm grabbing the chance to go to town," she said, putting a note of regret in her voice. "There are a few things I need."

"Tomorrow then?"

"I'd love to."

Hugh went off appeased and escorted the others on their early morning ride. Jamie came down, remarking that she felt quite well but vetoing the ride. She seemed to think that if she so much as sneezed she stood in dire danger of losing the baby. Mark went down to his office. He had occasion to ring Seven Trees and mentioned the proposed trip to Ashley.

The result of this was that after the plane had picked up Mark's party it also landed at Seven Trees to pick up Ashley. They already had a visitor staying so Sarah could not go and did not regret it. Hospitality came first at all times on the homestead.

The men grouped themselves up front near the pilot while the women got together behind them to consult how they would spend their day. Mark had told Jamie that the Savages had their base just outside the town so thought they could give them a ring as there would not be much time for a visit. Brooke did not like to mention that she was longing for another chat with Mary Savage. Her first great joy had subsided a little under the cloud of her present unhappiness. She foresaw a day hanging on the sleeves of her two women friends and resolved to bury all selfish introspective feelings in the pleasures of others.

As they came in over the town, Mark and Morris were locked in verbal battle over who should pay for the coming lunch. Morris wanted to do it in return for the hospitality being given to himself and his wife. Mark wanted to do it not only as host but to repay the hospitality he had been given in Brisbane. Ashley silenced the two wranglers by informing them that he was doing the shouting.

"What's an old bachelor like me got to spend his money on?" he demanded with surprising vehemence. "You two can go fight it out between you. Meanwhile I'm taking the three most charming women I've ever met to dinner at Camelot."

The ladies promptly accepted and that ended the argument.

"I don't know what's happened to you, Ash," Mark said as they settled for the landing. "First you stomp around shoving fellows over to get a dance with Brooke and now you're actually parting with some money."

Ashley aimed a blow at him which never landed and the plane taxied smoothly to a halt.

The restaurant was their first objective as the trip had made them hungry, especially Jamie who found that she could take a real interest in food by midday.

The Camelot Inne had only been opened recently and so far, they had never tried it. As they went in Jamie took Mark's arm and Allison took her husband's, Ashley turned to Brooke.

"Sorry you've got to put up with an old codger like me," he said with his shy smile and holding out the crook of his elbow.

Brooke tucked her hand in with a smile. "I told someone off once for calling you an old codger so you had best beware."

"Did you now?" Ashley looked confounded and Brooke fancied a flush deepening his tan.

"Yes, I told them I reckoned you'd give as good as you got."

"Well, now." Ashley smiled uncertainly down at her. Brooke turned the full battery of her rich brown eyes on him and his gaze faltered and dropped. "It might depend on what was being handed out."

Brooke chuckled as they caught up with the others and were soon busy with the menu. Camelot was done out in the style of what the proprietors thought was the England of King Arthur's day. There were imitation stone fireplaces that were never lit and great hangings on the walls which Jamie said were well done. Items like barons of beef and sucking pig were on the menu. The last was vetoed when Jamie said that she would throw up if she so much as set eyes on it. A mutton pie and a quail one were also offered and found to be delicious. With the roast beef came a Yorkshire pudding so tasty that they kept reordering.

"They're probably wishing us to the devil in the kitchen," giggled Brooke who seemed to be coming alive again.

It was the same with dessert. The men and Allison hesitated between Old English Plum pudding and Deep Dish Apple Pie and cream. Brooke and Jamie found fruit salad on the menu and conscientiously ordered it. When it arrived, the girls found themselves confronted each with half a large pineapple heaped with a delicious assortment of tropical fruits.

"I'll be yelling for help," gasped Jamie as she poked at one side with a spoon.

"So might I," murmured Brooke and glanced interrogatively at Ashley who promised to keep a corner if she had to give up. The men were given what was supposed to be old English ale in huge beer mugs and the ladies apple cider in elegant glasses. It was all very well done and they enjoyed it immensely. Coffee was only given if asked for, which they did and sat over it till the time for Jamie's appointment which was two o'clock.

As soon as the young couple set off for the doctor's rooms, Allison turned to the others.

"Morris and I thought we might have a look around for some things for Jamie's house…" She paused leaving the way open for Brooke to please herself.

"I thought I would just take a stroll around the town," said Brooke casually, not wanting to appear to pin Ashley down.

"Show you the sights if you like," he said diffidently. "Just got to take a look in at the bank first."

"Good," said Allison. "Supposing we meet back here in an hour's time. I reckon the others will be about through by then."

It was agreed and they went their separate ways.

Mark and Jamie were the first to arrive back, pale and uplifted with the importance of their session but Jamie's merry humour soon reasserted itself now she knew she would not lose her child if she rode a horse moderately, walked up more than six steps or teased her husband into making passionate love to her.

Allison and Morris arrived next with sundry large parcels and nothing to say about their doings. Ashley and Brooke then arrived with nothing to show for his satisfied smile and her radiance. Upon inquiry, it appeared that they had not got far in their meanderings. Ashley was well known and men had tried repeatedly to stop him and demand an introduction to the luscious beauty at his side. They had left behind them a wake of amazement and conjecture. Who was she and where on earth was Hugh? He must be paralysed in bed to let old Ash get away with this glorious creature.

As they strolled along they came across a baby shop and the three women promptly disappeared into it. Mark left the other two men to await their pleasure as he said he had some other business to attend to.

Jamie was brisk with her shopping after she had convinced the proprietors that she did not want pink or blue ribbons but would consider yellow or apricot or lavender. This meant a total ransacking of the goods available with Allison offering to rethread fresh ribbons into some of the tiny garments the expectant mother favoured. Brooke hung back a little, seeming reluctant to engage in this activity but Jamie caught the wistful glances. She picked up a tiny bonnet, covered in lace with miniature yellow roses tucked in and flowing yellow ribbons.

"That was a left over," the attendant explained. "All the ones with pink and blue ribbons were snapped up."

"More fool them," announced Jamie, deliberately passing the exquisite thing to Brooke and turning aside to other garments. As she held it, across Brooke's beautiful face came a look of ineffable sweetness and longing that had something of heartache in it.

Goodness, thought the attendant: one would have thought that, with that face and figure, she should have been snapped up long ago and been flat to the boards with bassinets and baby clothes.

The purchases were completed and packed up with the exception of the bonnet. This was popped into Jamie's handbag as she remarked, "Just the thing for William."

She was corrected. "Actually that is for a little girl, ma'am. "We don't put so much lace on a baby boy's bonnet."

"Don't you?" questioned a wide-eyed Jamie as she sailed out of the shop.

As they emerged outside they found Morris and Ashley bailed up by three new men, all well known to the grim Ashley, who had perforce to introduce them to the amused Morris, and all patiently waiting with them for the return of the ladies.

After the introductions were made and Jamie congratulated, the trio essayed to make painstaking conversation with Ashley while the whites of their eyes showed where their avid interest lay. As the conversation lagged and the three showed no signs of excusing themselves, mischief began to brew in Brooke.

When Mark finally appeared, striding swiftly towards them and breaking up the group, Brooke moved over to Ashley, slipped her hand into the crook of his arm, smiled up at him and said,

"You're not too angry with me because I went into the shop with Jamie, are you? I thought it a good idea to have a look-see."

Three pairs of eyes fixed her with an incredulous stare. Ashley looked down at her, his grey ones alight with comprehension and revenge.

"Have a care, my dear. You are not too old to spank and, if you were *my daughter*, I wouldn't hesitate."

Brooke gurgled: "Right between the eyes," she said and, as Mark claimed the attention of the others, she added softly, "Round one to you but watch out."

They then lost no time in shrugging off Brooke's three admirers and Jamie announced that they must find a bookshop as time was flying. One was found and they all separated to pursue their various interests. For some reason, Ashley and Brooke took a vast interest in the same subjects, Morris got lost in the world of art and Allison found a book on craft that she had been seeking for years.

Completing her purchase, she turned to the young parents-to-be to find Jamie deep in discussion with an attendant over various medical tomes on babies and Mark pop-eyed over an all too graphically illustrated book on The Hidden Nine Months of Baby's Life. Allison glanced over his shoulder and snatched at the book, exclaiming,

"Here! You don't want to be looking at things like that. It takes all the mystique away and –"

"But I want to," cried Mark, hanging on for dear life. "I must know all that Jamie has to go through."

"But not even Jamie can get a look at that," protested Allison still holding on. "Why they'd have to do a cross section of an unborn child to get a look at that."

"What's this?" demanded Jamie, going over to the struggling pair.

"This is too explicit, Jamie," began Allison. "It –"

"Here, let me see," ordered Jamie with all the authority of the newly pregnant. "We must have no secrets from each… Awk!"

She slapped the book shut and before her affronted husband could utter a word, remarked loftily, "The art work is shocking. Come and see the real thing."

Another book was opened before Mark at a page showing an exquisite pearly bubble with a little life floating dreamily in it.

"Now that's something like," breathed Allison with satisfaction.

"Just how did they get *that* picture?" demanded Mark.

"That's their secret," replied his wife airily.

There was an indescribable sound behind them and they all turned to find Mary Savage behind them desperately trying to smother her laughter.

"My dears," she gasped. "You're as good as a circus."

The circus promptly fell on her neck.

They hastily concluded their shopping and swept Mary off to a late afternoon tea. During it Mary presented Brooke with a parcel.

"It's a Bible," she smiled. "A modern translation that still retains much of the beauty of the King James. I was going to bring it out next week when we visit you but this is better."

Brooke was rather overwhelmed. It was a beautiful edition and would not have been cheap. Jamie nodded encouragingly.

"Mrs Savage has a right to give it to you as she led you to the Lord like she did Ashley and Mark. My friend, Helen, gave me the one I use."

So Brooke accepted it with becoming grace. "I shall treasure it all my life," she vowed.

"Good! That's the best thanks I could have." Mary was seated next to Brooke and, under cover of the general chatter, asked the girl how she was getting on.

Brooke smiled happily. "I did strike a rough patch but I'm on a bit of a high now."

Mary nodded wisely. "Just don't let yourself soar too high and lose your bearings because the landing could end in a nasty thud."

She saw, to her astonishment, something akin to panic leap to the beautiful eyes and the smile fade.

"My dear," she said quickly. "I was just giving some general spiritual advice. We are not meant to live continually on highs. Our human nature cannot sustain it. The land we go to possess is a land of hills and valleys. The visions we get on the mountain top are meant to be worked out on the plains."

Brooke's pretty mouth twisted in a wry expression. "It would take something special to work this vision out," she said soberly.

Mary looked puzzled. Brooke added: "I can't explain now but –"

"Leave it till I come out," advised Mary, "and, in the mean time I will be praying for you. I mean that. You are my nursling, you know."

The homely phrase comforted Brooke considerably.

They soon had to take their leave of their friend and hail a taxi to the airport. Their pilot had to get them out to Fairlie in time so that he would have enough daylight left to take off again for the return trip.

Once on the plane Morris frogmarched Mark to the back two seats. What he had to say would not brook any more delay. Seeing this Jamie sat with Allison. So Brooke sat in one of the pairs of seats and smiled invitingly at Ashley. He took the one beside her with some reluctance, as she noticed, and she straightway engaged him in conversation lest he thought better of it.

Jamie dreamed out the window while Allison took the wrapping off her prize.

"Now listen, Mark," Morris began quickly. "We've been here for at least a month and I can't spare more than a few extra days. I've a very important Show coming up and I don't want to leave it to my assistant. I *expect* this matter of where you and Jamie are going to build to be decided before I leave. Understand!"

His tone was sharp with some menace in it. Mark did not take offence.

"Yes, it has to be settled," he said slowly, "but I've waited hoping for a better attitude between Hugh and Jamie."

"Jamie is only reacting to Hugh's attitude," answered Morris brusquely. "It's no worse than mine. I was downright shocked yesterday when –"

"I know, I know," interrupted Mark. "I knew it would go deep with Hugh but I did not reckon that –"

"That he would hate your child?"

"I don't think it went as far as that."

"Well I do and furthermore –"

"No," said Mark firmly. "Not the child itself but the act of conception."

"The act of – *What?*"

"It's a first… of the next generation. Hugh has always come first in everything. Now, no matter how many kids he has himself, he can only come second."

"Like the America's Cup. No seconds. Only losers."

Mark nodded. Morris tried to visualise a state of mind so petty as to make an issue of so trivial a matter. He suddenly realised that to Hugh it was not trivial at all. Mark, being the eldest and siring the first child of the next generation, would now be the head of the direct line going through the Lawrence family; an unassailable position in the case of primogeniture. An unexpected coup and certainly unplanned. Well, thought Morris, wasn't that just too bad for poor old Hugh.

"Well, it's more than time the whole set-up was exploded," he stated. "You spoke of an alternative. Whatever it is, Jamie must have the house of her dreams."

"She will," Mark assented tranquilly.

"Well, now that's splendid," Morris said heartily, feeling that the battle was as good as won. "I take it she will have the choice of the two alternatives?"

"No, Hugh will."

"*Hugh?* Are you mad? Your wife demands the first consideration. You just said that she would have the house of her dreams and now you say –"

"The same thing. She will have her house, never fear. But Hugh has to make the choice."

Morris stared at him, nonplussed. Mark's jaw line was not that of a weakling. The set of his features had purpose in it but his eyes were hidden behind his dark glasses. He was giving nothing away and Morris fretted to be in his confidence. After a moment Mark turned to him and said:

"I'll bring it to a head tonight if I can but please don't interfere. What I am going to suggest constitutes a major change to Hugh and he'll need space to think about it. If I can engineer it that he is the one to make the final decision, he will not lose face and we should get by."

"What does it matter how many faces he loses? It's yours and Jamie's life and –"

"It matters to me. We don't want to be at loggerheads with my brother. Whether we like it or not our lives will continually interact with his and I have managed to live at peace with him for nearly thirty years. I'm not likely to throw that down the drain."

Morris was silent. What could he say? If it was a matter of finance he was prepared to settle a goodly sum on Jamie any time. She was their heir anyway. He decided to broach this side of the matter. Mark listened patiently then said that there was no need, as he'd been arranging finance that very day.

Satisfied that something definite was happening, Morris sat back to enjoy the flight. True, Mark had bound him to silence but there were enough of them to support the young couple if Hugh tried any of his tricks. It occurred to him that Ashley would also be present. In the interests of time he was going on with them to Fairlie and would later drive back to Seven Trees. Ashley was a good scout and had already shown that his sympathies lay with Jamie. Morris grunted his satisfaction and relapsed into silence to Mark's relief,

There was just enough light for the plane to take off for the return trip. After they had waved it off, Mark drove them back to the house. Hugh was in the shower when they trooped in and Jamie dashed off to the kitchen with her bundles as she sang her list of purchases.

"Good," said Mrs Howard briskly, "but dinner's ready to serve so be quick and have a wash. We'll have a grand showing after coffee."

"Yes, Mum," grinned Jamie and dumped her parcels into a chair in the lounge room. One small package she retained and sought out Mark.

She took out the tiny bonnet, placing the scrap of silk and lace on her balled fist.

"For William," she said softly. An exquisite glance passed between them. Allison caught the words as she passed and uttered teasingly, "Don't be too sure, my dears."

To her amazement, her remark brought on a guffaw from Mark and a snigger from Jamie.

The party was in such good spirits as they sat down to their meal that Hugh forbore to cast a damper on them. He wanted Brooke to be in a good mood tomorrow.

Mark waited till the meal was finished and then asked Mrs Howard to bring the coffee to the table. In all business deals the brothers invariably sat around the dining room table. Hugh was instantly on the alert as Brooke and Allison helped clear the final plates.

"Sure you don't want us to go into your office?" he asked with a deliberate glance around at the assembled company.

"No," said Mark quietly, "they're all involved one way or another."

Hugh took this to mean that Mark was already thinking of Brooke as part of the family so his expression was quite genial as he sat back and told his brother to fire away.

"It's about building our house," stated Mark and paused deliberately. Hugh reacted exactly as expected. His face hardened and he said shortly,

"There will not be a second house built on Fairlie Downs and that is my last word on it."

Everyone turned expectantly to Mark. Now was his moment. He did not leave them hanging.

"It doesn't have to be on this property," he said and everyone's jaw dropped. Hugh, who had been leaning back on his chair so that he was balanced on the back legs, sat forward with a bang. A wary look came into his dark eyes.

"You're not thinking of parking yourselves on Ashley and Sarah?" he rapped out.

"No," Mark shook his head. Then he calmly delivered his ultimatum. "A wing of this house is unacceptable to me." They all noticed how he kept Jamie's name out of it. "If I can't build a house on this property then I propose to sell out my share. Alec Cartwright is looking for a property to buy into, as you know. I reckon we could do a deal with him."

If his listeners had not been so avidly engaged with their own stupefaction they would have seen that such a happening had not remotely occurred to Hugh. He stared unbelievingly at his brother as though Mark had undergone some kind of metamorphosis.

Mark turned serenely to rescue his coffee from Mrs Howard who had nearly dropped the cup as she stood staring down at him.

Hugh recovered his voice and rasped out, "Are you telling me that you will sell *Lawrence property* to a – a damned stranger?"

"The choice is yours," replied Mark and stirred his coffee.

This was one of those dangerous moments in life. Two paths were immediately opened to Hugh. One path directed him to gracefully accede to his brother's wishes and so avoid all present conflict. The other immediately threw a dozen obstacles in his way, all contributing towards disharmony and ultimate disintegration of the family company. To those present the choice was obvious. It called simply for common sense and an act of grace.

Unfortunately, it was a gift that Hugh had never had to exercise. In all his spoilt and catered to existence he had never had his stated will thwarted. Circumstances in the form of Redmaster's ribbon and Mark's marriage had been out of his jurisdiction and both contributed to the present situation which threatened his status. Into his face came the mulish expression his family was familiar with, preceding the tantrum that had always got his way in childhood: the tantrum that never listened to reason.

"It's a bluff," he snapped. "It's legally impossible for you to opt out like that."

Mark sipped his coffee. Not once had he looked at Jamie. This was between his brother and himself. Jamie realised with a shiver that she was indeed well out of it.

"No it isn't," he said quietly. "I checked the deeds today. I can legally sell my share to you or anyone else you care to name. The bank will supply the adequate finance rather than drain the estate if you want it all."

Then the red light of anger lit Hugh's eyes.

"So… you've been plotting and planning this behind my back," he exploded. "Well, you've bitten off more than you can chew, this time, *brother.*"

He jerked to his feet, overturning his chair, and crashed his cup back on the saucer, splitting it clean across, as he strode from the room.

No one moved for several stricken minutes. Then Mark, whose glasses had misted from the steam of his drink, took them off and reached for his handkerchief. Jamie took them from him and a gleaming tear fell as she polished them.

Mark glanced around at the silent company and all could see his expression of calm purpose.

"There's nothing to worry about," he said kindly. "Hugh will make his decision and Jamie will have her house either way."

The cry came from several throats. There was plenty to worry about. One and all felt that there must be some other way and began to ply him with arguments. All except Brooke. All she could think of was what it must be like to be loved so sacrificially by a man that he was prepared to give up his home and possibly his way of life in order to please the woman he loved.

Ashley's voice was as vehement as the rest. He, himself, pushed the idea of their building on Seven Trees property. Mark shook his head.

"Hugh and I must live in peace side by side or not at all," was the only answer he would give and thereafter said nothing more. Mark never argued.

"But what will you do?" queried Morris eventually as Mrs Howard replenished the cups.

"Haven't decided yet. Got to wait on Hugh's decision." Mark said casually.

"You wouldn't go out on a property on your own, would you Mark?" asked Jamie humbly. "You couldn't work outside all the time."

Mark ruffled her hair. "No, but I might buy shares or go more into marketing the beef. There are several options with cattle. I've been thinking a few out."

Thinking a few out. And they had all, Ashley excepted, been chafing because they thought he would not come to terms with the issue.

"I feel downright ashamed," declared Morris and stretched his hand across the table, insisting on shaking Mark's hand. "It will be a terrible upheaval for you and —"

"Now don't cross your bridges yet," cautioned Mark, receiving his hand back with no little embarrassment, "Hugh may yet decide that the easiest and obvious solution is to let us have our house here."

There was no expression of agreement. They all remembered the closed look on Hugh's face as he went. At last Ashley spoke.

"And on that we'll have to pin our hopes," he said heavily.

"And prayers," added Brooke, suddenly coming to life.

"It'll take more than prayers to move that blasted Hugh," muttered Morris as the company rose.

They decided to call it a night. Jamie retrieved her purchases from the living room, dolefully informing Howie that she would show the things tomorrow. Mr and Mrs Lawrence departed arm in arm for their caravan.

Ashley drove off and the homestead settled down for the night. The quiet stars brooded over the desperately unhappy household and Mark and Jamie slept locked in each other's embrace.

CHAPTER TWENTY-THREE

Reaction

Breakfast next day was a silent affair. Everyone greeted everyone else punctiliously and thereafter took a rapt interest in the meal itself. Jamie was once again missing. Hugh was the first to rise from the table and addressed only Brooke.

"I'll come in for you about nine thirty. Right?"

"Hugh, I – I don't think –"

"You *promised.*"

Brooke gazed helplessly up at him and finally assented with as good a grace as she could muster. Satisfied, Hugh went out without a glance at the others.

Mark looked around at the morose company and there was a quirk to his lips as he said lightly,

"Nothing like a good ride to shake off the doldrums. Lead the way, Uncle Morris."

Morris smiled reluctantly and rose. Allison waited outside the caravan while Mark consulted Jamie. The usual morning convulsion had failed to materialise and she was feeling better. She went with them and they had a very sedate ride out of consideration for her. However, on the way home, Morris challenged Brooke and they had a fine race to the homestead, Brooke pulling up well ahead of him just as Hugh came in sight. Flushed and triumphant in her victory, her lovely hair tumbling free as she pulled off her neat little hat and fanned herself, she was enough to turn any man's head.

"Hope you've still got some energy left," Hugh remarked jocularly, leading a lively chestnut nearly the colour of Red up to her.

"Would you mind changing mounts? This fellow is more your style."

"Sure, he's a beauty," assented Brooke agreeably and the change was soon affected. She waved to the others and was soon moving swiftly beside Vulcan.

"Where are you working?" she asked

"Over the Ridge," he pointed with his crop to the right but they were heading towards a clump of trees on his left. Divining his intent, Brooke frowned but guessed she would have to face up to it eventually.

She was right. They rode to the centre of the clump where there was some space. He waited till Brooke came up with him, flicked the reins out of her hands, dismounted and secured both horses to a low branch. Then he turned and held out his arms to her.

"I can dismount myself," she said gruffly, preparing to do so.

"But I don't want you to." Hugh caught her by the waist, lifted her clear and brought her down into his arms. Brooke knew there was no escape this time. Nevertheless, she made a gesture.

"Did you have to bring me here – so far away from anyone?"

He nodded. "You're not getting away this time. Too many reinforcements at the homestead."

He settled her in his arms and, looking up as his mouth closed on hers, Brooke was shaken to see the blazing hunger in his eyes. She realised that he was in a dangerous mood and it would not do to try him too far. Then, as he crushed her to him, working his mouth, thrusting his tongue between her lips, a sudden anger flared in her, causing her to resist. She knew it all: that mad relentless physical pursuit till satisfaction was obtained and she was thrust aside. Brooke wondered if she could ever inspire the finer depths of love. Only one person had ever looked beneath her beauty and found something worthwhile. Thought of him caused the knot in her solar plexus to tighten into rigidity and Hugh felt the hardening. He lifted his head and stared down at her.

"How come I can't turn you on?" he demanded thickly.

"Too many husbands," said Brooke flippantly.

"I'll *make* you forget them." His passion consuming him, Hugh jerked at her blouse exposing more of her full breasts. His tongue tried to force itself between her now clenched teeth. Then, as he pressed his body hard against her, Brooke snapped.

There are few pains more painful than that of a bitten tongue as those who have inadvertently bitten their own can testify and Brooke was savage in her anger. Hugh released her sharply and reeled away as he combated his agony. It took him some moments to master himself and the blood was bright on his lips as he turned back to her, real hurt in his eyes.

"Whydithyouhavetodothat?" he got out, pressing his handkerchief to his mouth.

Brooke stared fixedly at him. "Some rights still remain for the marriage bed, if you don't mind."

Hugh moved over to a rock and sat down on it. Brooke stood there silently for a few minutes and then moved over to her horse. He made an imploring gesture to stop her.

"Pleathe don't go. I apologithe…. but you've teathed me beyond enduranthe."

"And you've deceived me," she said tartly. "I understood I was to ride with you to your work and that's what I'm expecting."

Relieved of his fear that she intended to ride back to the homestead, Hugh rose and approached her. He stood close, a rueful grin on his lips but the old masterful light in his eyes.

"Just a thweet one," he pleaded.

Recognising his need to always get his way, Brooke submitted resignedly and received a gentle hug and a cautious salute which made her smile inwardly. For all his bluster Hugh could be handled. As the pain of his maltreated tongue settled down he smiled at her,

"When I get this business with Mark cleaned up we'll be coming out here again to settle these rights. I'll be asking a question to which there will be only one answer, my girl,"

"Will there?" she asked lightly as she prepared to mount her horse. She fired an exploratory question at him.

"How long is it going to take you to settle this business with Mark?"

Hugh frowned. "It won't be long. I'm pretty sure he's bluffing. I'm going into town later today to find out a few things for myself. I'll soon put a spoke in his wheel. Coming?"

"And sit around while you talk business?" Brooke shook her head. Once mounted she smiled provocatively down at him.

"You seem to think that all you have to do to woo a girl is to smile at her across the table and take her for a few rides. I'm used to much more."

"Like what?" Hugh asked, mounting easily as Vulcan moved off.

"Oh…. champagne and roses, candlelight…soft music…" she suggested teasingly.

Hugh reached over, caught hold of her hand and kissed it. "I make you a solemn promise. You'll have it all and then some on our honeymoon."

Before his earnest intent gaze Brooke's own faltered and fell. Hugh was too far gone to play. He was going to be hurt badly. A fleeting sympathy welled up in her and a twinge of conscience. She had never played wantonly with a man's feelings and felt that even her desire to help Jamie was hardly justification for really breaking a man's heart.

"I hope you realise, Hugh, that apart from a bit of frolicking at Morris's house, I've not been guilty of flirting with you," she said gravely.

"I know, and I've never flirted with you either. In fact, I've held off till I couldn't stand it any longer."

Brooke felt that she had to get him off the subject somehow so she threw a lighted torch in his path.

"You told me once that you'd explain why Mark couldn't have his own house on Fairlie. Now's a good time."

Hugh picked up the flaming brand. "Because he's damned well not going to have the best house on the property."

"Why do you think it would be the best? They might want just a simple –"

"Because that bitch of a wife of his would see that it's the best."

Brooke kicked her horse and rode ahead, anger flooding her.

Hugh caught up quickly. "Sorry. That was a slip of the tongue. I know you're fond of Jamie – heaven knows why – but –"

"Whether I am or not, she's your brother's wife and-"

"A consolation prize. That's all Mark is. She couldn't get me so she did a line for him and the poor silly baboon fell for it."

At this typical evidence of his overweening conceit, anger just dropped from Brooke; also any latent sympathy or twinge of conscience. Let the beggar get what was coming to him. From then on Brooke played her part with calculated thoroughness.

"I wouldn't really mind if they had the best house," she remarked thoughtfully.

"Do you think I'm going to have that little upstart upstaging you in any way? You're going to be the queen of Fairlie Downs. First in beauty and first in consequence."

"Perhaps you owe something to the fact that Mark is the elder."

"Rot. He's always followed my lead and he was perfectly happy. We all were till Jamie showed up."

"I've never really understood how she came to be here at all."

"Just another example of her cunning scheming ways. I thought I was arranging with Morris to have her father, James Somerville, to come and paint Feldings Creek. Sarah had met him once and taken a fancy to his work. Jamie saw her chance and lied in order to get a free holiday up here and a go at me. Out of sheer good manners we couldn't do a thing about it especially as her father was dead. Sarah's never got over it. She can't stand Jamie of course."

Brooke was so shocked at the ugly twist he gave to Jamie's innocent prank that she said nothing for a while. Then she remarked in a vague voice:

"I thought Jamie said that there was a girl up here, Stella, that you liked."

"Stella? Known her for years. Always had a crush on me. We got things straight when she was here. I believe she's got a new boyfriend now." Hugh explained glibly.

"Oh, I see," said Brooke in a relieved voice. "Well now, what about Sylvia?" She looked at him sharply as she sprang it on him and noted that he flushed a little.

"Sylvia's family and ours have always been close. When her Dad took her Mum overseas for treatment for her cancer, Sylvia stayed with us and when her Mum died she continued with us for some time because her Dad stayed away for ages. She was like a little sister to us. There's never been anything between Sylvia and me."

"Or between Mark and Sylvia?"

"Certainly not," Hugh laughed derisively.

Yes, because you'd see there wasn't, thought Brooke. Well, it was all very revealing but she was sick of it.

"Let's have a race," she shouted and was gone on the words with Hugh's big black thundering behind her. They stayed with the men till lunch time and Brooke had to admire the way he handled his men and the cattle. The brothers made a good team but she wondered if Mark ever chafed at being tied to the administrative side. If he did no one would ever know. It was part of his nature, she guessed, to accept with equanimity whatever life handed him. If Jamie had not blown into his path like a fresh rejuvenating breeze he would have grown old at that desk, dependent on his brother for what little domestic warmth came his way like Ashley… here Brooke pulled up her thoughts sharply and dismounted from them.

Hugh only had time for a quick snack before the plane arrived to take him out. He repeated his invitation to Brooke softly but with greater urgency. Brooke, divining that he did not want to leave her to the influence of the others, was quietly adamant in her refusal but tempered it with a warm smile. Equally determined to leave his imprint on her, Hugh walked her out to the veranda and kissed her soundly.

"Behave yourself, my girl," he ordered and sprinted out to the plane.

After his departure, a cloud seemed to lift off the homestead. Jamie collected her purchases and was happily engaged in displaying them to the housekeeper when Mark informed them that he had been talking to Ashley on the phone and that he and Sarah were coming over that afternoon.

The cloud came back with the arrival of Sarah. Ashley had told her of Mark's ultimatum hoping she would get her first wails over before she saw him but she seemed to have an inexhaustible supply. Once again she took refuge in wonder: that Mark could even contemplate leaving Fairlie Downs; how Hugh would manage with a stranger; how they could ever recover from such a disruption; whatever would their friends be thinking and so on and so on ad nauseam. Anyone would think that it was Fairlie Castle and Mark the resident laird to listen to her until he stopped her short with one question.

"Would you rather it was Hugh than me, Sarah, who was leaving?"

Sarah shut her mouth.

Morris challenged Mark to a game of chess. They had not long discovered a liking for the game in each other. Ashley had brought his violin and he and Brooke settled down with their instruments.

Allison brought out her beloved craft book and soon Mrs Howard brought out her knitting. Heaven knew where she had got the wool but she was already embarked on a delicately patterned matinee jacket in white.

Jamie tentatively showed a couple of tiny garments to Sarah and the universal instinct of motherhood took over. Sarah was full of advice and, to Jamie's amazement, reminiscence. From placid and indulgent listening she moved to intense concentration, not missing a word. A little later, when the housekeeper moved to the kitchen to prepare supper, Jamie excused herself to Sarah and followed her.

Moving close to Howie as she got out the cups, Jamie whispered,

"How come I've never heard anything about Sarah's earlier life. I just thought she had been widowed and was childless but she's been referring to her son when he was a baby and –"

Mrs Howard turned sharply. "Well, you *have* made a hit. Sarah simply never talks about it. I guess showing her the baby clothes has done it."

"But what's the big secret?"

"Well, there was a divorce."

"That's nothing these days."

"It was to Sarah in her day."

"Come on, Howie."

"Okay. It's just that Sarah's marriage was a failure. More than that: a disaster. Sarah was far more a country girl than she herself realised. She was very pretty in a fair delicate sort of way when she was a girl."

"I can see that. Go on."

"A nephew of our lawyer came up with his uncle once and fell for her. He absolutely swept her off her feet. We had a big country wedding and away went Sarah right into a highly social city life. Her husband was a clever ambitious man after the big money in law. Sarah was appalled to find she was expected to do her part as a society hostess, charming his prospective clients. She'd always been shy and the strain affected her nerves. She tried to use her pregnancy as an excuse but Craig wasn't having any. His women employees apparently worked to the last minute before having *their* babies. So poor Sarah had to struggle on and six months after their son was born she had a proper breakdown. When she came out of hospital her mother went down and brought her home here so she could make a full recovery. And that was it."

"What was?"

"Sarah never went back."

"Never? What did her husband -?"

"Oh, he came and pleaded and threatened but there was no moving Sarah. She had found her safe haven again and was not shifting again for anyone."

"Did she have her son with her?"

"No. I think they made a mistake there: believing Sarah was not well enough to care for him. When Mrs Lawrence wanted to fetch him it was Craig's turn to be stubborn. He hung on to the boy thinking that it was the one thing that would eventually bring her back but even that could not move her. Finally, he sued for divorce and total custody of the child and got it."

"But surely they could have shared custody?"

"Sarah never lifted a finger even to get that. Her breakdown had so affected her confidence that she was paranoid about leaving the Downs even for a court appearance."

"Does she have any contact with her son?"

"That's the bitter part. Sarah would not go down to the city to visit him and Craig would not bring the boy up here. She never saw him again."

Jamie was appalled. She stood very still, recalling how wistfully Sarah had handled the little garments and how meticulous she had been in instructing Jamie how to care for the newborn. All her frustration with Sarah vanished as she saw her in a new light. Sarah was a damaged woman unable to manage change, finding her safety in set patterns. Jamie understood Ashley's patience with his sister and his quick assurance at the dinner table when Sarah's eyes had gone blind with panic.

"Do you mean to say she's never left Fairlie Downs?"

"Very rarely and then only occasionally to go down for the Show with the family. Which is a pity for Alec's sake."

"Alec?"

"Alec Cartwright – an old friend of the family. He'd marry Sarah tomorrow if she'd take him."

"Well!" Jamie sat down under this double revelation. She had met Alec Cartwright at her wedding celebration: a tall spare man with a humorous mouth. Maybe she could do some good work there.

"Did you ever find out what happened to the child?"

"Oh, yes. He's done well. Craig married again and had two daughters so young Terry has been the apple of his father's eye and follows in his footsteps. Craig's a QC now and works out of Melbourne."

"Do you think Sarah is happy?"

'Yes, I do – for her temperament. Ashley's brother Edward had been married a while and they had already had Mark. Then Hugh was born so there was a baby on the homestead. Marie wasn't too well after he was born so Sarah had a lot to do with caring for him. I think it was some compensation for her."

"So the pattern falls into place," remarked Jamie thoughtfully. This explained Sarah's decided partiality for the younger child.

When they took the supper in Jamie carried Sarah's cup to where she sat dozing as she listened to the music. One hand still held the tiny bonnet Jamie had been showing her. She smiled into Sarah's eyes with genuine friendliness and sat down beside her again.

Considering all the undercurrents and tension it was turning out to be a remarkably placid evening and Jamie thought wistfully that this was how it should be through the coming years.

Brooke and Ashley were in a cocoon built by their music. The lilting strains of old songs were providing a soothing background and a language for feelings that could not be spoken... or would not be.

As they gathered around the supper table there was constraint due to Sarah's presence and attitude that forbade a thorough discussion of what was on all their minds. Brooke longed to know what Ashley's private thoughts were in regard to selling the sacrosanct property of Fairlie Downs. Eventually she got up restlessly from the table where there was nothing but meaningless chitchat and wandered back to the piano.

When Ashley and Sarah prepared to leave, she was still there picking out tunes with one finger. Sarah's goodbye to Jamie was lengthy for she was receiving a most sympathetic response to the advice she was still keen to give. When Jamie finally turned to Ashley he was listening to Brooke, a half smile on his lips as they moved to follow the tune. Jamie caught the softly uttered words:

> *Hearing love's message as the organ rolls…*
> *its mighty music to our very souls.*
> *No life less perfect then a life with thee…*
> *oh, promise me…oh promise me.*

"It was lovely the way you played that at our Service, Ashley," she said warmly, her own sweet memories making her totally blind.

Ashley smiled down at her. "Had to do something to fill in time till that husband of yours brought you up for air. I've never seen the like and I've seen quite a few weddings."

"I'll have you know that Mark's technique is out of this world," asserted Jamie loftily.

"He certainly never learned it in this one," observed Ashley dryly.

Jamie gripped her sides as her laugh rocketed out through the room turning everyone to her. It brought Brooke out of a dangerous melancholy and ripped Sarah's smothering blanket off the others. They laughed with her but she would not divulge the cause, only saying mysteriously to Mark that she might let him in on it if he remained true to form. This caused Ashley to give a guffaw to the intense annoyance of everyone else. The party thus broke up on a light note.

CHAPTER TWENTY-FOUR

Suspense

Hugh now strained everyone's patience by staying away for two days. Morris was making plans to leave his wife behind for he would have to leave within the next three or four days or let a valued client down.

Mark spent his time in the office when he was not overseeing the men. Jamie, Allison and Howie talked themselves out more than once. Brooke took little interest in anything, mooning around the place once the morning ride was over. Morris worried about her and insisted on an afternoon ride as well. As the fit seemed to take her after Hugh left he wondered uneasily if Hugh's fatal charm had worked once more.

Meanwhile Jamie, when she had been resting in the caravan, had been studiously reading the first letter of John when curiosity made her refer to the Sermon on the Mount. There she came across some words to the effect that anyone angry with his brother would be subject to judgment. The arrow flew home and Jamie had to put the book down. When she did pick it up she deliberately jumped a couple of verses and was confronted by the statement that if she had anything to offer God and remembered that her brother had anything against her she was to go and be reconciled to him first. Jamie put the book down again. Did this mean that they must be content with the wing? For what else would bring about a reconciliation with Hugh? Forlornly Jamie went back to John's letter and read the verses that finally finished her: 'Anyone who hates his brother is a murderer'. Jamie got off the bed in tears.

Thinking it over when she was again alone in the caravan, Jamie thought she could be happy in their own little home if Brooke and Hugh were in the big house. Jamie's ideas were changing rapidly. What she would not give up for herself she could for Mark. A house that was not much bigger than the wing would surely satisfy Hugh, especially if he won Brooke, which now seemed very likely. Jamie had also noted Brooke's moodiness. She would not mind if Brooke was the main hostess of Fairlie Downs if Mark, with his simple tastes, was happy. Jamie made lots of conciliatory plans but all of them failed to deal with the main problem: the armed truce between her and her brother-in-law. Deep in her heart she knew she had to deal with this fierce unforgiving resentment of Hugh, and it was keeping her from real prayer for the situation. Like many others Jamie found she had to move from prayer for the problem, to prayer for herself that God would make her willing to forgive Hugh for the way he had hurt her husband.

On the second day of Hugh's absence Jamie was called to the phone and found her friend, Helen on the line, a very perturbed Helen.

"Jamie, dear, is everything all right? I've got a feeling about you."

"It is and it isn't," gulped Jamie.

"Look, I've got this terrific burden about you and when I told Dr Tracey about you he suggested that I ring you even if it means sticking my nose where you might not want it."

"Dr Tracey?" Then Jamie remembered. He would know how to deal with this matter with his theories about winning by losing, "I wish I could talk to him. Where did you hear him?"

"Well, actually he's here in the house. A friend of mine knows him very well and I was able to invite him to dinner. I just had to tell him about how I was feeling about you and I described you and Mark to him. He thinks he remembers you."

'Remembers *me*? But I –"

"Just sniffed," said Helen helpfully.

Jamie laughed a little and then a strong resolve took hold of her.

"Helen do you really want to help me?"

"That's why I'm ringing, dear."

"Well, will you tell Dr Tracey the circumstances of my marriage and what Hugh did to Mark?"

"As good as done. Then?"

"I'll give you twenty minutes and then I'll ring you back and if I could talk to Dr Tracey for a moment?"

"Of course. Take this number down."

Jamie did so and rang off. She hovered near the instrument to be ready to cut off any wayward call that came through. Right on the dot she rang Helen's number. Dr Tracey's cheerful voice answered her.

"Well, Jamie?" he said as though he had known her all his life. She nearly broke down on the spot but there was true metal in the girl. Without running down Hugh or justifying herself she gave a concise account of the present situation and the way Mark was handling it. When she had done, the Minister asked what teaching Mark had had.

"None," she said. "Just his Bible."

"Taught totally by the Holy Spirit," mused the Minister. "I'd very much like to meet your husband someday, my dear. He's a rarity."

"He can be a rarity without being right, can't he?" demanded Jamie. "He's prepared to give up everything rather than quarrel with his brother."

"Even you? Now, that surely can't be the case."

"Oh, not now," said Jamie impatiently. "When we first met he fell in love with me on sight but if I fell for Hugh he was determined to be happy for me without a fight…" Jamie ended on a sob.

"Total release," murmured Dr Tracey. "No wonder he won you, Jamie. He who loses his life will find it."

"I don't understand. How -?"

"No, you're too new a Christian to know much about the life of sacrifice but you have a great teacher in your husband."

Jamie was beginning to wonder if she had been wise to consult the Minister.

"Do you mean he's doing the right thing then?"

"He's following through on a spiritual law that few have the guts to do so these days. It's the Lamb life, Jamie. The sacrificial life. I think he's going to allow Hugh to slaughter him because he's trying to show Hugh the true Christ spirit. He's presenting to Hugh One Who was prepared to die to all His own desires in weakness –"

"There's nothing weak about Mark," interrupted Jamie hotly, a shade too hotly in Dr Tracey's opinion.

"You weren't listening. The weakness I'm talking about is displayed by great strength only through great meekness. Get it?"

After a moment Jamie said, "Do you mean that Mark is doing this not because he has to but because he wants to?"

"Right. Good scholar."

"Dr Tracey, I – I well, I could be happy with a smaller house but if – if you think I should accept the offer of the wing I –"

"Under no circumstances whatsoever. You keep out of this, Jamie. When God is dealing with a soul you interfere at your peril."

Jamie was silent, chastened by his sharp tone even though she was a long way from understanding him.

The Doctor continued in a more comforting tone. "Mark is working something out with his brother that has been going on all their lives. It has suddenly reached a flashpoint and it is really up to Hugh now. Either he will respond to Mark's innate generosity and goodness of heart or he will reject him. If he rejects Mark, he will be rejecting Christ."

"But he hasn't said a word about the Lord Jesus."

"When you live the Life like Mark is you don't have to. The spiritual challenge lies suspended between them even though it is invisible to other eyes."

"I wish I went to your church, Dr Tracey."

"It's Mark's church you need to go to, Jamie."

"I was afraid you'd say that. There's one other thing. I – I've got to tell someone."

"Now's the time, my dear."

In a low voice Jamie told the Minister of the cancerous hate in her heart for Hugh, of the verses she had read and how, condemned by her own heart, she could no longer enjoy her Bible. Edmund Tracey's heart was filled with compassion for the loyal and lonely little soul struggling in such deep waters.

"Listen, Jamie. You've had a very natural reaction and you just have not yet learned how to deal with it. That's all. You've tried to fight these feelings with your own weapons and that is why you feel such condemnation. You can't reason with hate. You have to flood it out on the tide of forgiveness and love."

"But I can't forgive him."

"Of course, you can't. It must be Christ forgiving through you."

"How do I know He'll forgive Hugh?"

"Well, He died for Hugh, didn't He?"

The girl was silent.

"Jamie, get a picture of Hugh in your mind. Now picture Christ beside him, putting His arm around him, and saying something like: Poor blind, naked, loveless Hugh –"

"But he's not poor and blind and naked. He –"

"Yes, he is. Think it through, Jamie. He is blind to the needs of his soul; unclothed of the robe of righteousness; poor –"

"Oh, yes, I see it… and – and he doesn't know anything at all about real love… at least –"

"Now you're getting it. That's what Mark sees and what he's trying to rectify."

"That means that Mark is rich… very rich."

"My word."

Jamie sat back, digesting this. The Doctor waited patiently. This would have a social cost by worldly standards, he thought wryly and, like Jamie, could not have cared less.

"If I could just get rid of this awful feeling in my heart towards Hugh. I don't feel clean enough to read the Bible."

"If you had kept on reading First John you would have found your answer to that."

"How?" Jamie was sceptical. "All I could find were things about hating my brother and felt condemned every time."

There was amusement in the Doctor's voice as he answered, "The verse that finally tripped you up was fifteen in chapter three, wasn't it?"

"Yes, about – about being a – a murderer if you hated your brother."

"Yes, well, verses nineteen and twenty go something like this: This is how we know that we belong to the truth and how we set our hearts at rest in His presence whenever our *hearts condemn us*. For God is greater than our hearts and He knows everything."

There was a long silence. Then Jamie said in a wondering voice, "If I'd only known. I feel better already."

"Well, you've a long row to hoe yet, my dear, but follow your husband's methods, keep reading the Bible and submitting yourself to the Holy Spirit's teaching. He is the greatest Teacher in the world."

"And you think that this hate for Hugh will eventually go?"

"Oh, yes, if you keep bringing it to the Lord. Also, keep out of Mark's way when he's dealing with his brother."

"Dr. Tracey, Mark seems to be suffering somehow in a way that doesn't seem to be about the property."

"You've sensed that, have you? Yes, I would say that he is travailing for his brother."

"I don't really understand."

"No, these are deep waters, Jamie. There is much below the surface in this case."

Jamie had another think and then at last, said reluctantly, "Well, I suppose I'll have to let you go. I'm so grateful for this chance to talk to you, Dr Tracey."

"So am I, my dear. I revel in being a part of a soul's expansion. Perhaps you could let me know how things turn out?"

"Oh, yes, indeed," replied Jamie eagerly, "and, Doctor, if you would –"

"Pray for you? Surely."

Jamie took down his own phone number and, with more stumbling thanks, finally rang off. She tore off the sheet from the small note pad and sat staring at it as one beholding rare treasure. How wonderful that God had given her this chance! He had been watching over her after all. She would have liked to share it all with Mark but there was a check on her spirit. As the Doctor had told her, Mark was working through something and, as in other matters, he had not needed any tuition, she thought wryly. He was a natural even in spiritual things.

So warm was Jamie's heart towards her husband that her ill feeling towards Hugh began to lessen from that moment. If he thought that his brother was worth all this, then she must find him so too. Jamie was just beginning to grasp the great simplicity of Mark's nature. The more or less isolated life on the station coupled with his natural reserve when at school and university had allowed the solid values of the Bible to take deep root in him and grow unmolested till he could see his path with greater clarity than most. The constant dying in this one situation had tempered the metal of his spirit till he could hold unswervingly to the course he considered to be right no matter how many voices urged him otherwise. This silent witness of his was having its effect on his wife, breaking down her own wilful ideas as to his behaviour.

Yet Jamie knew, when she woke in the night, close to her husband, that his breathing was not always that of a sleeping man. After her talk with Dr Tracey she used these odd moments to pray that God would make her more worthy of Mark and that her own selfish desires, justified as she thought them, had not the same power to distress him.

CHAPTER–TWENTY-FIVE

The Slaughter

The third day, to Morris's relief, brought the charter plane overhead and, as it landed, Mark drove out in his Landrover to pick up the occupants.

Four men got out. Besides Hugh and the pilot, there was the Lawrences' solicitor, Gavin Weyburn, and Alec Cartwright, a well-known cattle dealer and long-time aspirant to Sarah's reluctant hand. Gavin shook Mark's hand a shade too heartily and Alec did so with a troubled air. Hugh merely nodded to his brother who returned the nod and greeted the pilot, Jim McCracken, who did most of their charter work.

They had arrived in time for lunch and the pilot's presence at it meant that the talk was general. Hugh was the genial host as usual but he behaved as though his brother were not there. Brooke took a malicious pleasure in asking Mark's opinion as various subjects came up, thereby pulling him into the conversation but it did her no good. Hugh's eyes gleamed. He felt that he was getting wise to all her little games and anticipated with pleasure the bringing of her to heel. In the meantime, let her pull on the rein and cavort as much as she liked.

After lunch the pilot took off and Hugh, Mark and the two guests excused themselves and went down to Mark's office. Jamie was in fear and trepidation while they were away but Mark told her later, when they returned for smoko, that they had merely been going through the books.

Then the horses were called for and the four went off on a tour of inspection. Morris was a little hurt that he had not been included at least in the ride but held his peace.

By dinnertime the tension had mounted and conversation around the table was very stiff and disjointed, everyone much occupied with his or her own thoughts. It was with some relief that a car was heard but, when Ashley came in without Sarah, Hugh was disappointed. To his query, Ashley merely said that she wasn't feeling up to it. As she had no financial interests now, Hugh had to let it go but it annoyed him for he knew that Sarah was on his side. Numbers always helped. Actually Ashley, sick of Sarah's wailings, had ordered her to stay home. He wanted to catch every word tonight and knew that his sister's mewings would distract them all.

Once the table was cleared Hugh called for coffee to be brought in and looked pointedly at Morris and Alison. Brooke half rose but he motioned her back. Morris and Alison remained in their seats, returning Hugh's glare with bland smiles. Morris, still smarting over being left out of the afternoon's ride, made a big point of settling himself very comfortably and reminding Howie that he always had a second cup.

Gavin fetched his briefcase and took out a pile of documents. Alec scratched his chin with a nervous air and repeatedly glanced questioningly at Mark as though seeking some definite sign from him.

Hugh began to speak in a voice of quiet authority that had an inflexible ring to it. Everyone found themselves, like Alec, watching Mark, not Hugh, as the latter stated that he had accepted the alternative Mark had offered and arranged for Alec Cartwright to buy his brother out.

Then followed the complicated details of the division, something which had never occurred in the whole history of the property. It did not mean much to the onlookers as they went over the runs and poddy stations, the machinery plant and so forth. The first stab of Hugh's knife came when he stated that Alec wished to have choice of land on which to build his own home.

Mark did not flinch but the others did to hear Hugh offering Alec what he had denied his own brother. Gavin broke in here with a comment on the value of the land where the mine was to be and eventually the figure Alec was offering came out. Ashley frowned and glanced quickly at Mark. He knew how low the price was, something hidden from the others. But some of them guessed when Alec stirred uncomfortably and said that was the best he could offer as he did not want to disappear entirely into the bank's maw.

"I'd be glad to take less land and a smaller share in the plant and stock, Mark," he said on a conciliatory note but Hugh brushed him aside.

"It has to be divided right down the middle," he said brusquely, "as that's the way Dad left it."

Jamie longed to ask the solicitor if this were really fair even if Mark did accept the less valuation but she was abiding by Dr Tracey's advice. She looked meaningly at Mark but he had merely nodded. She glanced at Ashley who was frowning down at the table. Why didn't he say something? Surely he knew if the price was unfair. She groaned inwardly.

Morris was doing his own cogitations. Why was Hugh allowing Alec to take a full half of the property for less than its value? Did he imagine that this devaluing of Mark's share would give him the same say he had had with his easy-going brother? Morris arrived at the conclusion that Hugh had something up his sleeve.

They began to go through the papers, dealing with various matters that Alec, Gavin and Hugh brought up. Mark and Ashley still said nothing, Mark only nodding when his assent or approval was required.

Alison and Brooke had eased themselves a little back from the table and Alison whispered that she would like to hear Ashley and Mark having a conversation over the phone. 'One big silence,' I reckon, she averred and Brooke fought to hold back a hysterical burst of laughter. She did not know how the others' nerves were behaving but she herself could not stand much more. A forthright woman, herself, she could not understand Mark - or Ashley for that matter. Mark made her think of some dumb sheep being prepared for slaughter while the butchers chatted among themselves with never a thought for the quivering body in their hands. And Ashley was behaving as though he were the next victim in line. Brooke was seeing a different type of manhood in action and it tried her sorely.

They had been at it well over an hour when they finally got to the riding stock and vehicles. Everything was apparently running smoothly for Hugh as Mark never contested one decision. Everyone could see that it was beginning to nettle the younger brother. He moved his chair a little so that he was looking directly into Mark's face. Then he said deliberately,

"As the vehicles were all bought out of the estate money I intend to repossess all of them as part of my share. Alec has his own car and can have the use of estate ones."

Before Mark could respond Morris spoke up, too annoyed to realise that he was speaking out of turn.

"You'll hardly repossess Mark's new Falcon. Mark needs something to drive off the property with."

Watching Mark's eyes, Hugh snapped, "He can go with you."

There was a concerted gasp even from Gavin and Alec. Technically Hugh could do this but Mark had never taken what was due him in the way of holidays and personal expenses as Hugh had.

There was some hesitation before Mark nodded. To take his car from him was equivalent to taking a man's horse in the old days.

Hugh's tormenting smile hardened on his lips as Morris was heard to mutter, "Contemptible. Utterly contemptible."

Jamie could not believe either her eyes or her ears. Mark could easily buy another car but surely they could leave with some dignity and there was the caravan to be considered too. She could no longer keep silent.

"We've got to have something to pull the caravan. Surely…"

"Let Morris pull it out," was the flat answer.

Gavin looked disgusted. As a lawyer, he was used to schooling his features but Mark's forbearance in the face of what he could only term pure spite on Hugh's part was beyond him. He had earlier tried to reason with Hugh, wanting him to have a cooling off period but in the presence of the two brothers he was forced to wait for Mark's lead in order to renew his protests.

Actually, Hugh had expected Mark to protest long before this. He had been sure that once faced with the sale in concrete terms Mark would not be able to go through with it for it was not only breaking up a property but also a life partnership. His brother's continued silence was irking him to the point where he was having difficulty controlling his rising temper. But he was not done yet.

"Alec has arranged with his Bank to supply the finance," he said crisply, "so once we've settled the stock there's no reason why the papers can't be signed tonight – which means you can leave as soon as you like."

There was an agitated murmur of protest in which Alec's voice predominated.

"Hang on, Hugh. The Court's not serving notice on Mark. I'd like to go over the books more thoroughly and spend a few days with Mark. There is much he could tell me that I need to know. Everyone does things a bit differently." He looked entreatingly at Mark. "You're not going to just walk out and leave me in the lurch, are you?"

Appealed to thus Mark was forced to answer and his remark that he would see how things shaped up tomorrow allowed the others to hear his voice for the first time since the discussion began. And it gave him away. It was nothing but a slight huskiness making the light drawl a bit breathy but it was the voice of a condemned man who might gallantly request a cigarette to be put between his lips before he was shot. Jamie stared down at her clenched hands while a silver drop fell on them. Brooke stared stonily at Hugh and everyone else looked anywhere but at Mark. Hugh gazed fixedly at his brother and the scent of blood was in his nostrils.

"I'll be taking all the horses, of course. Alec will share the stock with me but a man likes to get his own horses."

Mark nodded.

"All the horses,' reiterated Hugh, "including Redmaster."

Jamie sprang to her feet.

"Oh, cruel! Cruel! Red's not just any horse. Mark trained him. He's a friend. You're just jealous of him and —"

Mark caught hold of her hand.

"Steady, Jamie," he said quietly.

Hugh completely ignored her impassioned outburst. He was waiting for the tolerance level to snap in Mark.

After a dreadful silence when everyone seemed to stop breathing, Mark nodded.

"Oh, no, no, *no*," wailed Jamie, snatching her hand away. "How can you, Mark? Don't let him do this to you. He's torturing you like the fiend he is. Mark —"

"Hush, Jamie."

"I won't hush." Jamie faced Hugh. "You're a dreadful, dreadful man. Selfish and mean and jealous! I'm glad I hate you! I'll never speak to you again as long as I live!"

She shoved her chair back and rushed out of the room. Mark rose to his feet quickly but Mrs Howard moved forward. She had naturally heard everything from the kitchen.

"I'll look after her. Don't worry, Mark."

Her kindly face lined with concern she disappeared after the girl.

Hugh watched her go with satisfaction. If Mark had not broken, Jamie had. In her upset state, she was his best ally. He could see the drawn lines about Mark's mouth as he settled in his seat again. He pressed home his advantage.

"Shall we get to signing the papers now?" he suggested smoothly.

"Right," Mark drew his chair in and felt for the biro in his shirt pocket. Everyone was immobile for a moment. Then Gavin slowly began to sort the documents. A queer look came into Hugh's face. It was he who hesitated now, wondering if it would have been better to postpone the signing till tomorrow which would give Jamie time to work on Mark during the night…but he had too much pride to back down now in the face of his brother's acquiescence.

Gavin was tight-lipped and Alec looked anything but a man who was making a very profitable deal. Mark read carefully through every line of the deed, signed his name and passed it over. The other men silently added their names, Hugh signing last but there was none of the usual flourish to his signature. Gavin gathered the papers, saying non-committally that he had a few details to check with the bank when he went back the next day.

"I'll get Jim to come back for me in a couple of days' time," said Alec as he put his pen away. "Better leave those papers with me. I'll bring them in."

Hedging your bets, thought Gavin as he rose from the table. Mark also rose and extended his hand across the table to his brother.

"I guess we'd better shake on it," he said quietly. "It'll be a new life for both of us after this."

Hugh rose too but stood staring at Mark's hand, his eyes narrowed to slits. In the act of breaking up the gathering paused.

Then Hugh savagely struck his brother's hand away and strode out of the room. Mark in turn stood staring at his hand as if wondering what was at fault with it. Then he turned to the company and said,

"Guess I'd better see to Jamie. G'night."

As he disappeared, Gavin at last gave voice to his thoughts. "That was a slaughter if ever I saw one. I can't think what has got into Hugh. They were such mates."

Alec stood, frowning deeply. When the proposition had been put to him he had not been able to resist the opportunity to buy into a magnificent property that would also give him better access to the long-time love of his life. Hugh had given him the impression that Mark was eager to go but that had dissipated as he witnessed the different attitudes of the two brothers. He drew nearer to Gavin and said worriedly,

"I don't feel somehow that it is all valid. I don't want to work with Hugh if Mark –"

"Look! If it hadn't been you it would have been someone else. I told you Hugh would have just about picked a man off the street, he was in that kind of mood."

Alec nodded uncomfortably. "Hugh took everything he could from Mark and Mark just let him. Yet – somehow – I felt Mark won the round. It's crazy."

"I don't pretend to understand it either but you know Hugh would not listen to reason. And it seems that Mark won't either. I felt sorry for his poor little wife. What a homecoming for a bride!"

The others had drawn together and were talking in low voices. Mrs Howard had come back and suggested a late supper. Nobody wanted it but Alec would not have knocked back a stiff drink. She set about settling the two visitors in their quarters as goodnights were said.

Ashley strolled out to his car. Brooke saw her chance and followed him.

"Ashley, could I walk down to your car with you?"

"Sure," Ashley fell into step beside her.

When they were near the vehicle and out of earshot, she turned to him.

"Ashley, couldn't anything have been done? Mark should have been handling the sale but he let Hugh do it and Hugh is obviously letting it go for much less than its value just to spite Mark. Half Fairlie Downs going for –"

"Hang on, Brooke. It's still a fair bit of money and actually it's a quarter share. Seven Trees constitutes half, which is in my name. We run the whole business as one."

"Oh," Brooke took time to think it over. Then she looked earnestly into the thin kindly face. "It's none of my business but – but what happens to your share, Ashley, if – if –" Brooke suddenly found the thought too dreadful to voice.

"If I die?" he completed matter-of-factly. "If I leave my will as it is, Mark and Hugh will inherit equal shares. Dad bought out Sarah when she married so she's okay. But I'm pretty sure Hugh will be over here, while his temper's up, to convince me that the property has been divided enough, that it will be much better now to change my will in his favour."

"But you won't, will you, Ashley? You'll favour Mark, won't you?"

She stared up at the man, quite unconscious in her appeal of the magnetism of her beauty. It brought a forlornness into his gaze as he stared down at her. Her lovely hair shimmered around her head in the moonlight; the line of cheek, throat and breast superb. Her hands were clasped together in the earnestness of her interest in her little friend's problems. Her red lips were slightly parted and the soft light picked up the gleam of her white teeth. It also picked up quite mercilessly her fatal flaw: her youth. He turned away and spoke through half closed lips.

"What do you want, Brooke?"

"What do you mean?" The woman began to tremble.

"What is your specific wish?" and now Ashley's voice was hard, "that I will all I own on God's earth to Mark, leaving nothing for anyone else?"

Brooke stood there horrified. What was she doing? What would come of her hasty interference now? A thousand incoherent thoughts rushed into her head. Was she actually trying to get Ashley to sign his life away for Mark. Such is woman – such is humanity – that the perspective of the whole business swung madly around and different values shot into the ascendancy. Brooke suddenly saw that Mark would be quite well off and, above all, he had the woman he loved. But Ashley…he had nothing but land and stock in trust. Brooke put her hands over her face.

"No, no… of course not," she exclaimed brokenly. "I don't wish that at all. Oh, Ashley, I've no business interfering. Forgive me but –"

"That's all right. Forget it. We're all a bit overwrought tonight."

There was a gentle pat on her shoulder and Ashley was getting into his car. The engine purred into life and the lights came on. He leaned out for a final quick wave and then the big car was turning and heading for the grid. Brooke stood there unable to move. She was still standing there when the lights finally dwindled but her blurred vision would not have been able to pick them up anyway.

Everyone else had gone to bed when she got in and Brooke was soon in bed but not to sleep. Within a few days, Mark and Jamie would be leaving, Morris and Allison would go too and so would she. There wasn't even a chance of coming back for a visit. Brooke had wept over her broken marriages but never had she felt such heartbreak as she did that night as the heavy tears welled slowly and trickled down the sides of her cheeks.

"My life is nothing but sorrow and disappointment," she whispered and in her despair turned to the God she was only just beginning to know.

"Oh, please help me," she prayed. "I've made such a mess of it tonight. Please show me what to do."

When Mark had arrived at the caravan Mrs Howard had got up from the side of the bed and slipped quietly past him and down the steps. She had been able to do nothing but try and soothe the distraught girl. Jamie was beyond all reasoning. Mark stood looking down at her and at last said tentatively: "Jamie?"

Jamie moved violently in the bed, her face well hidden.

"Go away! Go *away!*"

Mark did. He went and sat at the door of the caravan, his long legs stretched down the short steps.

Jamie had not wanted Mark to take her literally. She had wanted him to catch her up in his arms while she pummelled his chest and poured forth her rage, her frustration, what she thought of Hugh and the other men, all ogres in her eyes. She wanted to tell him what he should have said, what he should have done. She wanted to tell him to be a man not a wimp.

Instead he had taken her at her word. At that moment, he did not care what she thought or said. He had wanted her trust and she had not given it.

He sat there in the dark trying to think it through. He had followed the scriptural injunction to the letter: *If someone takes your coat, give him your cloak also.* With each assent, he had deliberately died the requisite death. *Unless a grain of wheat falls into the ground and dies it abides alone. But if it dies it bears much fruit.* The only fruit yielded had been Hugh's bitter antagonism and Jamie's desertion.

Mark sat on into the night in his misery and grief, trying to see why the divine principle had not worked. Eventually a still small voice began to speak. Had he really given the cloak freely or had it been a calculated gamble, simply a stake laid down confidently with the expectation of a win? Had he actually even anticipated losing? Mark saw into his soul under the searchlight of the Spirit. He saw now that he had not even contemplated leaving Fairlie Downs for good. In his subconscious mind, it had all been planned as a strategy, a method of victory conducted in a mechanical way. He put his head in his hands.

"Oh, God what you're telling me is that action isn't enough. My heart has to go with it. It has to be all the way."

This was it: the spiritual man battling against the flesh. Mark looked back on a lifetime of doing what he thought was right, only to have it questioned by the Spirit. Was it after all just for the sake of peace in what was really a successful partnership? Had there ever been an issue till now where the principle of the Lamb life had been really involved.

It was then that Mark at last faced his Gethsemane: the final battle before the death. In an agony, he yielded, releasing everything he held dear - not just into the hands of Hugh – but into the hands of God.

At long last the seed finally died and sank into the earth.

.   .   .   .

It was in the dark hour before dawn that the seed began to stir with the resurrection life. As he leaned against the doorjamb, rested and at peace, Mark felt a movement behind him. A soft form was kneeling at his back and two loving arms came around him and his head was drawn back against his wife's breast.

"Your God will be my God," she whispered. "The Lord do to me and more also if aught but death part you and me."

It was enough. Through those long dark hours God had dealt with her and Jamie had finally found her own victory. Her perfect trust lay like balm on his heart.

After a while she coaxed him to bed and as the dawn skies lightened the earth, she told him about her phone call to Dr Tracey for his counsel.

A far less happy Brooke woke from a disturbed sleep to that same dawn and the sound of someone tapping lightly on the glass door that led to the veranda. She got up, drew a few brush strokes through her thick hair and slipped on a brunch coat. As she opened the door she saw Hugh standing back against the railing. He smiled jauntily at her and there was a defiant gleam in his dark eyes.

"I thought we might take our ride a bit earlier than the others," he said.

Brooke looked past him. There were two horses, saddled and bridled and tied to the rail. One was Vulcan and the other was Redmaster, the polished black and red hides flashing in the sun with their movements.

Brooke drew herself up to her full height. So Hugh was going to take her out on Mark's beloved horse and no doubt propose to her in some fancy spot, was he? Brooke did not behave like a virago or a bad-tempered hussy. She was goddess-like, royal in her just anger. She delivered herself of her opinion of his methods and his morals, his cunning, his craft and his conceit. She informed him that she had never been the least attracted to him, that she would die rather than marry him, that he was not worth his brother's little finger and that if she never rode again she would *not* ride Redmaster. She told him that she would be leaving shortly with Mark and Jamie and that she earnestly hoped that their paths would not cross again. Then she quietly asked him to excuse her and went back into her room and shut the door.

Hugh stared around him as though suddenly finding himself in strange territory. It was the first time in his life he had been really told off, but for it to be Brooke, on top of the most uncomfortable night of his life – for Hugh was by no means at ease – drove such a wedge in his self-esteem that he could not get his poise.

Ever since Mark had held out his hand Hugh's thoughts had been in a kind of suspended animation. He had been so sure that he could break Mark that he had not even contemplated this kind of victory. The victory he wanted was Mark's capitulation. His submission would then have forced Jamie's submission and his own final triumph. His mind simply refused to accept what had happened so he had turned his thoughts to the winning of Brooke whose place at his side would definitely put his archenemy in the shadows. His animosity to his brother's wife was as strong as Jamie's for him with this difference: he neither fought it nor felt guilty about it. She was the cause of all his troubles…his Nemesis.

Now, in the face of Brooke's rebuttal, once again his mind refused to take it in. After a moment, he went back down the steps and, mounting Vulcan, he led the disappointed Red back to the stables and unsaddled him quickly. Then he went around to the kitchen to make up some food of anything he could find and rode off, to be seen no more for hours. He was perfectly convinced that Brooke was merely suffering some reaction from the dramas of the night before. Nevertheless, he was sufficiently shaken to want to retire till he could think through his next move.

He was unaware that a seed was stirring.

Brooke had no idea either. She could not go back to bed for her thoughts were tumultuous. The scene on the veranda engendered a resolve in her mind. A thought that had been growing wistfully in her heart suddenly took on an urgency. It was now or never.

When Mark came down alone to breakfast Brooke took her coffee up to Jamie and was relieved to find that Jamie was gaining control over her stomach but still sleepy. Sitting on the side of the bed she eventually led the conversation back to Jamie's courting days. Then she cleverly got around to Mark's shy nature, using a bit of her own natural guile.

"Mark must have been madly in love with you to defy Hugh and pop the question?" she said on an interrogative note.

Jamie gave a small secretive smile as she lay propped up on her pillows. Brooke found that smile very encouraging but she had to be sure.

"Now I come to think of it," she said with an air of doubt, "I can't imagine either Mark or – or even Ashley getting anywhere with a woman without some encouragement."

However, Jamie had her own pride and not even to her friend would she divulge the truth. She fell back on imputation.

"Could be," she said with a laugh. "I know I pulled Ashley on to the dance floor and just about had to bully Mark into dancing with me."

Brooke laughed too, remembering how Ashley had swept her on to the dance floor, pushing the young jackeroo aside.

"I guess once you get them started they can go on fine from there."

"You bet,' agreed Jamie with an introspective smile. Then she remembered Hugh's remark and added mischievously, "Just a touch on the rein and a bit of spur and he'll be right."

Brooke laughed. "I remember you telling me about Hugh's estimate of you. He couldn't have been more wrong."

Jamie looked anxiously at Brooke. Her friend's face had brightened in the last few minutes.

"Brooke, you haven't really fallen for Hugh, have you?"

"No way in the world," said Brooke, standing up. "He's gone off this morning with good sized flea in his ear. I told him off good and proper. I'd best be going. Don't rush up."

"Told him off? Brooke…"

But Brooke was gone.

CHAPTER TWENTY-SIX

Last Ditch Effort

Driving Morris's car, Brooke arrived at Seven Trees after the men had had their breakfast and were preparing to leave for their day's work. Parking the car, she came up the slope leading to the stables.   The overseer and two of the stockmen were adjusting their horses' harnesses. Seeing Brooke, they turned and leaned on the rails with one accord. Two of them, the overseer and the jackaroo, rarely got the chance to see such beauty. The third, a city boy sent out by his wealthy father in a last ditch attempt to instil some sense of purpose in him, knew well that Brooke would hold her own anywhere.

"Ashley here?" she asked briskly.

They all jerked their thumbs back at the stables. "Be here in a minute," they chorused.

"Oh, I'll catch him there,' she said nonchalantly and continued up the slope. Deeply appreciative eyes followed her till she disappeared.

Ashley was standing near his horse working a new bridle that was still a bit stiff. He heard a slight sound and peered around the rump of the big grey that was awaiting his pleasure. Then every movement stilled but the heavy thudding of his heart.

"'Morning, Ashley."

"'Morning, Brooke." He straightened and tried to go on with his work but the strap just would not go into the buckle.

Brooke drew a deep breath. Well, she was here with him and they were quite private. Reminding herself that her days were numbered at Fairlie Downs she plunged straight in.

"I – I'm leaving Ashley."

"L – leaving," Ashley stammered. "But you don't have to leave just yet. It will be a while before this mess is straightened out. I mean to have a word with Hugh today and –"

"I have to leave – and at once."

"Have to? But why?"

"You see," said Brooke, getting into her stride. "Hugh proposed to me this morning and I refused him." She was taking Hugh's intention as the deed. "So I can't stay any longer as his guest."

"Refused him?" The words seemed to be dragged out of his tight throat. Then the echo came. *"Refused him!"*

"Yes." Brooke waited till Ashley could adjust to her words.

"Refused him," he repeated for the third time, his hands fiddling mechanically with the bridle. "I reckon Hugh's never proposed to any girl before."

"Well, he chose the wrong one," said Brooke flatly, wanting to be rid of Hugh. "So you see I have to go straight away."

She looked straight into his eyes. He looked down so that she might not see their stricken expression but he was not quick enough.

"I see," he said slowly, wishing his wretched fingers were not all thumbs.

Brooke waited but nothing more was forthcoming. Just silence. She was now in Jamie's dilemma. The next step would have to be a crucial one. She hoped that the shyness that was tying her tongue was his problem too. Actually, it was the overwhelming thought of her going that had stricken Ashley dumb.

Still silence.

"Can't you put that stupid thing away?" she demanded irritably.

Ashley dropped the bridle in the dirt, bent and picked it up and hung it on a nail with hands that shook. The sight did Brooke no end of good.

"Ashley?" the softness and appeal in the voice compelled him to look at her. She was gazing at his hands.

"I don't know what to do with them," he said idiotically. He could not hide them in his pockets for there was still grease on them. He pulled out his handkerchief and made a great show of wiping them clean.

"There. That's better," he said with a feeble attempt at heartiness.

"Ashley?" Oh, that voice! He would hear it in his ears forever with its sibilant sweetness.

Brooke was trying hard to break the psychological barrier. Only a reigning Queen like Victoria had the right and authority to propose to a man, she thought miserably. If he would only give her some help. But he was looking at the ground again.

"It's – it's goodbye, Ashley."

He dragged his eyes up once again and his aching heart was in them.

Brooke moved closer and gently took both the hard calloused hands in her own and looked up at him.

"Ashley, is there – is there any chance for me?" she whispered.

The man stiffened in pure shock.

Brooke was past the point of no return. Ashley seemed encased in iron bands. Only his eyes, his piteous eyes were alive. Brooke drew his hands and placed them each side of her slim waist. Still Ashley did not move.

Wise in the ways of men, Brooke pressed his hands down on to her rounded hips.

Something was released in Ashley like the violent uncoiling of a spring. His arms enveloped her with crushing force and his lips burnt her forehead, her creamy eyelids, her cheeks till they found her mouth and fastened there. Nothing moved for a while. Then Ashley suddenly jerked back, aghast at the miracle. Brooke looked up into his stunned disbelieving eyes. She wriggled her arms free and clasped them firmly around his neck.

"More of the same," she ordered imperiously and lifted her delectable mouth.

Ashley stared down into those glorious eyes holding an expression he had not even dared to dream. A moment he hesitated and then, with the air of man prepared to drown in royal bliss, he complied.

How long they would have gone on with their ordering and reordering is anybody's guess but there was the sound of approaching footsteps and then a gasp that seemed to burst on the air behind them. Ashley lifted his head and spoke over his shoulder.

"Well, what is it?"

"N-n-nothing, b-boss," floundered the jackeroo. "I ju-ju-just –"

"Well, you can ju-ju-just take yourself off. Tell Matt to take over for the day. I won't be available."

There was no movement behind them.

"*Get!*"

Alan got.

Brooke's eyes were brimming with laughter. He grinned back and caught her hand.

"Come on. We've got to get away by ourselves."

He was racing her up to the house when he jerked to a stop. Brooke still running was swung right around on to his chest but he held her off.

"Brooke, this is impossible. I'm fifty-two."

"And I'm a hundred and two," Brooke declared. "I've lived two lifetimes to your one. Oh, Ashley, you don't know what it means to me to meet a man like you. A man with no guile, no hateful sophistication, no – why, darling, I only hope I am sweet enough and fresh enough for you."

Ashley drew in his breath sharply.

On skis and on horseback Brooke had been described as glorious. Standing before Ashley in her mature womanhood, pleading for her happiness, she had a glory so potent that it misted his eyes and deafened his ears with the pounding of his blood.

Love had come into his life with pennants flying and Ashley doubted no longer.

She pulled him on and they raced to the foot of the stairs.

"Wait here," he whispered and ran lightly up into the kitchen. The sound of the washing machine told him Sarah's whereabouts. He opened the fridge, found an esky and soon filled it. He opened another cupboard and pulled down a small picnic basket. Creeping out he gave the basket to Brooke and, hand in hand, they ran past the stupefied group to the car. Ashley took over the wheel and in a cloud of dust they were gone.

The two boys and the man continued to stare after the car with bemused expressions. After a while Matt pushed his hat to the back of his head and rubbed his brow.

"I don't know what's come over the place. First Mark comes out of his trance and grabs a peach… and now -"

"And now," grieved Alan, "Rip Van Winkle wakes up and makes off with a – with a –"

"Pêche Melba," said the city boy.

.   .   .   .

Back at Fairlie Downs they were at sixes and sevens. After the plane had taken Gavin away Mark had tried to get down to business with Alec. The new owner of half Fairlie Downs fussed around and finally decided that he wanted to go out to Feldings Creek to see what was going on. As nothing was going on as yet, Mark found it a nuisance. Morris suggested taking Alec out by car but Allison wanted her ride. Jamie did not want to go anywhere near the creek, saying that there was enough sadness around without breaking their hearts all over again. The truth was that no one had the emotional stamina to make any decisions. Finally, they all rode out to the creek except Jamie who announced that she had some domestic issues to discuss with the housekeeper.

Once she had her caravan in order Jamie spent the morning following Mrs Howard about and mulling over the whole awkward business again. She had expected a sympathetic ear. It turned out that Howie had her own grievances. She was fed up with both the brothers; she interspersed Jamie's groans with denunciations of Hugh's meanness and Mark's weakness. Hugh was an out and out bully and Mark was an out and out wimp, so there.

Brooke's absence was commented on at the lunch table when the others returned. Hugh's absence was noticed and some hazarded a guess that the two absentees could be together. Jamie shook her head but said nothing. After lunch Mark hauled Alec off to his office and later came up to tell the restless group outside the caravan that Ashley had rung to say that he and Sarah with Brooke would be over for dinner. Even then not one of the party entertained the slightest suspicion. They were satisfied with the thought that Brooke had in all probability gone over to Seven Trees to get away for a while.

Drinks were already being served in the annex when Morris's car was seen approaching with Ashley's following it. Rather to their surprise the watchers saw Ashley and Brooke get out of the first car and Sarah out of the second one. An altercation between brother and sister had caused this. Her shock at the news had been so great that Sarah had been downright rude to Brooke. The result was that Ashley had driven off with his fiancée, telling Sarah that she could follow if she liked.

Mark, Jamie, Morris, Allison, Howie and Alec watched the trio approach sedately with Sarah trailing behind the other two. Brooke and Ashley were not holding hands but he was supporting her elbow.

As they drew nearer, the radiant faces of the lovers could be seen and the woebegone one of Sarah.

Mark and Jamie jumped to their feet. Morris and Allison staggered to theirs. Alec's jaw dropped. Mrs Howard stared.

Mark leapt to shake hands with the man who seemed to have shed years while Jamie wrapped herself around Brooke, crying and laughing in her surprise and delight. Morris and Allison surged forward to join in what was obviously a family joy.

Not a soul had suspected. In the general hubbub of surprise and congratulation Sarah stood forlornly aside. Alec astutely summed up the situation and saw an unexpected chance for himself. He moved to Sarah's side and solicitously put a light arm around her shoulders. It was very gratefully received. Everybody talked and nobody listened. Ashley, secretly searching every face, could find no hint of doubt or criticism. Those who loved him were beside themselves with joy. In all her plans for him Jamie had not dreamed of such a prize nor that Brooke would find such a safe and happy harbour.

In all their excitement, they did not see Hugh come up from the stables and disappear into the house for his shower. He had heard the excited chatter and it fell ill on his ears. They should have been a dismal group and what was Alec doing hobnobbing with Mark? Anyone would think that they were to be partners. He was determined to separate Brooke from the others that night and find out just what was troubling her. The sooner they were engaged the better.

Freshly showered, he shaved again and took time to dress for what would be one of the happiest occasions of his life. He came up the slope unnoticed and the whole scene was etched on his startled brain with a pen of acid. Two people were the centre of attention. By now all were seated again. Ashley was on the caravan steps and leaning forward with his arm around Brooke seated close by in a cane chair. She was leaning toward him, one arm flung familiarly across his knees, her face tilted up to his in total absorption. They were the only ones actually facing Hugh's way but they had no eyes for anyone but each other. No one could mistake them for anything but lovers.

A queer gasping sound made everyone turn and all froze on the spot. Hugh looked straight into Brooke's eyes and then into Ashley's. Neither glance dropped. There was nothing anyone could do. Hugh turned on his heel and ran down the slope. Sarah got to her feet but Mark held her.

"He won't want anyone, Sarah," he said quickly. "I know."

Before she could answer and while everyone was watching, Hugh in his haste tripped and fell sprawling. With one accord, everyone except Sarah turned away that they might not witness his embarrassment. Sarah watched him as he struggled unsteadily to his feet putting his hand up to a badly cut lip. She wrenched her hand fiercely from Mark's restraining grasp and looked around to see whom she could hurt.

"You're finished, Mrs Howard," she snapped. "I'm taking over at the Downs. You leave with the others."

Before as much as a shadow could cross Howie's face, Jamie laughed and said,

"I've been wondering how I could persuade you to come to me. With a new baby, husband and house, I'll need all the help I can get."

There was some nervous laughter and Sarah stalked down to the house determined to minister to Hugh's lip and pride. She found Hugh in the bathroom washing off the dust and applying a washer to his bleeding lip. At sight of her he slammed the door in her face. Sarah never did have any tact. She stayed there wailing that she had never liked that awful Brooke and what a traitor Ashley was. She had dismissed that incompetent Howie and was going to look after him herself. Hugh wrenched open the door, shoved her roughly aside and fled the house. He ran around the outskirts of the buildings to keep out of sight of the others till he reached his car.

They heard the engine rev up and looked to see the vehicle disappear down the track.

"Probably going bush," suggested Morris. "A man needs to be alone at such a time." He turned to those around him and some of them nodded. It was in the minds of everyone but Alec that Hugh was getting a taste of his own medicine; nevertheless, they felt sorry for him.

Dinner that night was a celebratory meal as they resolutely put Hugh's troubles behind them. Ashley and Brooke protested laughingly at the eager questions about their future plans, saying that they had hardly had time to form any. Ashley finally did admit that he was taking a leaf out of Mark's book and they were going to see the

Minister about arranging the wedding as soon as possible, and then they were going to take a long long honeymoon. Everyone cheered except the dolorous Sarah but Alec was quietly working on her and she was turning more and more to him for comfort.

All this was birthing some new thoughts in Jamie's head. Under cover of the general chatter she whispered to Mark that these new events could pave the way for them to build on the Seven Trees property. Mark smiled into her eyes.

"This little game is not played out yet, sweetheart. Let's wait and see."

Jamie's returning smile was wholly sweet and Mark wondered why everyone raved over Brooke's beauty.

It just showed how much he was smitten with his own wife for Brooke was at her stunning loveliest that happy night. She seemed lit with an inner flame as she talked and laughed and spread her radiance around. True to form Ashley said little but his pride and joy were something to see.

CHAPTER TWENTY-SEVEN

The Reckoning

Hugh drove along the road towards Seven Trees, then branched off
and headed for one of the distant poddy stations. He found a group of
trees and parked under them. Climbing a boulder, he sat staring blindly
at the dying sun while he held a handkerchief to his still bleeding
mouth. For a long hour he never moved, his thoughts jammed on that
last scene. *Ashley and Brooke!*

At last the pain in his breast became so intolerable that he slid
off the rock and began to pace among the trees till he came to a small
clearing flooded by the rising moon. As he stood there, a still dark
figure marbled by the moon light which turned everything to black and
white, Hugh suddenly saw the situation with equal clarity. He saw his
love in the arms of another man living not twenty minutes from him.
He saw himself enduring the hideous situation alone without his
brother.

Then the first panic wave hit him.

Hugh had never had the tempering in his life that Mark had
endured. The constant adjusting to an unfair situation, the overcoming
of heartbreak had welded the fine steel that was Mark. Hugh's
character was flabby. The only major trauma in his life had been the
death of his parents and there he had blamed the plane rather than face
the fact of his father's fault.

He had nothing by which he could face his present situation. Not
only was he deeply in love for the first time, but Brooke stood out
above all the girls he had ever met. He would have laid his all at her
feet. To lose her was unthinkable. *But to lose her to his uncle: old Ash!*
Hugh burned with the humiliation of it. Ashley and Brooke would be
living at Seven Trees. Contact with them would be unavoidable.

The second wave of panic hit him. He would not be able to bear it.
Something had to be done. He'd talk to Mark and ...

Mark was leaving – and by his own hand!

The third wave forced Hugh into the shadows and brought him stumbling against the rock as terrible sobs shook him. NO! *He could not lose Mark!* Mark, who had walked with him all his life, first guiding and teaching, then following and supporting… his other self. The anguish he felt at the loss of his brother was as great if not greater than what he felt at the loss of Brooke. This was the real cause of the fear he was fighting. He wondered what kind of madness had seized him that he could even think of cutting his brother out of his life. He would sooner cut off his right hand.

Pain was knifing through him so badly that he ground his teeth and pounded the rock with his fists.

He could not be near Ashley and Brooke!

He could not let his brother go.

Where could he turn?

Shaken by his breakdown, startled by his tears, he tried to regain control. If only he hadn't insisted on the Contract being signed last night. Supposing Alec wouldn't back down! Supposing Mark insisted on going through with it. Then there would be nothing for it. He would have to leave himself!

Through those long dark torturing hours Hugh saw his whole life crashing down about him as those chilling waves of panic broke over him. Through all his despair one name beamed like a distant light in his darkness. Mark! He could barely wait for the morning.

The engagement party broke up fairly early. Ashley wanted to get Sarah home and out of the way. As he drove home, deaf to her moans, he was doing a lot of thinking. Amid the euphoria of the unexpected consummation of his dream of love he knew that dark clouds were looming. He could not see himself settling down with Brooke on the old property with Hugh on Fairlie Downs alone except for Sarah who was likely to have a breakdown over the loss of her personal security. He was detecting a very real fear behind his sister's whimpers and he did not want to hurt her. The winds of change were frightening her whereas they were blowing over him with the promise of distant and fairer harbours. He was also worrying about his nephew. How was Hugh going to cope? Also, he was well aware of Brooke's unconscious sophistication. Was Seven Trees the right setting for her

– or for them both in this wholly unanticipated situation? If Jamie and Mark did go Brooke would lose a dear friend, one of her own ilk. Hmm, there was much to ponder.

Everyone went to bed more or less brooding over the effect the engagement would have on the present crisis. It had added an unexpected element of excitement and suspense to the whole business. How would Hugh feel now with his brother gone? Eyelids eventually closed on a pleasurable sense of anticipation of what the morrow would bring.

When they returned to the caravan Jamie's happy chatter, as she went over the surprising event again and again, lay like a delicate quilt over the lumps and bumps of the breaking up of the long-standing traditions of the Lawrence family. Neither husband nor wife disturbed it as they prepared for bed. Sleep came early to Mark but Jamie took time to hand this new situation over to God. Would it be something He could use? Eventually she slept as the seed's delicate tendrils reached for the light.

In that solemn hour when the darkness held the earth in one last desperate grip and no bird note had yet tested the air, Mark was sound asleep in a tangle of legs and arms with Jamie. On his ear, quickening it with haunting memory, fell a fine sibilant note, repeated at spaced intervals. He stirred and there came the recollection of dawns when two boys had crept out with their lines and hooks and smuggled bait to freedom at one of the far billabongs, returning triumphant and in trouble to a late breakfast. Other times they had slipped out at night at the sound of a howl betraying the presence of feral dogs after the calves. He smiled in his sleep recalling the ringing shot that proclaimed their success and disobedience.

Persistently the note kept sounding and he raised his head, shaking off the wisps of sleep. Carefully he disengaged himself from his wife and peered through the glass of one of the windows. The shadowy figure of his brother stood there. Softly he returned the call. He had never failed to answer that soft whistle and now was not the time to do so - whatever happened. The vague outline straightened as if in relief and went back down the slope.

Mark dressed quickly and with a last glance at Jamie let himself out and followed his brother to where the horses were waiting. Hugh mounted and Mark followed suit without a word exchanged between them. The two riders guided their horses quietly till they were clear of the buildings. Hugh urged his mount forward and soon the two horses were at the full gallop, perfectly matched in pace and stride.

Jamie watched till they were out of sight and knelt by her bed praying that God would keep Mark strong against any ploys his brother had in mind.

As the sky lightened Mark was at last able to see Hugh's face. It shocked him: the closed set expression, the downcast eyes showed a man lost to everything but his agony. Hugh was desperately trying to ride out his pain and no one had the right to witness this but the one who had lived through similar suffering.

Mark saw that they were heading straight into the bush where the heat would be intolerable when the sun rose. He rode closer, intending to cause Vulcan to veer to the right but Hugh would have none of it.

On they rode… on… and on… It seemed Hugh would go on till Vulcan dropped.

At last Mark realised he had to take charge. He caused Redmaster to lean on Vulcan's shoulder turning the horse as he would a recalcitrant steer. This time Hugh did not resist, allowing the weary horse his way. They went in a wide circle heading back towards Feldings Creek. When the doomed trees eventually came in sight the pace slackened. Reining in under the canopy the two men moved as one, dismounting, loosening the girths and tethering the overheated horses away from the water till they cooled down. Then the men walked down to the creek and stood together as the rising sun delicately sent long fingers to pick them out.

At last Mark turned and took his seat on the rock where Hugh and Stella had once sat. Hugh stood staring ahead for a while longer and then turned towards the rock. Mark had made room for him but Hugh slid down till he was seated on the ground, his back to the rock, and leaned against Mark's booted leg.

An old memory stirred Mark. He was taken back to his early schooldays when the governess had had to shut his four-year-old brother out of the room so that some work could be done. Nothing daunted, the boy used to crawl in on his belly behind the closed in desk and creep in. There he would stay, snuggled up against his brother's leg well content with his act of disobedience and, more often than not, fall asleep.

Both had removed their hats and Mark glanced down at the tousled head and sweat beaded forehead and let one hand rest on the broad shoulders. Nothing disturbed the brooding silence, the waking birds cautiously surveying the intruders. Neither brother moved but Mark, so well attuned to Hugh's moods, sensed the irrepressible tension rising in the form beneath his hand. It grew like a violin string being remorselessly tightened to the point of snapping.

The break was heralded with an agonised moan and Hugh turned his head into his brother's knee. Words came in husky gasps.

"Markie, I can't…. I – I can't… go on… not now…"

The old baby name Hugh had used of him till teased out of it by older boys. Mark felt a scalding pity.

In his pain Hugh had dropped the façade of his dynamic manhood, the manhood that had so signally failed to win Brooke, and was again the whimpering boy that had run to his brother with his hurts.

"I – I can't… bear it… Markie… She'll be up there… *with Ashley!* I'll see her… almost daily… my God, *my God…*"

Hugh stopped speaking on a sobbing breath. Mark felt that the pain-ridden silence was almost too difficult to bear. Who can heal a freshly bleeding wound? His grip tightened but Hugh reared back and turned away, huddled over the loneliness of his heartbreak. Mark's hand slid away.

"*No!* You can't help. You can't know what it's like. You – you've got Jamie… You –"

"But I didn't have Claudia."

Hugh jerked his shoulder. "It's not the same. It – "

"Yes, it is."

The quiet words lingered on the air. For the first time Hugh was forced to view his brother's suffering from the viewpoint of his own.

"You didn't care that much. You –"

"I did care. Very much."

Hugh twisted and hunched his shoulder, dodging the blame as always. "Well, she couldn't have cared that much."

His thoughts veered off at a tangent.

"It's all Jamie's fault. She's brought all this trouble. If only she hadn't come here…"

"You invited her."

Hugh stood up, angrily determined to lay the blame elsewhere. "It's that damn painting Sarah wanted. If only Jamie hadn't –"

Mark hated the thought he was about to voice but it had to be said.

"Had I been married to Claudia, Jamie would have come and gone. Brooke would never have come here."

Stricken by these words Hugh stared at nothing, his thoughts shying at the tragic phrase: 'if only'… and all by his own doing. He had a blinding flash of insight: the roots of this whole present imbroglio reached right back to his selfish destruction of his brother's romance. He began to stride up and down, viciously kicking away any stones in his path.

Mark said nothing more, knowing full well that there was no way to get over the wall of Hugh's temper. Eventually the passion of his anger wore itself out and he came and stood over his brother.

"Something has to be done. I can't stay here if Ash and – if you go I go."

Mark said nothing.

Hugh reached down and shook his brother's shoulder. "Mark, what can we *do?* We can't let the whole Lawrence set up be broken like this."

"Sit down a minute and let me think."

It was obvious to Mark that when Hugh had tried to force his will on them he had not envisaged for one moment Alec actually taking his brother's place nor the horror of losing Brooke to his uncle.

Hugh subsided down onto the ground again and once more leaned on his brother, burying his head in his hands.

Mark too, was struggling for a solution. Ashley's successful romance had indeed thrown the cat among the pigeons. The present situation was unliveable for them all. Even if they persuaded Alec to renege on the Contract it did not relieve the hideous situation in which Hugh found himself.

His thoughts began to find the track that Ashley was already exploring. He once again put a steadying hand on his desolate brother's shoulder.

"Will you trust me to find a solution, Hugh?"

"Is there one?" the man mumbled through his hands.

"I believe God will show us the way."

There was a dismissive shrug.

"How could God help?"

"Because He understands your situation. He's been there."

Hugh glanced up for a surprised second.

"You're suffering from unrequited love," Mark said gently, "and Jesus knows all about it."

"How?" Sceptically.

"He came to His own people whom He loved dearly and they rejected Him to the point of crucifixion. He still loves and He is still rejected by many – even hated. He says to you: Hugh, I *know.* "

There was an intense silence which Mark made no attempt to break. Hugh's self-centred thought processes had been arrested. He was thinking deeply. Then he said in a different wondering voice,

"You know, for the first time God seems human to me."

Mark smiled and said nothing. There was nothing to say when the divine Comforter in the form of the human Jesus was at work. He sat there praying for his brother.

The seed was putting out a leaf.

Hugh was aware of an extraordinary sense of comfort and a momentary easing of his pain. At this moment, the strange alchemy of the Christian life began to work. Paul had said to his converts: 'We die daily that you might live.' Mark's total death to self was working its miracle. The spiritual principle of life from death was irresistibly in action. Hugh turned to lean his head against his brother's knee and nothing was said for a long time. Eventually he turned a wan face up to his brother.

"Do you think that Alec -?"

Mark stood up. "Let's see how the dice rolls," he said whimsically.

Hugh rose and the two went to fetch the horses and bring them down to the pool. As the two animals blew away the debris and lipped the water, the men stood companionably, the old harmony fully restored.

As one they brought the horses back and prepared to mount. Mark was tightening Redmaster's girth when Hugh spoke over Vulcan's back.

"How'd it be if we do a detour and inspect that land Jamie's got her eye on?"

Mark drew a quick breath. As an *amende honourable* it was superb. He nodded then turned to gaze far out to the horizon in deep thankfulness.

Hugh Lawrence had given in.

CHAPTER TWENTY-EIGHT

Surrender

The morning had brought Jamie rushing down to breakfast with the news of the early morning ride. The guests were just sitting down to a piping hot meal and there was consternation on every face, particularly Alec Cartwright's.

"Now what's that wretched Hugh up to?" demanded Allison, quite forgetting Alec's presence. Morris nudged her and remarked that Mark was a cool customer and not easily rattled. Then he found he was not satisfied with his own utterance and glanced apologetically at the prospective buyer. Alec kept his eyes on his plate and his expression was unreadable.

Having had a precautionary drink of her cordial Jamie told an amazed and gratified Howie that she felt she could stomach a boiled egg and dry toast. When this was served, she remarked that if her baby came out bright red the assembled company would know why.

Alec was rash enough to inquire the reason and found himself the embarrassed recipient of the various means of coping with morning sickness for the newly pregnant to the company's high delight.

Taking pity on him Morris swept him off to the veranda while the ladies cleaned up. No mention was made of the usual morning ride; the domestic chores were done in record time. Then the entire company sat down for the grand wait.

The first event was the arrival of the estate car bearing Ashley and Sarah. Ashley had wanted to come alone with the intention of carrying Brooke off so that he could put before her some ideas he had. However, Sarah had been distraught at the prospect of being left with her own thoughts. As they came up the steps Ashley looked meaningly at Alec. He rose to the occasion and took over the charge of Sarah, this time much more masterfully than the day before. Alec had his own row to hoe.

291

Learning the news Ashley joined the waiting group, content for the moment to converse in low tones with Brooke. Morning Tea came and went and Howie was just about to excuse herself in order to prepare the lunch when Ashley's sharp vision picked out the distant riders. The last twenty minutes were nerve snapping as the tired horses were brought in, stabled and rubbed down. Then the two tall men were seen making their way towards the house. Those who knew them well drew a breath of relief. Alec gave a wry smile, went and fetched the papers he had recently signed and dropped them on a nearby table.

What everyone was seeing was two people walking completely at ease. Hugh had his hand on Mark's shoulder as he often did when holding forth about something. Mark, with his thumbs in his belt, was glancing around as he listened. Brooke got up, whispered to Howie that she would start on the lunch and disappeared to stand just inside the door. She sensed that this was an occasion when her presence could be an unwanted distraction.

As they came closer everyone saw a different Hugh. The old bravado was gone. His face was that of a man who had been to hell, tasted its flames, and flung himself back. Mark looked at peace.

"How does he do it?" gasped Jamie. "Hugh talks and talks, Mark says nothing but –"

"He doesn't need to," said Alec. "He does it with smoke and mirrors," and with that he reached for the papers.

When the men came up the steps, Hugh addressed himself to Jamie.

"We've been looking at that plot you like and we both think it is ideal. We'll get a start on it as soon as you like."

"*Hugh!*" Jamie went quite pink while everyone else stared in amazed silence. She hesitated, then glancing at her smiling husband, she stood and, reaching up, kissed her brother-in-law's cheek before retreating to Mark's side.

Hugh coloured a little himself but turned to the expectant Alec.

"We're going to throw ourselves on your mercy, old son," he said with a grimace.

Alec nodded and tore the papers across and handed them to Hugh. A deep sigh passed through the entire group. Hugh took the papers, tore them again and passed them to Mark who also tore them and cast them aside.

"I always knew it was too good to be true," remarked Alec.

"Try Ashley," suggested Mark.

"*Ashley!*" exclaimed everyone.

Ashley grinned. "Now you just stop stealing my thunder, young 'un. I haven't even talked to Brooke yet."

He was peppered with questions mainly from Alec. Ashley stalled them all saying that until he had discussed the matter fully with Brooke there was nothing doing. At that Brooke reappeared and moved swiftly to his side.

"Just give me ten minutes with him, Brooke," Alec pleaded.

"Sure," she said. "I'll have the rest of his life."

"I'll handle this," announced Ashley. He put his arm around Brooke and ushered her and Alec inside to the lounge room.

Hugh affected to be blind and deaf to this. He swooped on Mrs Howard and pulled her from her chair.

"I'm famished, Howie. If you don't feed me I won't be responsible for what I eat."

The others rose too and went off to the kitchen herding the bemused Sarah with them. But Jamie held her husband back.

"I'm starving too, honey."

"It can wait. What did you do?"

"Nothing."

"*Mark!*"

He grinned down at her.

"Honestly. It was his passion for Brooke that broke him. With me leaving it was all too big for him. He was in a kind of blind panic. Wanted to cut and run."

"And so?"

"He was insisting that no one could possibly know what he was suffering. He did not seem to be aware of my suffering over Claudia. Then I just said that Jesus did because He knew what it was to have His heart broken… and it was still being broken."

Mark paused and rubbed his forehead. Jamie was silent.

"I don't know how it works, honey, but that reached him. After a while Hugh was able to master his emotion and began to talk coherently. Above all he wanted me to stay. He could not bear the future without me here to support him. He began to talk about appealing to Alec and suddenly the thought hit me like a bombshell that Ashley would want to leave and that would solve the problem of Brooke's proximity."

"You could have knocked me over with a feather when you said to try Ashley."

"Well, you saw that Ash was already thinking that way."

Jamie looked around helplessly.

"Things have taken an utterly different direction. It alters everything."

"I knew straight away that if Hugh was serious about Brooke – and he was – the situation for Ash and Brooke and Hugh on the same property would be untenable."

"It all seems to be taken quite out of our hands."

"I know. I guess that's what dying to self really means. If you really let go then God can work."

"Do you think Hugh has really grasped –"

"Not yet but a start has been made. There was a tremendous change in him and I could sense a leaning towards a higher strength. Let us say that the soil has been harrowed and is ready for the seed."

Jamie put her arms right around Mark and rested her head on his chest. "So, all our problems are solved. So is Brooke's. I'm so thrilled about her and Ashley. It'll be hard on Sarah –"

"Don't worry about Sarah." Mark replied as he returned her embrace. "Alec's got her cornered."

Jamie laughed and then sighed.

"It just leaves Hugh high and dry. I know that in a way he has come by his just deserts but I can find it in me to really feel sorry for him."

"Have faith, Jamie." Mark said as they turned to go inside. "I don't believe God is done with him yet. From all I have ever read it is a fruit bearing seed."

"But fruit trees take such a long time to bear," said Jamie.

"Maybe. But then in this case we have a divine Gardener."

"I guess we'll just have to have faith then."

Arm in arm they joined the others, each secretly marvelling at the mysterious ways of God.

In a matter of twenty-for hours the scene had changed completely. Ashley swept Brooke and Alec over to Seven Trees where a half-share in the property plus the Managership was swiftly negotiated. Then he swept Brooke back to Brisbane. In a kind gesture to Hugh but not to their friends he kept her there, married her quietly and then swept her off on that long long honeymoon.

Morris shot back to Brisbane to handle his important Show but left Allison to make sure the plans for the new house got under way. Everyone, including Hugh, took an interest in this by way of some much needed relief from the late tensions.

A bewildered Sarah was brought over to Fairlie as she was too upset to be left alone. This was very convenient for Alec who wasted no time in wooing her. Sarah had always liked Alec but had been paranoid about venturing into the wild seas of matrimony again. As Ashley had offered the house to Alec and she found she could do so while still within the security of the home she loved, she bravely took the plunge.

Things were still very hard for Hugh. The hurt over Brooke had gone very deep and his only solace was work and more work. He had known instinctively that Brooke was no gullible Claudia to be won away from her love and it stripped away a lot of his unconscious conceit. He turned almost feverishly to the house plans, entering thoroughly into every idea and innovation to Jamie's secret amazement and, be it said, apprehension. She did not realise that the long discussions and the consequent involvement in the building of their own house were a kind of therapy for him.

In the dark hours of the night, when his heartache threatened to overcome him, the pain acted like a catharsis, purging him of his shallow flirtatious ways and awakening him to an appreciation of patient and loyal values . . .

. . . and, there they were, as they always had been, waiting in the wings for his blinded sight to be cleared so that he could focus on the precious and hitherto unheeded treasure.

As always his brother walked by his side supporting and strengthening him, and drawing his chastened soul gradually to a richer fulfilment.

The End

295

EPILOGUE

A group of people sat patiently waiting on the front veranda of the new house. They had been alerted by phone to expect some special news.

Mr and Mrs Mark Lawrence were there keeping an eye on the baby crawling about and endeavouring to heave herself up against the various chairs. Sweet William, known to her immediate family by the working name of Willa, being her own bubbled attempt at her name, charmed all who met her with her golden curls, blue eyes and placid nature.

Mr and Mrs Ashley Lawrence were there having spent most of their time visiting his relations in the States with a view to buying shares into the cattle industry there. They had returned to Australia for the birth of their first child and Brooke was very near her time.

Mr and Mrs Alec Cartwright were there with Sarah blossoming in her husband's care into a more positive state of mind.

It was Ashley's keen sight once again that first alerted them to the approach of the distant car. Jamie caught up the baby and handed her to Sarah and she and Mark went to stand at the top of the steps. This time they had had their suspicions.

The vehicle swept up to the front of the house with something of a flourish. Hugh got out and went around to hand out his companion.

As he and Sylvia approached them hand in hand, there was a shout and Mark and Jamie ran down the steps, Mark to grip his brother's hand and Jamie to wrap herself around Sylvia in a tremendous hug.

All was babble and excitement for a while as the others joined them for a genuine happiness was felt all round. Eventually they began to return to the veranda, all talking at once.

Jamie found herself at Hugh's side and slipped a hand in the crook of his elbow. He glanced down and met her questioning gaze. He put one hand over hers.

"I know what you're thinking, Jamie. When I at last won free of my infatuation for Brooke I found that love for Sylvia was already there. In fact, I can't imagine a time when I did not love her."

Jamie's eyes had a sparkle to the lashes. "You probably both grew to love each other when you were very young and didn't realise it."

"That's probably it but I can't remember. All I know is that I was always ready to kill anyone who teased her – including Mark."

"Now don't try and tell me Mark was a tease."

"Well, he was. Used to tease our lives out. He had a lot more kick to him before… before…" his voice trailed away uncertainly.

"Before his heart was broken," Jamie finished softly.

Hugh nodded. "I guess so," he said huskily.

"I've every reason to forgive you, Hugh," Jamie said, the light of mischief in her eyes. "But you got your own come uppance. Now just a firm grip on the bridle and a bit of spur and you'll be right."

Hugh looked things not lawful to be uttered. Then Sylvia joined him, in her soft eyes the joy of love requited, and he continued to receive the good wishes of all who loved him.

---oOo---